Legion's War

Jon Roe

To
Andrew

from

[signature]

ISBN: 9798693560406

Cover art by: Karen Arnold

Jon Roe
45a Sun Street
Derby
DE22 3UL
ivellious@msn.com
07581418476

Andrew,

You may remember that many years ago you Alastair and me started a dungeons and dragons campaign, but didn't get very far into it before we all went off to uni. You may also recall that I said I was going to write the story as a book instead. Well that book is now available to purchase on amazon, since you helped inspire me to write it I thought you might like a copy. Also check the acknowledgements.

Also, in my initial manuscript I made a couple of formatting errors which I didn't notice until I got the physical copies, they've been fixed for future printings but they are still present in the copy I've sent you. Sorry. The story is still the same, just ignore the page numbers listed for the chapters, and there are some gaps at the bottom of pages which shouldn't be there. Although in a way it does mean that the copy you and the handful of other people I'm sending them too are kinda unique, which is cool I guess.

Yours Sincerely

For

Alan & Logan

Michelle & Helen

Acknowledgments

First I'd like to thank my family and friends who have graciously put up with my constant ramblings about this crazy obsession as well as having faith in me when I didn't have faith in myself.

I would also like to make special mention to:

Alastair Houldsworth
&
Andrew King

Without whom I may never have started on this crazy journey

Contents

Prologue

So you want to hear a story?

I can tell you a story, but which one? I have heard many a tall tale told here, perhaps one of those? Or maybe I should tell you of some of my own travels. What type of story do you wish to hear?

A romance? A tale of star crossed lovers with hearts entwined by fate?

Something political? A courtly tale of intrigue and betrayal?

I see by your faces that is not what you are looking for, you want to hear about adventure, a story of great heroes and terrible monsters. I can do that. But which story to tell, I would guess that you have already heard most of the great epics and I don't want to re-tred old ground for you. Hmm, I could tell you that tale, it is old but little know despite the tremendous impact it had on our world, on sweet Gallisium.

Gallisium hasn't always been the way it is now. It wasn't always as simple as it is today. There was a time when great wars were fought. Most of which were the same as yours, disputes over land, and petty rivalries. The occasional demonic incursion.

Some of the wars had much more to them though, some had much deeper meanings. Some of these wars endangered even the fabrics of time and space, threatening to erase existence itself.

I remember the time when the worst of these wars were fought. There was a time when a great darkness plagued the land.

I am not sure if I should tell you about these things, I am not sure you would believe me if I did. There are concepts you would not understand. Could you believe in what lies beyond, in the power of those *ideas* that exist in the void past the outer plains of existence Do you believe me when I say that the dawn of our world was not the beginning?

I'm not sure why I'm telling you this story; perhaps I want to prepare you, but why? The chances are that none of you will will have to face such trials, that none of you will have to witness the power of these *ideas* and the unthinkable entities they have become, for there are more of them out there, and one day they will stumble across this small corner of the void where Gallisium and all the other plains reside. I at least hope, for your sake that you are not here to bare witness.

Perhaps I am telling you because I can no longer keep the secret; perhaps I want to give you a vague idea of what is out there, and the potential dangers they pose.

I may not be so lucky, I understand now that it is my duty to stand watch for these things until the end of Gallisium, and long into the world that comes next in the cycle of Benii and Malus' great creation. I look forward to seeing that world, excited to see how it differs from our own and what stays the same. Though I hope it is still a long way off for I do love Gallisium, it is my home and always will be, I will mourn it greatly when it passes. I also hope I will be able to save that next world, as my predecessor saved ours, but I am getting ahead of myself.

So, where do I begin my tale? Should I explain how I came to be involved in the whole affair? No, I think not, not now anyway, another time perhaps.

I should begin my account when the first signs of the darkness were seen, but where was that? When was that?

I believe I should begin in the Cattle Shed.

Chapter 1
The Cattle Shed

The cattle shed is exactly what the name suggests, an old cattle shed. It was however renovated about twenty years ago, and made into a tavern. Since then, the cattle shed has become quite popular among the local farmers, and many people who are just passing through the small town of Calamshan.

There are two main types of people who pass through Calamshan, merchants travelling either too or from trading with the nomadic tribes who live on the plains to the west. A large fertile grassland between the borders of the Getandor Empire, the Four Kings Mountains, and the great Forest of Transeen. The other type of travellers who make frequent visits to Calamshan, and the Cattle Shed are adventurers, who are seeking to make a name for themselves against the goblinoid tribes of the Four Kings Mountains, or looking for treasure which is said to be hidden deep within Transeen.

There is a third type of traveller who visit the Cattle Shed, although this is not as often, are bards, who would trade stories with the passing adventurers. It was in this capacity that Roscoe Thorngage first came to be in the tavern.

Roscoe was a travelling musician, known among his kin for his skill with a Lute. However, with Roscoe being a halfling he always craved the creature comforts you can only find in a place you can call home. It was for this reason that Roscoe settled down in Calamshan. He made a deal with Zanian Alerteyes, the owner of the Cattle Shed, and in exchange for a room, and meals, Roscoe would perform to entertain the customers, using songs, poems, and some minor magic. This was like perfection for Roscoe, he had a place to call home, a place to perform, and he could trade tails with the many adventurers who passed through. However, he was soon to learn that nothing lasts forever.

It was a warm summer evening, and the Cattle Shed was surprisingly quiet for this time of year. Zanian had time to dust off the paintings behind the bar. Even Jannays, the young waitress, had the time to sit and watch Roscoe perform. The only customers were a group of local farmers who were in the tavern most nights, and two strangers.

Roscoe had been keeping an eye on these strangers since he had entered the main room for his performance. The first of the strangers was a human; he looked to be a young mage of some kind, wearing deep red robes, and always keeping one hand on his staff, which looked like a gnarled and twisted piece of wood. At the top was a large bird talon, made out of what appeared to be solid gold; this talon was holding a clear crystal. The mage sat talking with his companion, whom looked a little younger than the mage, but the chances were that this man was much, much older. It was quite plane to see by his slim build, fair skin, and pointed ears that he was an elf. This elf wore a pale green cloak, under which it was Roscoe could see he carried a sword. He also had a finely crafted bow and a quiver of arrows, both hanging from his chair.

Roscoe had decided that he would talk to with these two strangers when he had finished his performance, long before he had finished his first song. When he did finish Roscoe stepped forward and took his bow, and had a glance around the room to see the reaction of his audience. The farmers gave their usual claps and cheers, even the two strangers took the time to applaud Roscoe, and Jannays, Roscoe's ever-adoring fan, gave the usual cheers and whistles. As Roscoe left the stage Jannays met him.

"Another fine performance Mr. Thorngage." She said with a smile.

"Ah, my dear, how many times must I tell you? My name is Roscoe." Replied the halfling.

"Sorry Roscoe, its habit, can I get you a drink?" Jannays asked.

"Tell me, what are they drinking?" Asked Roscoe indicating the two strangers.

"They're both having wine."

"Then I will have the same my dear," they both began to walk towards the bar, "So, Jannays, what do you know of the strangers?"

"Well, the mage is apparently called Thoril Serpenthelm, and from what I heard while I was pouring their drinks, is that he's from that *Mage House* in Cemulion City." She said as she began pouring Roscoe's drink, "The elf is called Adokas Loreweaver, not sure where he's from."

"Loreweaver, that name sounds familiar."

"Your drink Mr. I mean Roscoe."

"Thank you my dear, I'll be back to talk with you later." Roscoe handed over a few coins for the drink, and started walking towards the two strangers.

"Greetings friends, perchance may I join you at this table?" Announced Roscoe. The two companions looked up at Roscoe, and after a moment's silence the mage replied, "Of course friend, your company would be welcome." And with that Roscoe sat down.

"My name is Roscoe Thorngage, and I was wondering, have you travelled far?"

"Well, my name is Thoril Serpenthelm, and my companion here is called Adokas Loreweaver. Personally I have come from the city of Cemulion, and Adokas is from Landorn Forest," replied the mage.

"You are a very talented musician Mr. Thorngage, I have not heard the lute played with such skill for many a year." Complimented Adokas.

"Ha ha, only Jannays calls me Mr. Thorngage, and I wish she wouldn't, please call me Roscoe, and thank you for the compliment, from one of your skilled people I am honoured by you words."

"Have you ever thought of travelling? Many would be happy to hear your music." Asked Thoril.

"I did travel once, but I settled here a few years ago." Answered Roscoe.

"It is a shame your music is not heard by many more people." Adokas said.

"Your words honour me again. Please tell, what brings you to this corner or Getandor?" Asked Roscoe. At this point the two companions swapped a nervous glance.

"I'm afraid we cannot say the full reasons for our presence here." Answered Thoril.

"However," began Adokas, "You may be able to help us, how much do you know of the surrounding areas?"

"I know these lands as well as anyone else, I've travelled them a little, and I've spoken to almost all who have passed through." Answered Roscoe curiously.

Thoril leaned back on his chair and took a sip of his drink. He starred at Roscoe for a moment, who felt as though the mage was looking straight into his soul. Thoril then turned his eyes to Adokas.

"We are searching for a temple," Adokas began.

Roscoe looked a little confused at this. "What do you mean a temple? There aren't any temples around here."

"That is where you are wrong my little friend," chuckled Thoril. "Somewhere within the forest of Transeen are the ruins of a temple to Sugalas."

"Ruins, there are some ruins in Transeen, said to hold some treasure, no-one knows what it was, but I should have guessed it used to be a temple." Said Roscoe, almost to himself.

"You know the place then?" asked Thoril excitedly.

"Of course, many people travel there." Answered Roscoe with a big smile on his face.

It was at this point that almost everyone in the Cattle Shed looked towards the door. The reason for this being the very heavy footsteps on the decking outside the door. The only people who didn't look at the door were Thoril and Adokas; they just looked at each other, and said in unison; "He's here."

Roscoe wasn't sure who "he" was, but from the sound of his footsteps he was big. The door swung open, and crashed into the wall. At the height Roscoe was looking all he caught was the top of a helmet. A little surprised Roscoe lowered his gaze, that's when all the pieces fell into place, those footsteps weren't those of a large person; they were the footsteps of a fully armoured dwarf.

This dwarf was a sight to see, he strode slowly into the room, the door swinging closed behind him. The dwarf was wearing full scale-mail armour, which Roscoe noticed was very finely crafted. He also wore a helmet, which looked to be designed around the shape of a dragon. On his belt, Roscoe could see that the dwarf was carrying a crossbow, and a large battle-axe. The most fascinating item the dwarf carried however was the shield he carried in his left hand. The shield was quite large, and circular in design. The main colour of the shield was silver, but the edge was rimmed in gold, and there was a picture of a gold dragon in the centre. The dragon was stood on its hind legs, and had its wings outstretched.

The dwarf took a few more steps into the room, before removing his helmet. After doing so his long blue beard fell from it's rolled up position by his chin, to reach almost to his waist. Squinting, the dwarf peered around the room, then pointing at Zanian he bellowed, "You, a mug of your finest ale," and then he strode over to the table where Roscoe, Thoril, and Adokas were sat.

"Greetings old friend, please pull up a seat," greeted Adokas. The dwarf just grunted and sat down. "It has been too long since we last met." continued Adokas.

"That's a matter of opinion," grunted the dwarf, "You must be this Thoril I've heard so much about." he finished, indicting the mage.

"I am, and it is an honour to meet you," replied Thoril.

The dwarf turned to Adokas, "Who's the thief?" he asked.

"Oh, do forgive me," Adokas began, "Davkul, this is Roscoe Thorngage, Roscoe, this is Davkul Gemcutter."

"Pleased to meet you," said Roscoe, extending his hand, "But you have me mistaken, I am no thief." He continued.

"Bah, you're a halfling ain't ya?" snorted Davkul.

"Why, yes, but..." Roscoe began.

"Well then, you're a thief," interrupted Davkul.

"Mr Thorngage is no thief!" Said Jannays in an angry tone Roscoe had never heard from her before. Nobody had noticed her approach, but with her sudden outburst she had certainly made her presence known.

"And who are you?" Davkul snorted.

"That's Jannays," piped in Roscoe.

"She's the waitress," added Thoril.

"Your drink," growled Jannays as she slammed the mug down onto the table, "And if you don't apologise to Roscoe for calling him a thief, then I'll make sure that by the time you leave this table, that big blue beard is no longer attached to your big fat chin."

Davkul stared at Jannays in disbelief, not even orc chieftain's dared talk to him in this way, and here was a young barmaid, threatening to cut off his beard.

Adokas laughed, "This is the first time I've ever seen you lost for words Davkul," he said.

"Well, are you going to apologise?" asked Jannays, still glaring at Davkul.

"Err, yes, of course, I do apologise, err, Mr. Thorngage," stuttered the dwarf.

"That's better, it'll be five copper pieces for the drink," said Jannays. Davkul rummaged through his pockets and produced a gold coin, which he handed over to Jannays, "And you keep the change for yourself," he said.

"Why thank you Mr. Dwarf," Jannays replied, in her usual cheery voice, and then she walked back over to the bar.

At this point Thoril was chuckling to himself, and Adokas almost fell off his chair laughing. Roscoe however was not laughing. He had only met dwarves on a couple of occasions, but he knew that it wasn't a good idea to laugh at ones expense.

Davkul grunted again, "Where were we?" he mumbled.

"You know that's the first time I've ever seen you give someone a tip," said Adokas, now composing himself a little.

"The girl has guts, she deserved it." Davkul snorted, "Now why exactly did you bring me all the way out here?"

"Well we can't say much here, but me and Thoril have been sent to find a particular item which lies hidden in the forest of Transeen," began Adokas.

"What's that got to do with me?" interrupted Davkul.

"We need you to set up an audience for us," answered Thoril. Roscoe sat listening to this discussion with great intent.

"An audience with who?" asked Davkul.

"Nasgaroth," answered Adokas.

"Ha, never happen," snorted Davkul, "Nasgaroth won't even grant an audience with that king in Cemulion."

"You have to try; everything depends on what we do. Our entire existence hangs in the balance," stared Adokas, with a very serious voice.

"You do have a flair for the dramatic, old friend," chuckled Davkul, "But I doubt that it will make much difference, you're not likely to get an audience with Nasgaroth."

"Tell him that time is running short, and if we don't act fast the shadow will fall," said Thoril.

A silence fell over the group. It was Roscoe who eventually broke this silence by nervously asking, "Err, excuse me, but who's Nasgaroth? And what shadow is going to fall?"

"I'd forgotten about you, where exactly does he fit into all of this?" asked Davkul.

"Oh, Roscoe is our guide," answered Thoril.

"Guide? What do you mean guide?" stuttered a surprised Roscoe.

"You said you'd take us to the ruined temple," answered Adokas.

"I said no such thing, I only said that I know where you were talking about," protested Roscoe.

"I do apologise, you are correct. I just assumed that you would show us the way," apologised Thoril.

"Well I could draw you a map," suggested Roscoe.

"It would be much easier if you could take us," pleaded Adokas.

"I wish I could," started Roscoe, "But I'm afraid that I can't. I have obligations here, also I haven't travelled in a few years, and I've grown out of shape."

"Well I suppose a map will have to do then," sighed Thoril.

"I have a quill and paper in my room, I shall be right back," said Roscoe, who then left the table and walked through the door which led to the upper rooms.

"Do you trust this halfling?" asked Davkul.

"We have no reason not to trust him, and the locals seem to have a bond with him no thief could gain," answered Thoril.

"And if his word is as good as his lute playing then I would trust him with my life," added Adokas.

"You may be doing just that," said Davkul.

"Is that a hint of concern I hear in your voice?" chuckled Adokas.

"Not bloody likely," grunted Davkul, "Personally I hope you get yourself killed, then I wouldn't have to put up with ya any more." Adokas just laughed at this, and drank some more of his wine.

It was at this point that Roscoe re-entered the room. He was carrying a rolled up piece of paper, a quill, and a jar of ink. When he reached the table he unrolled the paper, and began to draw a basic map of the area on it whilst explaining how to get to the ruins.

*   *   *

Meanwhile, there was movement in the streets outside. This movement was going unnoticed, but if someone had looked closely at the shadows from the buildings they would have seen several figures sneaking along. If someone had been listening carefully, then they would have heard the gruff whispers these figures passed amongst each other.

"Kevgeon, where are they?" If anyone had seen these figures it wouldn't have been difficult to see that they were orcs. Orcs are easily distinguishable by there protruding tusks, large muscular bodies, stooped postures, and coarse hair. There were eight of these orcs sneaking in the shadows, a tactic not often used by this brutish race. The leader, Kevgeon, looked smaller than the others, and his features suggested he had some human blood in his veins.

"There in the next building," Kevgeon declared, pointing towards the Cattle Shed.

Back inside the Cattle Shed, Roscoe was just finishing the map, Zanian was polishing his old sword, which he had mounted behind the bar, and Jannays was sipping a drink she had poured for herself, whilst reading some poems Roscoe had written. The farmers sat drinking their ale, discussing some strange behaviour the livestock had been exhibiting. One of the men finished his drink, and stood up and began heading for the bar. An arrow smashing through the window, and ripping into his shoulder cutting his trip short.

This was swiftly followed by other windows smashing as orcs jumped through them. The door swung open and more orcs came in. Seven orcs had entered the room. Four of these orcs were brandishing large axes, the other three were all holding bows, which were all strung, and aimed at different parts of the room.

After the first arrow had crashed through the window, Adokas, Davkul, and Thoril, all leaped into action. With his lightning reflexes, Adokas had leaped from his chair, grabbing his bow and quiver, and strung an arrow in his bow, which was now pointed at the orcs. Thoril was standing now, with his staff in one hand, and his other had outstretched towards the orcs. Davkul had replaced his helmet on his head, and had his axe and shield in his hands. Roscoe had fallen from his chair with surprise it was rare indeed to see orcs in the Cattle Shed. Zanian had grabbed the sword he was polishing, and Jannays had run behind the bar. All of the farmers had risen from their seats, but none of them moved now.

After a few moments of tense silence Kevgeon entered the room, he was carrying a large axe. This was no ordinary axe, the pole was very long, and it had a double axe head at both ends. Roscoe marvelled at this exotic weapon imagining the damage it can cause, if wielded correctly, which looked to be no easy feat.

"If you all co-operate, no-one will get hurt," Kevgeon yelled.

"The fact that you've already injured one of my regulars suggests that you cannot be trusted on that count," retorted Zanian.

"Don't test my patience barman, with one word from me you could have an arrow in your chest," threatened Kevgeon. There was another few moments' silence before Kevgeon spoke again. "All we seek are some directions," he started, "If you tell us what we want to know nobody will die."

"A little late for that don't you think?" grunted Davkul, indicating the farmer who had been hit by the arrow.

Kevgeon walked over to the man lying on the floor, and nudged him with his foot, at which the man groaned. "He's alive," Kevgeon said, "For now."

"There's no-one here who'll help you, now get out of my bar," shouted Zanian.

"Kill him," Kevgeon ordered. The orc nearest the farmers aimed his bow at Zanian, but he didn't have chance to loose his arrow before two of the farmers had jumped on him. One of the other orcs with a bow turned it to face the farmers, but before he could fire it, an arrow ripped through his throat, and he fell lifeless on the floor. Before the third orc could turn his bow in any direction he was hit by five small bolts of energy sending him crashing into the wall.

Davkul let out a battle cry, and charged at the nearest orc with his axe held high.

The axe wielding orcs also charged into battle, one went to help the orc who had been attacked by the farmers. Another charged to meet Davkul. A third ran towards the bar, which Zanian agilely jumped over. The fourth orc and Kevgeon ran towards where Adokas and Thoril were stood.

The orc who had been attacked by the farmers had little trouble throwing them to the ground, but the remaining two farmers charged in wielding chairs. The orc had no time to react before the first crashed into his head. A large axe however, intercepted the second chair before it could reach its target. After smashing the chair with his axe, the orc grabbed the farmer by the shoulder, and hurled him into the wall, where he slumped onto the floor. The orc who had been hit with the chair staggered backwards and fell over a table.

The orc who was heading for the bar received more than he was bargaining for. He thought he was moving in on some old, overweight barkeeper, not a man who had spent many years perfecting his sword arm, and he didn't expect the young barmaid, who had just retrieved her bow from behind the bar. The orc swung his axe, but Zanian easily avoided it. Zanian then brought his sword around in an arc, slashing the orcs side. The orc gave out a pained yell, and stumbled back slightly. Jannays now loosed her arrow, but not at the closest orc, she fired at the orc who was attacking the farmers, as it was plain to see that they were clearly out matched. Although she hadn't been training with a bow very long, her aim was true. The arrow hit the orc in the centre of its back, sending it stumbling forward, it then fell to its knees, and swearing in its own tongue the orc fell forward, dead.

Davkul made short work of the orc he charged at. He rammed his shield into the orcs stomach; the orc doubled over in pain, leaving his neck open as the perfect target for Davkul's war axe, the orcs life ended shortly after this point. Davkul now looked for his next victim, the orc he chose was the one who had been hit by the bolts of energy earlier, but now it had regained its composure, and was preparing for a fight, Davkul charged again.

Thoril was facing off against the orc who had run in his direction. He hadn't had time to cast another spell before the orc had begun swinging its axe, but he had been well trained in using his staff for more than just casting spells. However, Thoril was having a little trouble fending off the barrage of attacks he was suffering at the hands of the orc. Thoril's chance to finish his opponent came when Roscoe cast one of the few minor spells he knew, there was a blinding flash of light in front of the orcs face, the orc dropped his axe, and grabbed his eyes, screaming in pain, this gave Thoril the chance to cast a spell of his own, a stream of acid burned through the orcs chest, forcing him backwards. The orc fell backwards, and died, a very painful death.

Adokas was having a little trouble with his opponent; he hadn't had the chance to unsheathe his sword before Kevgeon had started to swing his huge weapon. Kevgeon was forcing Adokas backwards, using an agile manoeuvre Adokas leaped up onto a table, however Kevgeon had anticipated this move, and kicked the table out from under him, and so he was sent sprawling on the floor. Kevgeon now looked around to see the situation in the rest of the bar, this was when he noticed the map on the table where the companions had been sat, it didn't take him long to realise that it would lead him directly to where he had been told to go. Grabbing the map he ran for the door.

"We have what we came for," Kevgeon shouted, "Let's get out of here."

The orc who was by the farmers stood from where he had fallen earlier, and ran out of the door behind Kevgeon. The two remaining orcs did not have the chance to escape, the orc facing Davkul was made short work of, and Zanian did well to hold his own against the orc he was facing, until it received an arrow to the back of its head from Jannays' bow.

After the dust had settled Thoril removed a small vile from his robes, and proceeded to use the potion inside to heal all of the people who had been injured during the fight.

"They took my map!" called Roscoe.

"That's what they were searching for," Said Adokas.

"It would appear that we need you to take us to the ruins yourself Roscoe," Thoril suggested.

"But I can't," protested the little musician.

"The fate of our entire existence may depend on us making it to those ruins before the orcs do," warned Adokas.

Roscoe looked each of the three adventurers in the face, then he looked at the scene around him, and finally his gaze fell upon Jannays, then with a sigh he turned back to Adokas, "Okay," he said, " I'll take you to the ruins."

"Thank you Roscoe," started Adokas, "And you Davkul, must get us an audience with Nasgaroth."

"I'll do what I can," replied the dwarf.

"We must set off tonight," stated Thoril. The other companions all nodded, and began to prepare for their departure.

Roscoe gathered his old travelling equipment from his room. He said goodbyes to Jannays, Zanian, and the farmers, and then the companions began their journey.

Davkul heading back to his home in the Hardrock Mountains, and the other three set out for the forest of Transeen.

Chapter 2
The Meaning of Dreams

The dream came to him again this night. In all his years he had never truly remembered his dreams, even with a mind like his, but this dream was different. He'd had this dream every night for the past three weeks, and he remembered it perfectly even after the first night.

It started as it always did, with a great shadow falling over a land that was foreign to him. He could see a great battle being fought; he could see that both armies in this war were made up of the same four races. Both armies had the tall, slim windswept archers, and the short blue trident wilding mages. Both armies let the large rock like fighters lead the charge, as the red-cloaked assassins picked off the generals one by one.

After showing this battle the dream moved on to what looked to be the inside of a castle, there was a great chamber. In this chamber he saw a warrior from each of the four races he witnessed in the battle along with a larger bestial warrior. There was another being in this room as well as the four warriors; there was a monster in there with them, a demon of terrible power. The five warriors attacked the demon, fighting for what seemed like hours. It was at this point the dream became even more surreal, for the five warriors became him and two of the closest friends he'd ever had, one of the warriors remained the same however, the fiery assassin was still fighting alongside them. They continued to fight the demon; up until the demon's sword was thrust through the his chest, this was the time in the dream when he woke up.

Laucian sat up in his bed, sweat pouring down his brow. He knew he would get no more rest this night, for he had tried to when the dreams had first began. Laucian rose from his bed, he dressed in his usual black trousers, and sleeveless black tunic. Retrieving his boots he left his room and began to walk down the long spiral staircase of Magon's tower.

Laucian had lived with the eccentric mage for almost two months now, ever since he and Tanay had come to Getandor in search of Elana.

He had learned much from Magon; he could control his psionic abilities much better now. He had also found out about his true heritage. All his life he had been brought up as elven, but now he knew why he had never fit in amongst his "own" kind, it was not because he was abnormal, but because he was only half-elven. He learned that he was not actually born into house Galanodel, but rather he was the son of one of the house servants, a Miss Duskwalker, and his father was a planer traveller who had been visiting the Galanodel house.

After Laucian was conceived his father was never seen again, and his mother died just minutes after his birth, so he was taken in by the head of the Galanodel family, and raised as a son. Although he was never treated as an equal to his supposed brother.

Laucian finally reached the room he was looking for. This was the room Laucian had used the most during his stay in the tower. The room was about sixty feet long and forty feet wide, and it was filled with a variety of walls, bars, ropes, nets and beams. This room was designed to test a person's speed, agility, and stamina.

Laucian took a few steps into the room, letting the door swing closed behind him. He stood perfectly motionless for a few seconds, composed himself, and then he suddenly burst into a run, and leaped up onto the first rope.

He spent about an hour running around this room, swinging on ropes, leaping from bars to beams, climbing nets, and running along walls as if they were the floors.

He finally ended his exercise by swinging from one of the bars into a flip, and landing in almost exactly the same spot from which he started.

"It still amazes me to see you do that, and not be out of breath." Said Stomorel in a cheery voice. Stomorel was an elven druid, who spent much of her time at Magon's tower. She had entered the room quietly about twenty minutes earlier.

"And I keep telling you, you cannot get out of breath, if you don't breathe." Laucian's replied dryly.

"Oh yes, I keep forgetting your not actually elven. What was your real father again?" Said Stomorel sarcastically.

"What do you want?" asked Laucian, who had never really liked this nosey druid. She was always trying to make conversation with him, and was always trying to find *the person he used to be.*

"Why must I want something? I just heard some movement and wondered what it was."

"Well now you know, so you can leave me be." And with that Laucian headed for the door. Much to his dismay Stomorel followed him out into the hall.

"What you doing now?" The elf maiden asked.

"If you must know, I'm going to have some breakfast," and with that Laucian set off down the hall.

"That's quite a pace, you must be really hungry." Giggled the elf, who had to jog to keep up.

Laucian didn't reply to the joke, he was hoping that if he ignored her she would go away. He wasn't in the mood for her constant questioning this morning. Stomorel however, didn't plan on giving up so easily.

"I like your tattoo." Said Stomorel, indicating the intricate glaive and dragon design on Laucian's shoulder. Again Laucian ignored the elf, and carried on walking towards the kitchens. "It's the mark of Elvin isn't it?"

"Why do you keep following me?" asked Laucian, as he spun around to face Stomorel. By this point he was starting to get annoyed with the curious druid.

"I'm just trying to make conversation," replied Stomorel, "You know, it's called being polite, you might want to try it some time."

"Well I'm not in the mood to be polite, so why don't you just go away, and leave me be." and with that Laucian turned from Stomorel, and started off back down the corridor.

Again Stomorel was jogging in an attempt to keep up with Laucian. "You're not going to get rid of me that easily."

If Laucian were able to draw breath, at this point he would drawn a deep one, and let out a long sigh. At this time Laucian called upon an ability he assumed he had inherited from his father. He closed his eyes and began to concentrate, suddenly there was a cloud of dust by Laucian's feet, Stomorel, having never seen him do this before just watched in amazement as the cloud began to rapidly grow, within a few seconds the cloud had filled the corridor for twenty feet in each direction.

Stomorel began to cough uncontrollably and started to run back in the direction she had come from, in an attempt to get out of the cloud. Laucian however just continued walking as if nothing was out of the ordinary.

"Now that was just rude." the voice came from somewhere in front of Laucian, then a few more words could be heard, and a gentle breeze was felt by both Laucian, and Stomorel. This breeze cleared away the dust in the corridor at a swift rate. As the dust dissipated Stomorel's coughing ceased, and she turned to see who had cast the wind spell. Laucian however just carried on walking, without even a break in his stride.

"Are you okay Stomorel?" asked her mysterious saviour.

"She's fine." answered Laucian, "There isn't enough dust to actually choke a person." Stomorel's expression went from that of relief after dust had cleared, to one of miss trust when she saw who it was who had cast the spell. She had never trusted Tanay, the viperian sorcerer. Tanay looked almost human, with only a few tell tale differences that gave away his true heritage.

Tanay was Laucian's travelling companion; they had met a couple of years earlier in Krondmare, and had become great friends almost immediately after they had met. This was one of the reasons Stomorel tolerated Tanay, that and the fact that Magon seemed to trust him, but Stomorel still had her doubts about him, she still couldn't bring herself to trust a viperian, not a member of that sinister, devious race.

Laucian's pace never slowed as he walked past Tanay and through the door at the end of the corridor. Tanay turned to see where Laucian was heading.

"Hmm time for breakfast," Tanay then turned back to Stomorel "Care to join us?" Stomorel just stared at Tanay suspiciously, then without saying a word turned and walked back down the corridor, away from Tanay, who just laughed to himself before he followed Laucian into the kitchen.

"I see you're up early again," said Tanay, as he walked over to the stove, where Laucian was serving himself some stew. "Looks like Magon was expecting you'd be having an early breakfast today."

"It would appear so. There is stew and fresh bread, and more than enough for two," explained Laucian as he went to sit at the table in the middle of the room.

"Is that your way of asking me to join you for breakfast?" chuckled the sorcerer as he too helped himself to some of the stew. "Have you spoken to Magon about the dreams?"

"No, not yet, you're the only person who knows about them."

"Then how did he know to have a meal prepared early this morning?" Tanay moved over to the table, and took a seat across from Laucian.

"Well you know Magon; he always seems to know more than he lets on."

"Was it the same dream?"

"As it always is."

"Do you think it means anything?"

Laucian stood up and took his now empty bowl over to the water basin, "The only thing this recurring dream means is that some all knowing power doesn't want me to sleep."

"I thought you of all people would believe that dreams have meanings behind them." Tanay finished his food and took his bowl over to be washed.

"You have me confused with a seer, I'm a psychic, there is a difference."

"Is there?" came a voice from by the cooking pot. Both Laucian and Tanay span around to see who else was in the room with them. "Oh brilliant, you ate my breakfast." Tanay looked around in disbelief, as there was no one to be seen. Laucian just shook his head and walked back over to the table.

"Sorry about your breakfast Magon." said Laucian as he sat back down at the table.

"It's not you who should be sorry, I expected you to be up, I just didn't expect our reptilian friend to be up." came the voice again, as he spoke Magon began to make his appearance. The first thing to appear was his beard; it was long, grey, and looked as though it hadn't been brushed in years. Next came the rest of his head, he had long grey hair, and bushy grey eye brows. His nose was long and slightly pointed, on which he had perched his glasses, and perched they were as one of the arms and hooks were missing.

After his head appeared the rest of Magon's body began to come into view, he was quite tall, by human standards, he was thin, and wearing a long sky blue night robe, with many different coloured patches covering lots of small holes which had been made from the general wear and tare from the well used robe.

"You look amazed that an old mage can use magic." Magon chuckled.

"It's not that, I just find it odd that a man feels he should have to walk around his own home, invisible." replied Tanay.

"Well I heard someone stealing my breakfast, and I thought it may have been burglars."

"Burglars? Ha, we all know that it would take an army to penetrate these walls, and not even the craftiest of thieves could make it past your magical defences." Tanay retuned, laughing heartily.

"Well I have had a long time to make those defences." Magon adjusted his glasses, and looked at Laucian, who had now sat at the table, with his back to him and Tanay. Magon then turned his gaze to Tanay, and with a nod of the head indicated the door.

"Yes, well, I have to go and get my things ready, I'm setting off to see Nasgaroth in a few hours." said Tanay, as he walked towards the door. There was a long silence after Tanay left the room, Magon slowly walked towards the table, and sat down directly across from Laucian.

"With all the magic you know, with all the knowledge you posses, why don't you fix your glasses? Why do you wear a robe which is in tatters?" asked Laucian sombrely.

"Sentiment, when you have lived as long as I have you begin to cling to your past, you try to hold onto the good things in your life, the happy memories."

"Just how long have you lived?"

"Long enough to know when a friend is troubled." Laucian just quietly laughed at the comment, "What's so funny?"

"You have known me for less than two months, and yet you call me friend."

"You don't call me friend?" Magon leaned back on his chair; he adjusted his glasses, which had slipped off his nose.

"To me a friend is someone I can trust implicitly."

"Ah, now I see, you feel you can trust me, so I'm your friend, but you don't think that I'll be able to trust you." Magon sat up straight now, with a large grin on his face, Laucian thought that he looked like a child who had just outsmarted its tutor in some logic puzzle. A slight grin found its way onto Laucian's face as he looked at Magon, and he chuckled to himself.

"You know, I think that could possible be the first time I've seen you smile," said Magon with a reminiscing tone. The smile quickly disappeared from Laucian's face and was replaced by his usual emotionless expression.

"So why are you up so early?" asked Magon who had decided that he had best try to get to the point of the conversation.

"I couldn't sleep" was the simple and direct answer he received.

"Like you haven't been able to sleep for the past three weeks?"

"You know about that?"

"Of course I know. I know everything that goes on in my tower."

"Then how come you thought it was burglars eating your breakfast?" It was Magon's turn to chuckle now, and he promptly re-adjusted his glasses as they slipped from his nose again.

"So anyway, are you going to tell me about this dream or not?" asked Magon, deciding that he had best get down to business. Laucian however was still unsure if he wanted to talk to Magon about it, he had told Tanay, but he was his best friend, he had only known Magon for less than two months, how could he know if he could really be trusted?

"Now come on Laucian, have I given you any reason not to trust me?" Laucian was again amazed at Magon's seeming ability to know what a person was thinking, even though he always denied being psychic.

Laucian decided that he had nothing to lose by telling Magon what he had been dreaming, it's not like it actually meant anything, and so he explained the dream to Magon, and how it had occurred every night, always exactly the same.

"Well, where do I begin," Magon re-arranged his glasses, which had again slipped from his nose. His face had now taken on a more serious look, one that was not often seen on the old wizard. "I'm not sure that there is much I can do to help you with your sleepless nights, I cannot stop dreams, but maybe I will be able to help a little with the meanings behind them."

"Do you believe that all dreams have meanings?"

"Oh no, not at all. A couple of nights ago I dreamt that I was an apple, and that a man picked me from the tree and took me to market."

"You have strange dreams old man."

"Yes I know, but what I'm trying to explain is that my dream had no meaning, it was all part of my mind, and therefore doesn't have any real reason behind it. Reoccurring dreams however do generally have a meaning; there is a purpose behind them."

"Then what does my dream mean?"

"Well how should I know? I'm a wizard, not a seer, there is a difference." Magon laughed, and nearly fell from his chair as he tried to catch his glasses as they again slipped from his nose. "Now, seriously, I cannot be sure about what your dream means without looking into it, I do have an idea about why you are seeing the war of the elements, but I thought there would be more time."

"More time for what? What is this war you speak of?" Laucian was now more confused than he was before he had decided to speak with Magon about the dreams.

"I'm afraid I cannot say any more at this time, but this matter will require more reading, and that could take some time."

"Then what am I suppose to do while you do this reading?"

"Well my suggestion would be for you to go to see Nasgaroth with Tanay, I'm sure he would welcome the company."

Laucian leaned back in his chair; he stared at Magon for a few moments. Laucian was sure that Magon knew more than he was letting on in this instance, but he didn't know why Magon was holding back this information. "Perhaps some time on the road will take my mind off these dreams." He said, knowing that there would be no point in trying to gain any more information from the old wizard.

"Well you had best get a move on my young friend, Tanay is wanting to set off quite soon." With this final suggestion Laucian stood, gave Magon a respectful nod of his head, and walked over to the door.

Laucian opened the door to find himself face to face with Stomorel, who looked slightly shocked at the door opening; she still had her arm outstretched towards the handle. Laucian took a step back and to the side, barely looking at her as she walked through the door.

"Ah, my dear Stomorel, would you like to join me for breakfast, I was just about to make some stew, since someone ate mine." Laucian did not react to the obvious joke Magon was making towards him, and just walked through the door and headed to prepare for his forthcoming trip with Tanay.

*   *   *

The room was dark; it had large stoned walls, and no widows. The light for this room was supplied by two torch's, one at each side of the large wooden door which stood in the centre of the eastern wall, a fire in the hearth, which was directly opposite the door, and there were some lit candles on a blood stained alter to the north of the room. There was also a large wooden table in the centre of the room; it was very long, with five chairs on the sides, and a large elegantly carved chair at the head.

There were two men in this room, the first was a tall, broad shouldered man, who was wearing a suit of black armour that covered him completely, many skulls decorated this armour, and the helmet had large bat wings on the side. The second man was much shorter and slimmer than the first; he wore a simple robe, in a deep patterned green.

"I have news from the spy my lord," said the shorter man.

"And what might that be Deventis?" asked the larger man.

"I have been informed that the psychic has been having the dream," replied Deventis. The armoured man now walked over to his alter.

"So Magon is now aware that the time is at hand"

"Yes my lord."

"This boy who is having the dream, he must be killed, he could be troublesome if he is not."

"My spy tells me that he will be on the road shortly, travelling to see one named Nasgaroth."

"Will he be travelling with his usual companion?" the man now turned to look at Deventis, although through the darkness he could not be seen too well.

Deventis took a deep breath before answering, "Yes my lord."

"Go, send the three to me, and then go and tend to the king."

"Yes my lord." Deventis bowed low before turning and leaving the room.

The man now sat in his chair at the head of the table, and waited for the three to arrive. He did not have long to wait before there was a gentle knock on the door.

"Enter." The door opened, and three women walked in, the first of which wore red trousers and a low cut red top, she had pale skin, and her hair was long and rich blond in colour and large pointed ears. The second two had pale red coloured skin, with long dark hair not quite covering their pointed ears, or the ring of small horns circling their heads, the clothes they wore were identical to then the first had, in all but colour, their clothes were black.

The first of the women walked over to the table and hopped up onto it just in front of the man, and leaned close to him, the other two stayed standing at the other end of the table.

"You sent for us, Markus," said the elf as she leaned even closer to the man in the chair.

"You will refer to me as either General Markus or my lord." he replied, as he pushed the attractive woman away from him. General Markus now stood and walked towards the fire. He laughed to himself as he walked, even though he had sent these three to assassinate many people, he still always found it odd to see two graws answering to an elf. Graws were a race of lesser demons that managed to break free of the abyss making the material plane their home. Many believed them to be a twisted reflection of the ancient elves created back when Gallisium was still a young world. None could say if this was true or not, but it was certainly true that for as long as was recorded the elves and the demonic graw had despised each other. Yet here before him those ancient hatreds were put aside by these three to do the bidding of General Markus.

"I do apologise, my lord." The elf now stood from the table, "What is it you wish of us." she asked.

"I wish you to travel to country of Getandor. The psychic known as Laucian, he will be on the road between Magon's tower, and the dwarven mine in the Hardrock Mountains. I want him eliminated."

"When are we to set off, my lord?"

"Immediately."

"Then we will take our leave." The three now began to walk towards the door.

"Aluthana, there is one more thing."

The elf turned to face General Markus, "And what is that my lord?"

"Laucian will not be travelling alone; he will be with the young sorcerer Tanay, Deventis's son."

"And what do you wish me to do with him?"

"Kill him."

Chapter 3
Cloak and Dagger

The road was easy to travel, which was lucky as it was going to be difficult to catch the orcs, who had a big head start. Even though Zanian had supplied the three companions with horses, they would be hard pressed to catch up.

Despite their chaotic nature orcs can be quite remarkable creatures. Even with their stocky, heavy build, they have the ability to travel great distances in very short amounts of time. The companions knew this, and had been riding hard, but the orcs were still no-where in sight.

It had been a very uneventful ride across the plains, at this time of the year the nomadic tribes can usually be found close to the mountains, following the herds of deer they hunt. Which means that most of the caravans took the north-western road, where as the companions were heading south-west.

They rode for three days before reaching the forest, only stopping for short periods of time, to sleep and eat. This wasn't exactly to Roscoe's taste, as he had gotten used to the easy life of three meals a day, four on some days. He was also used to a full nights sleep, not just the couple of hours the companions could afford to have.

Finally they reached the edge of the forest. They hadn't seen the orcs since the night in the bar, but they hoped that it would be easy to pick up there trail when they entered the forest. Orcs may be able to travel quickly, but being discreet is not one of there strong points. These orcs would not be able to travel through this forest without leaving an easy trail to follow.

Travelling through the forest wasn't going to be easy, the companions would not be able to take the horses with them, as they would slow their speed greatly, making it even harder for them to catch the orcs as they would still be able to keep up their quick pace, even through the dense woodland.

Adokas was the first of the of the companions to enter the forest, he spent a short time examining the forest, looking to see if he could pick up the orcs trail. Roscoe and Thoril started to unload the horses. It didn't take Adokas long to pick up the orcs trail, they were following exactly the same route Roscoe had drawn on his map.

"Can you tell how much time they have on us?" Thoril asked as he walked up to his elven friend.

"About an hour, we have been gaining on them," replied the skilled ranger.

"Can you tell how many there are?"

"You don't want to know." By now Roscoe was stumbling over to where Thoril and Adokas stood.

"What don't we want to know?" He asked, trying to compose himself slightly.

Both Adokas and Thoril looked to each other, neither wanted to tell the little bard what odds they were facing. "We should get going." Thoril suggested.

Adokas took the lead through the forest, following the trail left by the orcs. He occasionally asked Roscoe if they were heading in the direction of the ruins, which they always were, in exactly the same way Roscoe had shown on his map.

Their pace had slowed greatly since the trio had entered the forest; Adokas was still able to travel at high speed, having spent most of his life wandering his woodland home. Thoril and Roscoe however were not used to this type of terrain, although both had done their share of travelling in the past Roscoe much preferred country lanes, and Thoril spent most of his time experimenting with his magic in the luxurious mage house.

"Hold up," called Adokas from a little way in front of Roscoe.

"Be quiet, do you want the orcs to hear us?" snapped Roscoe, more than a little worried.

"Don't worry so much my little friend, there's only one orc likely to have heard me, and he is quite dead."

"What are you talking about?" asked Thoril, who was bringing up the rear.

"I'm talking about the poorly hidden corps over there." replied Adokas with a grin. Adokas pointed over to his left, where there was a large pile of freshly ripped up foliage, half covering the corps he was talking about.

"What do you think happened?" Asked Thoril as he took a closer look.

"Does it matter? Its one less orc for us to worry about." chuckled Roscoe.

"It matters because someone or something killed it, and although it may be intelligent enough to try to hide the body but isn't too bothered if it is found." explained Thoril.

"Perhaps it was just killed by the other orcs, as punishment for something," suggested Roscoe.

"No, if that was the case this poor soul would have been strung up for everyone to see, as a warning to others, no he was probably a scout of some kind, killed by someone who doesn't like orcs much." said Adokas, "By the look of his injuries it was an experienced swordsman who did this, they knew exactly where to strike so the creature died quick and easily."

"Well if it was someone who doesn't like orcs then that's a good thing isn't it?"

"Not necessarily my small friend, there are many things in this world that dislike both orcs and Halflings alike." chuckled Thoril.

"We should keep moving," said Adokas, "About how far are we from the ruins?"

"We're getting close."

"That explains why there was a scout; he was probably keeping watch for us as the others searched the ruins."

The three companions continued through the forest, now trying to move much quieter than they had been, hoping that they could sneak up on the orcs, hoping that the orcs hadn't found what they were looking for.

It didn't take the companions long to find the ruins, but they did not expect what they found. The ruins were in the middle of a large clearing; there was a surprisingly small amount of plant growth in the area, even after the centuries this place had been abandoned. The only vegetation that thrived in this area was a thick green vine that covered the crumbled foundations of the ancient temple.

It wasn't the lack of foliage that surprised the companions when they caught their first glimpse of the clearing; it was the large number of orc corpses. By the looks of things all of these orcs were killed by only two men, the two men who were still in the clearing, and the two men who were still fighting against what looked like overwhelming odds.

The first of the men was a knight of some kind, he was wearing full plate mail armour, the sun was shining off of his large polished silver shield and his blood stained sword. The second man was cloaked and hooded; he was wielding a long slender sword in one hand, and a curved dagger in the other.

The three companions slowly took a few steps into the clearing, staring in disbelief at the scene before them. By the looks of the amount of orcs there, these two warriors had been against an entire orc raiders tribe, and by the amount of these orcs that were already dead, they were winning.

"It would appear we have an audience." called the hooded man.

"If we ask nicely they may be kind enough to help," replied the armoured man, in a low gruff voice. It didn't take long for Adokas to pick up on this hint, with lightning speed he had his bow in hand, and by the time the closest orcs to where he was standing had turned to face him, one of them already had an arrow in his neck.

The three companions now found themselves in a fight for their lives, and so dropped their packs, and prepared to face the orcs. After Adokas had killed the first of his new foes he drew his sword and charged into battle, Thoril raised his staff and began chanting the beginnings of a spell. Roscoe however retreated back into the woods slightly, knowing he would be no good in a straight fight, so he decided that he would be better suited to stay away from the main action and use his crossbow.

From Roscoe's position he had a good view of the entire battle, he spent the first few moments looking to see where his crossbow could be put to the best use. He first thought to help the two strangers, as they had quite plainly been fighting for a while, but after a few moments watching them he realised that they in no way needed his aid. The hooded man first appeared to be in the most trouble, as there were a great deal more orcs around him than any of the others, but upon closer inspection Roscoe saw that he was in complete control of his situation. His swift movements and the precise strikes of his blades meant that he was more than a match for the orcs, each swing of his sword; each thrust of his dagger either maimed or killed one of his enemies.

The armoured man also appeared to be handling himself well too, although he was not as efficient in his fighting style as the hooded man was, he was still having little trouble dealing with the orcs he faced. His fighting style was very methodical, and precise, he looked as though he had been trained in one of the great knight schools.

Roscoe now turned his attention to his companions; Adokas was using his speed and agility to run rings around his opponents. Thoril however was having a little bit of difficulty.

Thoril was not as well trained in close combat as the others; he needed more space so he could cast his spells. This was the reason Roscoe decided to try to keep the orcs at bay from Thoril. It had been a long time since Roscoe had used his crossbow in combat, but he proved on this day that he had not lost his touch. Each bolt he fired hit its target, although he was not as accurate as Adokas with his bow, he did drive the orcs back away from Thoril, most were just clutching at painful wounds, but it gave Thoril the chance he needed to put his powerful magic into action.

The battle raged for quite a time, swords clashed, bolts flew, and magic was thrown. The numbers of orcs fell swiftly, which made Roscoe's confidence grow greatly. As his confidence grew, Roscoe began to move closer to the fighting, as he tried to get a better aim at his enemies. This extra confidence Roscoe gained meant that he began to be less cautious, which almost became his undoing.

Roscoe had completely left his concealment by now, and was still taking aim at the orcs closest to Thoril. There was a loud grunt behind Roscoe, and with a quick glance over his shoulder Roscoe realised the folly in leaving his concealed position. The halfling spun around swiftly, aiming his crossbow at this new foe. He was not fast enough though, the orc just laughed, and knocked the crossbow from Roscoe's hand, and sent him sprawling backwards.

Roscoe saw the orc advancing on him; the orc raised its large serrated blade, the halfling closed his eyes tightly as the orc brought its sword down in an arc, "*Hashnay!*" he cried as he expected to feel the orcs weapon to strike, but to his surprise the blow never came.

Roscoe opened his eyes to see what had happened, and he was surprised to see the hooded warrior before him, arm extended.

"That was close my small friend." said the hooded figure as he helped Roscoe to his feet.

"I'm just glad you arrived before he finished his swing." Roscoe replied gratefully.

"Yes, thought you would be," said the man, sounding a little confused. They both now turned their attention to the rest of the fighting. Most of the orcs were now dead, and many of those which did remain looked as though they would be dead shortly, the rest were beginning to make a hasty retreat into the forest.

After the fighting was over everyone made their introductions Roscoe took a moment to have a closer look at the two men, it was at this point that he realised that because of their clothing he could not actually see any part of either of them.

It was the hooded man who introduced himself first, "My name is Solaris," he said as he lowered his hood to reveal a pale-skinned face, with long fiery red hair, on the left side of his face there was a tattoo of flames, this tattoo came up from his neck, and went up around one of his pale yellow eyes.

The armoured man now stepped forward and introduced himself. "I am Jamaan, son of Jameel, paladin of the highest order of Sugalas."

"Well met, my name is Thoril Serpenthelm, and these are my companions Adokas Loreweaver, and Roscoe Thorngage."

"Many thanks for your aid, but what brings you to this remote place?" asked Solaris.

"We were actually tracking these orcs, hoping to find an artefact which they were also searching for," replied Adokas.

The main conversation started to dwindle; Adokas and Thoril began to search the crumbled foundations. Jamaan started to pile up all of the orc corpses at one end of the clearing. Solaris took this time to speak with Roscoe.

"Tell me Roscoe, what does *Hashnay* mean?" he asked.

"Excuse me?" Roscoe replied, slightly confused by the question.

"Hashnay," clarified Solaris, "You called it out when that orc was attacking you."

"I don't know, I didn't realise that I had said anything."

"Interesting." Solaris seemed slightly preoccupied for a moment, "I think your friends may need a little help in their search." Roscoe looked over to his two companions.

"You're probably right," he said, not knowing exactly how much use he would be, but he still went to offer his services.

Roscoe had almost reached his companions by the time Solaris heard the voice from behind him.

"You are not welcome here." came the voice.

"I proved your people could trust me a long time ago." Solaris replied.

"But they have not, the wizard digs too close to that which is hidden, and we cannot allow it to be disturbed."

"They will not disturb the gateway, I promise you this."

"How can you make promises for people you have just met?"

"Do you doubt my word?" asked Solaris as he now turned to face this man.

"No, I doubt your judgement." At this point everyone in the clearing, bar Solaris and the man he was speaking to, found several swords pointed at each of their throats, these swords were held by warriors, who appeared from no-where.

"What is the meaning of this?" called Jamaan.

"Is this really necessary?" asked Solaris.

"Why do you draw swords on us?" asked Adokas.

"You trespass upon our land." Spat the man closest to Adokas.

"This forest has long been uninhabited, who are you?" asked Roscoe, more than a little confused.

"Look closely Roscoe, and remember the tales spoken by old bards." called Solaris from where he stood. Roscoe did as instructed. The warriors were about the same hight as humans with strong corded muscles. The beautiful weapons the held, some with lightly glowing runes, showed that they were well versed in the crating arts, but their thick wild mains of hair, horns and long additional canine teeth gave them a slightly bestial appearance. It was their eyes that really drew Roscoe's attention though, they were both haunting and beautiful, with no iris or pupil they were instead deep pools of silver or gold.

"Etharii?" Roscoe said almost to himself. "But I thought you were just a fairy story."

"Not fairy stories, just somewhat reclusive, they often go unnoticed since they mostly dwell on the ethereal plane." Explained Solaris as he approached the others.

"You are trespassing in our lands, we are bound by an ancient oath to protect these ruins, and that which is hidden within them." said the etharii which had been talking to Solaris.

"We are sorry to trespass, but perhaps you could help us," started Adokas.

"And why should we help you elf? You who invade our home." asked another of the etharii bitterly. There was a long silence after this, and the tension began to grow.

Solaris eventually broke the silence, "I was wondering if you could tell me where the Sugalas' flair lies?" he asked the etharii he had been speaking with. The mention of this fabled weapon caught the attention of Jamaan, and Roscoe's two companions.

"Jovan's bow no longer lays here." was the reply.

"Where is it now?" asked Thoril urgently.

"It was taken by the orcs, along with Malkay's sword."

"You would let orc raiders lay their filthy hands upon Jovan's mighty bow? How could you let them take it?" Asked Jamaan, sounding more than a little angry.

"The bow is no concern of ours, we were only charged to protect the gateway, anything else that was left here matters not to us."

"How long ago did they take the bow?" asked Thoril.

"Why are we answering their questions?" asked one of the etharii.

"Because they are with a trusted friend to our people."

"If it was the orcs who found the bow, won't it still be hear somewhere?" asked Roscoe.

"Not necessarily, do you see that leader who was in the bar?" replied Adokas.

"If you are searching for the bow, then it is no longer here, which means you have no reason to remain."

"If we leave quickly we may be able to catch them." Adokas suggested.

"The quicker you leave the better." said another of the etharii.

"You will not catch the orcs, they have used some strange magic to speed up there escape. They are already far from the borders of our forest," informed the man who had been speaking to Solaris.

"Then our mission has failed." said Thoril.

"We should still go to seek Nasgaroth's council." Suggested Adokas.

"Fanell," started Solaris as he turned to face the etharii he had spoke with earlier, "Tell your men to lower their weapons; there is no need for any violence here. I would speak to you privately." The etharii thought for a moment, and then turned to his men.

"Lower your weapons, but stay on guard," Fanell then turned back to Solaris, "They have not yet earned our trust."

"That is fair, now can we speak?"

"Certainly." Both of the men walked to the far side of the clearing and began to talk.

The etharii backed off from the others, who all moved in closer together so they could speak.

"Tell me Jamaan, who is this Solaris, and why does he seem so friendly with the etharii?" asked Adokas.

"I'm not too sure, I only met Solaris a month ago, and he does not speak too much of himself." Jamaan explained.

Roscoe was only half listening to the conversation; he was watching the conversation across the clearing, which seemed to be becoming a little heated. Adokas and Thoril began to plan what they would do next.

"Do you wish us to leave you back in Calamshan Roscoe?" asked Thoril.

"Well, yes, I guess so." Roscoe replied. At this point Solaris returned to the group, Fanell went to speak with his men.

"He has agreed to aid us." Solaris began, "You know Roscoe I think you will enjoy meeting Nasgaroth, it is quite a unique experience."

"I'm not going to the meeting; I was only guiding the others here." Roscoe explained.

"No, I think that you should come with us to the meeting." said Solaris.

"You will be joining us?" asked Adokas.

"It has been a long time since I last saw Nasgaroth, and I think it could be an interesting trip." The etharii now started to disappear, as they began to return to the ethereal plain. Fanell approached the group.

"Our steeds will take you as far as Calamshan, but no further." he said.

"Many thanks, it will cut days from our journey." said Solaris gratefully as four griffins appeared as if from no-where. Each of the griffins had one etharii rider, and looked to have room for one passenger.

"The halfling will have to share a mount," explained Fanell.

"He can ride with me," said Solaris before anyone else could make an offer, "Perhaps I can take the time to talk him into joining us on our visit to Nasgaroth." The now five strong party mounted the griffins. It took them only mere hours to reach Calamshan on the griffins.

When they arrived in Calamshan the companions dismounted, and the etharii took no time in shifting back to the ethereal plain and set off back to their woodland home. The companions decided that they would stay the night in Calamshan, and set out to see Nasgaroth in the morning. Roscoe spoke to Zanian and got the party some cheap rooms in the Cattle Shed. During the trip back to Calamshan Solaris had succeeded in talking Roscoe into travelling with the rest of them to see Nasgaroth, so he turned in early, realising that he was in for a long and interesting journey.

Chapter 4
Friend or Foe?

It didn't take the pair long to gather their things for travel, neither of the men were planning to take much on this trip as they would be returning to the tower. They didn't need to take many supplies as the journey to the Hardrock mountains would only take about ten days, and with the root Magon had suggested meant they would be passing through a small village or farming community every day or two.

Tanay was an interesting site in his travelling clothes, most people wear dull clothing, which didn't show the fading caused by long times spent in the wild. Tanay however wore a bright red cloak, with an even brighter yellow lining. Under his cloak he wore brown leather trousers with extravagant buckles, and a white shirt, with frills on the collar and cuffs. He wore his pack on his back, and held a spear in his hand. The shaft of the spear was gnarled and twisted, and instead of showing the brown colour of the wood it was made from it was a deep orange colour, with a flame yellow head.

Laucian looked much more like the usual travellers, he wore a muddy brown cloak over the top of the black trousers and sleeveless top he had been wearing earlier in the training room. He too had a pack on his back, but unlike most travellers he was carrying no visible weapons.

"Will Coran be joining you on this trip?" asked Magon as he followed the two out of the main door to his tower. Most of the people currently staying in Magon's tower had come to see off this pair, Tanay was well liked be the serving staff, and a mysterious bald mage had taken a bit of an interest in Laucian, this interest had largely gone unnoticed, as the mage had remained in his room most of the time, Laucian and Tanay did not even know his name.

"Of course he will," answered Tanay "He's quite excited about meeting Nasgaroth." At that very moment, a shadow passed overhead, everyone glanced skyward to see Coran swooping down. Over the years Coran had become more of a friend to Tanay than a familiar, the small winged reptile had always been curious of magic users, so when he came across Tanay in a meditative state trying to summon a familiar, Coran decided to answer to young sorcerers call.

Coran flew around the trio before he finally landed on Tanay's shoulder, wrapping his long tail around the young sorcerer's neck. Coran looked like a small version of a dragon, he had dark blue scales down both his sides, which faded up to a red line down his back, and faded down to a shining silver on his underside. He folded his blue and red wings on his back and asked, <When do we leave?> projecting his question telepathically into all those around him.

"I know that I needn't tell either of you to be careful on your road," began Magon, in a much more serious tone than he normally used, "But you must remember the reputation of your race Tanay. Most of the people in this area have never met a Viperian, but they will have heard of them. If you are lucky the farmers will pay little attention to you, and if you give them no cause to think otherwise then they will just assume that your eyes are a product of some draconic heritage in your past."

Tanay was a Viperian a race related to snakes, in appearance he looked very similar to a human, there are some differences though. The snake nature can appear in many different ways in the viperians, ranging from forked tongues to patches of scales. This snake heritage had appeared within Tanay with scales on the top of his arms and back, which are easily hidden, but his eyes were not so easy to hide, for he had not the eyes of a man, but the eyes of a snake.

"Well there is always the possibility that I do have some dragon heritage anyway, they do say that sorcerers gain their magic from dragon blood running in their veins." Tanay replied with a grin.

"That is just a rumour started by a terrible sorcerer, who wished people would pay him a little more respect." Corrected Magon.

"We had best be leaving, if we wish to reach the first settlement by nightfall."

"You are eager to leave my friend. Is Stomorel not coming to see us off?" Tanay asked with a rye smile.

"I hope not." Laucian replied, scowling at Tanay as he began to walk away from the tower. Both Tanay and Magon laughed at this. They had both noticed the young elf maiden following Laucian around, trying to spend as much time as possible with him, they could both see that she had some kind of feelings for him. The pair could also see that Laucian had no interest in her, and that he had only been getting irritated by her constant presence.

"I'm afraid Stomorel will not be seeing you off this day, see apparently had to attend some important business in her grove." explained Magon.

"That's probably for the best," said Tanay, as he shot a glance towards his travelling companion, "I bid you good day, and now must take my leave, before Laucian gets too much of a head start on me."

"Then I too bid you a good day, and wish you luck on you quest."

"My thanks for your hospitality Magon. Come Coran, let us depart." At that point Coran leaped from Tanay's shoulder, spread his wings and soared in the direction Laucian had begun to walk. Tanay too started after his friend, jogging slightly until he caught up.

*   *   *

The large circular room was very luxurious; there were many large cushions scattered about. To one side of the room was a large four-poster bed, and to the other a desk. The desk was covered by many scrolls and bits of paper, to one side of the desk was a large book self, and on the other side were many shelves, on these shelves stood glass jars, the contents of which bare not mentioning. In the centre of the room was a fire pit, over which a large cauldron hung.

This was the room of Baknul Panthos, a necromancer of moderate power, and a loyal servant to General Markus.

"So who is it you hunt?" asked Baknul. It was not often that people visited this mage in his personal quarters, but today he had the company of the three, and Deventis. Baknul stood by the cauldron, on the bed laid a beautiful young maiden, one of Baknul's personal slaves. The three were all sat on the cushions, and Deventis stood by the door.

"We are hunting an old acquaintance of yours, Laucian Galanodel," replied Aluthana. Baknul turned to face the elven assassin, his lips curled into an evil smile. The woman on the bed also reacted to the name, sitting up, and moving to the edge of the bed, a look of great interest on her face.

"Silvana, leave us." Baknul ordered, without even looking at the woman on his bed.

"Yes my lord." The woman replied, and she immediately stood and left the room.

"You have her well trained," laughed Aluthana as the door closed.

"All of my creations are," Baknul replied. "Now how is it I can help your hunt?"

"We are in need of transportation; we need to get to Getandor, with great haste."

"My spy tells me that he will be passing through the village of Faknell in a matter of days, it'll be there last stop before they head to the mines in the Hardrock Mountains." explained Deventis.

"It's a long way, the sea voyage alone takes at least fifteen days, and that isn't even a third of the journey." Baknul mused as he sat on one of the numerous cushions.

"That's why we need your expert help," said one of the two graw members of the three, as she walked over to Baknul, and draped herself on the cushion next to him, rapping her arm around his neck.

"Well that's what I'm here for isn't it."

"So what do you suggest?" asked the graw as she ran her fingers through the necromancer's hair.

"Well first I suggest that you go back to that cushion over there," this remark surprised the graw, she had a shocked expression on her face as she walked back to her original cushion, "Don't take offence my dear, your just not my type. As for travelling to Getandor, I would suggest wind walking, fast and easy, you'll be in Faknell within two days, three at most."

"Make the arrangements," Deventis began, "And Aluthana, my son will be with Laucian, he will try to defend his friend, but I do not wish him harmed." Both of the graws smiled at this comment, "I will tell the General of the plans, report in when you return." At that point Deventis left the room. Baknul stood, and went to gather the components he needed to cast the wind walk spell, while the three started to plan their mission.

*   *   *

Magon had been correct; the people living in the small communities had paid little, if any attention to the two friends as they travelled their road. They had one more stop planned on their journey to the dwarf's mines, where Nasgaroth resided. That stop was Faknell, the largest of the villages they were passing through. They would reach the village a little before nightfall, and planned to spend the night there, and set off on the final leg of their journey early the following morning.

Faknell had originally begun as a small farming community like most of the other surrounding settlements, but it had grown over time through trading with the dwarfs. Faknell had grown so much that it had even had a garrison stationed there; a small trained fighting force that kept the peace in the area.

The wooden walls of Faknell came into view as the three friends came over the small rise. Coran flew on ahead a short way, before landing in the shade of a lone tree to the side of the road, Tanay and Laucian stopped in the shade too. Tanay took out the last of his water and drank most of it, then gave what was left to Coran, Laucian did likewise, and the three of them carried on along the road. It wasn't long before they were approaching the gates of Faknell.

"Halt! Who goes there?" called one of the guards from the wall above the door.

"We are friends," replied Tanay. At that point the gates opened and an armoured man walked out towards them followed by six more men, all with weapons drawn, several more figures appeared on the wall, each with bow in hand. The armoured man stopped a little in front of Tanay and Laucian, he folded his arms and looked the pair over.

"I don't care if you are friend or foe, it is who you are friend or foe too that matters to me." He said, staring Tanay in the face.

"We are friends to Magon of the tower, we wish to…" Tanay began.

"And you expect me to take your word on that?"

"Well it is all I have to give."

"The word of a Viperian does not count for much here, master Tanay."

"It appears you have me at a loss, for you know of me yet I do not know you."

"I am captain Holdak, commander of the Faknell garrison. We received word of your approach, and now I ask you to move on, I will not have one of your kind within these walls."

"Neither I, nor my people have committed any crimes here and all I wish…"

"The fact you have committed no crimes is the only reason I have not had you clamped in chains, now I advise you move along." Tanay could see the tension growing in the soldiers behind Holdak, and did not wish to push his luck, but he and Laucian were in need of water.

"We will leave then, if that is your wish."

"It is."

"But first I ask if we can have some water, for we have run out." Holdak thought for a moment before turning to one of his men.

"You, your water skin." The soldier stepped forward and handed his water skin to Holdak. "Here, I advise you make it last, I doubt the dwarves will be quite so generous to a Viperian." He handed the water to Tanay before turning and walking through the gates followed by his men, who promptly closed them.

Laucian turned to his companion, "I ask only one question, how did he know our destination?" This was a question Tanay was already asked himself, Holdak may have received word that a snake eyed sorcerer was heading this way, and he may have realised that it was a Viperian, but neither he nor Laucian had mentioned their destination.

The companions turned and walked away from Faknell, increasing their speed, it was beginning to grow dark, and they needed to find a safe place to make camp. It wasn't long before Faknell was out of sight; the terrain became much rockier as they got closer to the mountains. The surrounding area became much steeper as they entered the foothills, creating many outcroppings and small rock faces, and many large boulders lying around.

A little after they had lost sight of Faknell the companions noticed a cloaked figure sitting cross-legged in the middle of the road, with tall rock faces to either side of them. Both Laucian and Tanay found this scene suspicious. Laucian walked closer to the figure, where as Tanay stayed back, running his spells through his head, making himself ready for any possible ambush.

This was exactly what Aluthana had expected to happen, and just as soon as there was a large enough gap between Laucian and Tanay was big enough, one of the graws muttered a few words of magic, creating a wall of earth, as tall as the rock faces, between them.

Laucian spun around just in time to see the wall finish growing. "Do you always travel unarmed Laucian?" asked Aluthana. Laucian turned to see her still sitting on the ground, she removed her cloak, throwing it to her side, and then picked up two large daggers from the floor in front of her, before rising to her feet.

"I am never unarmed." was Laucian's reply as he turned back to face the woman, he dropped his pack to the ground, and threw his cloak off to the side, revealing the same clothes he had been wearing earlier in the training room, with only a couple of differences. He now wore a pair of leather bracer's on his wrists and a belt around his waist.

"That is good to hear, I do so enjoy it when the hunt ends with a good fight, I never was one of those easy prey assassins."

Laucian smiled "It's good to know that I've annoyed someone enough for them to send an assassin after me." Laucian reached behind his back and took hold of the two knives attached to his belt and brought them round to his side. "So, before you die, who is it that wants me dead? I'll have to pay them a visit, and annoy them some more."

"Oh don't you worry, I don't think you've met my master." At that point Aluthana launched herself forward, bringing one of her daggers in high, aimed for Laucian's head. With lightning quick reflexes Laucian easily blocked this first attack, blocking the second dagger was slightly more difficult though, Aluthana brought it in low and Laucian was hard pressed to bring one of his knives across to block it.

"Good move." Laucian said with a grin.

"I thought so"

Laucian's grin disappeared, and he pushed hard, forcing his opponent to step backwards quickly.

"So, if I haven't met your master," it was Laucian's turn to attack, he swiped across in front of himself, but Aluthana easily spun away, Laucian also spun, bringing his other knife round straight towards her gut, but Aluthana crossed her arms down low, stopping Laucian's attack from getting too close. "Why do they want me dead?" Laucian finished.

Aluthana forced Laucian's trapped arm up high, leaving his body unprotected against her knee, which she brought in hard and fast, scoring the first real blow in this fight. "The general wants you dead before you can interfere with Legion's plans."

Laucian fell backwards; he continued the movement rolling backwards until he had his feet under him again. "And which legion would that be then?"

Aluthana just smiled "I do like it when the damned try to make conversation."

"The damned? You're talking as though you've already killed me."

"Well I do have the upper hand, if you hadn't noticed."

"The upper hand," Laucian chuckled "I haven't even begun yet." He launched himself forward, and started what looked like an intricate dance with Aluthana, as they spun and twisted trying to find an opening in each other's defence.

Tanay was inspecting the wall that had appeared between him and his friend. He could hear voices from the other side of the wall, and the sound of metal clashing. He took a step back from the wall, "Coran, fly over there, see if Laucian needs help, I'll see what I can do about this wall." Coran launched himself upwards, but before he could reach the top a net was thrown over him.

"The wall is the least of your troubles." Tanay looked up to see Coran slowly descending with the net over him. That's when he also noticed a figure sat on top of the wall. This woman was the obvious source of both the comment and the net.

"So what trouble do you think I should worry about then?"

"Me," was the only reply he got, but not from the woman on the wall. Tanay spun around to see where this voice had come from, and he found himself face to face with one of the graws, who already had a sword and dirk in her hands.

Tanay dropped his pack and took a hold of his short spear with both hands. "And to what do I owe the pleasure of a graws company?"

"You keep bad company." The graw started to walk forward towards Tanay, who swung his spear to one side, extended one of his arms and muttered a few words of magic, causing five bolts of energy to emerge from his fingertips heading towards the graw, who used all her agility to try to avoid them, but they were too close. Where she was able to dodge the first couple of the energy bolts, the other three however hit their target, although not causing much damage, they did knock her back hard, causing her to stumble backwards.

Tanay strode up towards the fallen graw, "Terribly sorry about that, but I don't really get on with armed assailants." At this point Tanay felt a sharp stinging pain in his back, and fell forwards as he heard laughter behind him.

Aluthana spun away, giving herself a few yards from Laucian as she tried to catch her breath. Laucian smiled, "Getting tired?"

"Do you not loose your breath?" Asked Aluthana, as she again launched herself forward.

"It is particularly difficult for me to loose my breath," chuckled Laucian as he easily deflected the attack.

"And why is that?"

"Because I don't breath."

"Well that explains that then, although it's not going to help you I don't think." Aluthana slashed at Laucian back and forth, causing him to step backwards as he blocked the attacks and eventually made him drop one of his knives. She forced him back even more, until Laucian suddenly quickened his pace, making a slight gap between the duelling pair.

"Well I guess this is the end," said Aluthana as she moved in for the kill, thinking that Laucian no longer had ample defence against her attacks.

"You seem to be forgetting one thing."

"And what's that?"

Laucian smiled, before quickly extending his arm towards the assassin, conjuring up his psychic abilities and sent Aluthana flying backwards at least ten feet. Laucian retuned the knife he was still holding back to its sheath, as Aluthana staggered back to her feet, Laucian reached one of his bracer's, and pulled out a throwing knife and launched it towards Aluthana. The assassin quickly dodged to the side, narrowly avoiding the flying blade. She wasn't expecting the second knife though, which flew in fast, hitting Aluthana in the shoulder sending her to the floor.

Laucian walked towards his fallen foe, collecting and sheathing his knife on the way. He crouched over her and said, "Looks like you loose," as he took hold of the blade in Aluthana's shoulder and pulled it free.

Aluthana cringed with pain, "I want you to do something for me," she stuttered.

"And what's that?"

"Tell Magon from me, Legion is coming."

"Well I was thinking that maybe I'd take you back with me, you could tell him yourself."

"I'm afraid I can't allow that." Aluthana then hit Laucian in the groin with her knee, the pushed him backwards with both feet. The assassin rose to her feet, picked up her knives and ran along the footpath and disappeared into the darkness.

Tanay rolled over onto his back to see the graw from on top of the wall was now stood a few yards away from where he had fallen. As she walked towards him, Tanay noticed that she was now holding a spear of her own.

It wasn't long before both of the graws were standing over their prey. "Well, that was much easier than I expected."

"His father is supposed to be a great warrior; I guess he wasn't a very good teacher." Both of the graws laughed.

"So you've heard of my father then?"

The graw holding the sword bent low over Tanay, "I'll let you into a little secret before you die, we work for your father." The graw put her sword to Tanay's throat, "It seems a shame to kill someone so cute." Before the graw could strike though an arrow streaked into her chest.

"I agree, it is a shame to kill someone so cute, but graw are not welcome in these parts," came a gruff voice from within the darkness. "And I advise if you don't want to end up the same way as your friend, you drop your weapon." Holdak walked into view, flanked by two other soldiers both with bows aimed at the graw.

The graw looked from Holdak to the soldiers, and then to Tanay, he was only a secondary target, if Aluthana could finish off Laucian then there would be no trouble back when they returned to Markus. She uttered a few words under her breath and some smoke swirled around her.

"Kill her," yelled Holdak, and both soldiers loosed their arrows, but she was gone, and the arrows shattered on the wall behind where she had been.

Holdak approached Tanay, and helped him back to his feet. "Why is it that I thought if I followed you I would find some kind of trouble?"

"After our earlier meeting I'm surprised that you would help me."

"As I said before, I've never met a member of your race, only heard tales of the evils that occur within the homeland of your people."

"Ah yes, a common problem I face," Tanay replied with a smile, "A somewhat apt reputation for Sslishka's zealots who rule my homeland, but those of us who manage to escape that deities grip can be quite charming."

"That remains to be seen, but I have seen the evils of the graw first hand, and if you are foes to those demons, than that means you are a possible friend."

"Well that is good to hear."

"How is your back? It looked like a nasty spell she hit you with."

"Its fine, just stings a little."

After collecting his other throwing knife, Laucian approached the wall, "Tanay!" he called, "You okay over there?"

"I'm fine, stand away from the wall." Tanay spoke a few more words of magic and sent fireball flying towards the centre of wall, exploding on contact creating large hole.

Captain Holdak escorted Tanay, Laucian and Coran back to Faknell. Although he still was not prepared to trust Tanay completely, he had seen that Tanay was enemies with the graw, a race Holdak held much hatred for.

Chapter 5
Meetings

Captain Holdak showed the pair to The Sleeping Dragon Inn, which was located next to the soldier's barracks, and just happened to be the tavern in which most of the off duty soldiers spent their evenings.

"I was wondering," began Laucian, "Why have you now decided to let us stay in your town?"

"You must understand, under normal circumstances I would have not turned you away to begin with."

"But because of my race you did." Tanay said, sounding surprisingly cheerful about the topic.

"That is not entirely true." Began Holdak as they entered the Inn, "If it wasn't for the fact I was told of your arrival I wouldn't have even known that you were Viperian."

"So it was because of my race."

"Not exactly, as I said before, I have never met one of your race; I have only heard the tales told to me. I have always believed to give people a fair chance before judgement." By this time they had reached the bar, behind which a fat bearded man stood.

"And how can I help you tonight mister Holdak?" the bar keeper asked in a very cheerful voice.

"Well these men need a room for the night, and I would like a mug of ale."

"A room you say, let me see, yes, room seven. There's two beds in that one," the bar keeper rummaged behind the bar, and produced a key which he handed to Laucian, "It's up the stairs and down the corridor on the left." The bar keeper then poured Holdak's drink, and took a couple of coins for it. "Is there anything else I can get you gentlemen?"

"Do you serve Maldraw?" Asked Tanay hopefully.

"Why yes, not often we get a request for it, but I do like the odd nip myself, I'll get you a glass."

"Please sir, two glasses, and the bottle."

"Why certainly sir, that'll be two silver coins, and you can settle the bill for the room in the morning." Tanay handed over the money for the drink.

"You don't worry that people will leave in the morning before they pay?" asked Laucian curiously.

"Well, with a garrison of soldiers living just next door, most people feel its best to settle the bill before they leave." All four men laughed before the bar keeper had to go and serve another customer.

"So, Captain, if you believe in giving people a fair chance, why did you turn us away to begin with?" asked Laucian.

"Because I was asked to." began Holdak as he leaned on the bar, "A few hours before you arrived an elf maiden came to tell me of your arrival, and that I should send you straight away so the elves could deal with you."

"So why did you follow us?"

"I have worked alongside the elves of the area many times, and never have they told me to just stand aside and let them deal with a threat."

"So you were slightly suspicious, and that's why you followed."

"And when I saw graw attacking you, I realised that you couldn't be as bad as I was told." Just then a soldier walked into the tavern, and approached Captain Holdak and whispered something in his ear. "It would appear that duty calls gentlemen, good evening." Holdak then headed for the door, and Laucian and Tanay found an empty table in one corner of the room, where Coran curled up on one of the chairs and went to sleep.

It didn't take Captain Holdak long to reach the gates of the town, where he was met by the two guards posted there this night. "What do we have now gentlemen?"

"A group of five sir, heavily armed." Replied one of the soldiers.

Holdak walked forward "Open the gate." The soldiers did as he ordered, and Holdak walked out to face these new arrivals. "And how is it I can help you gentlemen tonight?"

Adokas stepped forward, "We wish to stay at one of this town's Inn's."

"And what brings you to our town at this late hour?"

"We are heading to the dwarven mines of Hardrock."

"Well the dwarves are popular today aren't they? If you would follow me I will show you to the Sleeping Dragon Inn." Holdak turned and walked back in through the gates and back up the streets to the Sleeping Dragon, followed closely by Adokas and his friends.

Holdak booked the party into the Sleeping Dragon in much the same way he had with Tanay and Laucian. Thoril and Jamaan decided to retire to their rooms early, where as Adokas, Roscoe and Solaris planned to have a few drinks before they slept. After they had purchased drinks Solaris approached Holdak, "Tell me sir, do you always bring weary travellers to sleep next to your garrison?"

"Only when they are as well armed as yourselves." Captain Holdak replied calmly.

"If you don't mind me asking, what did you mean when you said that the dwarves were popular today?" asked Adokas.

"I meant master elf, that you are the second set of people to come here tonight on their way to see the dwarves. Now if you would excuse me, I have duties to attend to." Holdak bowed his head respectfully to the trio before leaving the Inn.

Roscoe took a quick look around the tavern area, trying to see an empty table where they would be able sit, "It appears there are no seats."

"There may be no empty tables, but that does not mean there are no empty seats," explained Solaris, "Which table looks to have the most interesting people sitting at it?" Roscoe took another look around the room, but before he could answer Adokas did.

"I'd say the pair in the corner," he said pointing to where Tanay and Laucian were sat, "Unless you want to hear drunken tales of how the soldiers keep the peace."

Roscoe looked at the pair for a moment before he too said they looked by far the most interesting patrons. Thus it was decided, and the trio walked across the room to where they were seated.

"Excuse me gentlemen," began Roscoe, "I was just wondering if we would be able to join you at this table?" Laucian looked at all three of them before silently turning back to his drink, Tanay just looked at Roscoe, and then smiling nudged Coran.

"Come now Coran, won't you let these men have a seat?" Coran slowly looked around, stretched a little and jumped to the floor, where he curled back up on the end of Tanay's cloak. "My name is Tanay, and my companion here is Laucian." Tanay extended his hand towards Roscoe.

Roscoe shook Tanay's hand before sitting where Coran had been curled up earlier; he introduced himself, and his two companions. The group then spent a long time in the bar, Adokas, Roscoe and Tanay swapped tails of some of their past travels, Laucian and Solaris kept quiet, both of them sat silently observing the other people sat at the table.

"Tell me, judging by your eyes, and your sorcerers powers, do you have some dragon heritage in your past?" Asked Roscoe.

"Well we sorcerers do have dragon's blood in our veins." Tanay replied.

Solaris laughed, "You are not serious, that is just a rumour started by a terrible sorcerer, who wished people would pay him a little more respect." This was the first thing Solaris had said since sitting at the table, and it sounded very familiar to both Tanay and Laucian.

"Well we can never be so sure about that, although there is no record of dragon blood in my ancestry," laughed Tanay. Laucian stared at Solaris, he new that if a person didn't speak, it wasn't always because they had nothing to say.

"Solaris, have you ever met a man called Magon?" Asked Laucian as he sipped some of his drink.

"Magon?" Began Solaris, "Do you mean the shepherd?"

"No, the wizard."

"Well the name does sound familiar, but then I have met many people in my travels."

The conversations began to dwindle from this point, it was getting very late, and most of the other patrons had long left the bar. The group also decided that it was time to sleep, and all headed for their rooms.

*   *   *

Laucian's sleep was again cut short by his dream, although this time he recognised the assassin he fought alongside in the end, he knew who this great warrior was.

Laucian went down to the bar, behind which a young woman was serving, glancing around the room he saw a number of soldiers eating breakfast, and Solaris sat in a solitary corner. He quickly bought a drink, and made his way to where Solaris was seated.

"We need to talk." Laucian sat down at the table staring intently at Solaris.

"I guess you too are having trouble sleeping. I know of what it is you dream."

"How?"

"Because I have been dreaming the same thing."

"Who are you? What does it mean?"

"Those are questions I cannot answer right now." Solaris stood and began to walk around the table. "All will be explained in good time, but sharing information so soon could prove disastrous." Laucian watched Solaris walk from bar, even through his suspicious nature Laucian found himself trusting Solaris, and didn't even think to question he reasons.

It wasn't long before Tanay and Coran joined Laucian in the bar, they did not tarry long this morning. They paid the bill for their room, and set out for the dwarven halls.

They travelled swiftly this morning, always on guard for any sign of their unknown assassins from the night before. Despite their concerns the trip was rather uneventful, and they reached the rocky slope leading to the lower entrance to the dwarven mines.

This slope served as a great defence from any would be attackers, as it meant that any force would be out in the open as the struggled up the steep hill, constantly slipping on the gravel and slate, as well as the large piles of broken rocks, or they would have to climb down the hundred foot cliffs above the entrance. There was another entrance to the mines, higher in the mountains, but to reach that one you had to travel through some very treacherous terrain, before having to pass through a dungeon like entrance laden with traps.

By the time Tanay and Laucian reached the top of the hill there was already a small group of dwarves waiting for them.

"Greetings travellers, what brings you to these halls?" Asked Davkul.

"Greetings master dwarf, I am Tanay and my companion is Laucian, may I ask to whom we are addressing?"

"My name is Davkul Gemcutter, and I ask again, what is your business here?"

"We wish to speak with Nasgaroth."

"And you think that you'll just get an audience with him because you show up at the door?"

"I believe Magon sent word of our arrival, we should be expected."

"I see, you had best follow me then." Davkul turned and walked through the large stone doors into the mines followed closely by Tanay, Laucian and Coran. They passed the large winch and pulley system used to pull carts up the gravel slope.

They walked deep into the mountain; Davkul led them through long twisting corridors, each one delicately carved through the natural rock of the earth. It took a long time to reach Nasgaroth's chambers; no-one spoke as they walked, until they reached the large golden doors leading to Nasgaroth's chambers.

"I'll have to take your weapons; we do not allow outsiders to enter the great hall so armed." Davkul said as he turned to face Tanay and Laucian. The pair glanced around at the dwarves around them, before they both handed over their weaponry.

"And I'll be taking that pouch of yours." Davkul added pointing to the blue pouch hanging from Tanay's belt.

"Do you always take peoples personal possessions?" Asked Tanay with a grin.

"According to Magon you're a sorcerer, and that means you have a pouch for storing spell components, and you being a fancy sort tells me that the bright blue pouch with funny white symbols on it is where you keep them."

"You know, you're bright for a dwarf." Laughed Tanay as he handed over the pouch. Davkul placed the weapons on a table to the side of the door, then he pushed open the door and walked through, followed by Tanay, Laucian, and Coran, and they were followed by several, heavily armed dwarves.

The room they walked into was awe inspiring, not because of the many statues beautifully made out of precious metals, and many different types of stone. It wasn't because of the large number of jewel encrusted chests. What made this room so impressive was its size. From where Tanay and Laucian stood they couldn't see the roof, or any of the walls, the only light came from a large fire about thirty feet into the room, yet even with this the walls were in shadow.

"Who is this? Coming to disturb my slumber." Boomed a deep growling voice from the shadows at the far side of the room.

"These men seek your council my lord, they are friends of Magon." Replied Davkul.

"Magon's choice in friends seems to have changed greatly since I last spoke with him."

Tanay walked forward into the chamber, "I wish you to help me find a mutual friend we share Nasgaroth." A deep throaty laugh was heard from the shadows.

"And why should I help you serpent blood?" Spat Nasgaroth.

"My blood isn't all that different from yours." Retorted Tanay. There was a flash of light from within the shadows, just before Nasgaroth launched himself forward, the dwarves all took a couple of steps backwards, but Tanay and Laucian both stood their ground as the dragon landed a few paces in front of them.

"My blood is nothing like yours!" Nasgaroth roared, "Mine is not tainted by the evil of the snake." Nasgaroth was an impressive sight to see, the light from the fire glistened off of his golden scales, he stood tall and majestic, with his wings folded on his back.

<Dragons are reptiles, the same as snakes, your blood is not so different to Tanay's blood> Coran telepathically projected into everyone's mind.

"Why do you keep company with evil? Little one." Asked Nasgaroth turning his eyes to Coran.

<My friends are not evil; you should not be so keen to judge them.>

"I am looking for Elena of Krondmare," announced Tanay, "She often spoke of you, and I thought you may know of her whereabouts."

"I ask again, why should I help you?"

"Elena may be in danger."

"There are few things in this world more dangerous that the devious viperian's, I would never help you find Elena."

"Then you do know where she is?"

"And if I did, you think I would tell you?"

"Where is she dragon?"

"You will leave now." Said Nasgaroth as he turned away from Tanay.

"Do not turn your back on me dragon." Yelled Tanay. Nasgaroth spun back around, he extended one of his front legs towards Tanay, knocking him to the ground and pinning him there.

"And why shouldn't I turn from you snake?" Laucian launched himself forward, as he did a sword materialised in his hand, forming from a black mist, the long slender blade was slightly curved, and pure black in colour, with what appeared to be dark translucent flames covering the blade.

Laucian sliced the blade across Nasgaroth's foot. The dragon recoiled his leg and roared in pain. Davkul and the other dwarves started forward, weapons in hand.

"Hold!" called Nasgaroth, "I thought you took their weapons."

"They did," replied Laucian, "But this is no normal sword."

"A psy-blade? You are a psychic?" Asked Nasgaroth.

"I am." Answered Laucian as he calmly stared at Nasgaroth.

"You will leave now, and I will spare your miserable lives."

Tanay got back to his feet, "You will tell me where she is."

<Don't waste you time, this stubborn fool will not help us this day> Nasgaroth had made his way back into the shadows by now. Tanay stood staring into the darkness for a short while before he turned and walked from the chamber, Coran flew and landed on his shoulder. Laucian glared into the shadows for a moment longer before he too turned for the door, and his psy-blade disappeared back into the nothingness it had been forged from.

The pair collected their weapons and were led back out of the mines. They slid down the slope where they met Roscoe, Solaris and the others from the night before.

"Greetings travellers, you too seek these dwarven halls?" Asked Tanay, now with a big grin on his face.

"We are seeking Nasgaroth's council." answered Solaris, a comment that attracted nervous glances from his companions.

"Well you should know that he is not in a good mood," warned Tanay.

"How bad a mood?" Asked Adokas.

"He's currently nursing a wound from a psy-blade." Answered Laucian.

Solaris' face dropped, "Well he is probably not going to like some of the news I bring, for we are not the only people who will be seeking his council in these next few days."

"Who else will be seeking his council?" asked Tanay.

"Some people from Cemulion. I doubt he will be happy to learn this." Solaris raised the hood of his cloak, "Where are you two heading next?"

"We will be heading back to Magon's tower I expect." Answered Laucian.

Solaris turned to Jamaan, "You should go with them, I feel you're presence in this meeting could cause tension."

"I think you are right, I have been meaning to visit the mages tower, and seek his council, and this is my opportunity to do so."

"Well I bid you good day gentlemen; we should make our way to see Nasgaroth." Said Solaris. Everyone said their farewells, and they each went their own ways.

Tanay decided that he would travel to Cemulion to meet these people who would be having a meeting with Nasgaroth in the near future, so he headed in the direction of Getandor's capital city, where as Laucian and Jamaan headed for Magon's tower.

This left Solaris, Roscoe, Adokas, and Thoril to climb up to entrance to the dwarven mines. When they reached the top of the hill they were greeted by a grim faced Davkul.

"Hello again my old friend." Said Adokas, grinning broadly.

"You certainly pick your moment's elf."

"It's a gift." laughed Adokas, "You know why we are here."

"He will not see you today."

"But we must speak with him; it is of the up most importance." Interjected Thoril.

"There is nothing I can do; he will not see you this day."

Solaris had stayed back though this conversation, but now he stepped forward and lowered his hood, "Perhaps he will make an exception to see me."

Davkul's eyes widened, "My lord," Davkul bowed low, "I did not know you were travelling with these men."

"That is okay master Davkul, but it is very important that we speak with Nasgaroth."

"Certainly my lord, if you would follow me." Davkul spun on his heals, and headed back into the mines.

Roscoe was the first to ask the question that he, Adokas and Thoril were all thinking, "Mr Solaris sir, what is it you have done to inspire so much awe in a dwarf?"

"That is a long story, but it is all to do with when Nasgaroth was but an egg."

"An egg?" asked Roscoe, "Is Nasgaroth not a dwarf?" No-one answered Roscoe's question, they all just smiled, feeling that Nasgaroth's true nature would best be left as a surprise.

They eventually reached the golden door leading to Nasgaroth's chamber, Davkul took the weapons from Roscoe, Adokas and Thoril, but he left Solaris' alone, and they all entered through the door.

"Who dares to disturb me again?" Bellowed Nasgaroth.

"That would be me." Answered Solaris. Nasgaroth stepped into the light; Roscoe stared at the dragon in awe.

"And what do you want fire man?"

Adokas stepped forward, "We come to seek your aid." He called.

"And why should I help you elf?"

"Show some respect dragon," Spat Solaris, "You are in the presence of greatness."

Nasgaroth laughed, "Greatness, they do not look so great to me."

Solaris smiled, "Appearances can be deceiving, this is Adokas Loreweaver, son of Adolane Loreweaver, king of the Landorn elves." Roscoe looked at Adokas in surprise, now realising where he had heard his name before. "And this is Thoril Serpenthelm," Solaris continued "Keeper of the Helentar crystal." Roscoe turned to Thoril, with the same surprised look on his face as when he realised just who Adokas was. "And finally, this is Roscoe, master of the Wentar words."

Adokas and Thoril both turned to face Roscoe, who had a very confused look on his face, "Master of the Wentar words?" he asked.

"I will explain all later my small friend, but right now we have more important issues to deal with." Answered Solaris.

"So you have distinguished friends, but that does not mean I should help you."

"There is a great war coming, and we will need your help if we are to survive it," Adokas began, "This war has been prophesied, and we have already failed to find the weapon needed to help us destroy the demon that will lead our enemy."

"Not all weapons are blades or bows, you have found what you were seeking, you just do not realise it. As for my help, you will not receive it. This war you speak of is no concern of mine, or my subjects."

"Your subjects?" asked Solaris, he looked around to Davkul, "I thought these were dwarven mines, not dragon's mines."

"Enough!" Yelled Nasgaroth, I tire of your incisive chatter fire man, my dwarves may hold you in high regard, but I do not, I would advise you to leave before I become angry."

"My lord, forgive my insolence, but will we send no aid for this prophesied war?" Asked Davkul stepping forward.

"If you feel so strongly on this matter Davkul, then why don't you help these fools in their war, but me and the rest of my dwarves will not be taking part in the fight to come." Nasgaroth walked back into the shadows.

"There is one more thing Nasgaroth," called Solaris.

"No, there is nothing else, you will leave now."

"You will be receiving more guests soon, and you will aid them." Said Solaris calmly.

"Why should I help more of these mortals who disturb my peace?"

"Because I am telling you that you will."

"Insolent fool, you dare give me orders?" Nasgaroth spun to face Solaris, swiping his still bleeding foot towards him. Solaris drew his sword, and swung it towards the dragon, who quickly retracted his leg.

"I see you remember that last time we came to this. You will speak with the travellers when they arrive, and you will aid them, or you will have more to worry about than a bloody paw." Said Solaris as he sheathed his sword. Nasgaroth just growled and walked back into the shadows. Solaris turned and walked out of Nasgaroth's chambers followed by Roscoe, and the others.

Roscoe, Adokas and Thoril collected their weapons from by the golden door, and made their way with Solaris and Davkul to the entrance to the mines.

"Why do you allow Nasgaroth to treat you and the other dwarves as he does Davkul?" Asked Solaris as they stood in the afternoon sun. Davkul answered only with a grunt as he started down the rocky slope.

"You now plan to travel to Cemulion?" Asked Solaris as he pulled a scroll from his cloak.

"Yes, we have to inform the king of our progress." Answered Adokas.

"Or lack of progress." Added Thoril bitterly.

"Can I ask you to do something for me," Solaris handed the scroll to Adokas, "Travel quickly, and give this to Tanay, tell him that it contains a picture of the people he is looking for."

"You are not coming with us?" Asked Roscoe, sounding a little disappointed at the prospect.

"No, my path currently lies with Jamaan, but I expect we will meet again soon my small friend."

"I will run ahead and give him the scroll before nightfall," announced Adokas. They all said their goodbyes, before setting off to their separate directions. Adokas ran in the direction of Cemulion, followed by Roscoe, Thoril and Davkul. Solaris set down the road, following Laucian and Jamaan.

Chapter 6
Cemulion City

It hadn't taken Adokas long to catch up with Tanay to give him the scroll. It did however take the others a long time to catch up. Tanay had decided to travel with the others to Cemulion, after all the road is dangerous to travel alone, he also thought it wise to see if any of the others recognised the men it depicted. Tanay was pleased to find that Thoril did.

Thoril explained that the men on the scroll had also been recruited by the king to find a collection of ancient prophesies that had been hidden in the royal tombs, and old catacomb filled with death. Thoril told Tanay that that one of the men was a half-elven paladin named Aramil, and the other an elven ranger named Larenor, but beyond this he knew nothing of the men.

It took the group about ten days to reach Cemulion. Upon entering the city everyone went their separate ways. Tanay went in search of the men on the scroll, Adokas Thoril and Davkul went to speak with King Augustus IV, the ruler of Getandor. This left Roscoe, who arranged to meet his companions at the Mini Palace, an establishment owned by an old friend of Roscoe's from his travelling days.

It had been many years since Roscoe had walked the streets of Cemulion, so he decided to reacquaint himself with the city before going to the Mini Palace. He wanted to get a feeling for the city again, and he was curious as to how it had changed over the years.

The noble houses were just to the north of the of the city gates, so Roscoe decided this would be a good place to begin. He wondered around these tall, elaborately built buildings, several new ones had been built since Roscoe's last visit. For all of the wealth the nobles had spent building their fancy houses, not one of the could compare to the extravagance of the mage house.

The mage house was the home of the most powerful mages in the city, and their apprentices. It was at least twice the size of any of one of the noble houses, around its walls there were what at first appeared to be beautifully carved statues of old mages and gargoyles, but if you stopped and watched them you would see that they were all changing. They were each morphing form one statue to another, each staying for a few moments before it seamlessly transforming into the image of something new.

Roscoe made his way through the hustle and bustle of the market before heading down towards the docks. There were several fat merchant ships at the docks along with a handful of fishing boats. The ship that caught Roscoe's attention however was the *Guillotine*. It was smaller than the merchant vessels and was built with dual masts, this ship had obviously been built for speed. Roscoe could also see that the ship had a large number of cannons running down the sides. He was so in awe of this amazing vessel that Roscoe hadn't noticed the woman standing next to him.

"She's a beautiful ship don't you think?" The halfling turned and looked up at the woman. She was quite tall and slim with long brown hair and dark skin.

"That she is," Roscoe replied, "But by what cause have the navy gained a presence in Cemulion?"

"She is no navy ship, the *Guillotine* was commissioned by the merchants guild, she's a pirate hunter." The woman explained.

"Really?" Roscoe turned back to he ship with renewed awe, "But what man would dare captain such a vessel? He would be the target of every would-be assassin along the coast."

"Captain Urthandor dares captain this ship." the woman answered with a grin.

"Captain!" Roscoe and the woman both looked up at the *Guillotine* to see a large bald sailor leaning over the side, "We've just received word, Kheldun's ship has been spotted heading north!"

"Prepare to make sail!" The woman called back. The sailor ran from the side of the ship and began barking orders.

Roscoe turned and looked sheepishly at the woman, "Captain Urthandor I presume."

The flashed the halfling a wry smile, "I'm not one to stand on ceremony, please call me Janemita."

Roscoe laughed nervously, "I guess there really was no man who would dare captain such a vessel."

"Do not worry my friend, you are not the first to make such an assumption, and I dare say you won't be the last. Now if you could excuse me, I have a pirate to hunt." Janemita turned and ran to board her ship. Roscoe watched as people ran about on board preparing for departure, before he decided to continue on with his re-acquaintance with the city.

Roscoe walked past the large warehouses at the side of the small port, then down dock street towards hangman's square, where the public trials and executions took place. This also brought the halfling close to the slums, a small corner of the city where the poor huddled together to keep warm.

"Could you spare a few coins little master?" Roscoe hadn't even noticed the hooded man standing in a boarded up door way; he hobbled slowly towards Roscoe. "For a poor man to buy a meal."

"Of course," Roscoe answered fishing through his pockets for some loose coins as the man hobbled a little closer.

"Lower your hood beggar." Roscoe turned to see a large armoured man, whom he recognised to be Medlich; a member of the city guard he knew from previous visits to the city.

"Please sir, I only need a few coppers to buy some food." said the man, as he now shambled back towards the the doorway from which he had emerged.

"Lower your hood!" Medlich repeated in a clam but stern voice as he took a couple of steps towards the beggar. The man stopped and looked from Roscoe to Medlich, who took another step towards the man. The beggar slowly lowered his hood; he had short dark hair and a scruffy beard. His most prominent feature however was the rough scars where his ears should have been, it looked as though they had simply been ripped from the side of his head.

"Scurry back to the shadows, you'll be getting no money this day." Medlich spat before turning to Roscoe, "You see Roscoe, those scars mean this man is a known criminal, he would take the coins you offer, just before he slits your throat and takes anything else you have of worth."

The beggar waited until Medlich had his back to him before pulling a dagger out from under his cloak and running at Medlich. The seasoned soldier spun around catching hold of his attackers wrist, he hoisted the man from the ground before slamming his other fist into the beggar's face. Medlich dropped the man to the ground, who promptly scrambled back to the shadows. Medlich turned back to face Roscoe.

"If you know that man is a criminal, then why is he still on the streets?" Asked Roscoe, who was still a little shocked by what had just transpired in front of him.

"Some new magistrates, they decided that instead of keeping *lesser* criminals in the jail, we should cut off their ears as a sign of their crimes, and then let them go. Its all part of their grand plan to stop over crowding in the cells."

"Did it work?"

"Of course, and now the magistrates are trying to think of a way to combat the sudden rise in crime rates. They haven't seemed to notice that this sudden rise just so happens to coincide perfectly with their new release scheme, they find it easier to blame us in the guard instead."

"So you are still a member of the guard then."

"A member my small friend? I am now the commander of the city guard." Roscoe looked up at his old friend with a broad smile.

"A lot has changed, I remember when you were but a young upstart, working your first case, and now you are in charge."

"That is not all that has changed, the streets are not as safe as they used to be, these new magistrates have not done much to help the city, but they are doing a grand job of destroying it. Letting petty criminals walk free, and giving immunity to more dangerous ones. My men are doing what they can, but we're just having our hands tied at every turn." Medlich explained bitterly, "If I didn't know any better I'd say they were trying to weaken the city."

"It sounds like I have returned in dark times." Said Roscoe.

"That is one way of looking at it. Now if you would excuse me I'm running late for a meeting. I'd advise you to get to wherever you are heading, as I said the streets are not safe."

"Thank you old friend. It has been good to see you again, we will have to catch up properly some time, over a few drinks."

Medlich smiled, "I like your thinking Roscoe, but I am going to be away from the city for a few days, I'm planning a little *hunting* trip. There is an ogre which has been terrorising the local farmers." The old friends bid each other good day and went their separate ways.

Roscoe heeded his friends words and turned straight down main street and headed for the Mini Palace at such a pace that he ended up bumping into a rather large half-orc.

"Watch you step little man." the half-orc grunted, Roscoe stumbled backwards looking up at the huge brute.

"You really should watch where you are going little one," chuckled the half-orc's companion, a roguish looking half-elf.

"My apologies," said Roscoe bowing his head to both men as he passed them and walking straight to the Mini Palace.

*   *   *

The half-elf was called Ivellious, a talented thief who had spent most of his life in Cemulion; his half-orc companion was Branack, originally from one of the barbarian tribes in the far north. The pair were heading for The Pit and the Pendulum, a bar known for its cheep ale, and pit fighting, a sport which attracted a less than friendly crowd. Ivellious and Branack were regulars at the bar; Branack was also the only undefeated regular of the pit fights. This time however the pair were going to meet someone, this time they had the prospect of a rather well paid job.

"Greetings gentlemen, please do sit down." Ivellious and Branack sat at the table opposite the man.

"You must be Antonema." said Ivellious offering his hand to the man. Antonema Christortus was a foreigner, who had made quite an impression on the city since he had arrived a year or so previous. He was unlike anyone Cemulion had ever housed; he had come from farther east than anyone had ever travelled before. It had not taken him long to become well known in the city. The nobles had welcomed him with open arms, probably because of his seemingly endless flow of gold. Even the king had taken an interest in the man, and was consulting him on matters of state on an increasingly regular basis.

"To what do we owe the pleasure of meeting such a distinguished man as yourself?" Ivellious asked.

Antonema placed his sword on the table before him, it was an impressive weapon. The blade was long and slender with a slight curve. It had a red sheath and the handle was carved into the shape of a bone, with a skull pommel, Ivellious suspected that it was carved from actual bone. "I hear that you were recently hired by two men as guides, you took them to the royal tombs."

"That's a nice sword, do you always keep it on the table?" Asked Ivellious with a little laugh.

"It is tradition where I come from to put you weapons in the open when in a busyness meeting." Antonema explained. "Now can we continue?"

"Certainly, how can we be of service."

"The men you took to the tombs, tell me about them."

"There isn't much to tell," Ivellious began, "We took them to the tombs so they could collect some scrolls, we brought them back, they paid us. That's about all there is to tell."

"They were good men, honourable men." Branack grunted, who was not liking where this conversation was heading.

"Do you think you will be hired by them again?" Just then the trio were joined at the table, they were joined by Kevgeon.

"I hope I'm not disturbing you." Kevgeon said as he sat down.

"Not at all, I was just about to offer my guests here a little deal." Antonema replied. "As I was saying, do you think they will hire you again?"

"Its a distinct possibility."

"In the not too distant future I believe they will be collecting some rather special stones, I would like you to acquire them for me. Do this and you will be generously compensated."

"I like your choice of associates Antonema, no-one can get a job done better than an orc, eh brother." Kevgeon extended a hand towards Branack. To everyone's surprise, apart from Ivellious, Branack did not take the hand, instead he leaped to his feet sending his chair flying backwards.

"I AM NOT AN ORC!!" he roared, he was staring at Kevgeon his teeth bared and axe in hand. Both Antonema and Kevgeon also leaped from their seats, drawing their weapons.

"I must apologise for my friend," Ivellious began calmly, "He can be a little touchy when it comes to orcs." The half-elf had remained seated during the exchange, and now had a wry smile on his face.

"You deny your heritage?" Kevgeon asked.

"Might have cursed orc blood," Branack spat, "But not make foul beast." Branack slowly lowered his axe as he spoke, and the two opposite followed his example.

"So you turn your back on your strongest feature." Laughed Kevgeon as he sat back down.

"I turn back on savage murder. I not work for fool who think that make them strong." Branack turned and walked away from the table.

Antonema now sat back down, "And what of you?" he asked, "I am willing to pay a thousand gold for these stones."

Ivellious had fewer reservations than Branack when it came to deciding who to work for, he had always believed that any job was worth doing if the pay was good enough, and a thousand gold was a hefty sum. "You are very generous good sir," Ivellious glanced over to Branack; the pair had met many years before, during which time the half-orc had saved Ivellious's life many times over, and vice versa, Branack was the closest thing to family Ivellious had ever had. A thousand gold however was a lot of money, and would last him a long time. "But I am afraid I will have to decline your offer."

"You would turn down a thousand gold?"

"Well it does go against my better judgement,"
Ivellious replied with a grin, "But if I take your job I'm afraid I
may loose more than your money can buy. Good day
gentlemen." With that said Ivellious left the table, and walked
over to his friend.

"What news do you bring?" Asked Antonema, without
even looking at his companion.

"We collected the weapons, my orcs have them. I sent
them to make camp with your ogre. We lost many though,
there was some unexpected problems."

"What kind of problems?"

"Two men, a knight and some hooded warrior, they
killed most of my orcs."

Antonema thought on this for a moment, "I will head
out to meet your remaining orcs, I want you to keep an eye on
those two," he indicated Ivellious and Branack as he spoke, "I
feel their part in this is not yet finished." Antonema stood and
walked from the bar.

"Thank you Branack, you've just cost us a lot of
money." Ivellious said as he stood by the bar waiting to be
served.

"Other ways to make coin."

"That is true, but I think we have also gained a new
enemy. From what I've heard that Antonema doesn't like it
when people turn him down."

Branack grunted, "Not worry about him. He care about
reputation too much."

"Did you notice that both of them had the same tattoo
on their arms?" Ivellious asked thoughtfully.

"No."

"I could be mistaken, but I think it was the symbol the
legion of Strakstaw wear."

"What? The mercenaries?"

"Yes."

Branack glanced back to where Kevgeon was still sat, "But why they in Cemulion? And why they asking about Aramil and Larenor?"

"I don't know."

*　　*　　*

The Mini Palace was a very grand establishment. There were large arched windows and fake spires, and it had been painted in bright colours. The inside was even more extravagant, with large chandlers hanging from the high ceiling. The main room was huge, with an abundance of extremely comfortable seating. At the far side of the room was the bar, next to which was a grand staircase leading up to the rooms for rent. To spend a night in one of these lavish rooms was deceptively cheap, this was because under normal circumstances you could not stay in one of these room unless you were accompanied by one of the establishments employees, and the company of these particular men or women did not come cheap.

There was an exception to this rule however, if like Roscoe you were very good friends with Victathana Foechuckle, the halfling owner of the Mini Palace, then you were in with a chance of renting rooms for you and your friends without having to hire any other *services* for the night.

Roscoe spent several hours sitting at the bar with Victathana as they laughed about old times; he had forgotten how much he enjoyed the woman's company. It was getting late by the time Adokas and Davkul walked through the door,and quickly made their way to where Roscoe and Victathana were sat.

"Greetings Roscoe." Said Adokas as they approached.

"Ah, Adokas, Davkul, I'd like to introduce you to Victathana, the owner of this fine establishment."

"A pleasure to meet you," said Adokas with a slight bow, Davkul just grunted as he examined the interior of the Mini Palace.

"These are two of my travelling companions." Roscoe explained, before turning to Adokas "Where is Thoril?"

"He went back to that mage house." Davkul grunted, "What are the rooms like here?"

"Very comfortable, and reasonably priced if memory serves." Roscoe replied.

"For you and your friends Roscoe, they are free." Victathana said with a smile.

"You are too kind." Roscoe kissed the woman on the hand before they made arrangements for the rooms.

When everything was arranged, Roscoe, Adokas and Davkul sat down with drinks and Adokas explained what had happened in the meeting with King Augustus IV. Apparently the king had been just as confused as they were about Nasgaroth's announcement that they had found the weapon they were looking for. He had also asked them to stay close in the city while his scholars translated some ancient prophecies.

Not long after their discussion the trio each went to their rooms. Roscoe had not been lying when he had described the rooms as comfortable; each of them having a large four-poster bed, which was fit for royalty.

It wasn't long after they had gone to bed that Roscoe was joined by his *old friend*.

Chapter 7
Uninvited Guests

The trip back to Magon's tower was largely uneventful, Captain Holdak had shown a little interest in Laucian's change in travelling companions, but beyond that no-one paid the three men any heed. Although Jamaan did receive a few stairs, sitting in taverns and yet never removing his helmet.

By the time they finally reached the tower, Laucian was becoming very curious as to why the knight never relieved his appearance.

Laucian approached the main door to the tower and banged hard. After a few moments the large wooden door swung open to reveal Magon's tall slim butler. The butler welcomed them into Magon's home and led them to one of the many comfortable seating areas, where Magon, Stomorel, and the bald mage were already seated.

"Well this is a surprise Laucian, had you noticed that Tanay has gotten rid of his pretty red cloak and replaced it with a boring old black one, and Coran has turned into a rather large armoured man?" Chuckled the eccentric old mage.

Solaris stepped forward and lowered his hood, "You never change do you."

"Ah, the immortal. Welcome to my humble abode."

"Ah the shepherd. Thank you for welcoming me to your not so humble abode."

Magon laughed again, "I'm a little more than just a shepherd don't you think."

"That depends on your prospective of things." Solaris answered with a wry smile. There was a few moments of silence as most people in the room looked at each other, all a little confused. Jamaan decided to take this opportunity to introduce himself to Magon.

"Greetings good sir, I am Jamaan, son of Jameel, paladin of the highest order of Sugalas."

"Of course you are," Magon looked at the warrior for a few seconds before continuing, "I'm afraid I do not allow people to hide their faces in my tower, I must ask you to remove your helmet."

Jamaan was a little surprised at the mage's request, he had never been asked to remove his helmet before, people had always respected his wish to keep his appearance hidden. "I would prefer it if I could keep my helmet on."

"Now now Mr Jamaan, your appearance is part of the reason you have come seeking my council, is it not?" Stated Magon, again showing that he knew more than he necessarily should.

Jamaan thought for a moment, before deciding that it would probably be in his best interest to do as the mage wished if he was to get the help he needed. The knight slowly unclasped his helmet and lifted it from his head. Stomorel let out a gasp of shock, and the bald mage sat forward in his chair amazed by what he saw. Jamaan's head was covered in dark red scales, his eyes were a deep orange, and his teeth were all sharpened to points, though without a protruding snout he was clearly not lizard folk or any kind of dragon kin..

"By the abyss," the bald mage stood and walked up to Jamaan, "What are you?"

"I was a man once," Jamaan answered, "And hopefully with Magon's help I will be again."

The mage began to slowly walk around Jamaan, taking in every detail of the man's appearance, "This is amazing. How did this happen to you?"

"Come now Fruril, leave our guest be. He's had a long trip, and I doubt he wants to discuss the details of what happened to him with people he has only just met." Fruril looked around at Magon, and then back to Jamaan, before shrugging his shoulders and returning to his seat.

"Please gentlemen, do sit down." Magon said, indicating the empty chairs. Laucian sat in the chair closest to the door, which also happened to be the seat furthest away from Stomorel. Solaris took a moment to see which chair looked most comfortable before sitting close to Fruril. When Jamaan took his seat there was a cracking sound heard from the seat. Jamaan jumped back up and turned to see a pair of glasses on the seat, he picked them up and to face Magon.

"I'm very sorry," Jamaan held out the glasses, "I didn't see them."

Magon leaped forward, "Oh, I've been looking for those." Magon took the glasses from Jamaan, but as he did the one remaining arm fell to the floor. "Ah, that's not very good is it? Oh well never mind." The old man returned to his chair and perched the broken glasses on the edge of his nose. Jamaan paused for a moment, expecting some kind of reprimand for breaking Magon's glasses. When it was obvious one was not coming he sat back down.

"Tell me Laucian, did Tanay find what he was looking for?" Asked Magon as he adjusted the glasses on his nose, trying to make them stay in place.

"Nasgaroth refused to give him any information, because of his race." Laucian answered coldly. Stomorel let out a slight laugh; she had never hidden her dislike for the Viperian sorcerer. Laucian shot her an angry look; he had never hidden his dislike for the elven druid, much to Laucian's disappointment however Stomorel had not seemed to notice.

"Nasgaroth is a stubborn fool." Solaris said as he made himself more comfortable in his chair.

"I agree with you on that," chuckled Magon, "I have my doubts as to if he even could help, he's not as all knowing as he likes to think he is."

Laucian was beginning to grow tired of the conversation, he wished to spend some time alone. The only company he could stand as of late was that of Tanay, but with his friend seeking aid in Cemulion Laucian planned on spending much of his time in his room, or in Magon's training rooms. "It is growing late," he began, "I think I will take my leave of you, good evening." Laucian stood and walked towards the door which led to the higher levels of the tower.

"Are you not hungry good sir?" Stomorel stood from her chair as she spoke, "You have travelled far, I could make you some food."

"No, I am tired, and wish for some peace." Laucian pulled open the door and stepped through.

"Well..." Stomorel began before Magon interrupted her.

"Leave him be my dear, let him get some rest." The druid looked around at Magon and then back to the door, which by now had swung closed. She let out a sigh of resignation before returning to her seat.

"I too think it is getting late, I will also take my leave of you." Fruril declared as he rose to his feet, he took one more look at Jamaan before leaving through the same door as Laucian.

"Well I think I can guess why Mr Jamaan has come to my home, but you, tell me immortal what brings you to my tower?" Magon asked. The old man was still fiddling with his glasses, he was having a great deal of difficulty getting them to stay on his nose.

"I am making new friends." said Solaris with a grin, "Oh, and I answer to Solaris now."

"Really, I think I preferred Mandar."

"Well I felt I had to change with the times." Stomorel and Jamaan were both getting a little confused by Solaris and Magon's banter. They continued to chat like this for a while; it was obvious that they had known each other for a long time, however it was difficult to tell if they actually liked each other, neither of them openly criticized the other, but neither was it a friendly conversation.

Eventually Stomorel grew tired to this and decided it was time for her to go to bed, and so she took her leave of the others and left the room. Solaris waited until she had left the room before he asked Magon if there was a room he too could sleep in, Magon sent for his butler who showed Solaris to his room. This left Magon and Jamaan sat alone together.

"So, how about you tell me why you have come seeking my help."

Jamaan just looked at Magon, his orange eyes narrowed slightly as he tried to work out if this eccentric old man was actually the wise mage he had heard so much about. Jamaan had never met a mage of any real measurable power that was as strange as Magon, who was still attempting to make his glasses stay on his nose.

"I want you to help me become a man again." Jamaan eventually replied.

"Well how did this happen, any idea what spell was used?"

"It was a ritual, performed by some cultists."

"Please do explain."

"My temple sent me to investigate a cult of demon worshippers," Jamaan began, "I was searching some catacombs just outside Keglee when I was ambushed. The next thing I remember was being chained to an alter, and there was a demon towering over me. Its priests then performed the tainting ritual, mixing the beasts blood with my own. The tainted usually become the demons most obedient servants, I spent months in a cell fighting the monsters evil in my head, until eventually I won, but as you can see my body had already taken on the physical traits of the tainted. I eventually escaped the catacombs, and I have been searching for the demon and a cure ever since."

Magon sat fiddling with his glasses, the old man looked as though he hadn't even noticed that Jamaan had finished talking. Jamaan sat staring at Magon, his eyes narrowed as he began to think that Magon hadn't even been listening to him. The paladin opened his mouth to say something else, but he was cut off before he found the words.

"I'm not sure that this situation falls within my domain." The mage began. "This sounds more like a divine matter than an arcane one. Have you tried speaking with your temple elders?"

Jamaan leaned back, realising that the mage had been listening to every word he had said. "No members of the temple will listen to me. They do not believe that someone who has been tainted can still remain good, and Sugalas is not answering my prayers. He will not show me the path I must take."

"Well temple elders can be stubborn, but I'm afraid that I know no magic that can help you. However, seeking the guidance of your god would be my advice."

"But he is not answering my prayers; I fear he too has deserted me."

"Are you still able to cast your priest spells?"

"Yes."

Magon cocked his head and looked at Jamaan for a moment, his glasses perched precariously on his nose, "Did you ever stop to think, if Sugalas had deserted you then you would not be able to cast those spells?"

"I hadn't thought of that. But why then would he not give me guidance?"

"Perhaps Sugalas won't tell you which path to tread because you are already walking the correct one."

"Then I should continue hunting the demon that did this to me?"

"Now demon's can be pesky little critters to find, unless you know their names" Magon paused for a moment, "You don't happen to know the name of the one who did this to you?"

"No, I only know that it was a powerful beast, I believe it was a prince of the abyss."

"Then I would suggest that you carry on walking the path of your calling, and let the beast find you. Demon prince's don't soon forget, and if one lost one of its tainted to goodness then I imagine it will be wanting to rectify that loss."

Jamaan contemplated Magon's words for a while, before he decided that he would have to sleep on the advice. Magon showed his guest to a room before retiring himself.

*   *   *

The small mirror was very ornate; the golden edge was encrusted with pale green gems. There were also eight slots which looked as though they should also contain gems, one in each corner and one in the middle of each side.

Aluthana was holding the mirror in one hand and retrieved a small blue and a small red gem from a pouch. She placed the blue gem in the top right slot, and the red one in the middle left. The beautiful woman's reflection began to fade, and the image of Deventis replaced it.

"It has been a long time, we feared the worst." Said Deventis. "I received word a short time ago, Laucian is back in Magon's tower. You failed."

"He had help, soldiers from Faknell, we lost Vandex." Aluthana replied defensively.

"Well do not underestimate him tonight." Said Deventis coldly..

"Tonight? And how do you expect us to enter Magon's tower?"

"My contact will get you in. you will need to place the red stone in the top centre slot, and the blue stone in the bottom left."

"So I finally get to meet this mysterious spy of yours."

"There is a new target."

"What! Not only are we expected to enter Magon's tower, under the nose of one of the most powerful mages there is, and kill a very dangerous target, but you expect us to kill someone else as well?"

"The immortal is within the tower. His death would serve to greater secure our master's victory."

"You want us to move against the immortal? That is madness." Deventis just looked at her through the mirror without saying a word, before his face slowly faded away and was replaced by Aluthana's own reflection. The assassin replaced the two coloured stones as Deventis had instructed, and her reflection was replaced again, this time by the face of Deventis's spy.

*   *   *

Laucian's dream was exactly the same again this night, except for one thing. This time it did not run its full course. Laucian woke before it ended, he sat bolt upright in his bed; there was someone else in his room, he could sense their presence.

Laucian stood from his bed and retrieved his trousers. He looked around the room, trying to spot the intruder he knew was there. He casually walked over to the chest where his weapons were stored; he opened the lid to find his knives had been removed from their resting place. Laucian heard a quiet laugh from across the room.

Laucian stood stone still, whomever was in his room was not visible to the eye, so he closed his. Listening carefully he could not hear any movements. Whoever this intruder was they were greatly skilled at masking themselves from the senses, but Laucian knew they would be hard pressed to hide themselves from his mind.

Laucian concentrated hard; he had followed the path of a *psychic warrior*, which meant that his psionic abilities were focused on combat manifesting in such a way that many had confused them with magic. This meant he had not developed any reliable mind reading abilities, but with focus he could track nearby people, without having to see or hear them.

Aluthana made her way silently across the room, holding her breath to minimize noise until she was a matter of feet away from her target. Suddenly Laucian opened his eyes, his head snapping round to look directly at the assassin, his lips curling into an evil grin, "I can see you."

Aluthana glanced down to where her hand should have been, her invisibility still held, and she looked back up at Laucian thinking for a moment. Surly if he could see her then he would have made some kind of move against her, but he just stood there, looking straight at her.

With lightning speed Aluthana launched herself forward, she brought her left arm around in a wide arc, aiming the blade she held straight for her targets head. Laucian's reaction was just as quick, catching the assassin by the wrist. In the moment of impact Aluthana's invisibility spell ended and the woman became visible. In her left hand she was holding a large dagger which Laucian has managed to stop barely before it had struck his temple. Laucian was more concerned however with the sword the assassin held in her right hand, which she now thrust towards his gut.

Laucian span away from the attack, twisting Aluthana's left arm as he did, the hold making her double over. "So we meet again. Am I still annoying this legion of yours?" He asked.

"Your existence is enough to annoy anyone."

"What? Don't you like me?" Laucian asked sarcastically, "And I thought we were getting on so well." Aluthana let out a dry laugh before kicking out, she manage to catch Laucian on the ankle knocking him off balance, giving her the chance to break free of his hold.

Both of the seasoned fighters quickly regained their balance, facing each other. Aluthana held her weapons out before her, "Guess I really have caught you unarmed this time." She chuckled.

Laucian smiled, "I'm never unarmed."

"Is that so?" Aluthana launched herself forward swinging her sword at Laucian, who easily blocked the attack with his psy-blade; the most dangerous weapon in his arsenal, summoned at will with just a thought.

"Just wondering," Laucian began as Aluthana stared the Laucian's burning black blade, "Where did you put my knives? I'll be wanting them back after I'm finished with you." Laucian forced Aluthana's sword arm out wide as he spoke, aiming his other fist at Aluthana's face. The woman snapped back to her senses, leaning back to easily avoid the attack, slicing Laucian's arm with her dagger as she did.

Laucian retracted his arm in pain and kicked out at his attacker forcing a gap between them. Lucian glanced at the line of blood now forming on his arm.

"That looks nasty, perhaps you should get some armour." Aluthana laughed.

"Maybe I will," Laucian closed his eyes for a split second, and when he opened them a shimmer of light flowed over his body.

Aluthana attacked again bringing her sword in high. Laucian blocked the strike with his arm, angling it so the sword would slide down the invisible barrier which now covered his skin.

"That's an impressive trick," the assassin said, realising what the shimmer had been, "But it won't save you, that armour doesn't look too thick." Laucian smiled again; it had been a long time since he was really tested in combat, but this was the second time this woman had matched his skill and he was thoroughly enjoying the challenge.

The pair sprang into motion again; each twisting and turning, attacking high, striking low, each of them parrying and countering in what looked to be an elegant dance, but neither able to gain the upper hand. Laucian thrust his blade forward but Aluthana knocked it out wide with her sword and stabbed forward with her dagger. Laucian caught her by the wrist and pulled her in close, trying to stop the woman from being able to attack with either of her weapons. This turned out to be the first mistake either had made though; Aluthana brought her knee up hard, straight into Laucian's groin.

Laucian let out a groan as he doubled over in pain, loosing his concentration. There was another shimmer of light over his body as the psionic armour dissipated, and his mind blade faded into nothingness. Aluthana took a step back before kicking out forward, catching Laucian in the face which forced him upright. Blood poured from his nose; he shook his head trying to regain his focus through the pain. Aluthana took another step back before launching a hard side kick, sending Laucian sprawling backwards onto the bed.

Aluthana walked to the bed, easily hoping up onto it, the assassin kneeled across Laucian's stomach and smiled. Her victim tried to sit up, but Aluthana forced him back down with her dagger at his throat.

"It would appear that you finally get your kill." laughed Laucian.

"You laugh at your own death?"

"I laugh at the pointlessness of it all; you killing me for a master I've never met." It was Aluthana's turn to laugh.

"I like you." Aluthana put her sword down on the bed next to her and ran her hand over Laucian's naked chest, stopping just by his shoulder. The woman leaned forward, still holding the knife tight to Laucian's throat. "It seems a shame to waste such a specimen." she whispered into his ear before kissing him on the forehead and sitting back up.

"Do I at least get to know the name of my assassin before I die?"

"Excuse me?"

"We have fought twice now, and you have always known me, but all I know of you is that someone is paying you to kill me."

"My name? You are about to die, and you ask me my name?"

"Yes."

The assassin smiled again, "My name is Aluthana."

"That's a nice name."

"Goodbye Laucian."

"Thank you Aluthana."

Aluthana paused, "That you? For what?"

"Time." Laucian smiled, "Time to regain my composure." Like lightning Laucian again grabbed Aluthana by the wrist, but not before she cut into his throat. This didn't bother Laucian too much however, in the time Aluthana had been talking he had called upon another of his many psionic abilities. Laucian's fingernails had elongated into sharp claws which now dug into Aluthana's flesh. As the claws cut into her wrist the wound on Laucian's throat began to heal, it was as though the injuries caused by the claws drained the life from Aluthana and gave it to Laucian.

The woman went for her sword but Laucian pushed it to the floor. He forced Aluthana backwards as he sat up, grabbing her by the throat, his nails scratching her neck.

"Now you are going to drop the dagger and slowly back off the bed." Aluthana looked Laucian in the eyes for a moment before glancing at the hand gripping her wrist. She was in quite a predicament, feeling it was in her best interest to do as she was told, for now, she dropped the blade and slowly moved backwards.

Laucian forced the assassin up against the wall, still holding her by the throat and wrist. "Now you are going to tell me everything I want to know," the woman just looked at Laucian, "Who sent you?"

Aluthana smiled and tried to knee Laucian in the groin again, but this time he had been expecting it, and blocked the attack with his own knee.

"Did you really expect that to work again?" Laucian asked coldly, "Who sent you?"

"Screw you!" Aluthana spat, loosing her composure for the first time.

"I'm not going to ask you again." Laucian dug the claws a little deeper into Aluthana's throat causing her to wince in pain as blood trickled down her neck.

"Markus, General Markus!"

"I don't recognise the name. Why does he want me dead?" Aluthana tried to push forward, but Laucian just slammed her back into the wall. "Why did he send you?"

"He wants you dead before you can interfere with the legion's plans."

"And what legion would that be?"

Aluthana screwed up her face and tried to break free again, but Laucian just tightened his grip. "The legion of Strakstaw." She spat.

Laucian's eyes narrowed, he knew of the legion of Strakstaw. They were possibly the largest mercenary organisation in the known world. Its members were drawn from all races, some who volunteered and others forced into its ranks. All of the members were put through a ritual to erase their memories, leaving them open to the suggestions and orders of their masters. Every member of this legion were also tattooed to show they were members, meaning that someone from a less trusted race could walk city streets without trouble as people could see that they were different from their people, who the mercenaries allies were often at war with.

Laucian released Aluthana's wrist and moved her sleeve to see there was indeed a tattoo. He used his claws to cut the sleeve, letting some of the material fall away. This revealed the full image on her shoulder, which was the mark of the legion of Strakstaw.

Laucian's extensive knowledge of the legion came from the fact that the father of his best friend, Tanay, was a member. Deventis was a long serving member of the legion and was a permanent presence for them in the court of Krondmare's capital, and advisor to the king there.

Tanay had never been made a member of the organisation. He was too young when his father had joined, and the legion of Strakstaw wished to wait until he had reached his full potential before inducting him into their ranks.

"You expect me to believe that the legion of Strakstaw wishes for my death? You do realise that my travelling companion is the son of one of the legion's high ranking members."

Aluthana laughed, "You think that will save you? It was Deventis's spy who allowed me to gain entry to this tower."

"And what spy would that be?"

"That's not for you to know."

Laucian shook his head, "I thought we had covered this, you are going to tell me everything I want to know."

Aluthana smiled, "No, I will not be staying long enough to answer any more of your questions."

"And how exactly do you plan on leaving?"

"With this." Aluthana brought her now free hand up near Laucian's face, showing him a silver ring with a blue gem embedded in it. She smiled as she stared at the confused look on Laucian's face. "Vasderock!" The instant Aluthana uttered the activation word the blue gem began to glow, and she began to fade. Laucian tried to grab hold of her wrist again as he realised what was happening, but it was too late and his hand passed straight through her as is she wasn't there, as did his hand holding her by the throat.

Aluthana had faded almost from view, Laucian could now see the wall trough her ghost like form. She began to laugh as she passed backwards through the wall. Laucian ran for the door and out into the corridor, where he tripped over his own weaponry which had been placed just outside his room. Regaining his balance quickly he looked up and down the corridor for his attacker but she was nowhere to be seen, and because the spell she had cast with the ring she could have been almost anywhere in the tower by now. Also if she had had help from someone in the tower, then it would not be difficult for her to find a good place to hide.

Chapter 8
Allies

"The hunt went well my lord." The hobgoblin bowed as general Markus approached.

"I am glad to hear that Grandar. Did you take the new recruits for training?"

"Yes my lord."

"Then why have you asked me to come here?" Markus looked down the long dark corridor, the only light coming from the sparsely placed torches. Grandar had asked Markus to meet him here in the catacombs beneath the palace of king Sireanor, the ruler of Krondmare.

Those living in the palace never used the catacombs; they had been blocked off over a century earlier. They were now being used by the legion of Strakstaw as their base of operations for the area's surrounding the kingdom of Krondmare.

The legion's presence in the catacombs was largely unknown to anyone outside of the organisation; since they had been blocked off only four people who were not a part of the legion had entered them. One of the four had died in that expedition, the other three only surviving because of pure rage. A few days after they had escaped the catacombs the second of the group had disappeared, leaving Tanay and Laucian to look for their friend Elena, the daughter to king Sireanor.

Grandar shifted uncomfortably looking at the floor. Markus removed his bat-winged helmet so he could better see the hobgoblin. The large man had short brown hair, dark skin and a long scar on his left cheek. He narrowed his eyes, what was bothering this hobgoblin?

"Why have you asked me down here?" Markus asked again more forcefully.

"One of the new finds my lord." Grandar finally looked back up at his master, "One of them is here."

"Why?"

"It, well, it demanded to speak with you."

Markus cocked his head slightly, "It demanded to speak with me?"

"Yes my lord," Grandar was looking at the floor again, "It asked for you by name."

Markus thought for a moment, "And what exactly is *it?*"

"I don't know, I've never seen anything like it before."

"Where did you find it?"

The hobgoblin looked around nervously, "We didn't find it my lord, it found us." Markus's eyes narrowed even more. "It walked into our camp three nights ago, demanding to be brought to you. It bares the mark of our legion, my lord."

"Well you had best show me this creature."

Grandar led Markus through the winding passages of the catacombs. He led Markus to the deepest of the tunnels, a place where even members of the legion rarely went. Grandar and Markus turned a final corner leading into a large room which was lit by a single fire in its centre. Around the fire were eight large animals, they looked similar to the hunting hounds used for catching big game. These however were larger, much larger than any hounds Markus had ever seen. Their eyes shone red in the firelight; the light glistened off of their black fur and long claws. The joints on the animals fore legs each had long pointed bones erupting from them, and still more down their spines making the creatures look like fierce combatants.

"What are these?" Asked Markus as he examined the creatures.

"They are war dogs." Markus looked over to the shadowy corner where the reply had come from, the voice was deep and sounded like it was gargled through water, "I breed them myself." Markus could see two red eyes glowing in the shadows, they were a little lower than the general's hight.

"This is Havak my lord," Grandar explained, "He is the one I was telling you about."

The eyes glowed brighter, "You are general Markus?" Havak asked, the glowing orbs of its eyes rising up as it spoke until they were a couple of feet above Markus's hight.

"I am." the general replied, not fazed in the slightest by Havak's apparent large stature, "And who might you be?"

"I am a messenger." Havak stepped out of the shadows; he stood easily nine feet tall despite the fact he was still slightly crouched because of the ceiling. The beast looked humanoid in shape with a black leathery hide. Its body was highly muscled, and its hands had elongated fingers with long black claws, its mouth was large and seemed oddly shaped, and barely able to contain the several rows of razor sharp teeth. Havak also had the mark of the legion of Strakstaw branded across its back.

"A messenger from whom?"

Havak appeared to smile, showing its teeth, "I bring word from *Legion*, it is time." Markus's eyes widened and a bread grin crossed his face as he realised what the beast was telling him.

"The legion sends word? You mean the big bosses?" Asked Grandar. Markus had almost forgotten in his moment of excitement that the hobgoblin was still there, the hobgoblin who knew nothing of the general's true motivations.

"Go to Deventis; tell him to summon the council." Markus ordered Grandar, mainly to just get him out of the room. Markus wished to speak with Havak alone, to see just what this beast knew of Legion.

"Right away my lord." Grandar bowed before turning and walking back off through the catacombs.

"You command your troops well." Havak moved to sat by the fire and began to stroke one of its war dogs.

"I demand complete obedience." Markus moved further into the room and also sat by the fire, across from Havak. "Tell me what you know of Legion."

Havak laughed, "You speak to me as though I am one of your subordinates, do you not think that Legion may have sent me to take command in the time before his arrival?"

"Are you here to take command?" Markus asked without missing a beat. Havak laughed again.

"I like your attitude, straight to the point." Havak shook his head, "No I am not here to take command."

"Then why did Legion send you? Or are you just a messenger?"

"I am here as an adviser, and to instruct you on the finer details of the summoning ritual." Havak explained.

"Tell me how you came to be in the service of Legion."

Havak cocked its head and thought for a moment. "I have served Legion from the beginning, I was one of his first disciples. I have been leading Legion's armies into battle since before your world was a dream within a dream within a dream." Havak grinned widely, "Me an my pets have caused more destruction than your world has seen since its birth, all of it in Legion's name."

"And yet even with all your loyal service Legion's plans have always remained unsuccessful." Havak's grin disappeared, his glowing red eyes narrowed and he let out a low gurgling growl. Markus realised that had raised a point Havak did not appreciate.

"You need not worry about past failures. Legion has learned from past mistakes. He knows exactly how to accomplish his goals. The very chaotic nature of this world acts in our favour." Havak explained, "In the past the forces of power have always united against us. In this world though, while Legion's power can unite this chaos under his banner, it will never unite against us. Not only that, the only element able to seriously harm Legion is not abundant enough to harm our master."

Markus contemplated Havak's words, this creature claimed to have been serving Legion since he had begun his campaign of destruction, and it would appear that Legion had been attempting to fulfil his destiny for much longer than he had let on to the general. "What is this element that can harm our master?" Markus knew that asking this question may not be well received, but he would not be intimidated by this beast.

To Markus's surprise Havak grinned again, "All elements can harm Legion, but some can harm him more than others."

"Such as?"

"Fire."

"But we have fire in this world, and it is in quite a high abundance."

"That is true, but it does not burn with the intensity that it did in previous worlds, here it is far less harmful." Havak was not worried that he was explaining Legion's greatest weakness to this man. Havak knew from his master that Markus was loyal, and would never use the information he gained here against Legion, it was more likely the man was trying to find any ways he could improve the defences against any foolish enough to try and attack their master.

"Why did Legion not tell me himself how to summon him into our world?" Markus asked, deciding to bring the conversation back to the point at hand.

"Our master is not able to pass on that information through the dimensional walls; summoning rituals do not translate across the void."

"Then how was he summoned into the first world?" Markus asked, "Without you to tell anyone the details."

Havak laughed, "Legion was not summoned into the first world, he was born into it." Havak suddenly looked distant, as if he was looking into the past, "Our world was a hell. It was filled with demons of terrible power and evil, creatures that spent an eternity torturing the mortal inhabitants. Legion believed that this was wrong."

It was Markus's turn to laugh, "If Legion is so moral, then why is he trying to wipe out the whole of existence?"

"What better way to destroy immortal beings? What better way to end suffering forever?" Havak's grin faded as he decided to explain exactly why Legion was attempting to end everything. Markus had been a paladin once, until his god turned his back on him, before Legion had found him, and saved him from the abyss. Markus knew what it was like to walk a path of righteousness, only to find that it was folly. Havak believed that if anyone in this world would understand Legion's motivations, it would be this man.

"Legion believed it was wrong to treat the mortals with such contempt, he believed that we immortals should guide the *little people*. He believed we had an obligation to help the mortals reach their full potential, to help them become as great as they could be." Havak began.

"Legion has a gift for persuasion," the beast continued. "It wasn't long before he had a great many followers, all wanting to guide our world towards a better future. The future Legion envisioned did not appeal to many of the other, more powerful demons though and they stood against us. This led to war, with the mortals suffering all the more because of it.

"The war raged for a millennia, and we saw no way for victory over our enemies so Legion changed his plans. If we could not save our world then more drastic measures had to be taken, he found a way to end existence, a way to eradicate everything."

Markus smiled, "And how exactly does he plan to do that?"

Havak laughed again, he always found the curiosity of mortals amusing, "Our master found a ritual that could be used to destroy all life that contained a shred of evil."

"And that would destroy all of existence with it?"

"You mortals know nothing do you?" Havak mocked, "If any one alignment is destroyed, be it good or evil, law or chaos, the balance would falter, it would cause oblivion. Evil, good; without one there cannot be the other.

"We were so close to victory that first time, closer than we have ever been since. It takes time for Legion to gain the power and ingredients he needs for the ritual. We were so close." Markus could see the look of pain on Havak's face. "We were half way through the ritual when they attacked, we had been betrayed, our location given to our enemies. We were not prepared for such an assault, the most powerful of our enemies cast Legion across the void, banishing him out of the conventional plains of existence." Havak's grin returned, "Little did they know that by doing so they gave Legion true immortality. He could be summoned into each new world, though only once. But it did mean that when their world did eventually die out to make way for the next, taking them with it, Legion lived on. Because of his banishment he is unable to be killed, if he dies in this world then he is simply returned to the plain in which he currently resides, where he waits until he is summoned again into the next world."

"How did you escape the end of your world? And those worlds you have inhabited since?" Markus asked, truly curious as to how this creature could have lived through so many.

"I too am immortal, as all demons are, however even we cannot survive the end of a world. After Legion was banished most of his followers began to return to their old ways, I however dedicated myself to finding Legion, and eventually I did. When I was finally able to contact my master he had learned much more about the nature of existence, and he showed me how to survive a world's fall.

"That is enough of my past for now though. Now I must prepare you for Legion's summoning..." Havak began to explain the summoning ritual to Markus, explaining exactly what he would have to do to bring Legion into this world.

*   *   *

Deventis sat looking at Markus; he was trying to work out what the man was thinking. Deventis had known Markus for many years, ever since he had joined the legion of Strakstaw. Markus had been the first member Deventis had met directly after Legion himself had set him on the path out of his nest.

Legion had been watching Deventis for some time before he had decided to take the Viperian into his confidence. Legion saw in Deventis a quality he had himself. Deventis did not approve of the way his people behaved, he did not approve of their cruel treatment of their slaves, in much the same way Legion had disapproved of his peers treatment of mortals.

Deventis however was not like most of the people who Legion had seen throughout history. When he saw people who disapproved of slavery in the way Deventis did he knew that they would also be the type of person who oppose him at every turn. Deventis was different though, he was a Viperian, he had been raised by the worshippers of the murderous deity Sslishka, Deventis would understand what he was doing.

Deventis continued to stare at Markus; he had been speaking with this Havak creature for hours before returning to his private study where Deventis had been waiting. He had not said a single word, he just sat at his desk across from the Viperian, smiling.

Deventis was growing impatient, "So, what have you learned?" Markus finally looked back at Deventis. This Viperian was the closest thing Markus had to a friend, but his shear excitement at the prospects of what was soon to happen had overwhelmed his usual stern composure that he was finding it hard to put what he had learned into words. Deventis watched him a little longer before leaning forward on his chair, he was grinning himself now; Markus knew something, something that was making him very happy indeed. "What have you learned?" he asked again.

When Markus finally spoke his voice was little more than a whisper, "Within the next thirty days," he began, "Legion shall walk amongst us." Deventis leaned back in his chair, trying to process what Markus had just said. "Our master is also sending us another mighty ally." Markus continued, "Slantary is already on her way."

"And who pray tell, is Slantary."

Markus laughed to himself, "Slantary is a dragon, a very old red dragon."

*   *   *

It was barely dawn when commander Medlich banged on the front entrance to the Mini Palace, and shortly after that he was banging on the door of the room Adokas was staying in. Medlich explained that King Augustus required that he and his companions come to the palace as soon as possible. Adokas began to collect his things together as Medlich departed to collect Thoril from the Mage House.

Adokas roused Davkul, which was not appreciated by the grumpy old dwarf. Davkul began to gather his belongings and Adokas went to wake Roscoe. The elf knocked lightly on the door and waited for a short while. His keen ears could hear movement in the room, he listened as the footsteps got closer to the door, he was a little surprised however when the door was opened and Victathana was standing there instead of Roscoe.

"I'm sorry to disturb you my lady, I thought this was the room Roscoe was staying in." Adokas bowed and began to turn; he was trying to think which room Roscoe could be in if not this one. That's when it struck him, Roscoe had most certainly entered this room the night before. This thought was confirmed when Roscoe stuck his head round the door.

"Wait, wait. You have the right room," Roscoe stuttered, "How can I help?"

Adokas had a big grin across his face, "Well Davkul and I have been summoned to see the king, I thought you might have liked to attend, but I can see that you are... busy."

Adokas could hear Victathana laughing behind the door as Roscoe attempted to stutter a reply. "He is not busy." the female halfling said as she pushed past Roscoe into the corridor, Adokas noted that she was wearing the same stunning dress which she had the nigh before. "I was just taking my leave." she continued, "There is much to be done before the other guests wake." The woman offered a slight bow, which Adokas mirrored before she turned and walked off down the corridor.

"I will be ready shortly." Roscoe said.

"Take your time my friend, it seems you had a long night." Adokas chuckled. Roscoe's face turned bright red as he ducked back into his room, where he prepared himself for meeting a king.

It wasn't long before the trio were all stood in the main lobby of the Mini Palace, Davkul was still grumbling to himself about being woken up so early. Roscoe wasn't saying anything at all, he didn't even complain about the fact he was missing the incredible breakfast Victathana had promised him. Adokas just laughed to himself, finding the early morning behaviour of his companions most amusing.

"We had best make our way to the actual palace." Adokas led the way to their meeting with the king. The palace was in the centre of the city, as they approached the entrance the trio saw that Thoril and Medlich were already waiting for them.

"Good morning gentlemen, glad you could join us." Medlich said as they drew near, Thoril looked as though he was still half asleep.

"A late night my friend?" Adokas asked, his smile widening even more as he realised that he was the only member of the group who had actually had more than enough sleep during the night.

"I was up late aiding the grand mage with one of his experiments." Thoril explained through a yawn.

"Did it go well?" Adokas was now studying the mage, looking for any signs to answer his question, as he knew exactly what Thoril's answer would be.

"Of course it went well. All of the grand mage's experiments go well." Adokas could easily tell that Thoril's answer was not entirely accurate. He could see scorch marks on his robes despite the mage's attempt to hide them. Also Thoril's hair was shorter, and his eyebrows were singed. To the elf's keen eyes something had obviously burned very hot in his direction, which suggested that something had gone very wrong with the grand mage's experiment.

Medlich showed the four companions into the palace and lead them towards the king's audience chamber. Roscoe took this time to chat with his old friend.

"I thought you were supposed to be hunting some ogre," Roscoe began, "Could you not get your hunting party together?"

Medlich smiled, "I got my party, and we got our ogre." He explained, "The beast was easy to track, and even easier to kill."

"That is good to hear, it is always good to know there is one less beast prowling the area. Did I know any of the people in your party?"

"I doubt it. I asked for the help of two new comers to the city. An elven ranger by the name of Larenor, and a half-elf paladin known as Aramil." This caught the attention of everyone, they had all seen the scroll Solaris had given Tanay, and heard from Thoril who the men were. "We were aided by some others we met on the a cleric called Kimanay, a monk called Delensa, who have decided to carry on working with the others for now. There was also a curious reptile eyed sorcerer too, but I never managed to catch his name." Medlich explained, "The only real problem came in the form of *the Shadow*."

"The shadow?" Roscoe asked.

"Some assassin type claiming to be an imaginary killer. But with the party I had with me we sent him running off with his tail between his legs."

"He was a legendary killer?"

"No, just some fool using the name. The Shadow is just one of those made up names people tell their kids about, you know the type 'if you don't do your chores the the shadow will get you'" Medlich laughed.

They eventually reached the extravagant set of double doors leading to the king's audience chamber; they were large wooden doors with gold bracing, each of the doors had the likeness of an ancient king carved into it. As he passed through the doors Roscoe could see that they were entering a very large, well decorated room. There were large tapestries along the two side walls depicting scenes of battles and coronations, dragons and men.

The main source of light of light in the room came from the ceiling, which was largely transparent. Roscoe had never seen such a large glass panel, he presumed it was some gift from the cities mages. At the far end of the room Roscoe could see the king seated on a large golden throne. There was another man stood next to the king who did not look to be from Getandor, his eyes were narrower and his skin tone slightly darker than the native born.

"Good morning gentlemen, my apologies for summoning you all so early." All of the summoned men bowed, showing their respect for the king. "Now now, that is not necessary." Everyone looked up; the king had risen from his throne and was standing in front of the group. He was about average hight for men of the region with short grey hair and a kind face, judging by his waist line he was also very well fed.

"It is good to see you again so soon, your grace," Adokas said, very politely, "May I introduce Roscoe Thorngage, he has been travelling with us for some time now."

"Well met little one, I am King Augustus IV." The king proclaimed with a warm smile.

"I am honoured to meet you, your grace."Roscoe said, returning the smile.

"And who might he be?" Davkul asked in his rough tone. The dwarf was still not over the fact that he had been woken up so early, and was in no mood for pleasantries.

"This is Antonema Christortus," the king explained, "He is one of my most trusted advisors."

"May I ask why it is we have been summoned my lord?" Thoril asked. The mage wanted to get this meeting over with as soon as possible, he was hoping to be able to get some more sleep.

"Ah, straight to the point," the king's smile dissipated and he returned to his throne. "We have translated some ancient scrolls, they are prophecies concerning the war we are soon to face."

"And what do they say?" Adokas asked, now sounding very serious.

"We need more allies." King Augustus answered bluntly, "The scrolls speak of the army we will face, and it is far greater than anything the world has ever seen before. If we don't find more forces we will be completely overrun." The king turned to face Davkul, "Are you sure the dwarves will not aid us?"

"Nasgaroth does not see this fight as any of his concern, he will not send help." Answered the dwarf, lowering his gaze shamefully.

"My father will send aid; he is just waiting to receive word." Put in Adokas.

"That still will not be enough." said the king sombrely.

"What about the nomads from near Transeen?" asked Roscoe, " If you send an emissary to them they may answer your call for help." All eyes turned to Roscoe, none of them had expected the halfling to contribute to the plans, least of all Roscoe himself.

"They will not help," Antonema said, "They are barbarians, and would use this trouble to simply further themselves."

"I disagree." Roscoe said, "They may not be civilised by your standards, but I have met many of their chiefs. They are both honourable men, and able warriors." Roscoe turned to the king, "If asked correctly, I believe they would help."

The king smiled again, "This is the very reason I have asked you all here. I have sent the paladin Aramil, and his companion Larenor in search of some artefacts that will summon an army of *elements* that the scrolls spoke of. What I need from you is to find us allies who are already here, and bring them to our aid." The four companions looked to each other, "I would suggest that your first stop should be at Magon's tower. The old mage may know of some others who would be able to help."

There was little else that needed saying. King Augustus IV told Medlich to provide his emissaries with horses for their journey. It was not long after this that Roscoe, Adokas, Davkul and Thoril were back on the road, expecting to reach Magon's tower in a matter of hours.

Chapter 9
New Roads

"Your choice of guests is rather peculiar of late. First a viperian, then a devil, and now a graw." Stomorel had just entered seating area where Magon and Solaris were sitting, along with the female graw Stomorel's spiteful comment had been aimed at.

"Devil?" There have been no devil staying in my house." Magon replied in his usual cheery tone.

"Well that *paladin* looked fairly devil like to me."

Solaris quietly laughed to himself, "Jamaan may be tainted, but he is no devil."

Stomorel glared at Solaris, "He may as well be a devil."

Solaris laughed again, "For a child of nature who is supposed to understand the delicate balance of this world, you are very quick to judge."

"So you expect me to believe that there is a truthful viperian, a good *tainted* man, and a well meaning graw. All of which just happened to visit you?"

"Not at all my dear." Magon chuckled, "This graw is in no way well meaning."

"She attempted to assassinate me last night." Added Solaris.

"Oh, I see," Stomorel appeared more than a little taken aback by Solaris' proclamation. "So you are going to interrogate her?"

"That is just what we were doing before you arrived, my dear." Magon explained with a smile. Stomorel took another look at the scene before her. This did not look like any interrogation she had ever seen, the graw was sitting in one the more comfortable seats, and even had a drink in her hand.

"Has she said anything useful?"

"Not yet," Magon answered, still sounding very cheery.

"She is a stubborn one," added Solaris.

"She is part of the group who attacked me and Tanay on the road to see Nasgaroth." All eyes turned to the door, where Laucian now stood.

"I didn't know you were attacked on the road." said Stomorel, sounding a little shocked, and concerned.

"You would be surprised at the amount of things you don't know." Laucian said coldly as he walked past the woman towards one of the seats.

The graw glared at Laucian as he walked across the room, her eyes narrowing as he sat down. Laucian looked straight back at the grew, his lips curling into an evil smile.

"Your friend failed to kill me, again." The graw snarled as Laucian spoke, "You and your friends really are very bad at this assassination game. Perhaps you should find a new line of employment, before you get yourself killed as well."

The graw growled, she threw her drink to the side and launched herself from her chair. She would show Laucian just how good she was at her chosen career path. The graw only made it a few feet from the chair before she suddenly stopped in mid-air for a fraction of a second, then flying backwards until she was safely back in her chair. The sight of this had Magon curled up in his own chair laughing. Even Laucian laughed, Solaris shook his head smiling, Stomorel just stares in disbelief.

Magon eventually stopped laughing and looked at the dumbfounded elf, "What do you think? I call it springy air."

"It seems to be very effective." Stomorel answered slowly. The graw was growling again. Stomorel judged by the look in her eyes this wasn't the first time the graw had tried to move, and was getting frustrated by the old mage's trick.

"Do you know how they got in?"

"But of course I do." Magon answered, sounding a little insulted by the question.

"Really?" Stomorel asked, "How?"

"Oh its quite simple, she was let in." Both Laucian and Stomorel turned to look at the old mage, both of them confused by his statement.

"We were just about to ask who opened the door." Solaris leaned back in his chair; all eyes fell on the graw.

"Do you really think I'm going to tell you anything?" She looked at the other people in the room; she had an evil smile as she looked at Magon and the Solaris., as she turned to Laucian she bared her teeth screwed up her nose and growled at the man her companion had failed to kill, twice. She didn't even look at Stomorel, the contempt that graw felt for elves was well known, graw had a deep hatred for all non-demons, but none more so than elves. This graw didn't even deem to look at Stomorel, those gathered could only assume that her hatred ran so deep that it did not need to be shown.

Solaris laughed to himself, "Do I think you will tell me anything?" his expression suddenly turned serious, "You have already told me everything I need to know."

The graw laughed this time, "Is that so?"

"You have told us more than enough." Magon said, "Gregor!" the mage called.

"Yes my lord?" Everyone turned to the back corner of the room, no-one had noticed Magon's old butler sitting there. The old wan walked over to where Magon was sitting. Gregor was a tall thin man with short grey hair and a well trimmed moustache. The old butler stood very straight and ridged, but still appeared to be very frail.

"If you would be so kind, could you take our guest down to her private room?"

"Certainly my lord." Gregor walked over to the graw, "If you would follow me miss." The graw just looked at the man thinking this was just a trick by Magon, an attempt to humiliate her by making her stand up just to be dragged back to her chair.

"Don't worry my dear, the spell has worn off now. You can quite easily leave the seat." Magon said politely as if he had read the demon's mind.

The graw slowly got up from the chair, still not sure if she trusted that the spell had run its course. "If you would come this way please." Gregor extended his arm towards the door, the graw slowly walked past the butler towards the door.

When Solaris had first caught the graw she had been ecstatic at the fact he had not done a thorough search, meaning that he had missed the small knife concealed within her top. The graw realised that without her companion she was not likely to escape this tower, Vandex had fallen at the hands of captain Holdak, and now it appeared as though Aluthana had been finished off by Laucian, her mark. The graw knew that the spy within the tower would not help her either; they would not risk their cover to save her. She also had no intention of remaining a prisoner within this tower, and with no chance of escape she decided that she would use this last chance to do her job, she would kill the missions primary mark.

The graw slowly reached for the knife and pulled it from its concealed position. She span round quickly thrusting the blade into Gregor's gut, planning to kill the butler before throwing the knife through Laucian's throat. Hey plan did not go as she had expected however; as the blade penetrated Gregor's gut it seemed to hit nothing, the butler's gut had just become a swirl of smoke.

"Now that was not very polite miss." Gregor was looking down at the knife as he spoke. The graw looked down in surprise, as she retracted the blade Gregor's gut returned to normal. "Now if you could please put the knife down." The graw swiped the blade at the butler, twice across the chest, each time it swiped through nothing but air and smoke where Gregor's chest had been.

Magon laughed at the scene along with Solaris, Laucian just shook his head as Stomorel stared in disbelief. Gregor smiled at the graw, "Miss, I would greatly appreciate it if you could stop doing that."

The graw backed off slowly, "What are you?"

"I am a butler, miss." Gregor answered with a slight bow, "Now I am going to ask you again, could you please drop the knife?" The graw responded by lunging forward, Gregor just stepped to the side and placed his hand on her shoulder, the graw's arm began to loose strength and grow numb, it was as though Gregor was draining the life from her arm until it fell limp at the side, her hand relaxed and the knife dropped to the floor. "Thank you miss, now if you would please come this way." Gregor led the graw from the room, taking her to the lowest level of Magon's tower, where the mage had a number of cells.

After they had left the room Solaris and Magon turned to Laucian, "So where is the other assassin?" Solaris asked.

"I expect Magon will have a better idea of that, she is loose somewhere within the tower."

"I'm afraid I am at as much of a loss as you are on that count, this assassin is staying very well hidden." Magon replied.

"And I thought that nothing happened within your tower without your knowledge." laughed Stomorel as she decided to finally sit down.

"It would appear that whomever is helping our assassin is doing a rather good job at keeping her hidden from me." Magon explained sheepishly.

It was not long before Gregor re-entered the room, "Your pardon my lord, you have some guests."

"Is that so? And who might they be?" asked Magon, sounding very excited by the prospect of more guests.

"They claim to be an envoy from King Augustus IV, my lord."

"Well then, you had best show them in."

Gregor turned and opened the door, "This way please gentlemen." Through the door walked Adokas, Thoril, Davkul and Roscoe.

"Good day to you gentlemen, please do sit down." Greeted Magon with a smile.

"Well met my lord," said Thoril with a bow. The four men each found themselves a seat and introductions were made for those who had not met before.

"Gregor, if you would be so kind as to rouse Jamaan, I think he should be present for this meeting." Magon asked politely.

"Certainly my lord." Gregor bowed before leaving the room.

"So, how may I be of service to you?" The old mage asked, now turning to face his four new guests.

"The king has had some ancient prophecies translated; they tell of a great army that will sweep across the land, if we cannot build up our own forces to stand against it then all will be lost." Thoril explained.

"And how can I help?"

"We wish for you to join our cause, to help in the coming battle." Adokas replied.

Magon closed his eyes and bowed his head, letting out a sorrowful sigh as he did. "I am afraid that I can be of no help in any coming battle."

"But my lord, it is said that you are a most powerful mage." said Adokas.

"That is very true, I do possess great power. With my magic I could easily lay waste to an entire army."

"Then why will you not help?" Roscoe piped in.

"It is not permitted; I am able to guide the people of this world, to help them reach their true potential, to set them down the roads of their destinies. I cannot however actively participate in the events that mould those destinies. I suppose I am as my old friend so eloquently describes me," Magon indicated Solaris as he spoke, "A shepherd."

"Are you saying that you will not help us either?" grunted Davkul. Just then the door opened and Gregor entered the room followed by Jamaan, a sight which shocked Roscoe and his companions as they had not seen the man without his helmet before, they had not seen his true nature.

"I may not be able to help you directly, but I can offer you some new roads to tread." Magon explained defensively. He suddenly felt rather useless, all of his great magical powers seeming redundant.

The people Magon was trying to explain himself to however seemed to barely notice his words, they were all fixated on Jamaan. They were all staring at the man's red-scaled face, they were mesmerised by his deep orange eyes.

Jamaan couldn't help but notice the look of shock on the faces of Magon's guests and forced himself to smile, "Well, I guess this is a face you were not expecting to see."

"What happened?" Roscoe asked, genuinely concerned for the paladin's well being.

"Nothing has happened since we last met, except I have removed my helmet." Jamaan walked over and sat in one of the seats, whereas Gregor remained standing by the door. "Could I ask what this meeting is about?"

"We've been sent by the king, we are searching for allies to help fight in a war." Roscoe explained, never taking his eyes off of Jamaan.

"As I was saying, I might not be able to help in the fight directly, but I can offer you some advice." Magon said, feeling that people had stopped listening to him.

"What are you planning?" Asked Jamaan. Solaris and Laucian both laughed to themselves, having noticed the look on Magon's face. He had pulled the same face an attention-seeking child would pull when it was being ignored.

"Well the elves of Landorn will send aid," started Adokas.

"Nasgaroth however will not send the dwarves," Davkul grunted, seemingly irritated by his own statement.

"We are also heading to see the nomadic tribes past Calamshan." added Roscoe.

"We were hoping that Magon would also lend us his help, but..." Thoril started.

"But I am not permitted to interfere," said Magon bitterly, "If you would take the time however I may be able to make a few suggestions." Solaris laughed again, he could see by Magon's face that the old man was annoyed by the tone Thoril had used when speaking about him. It was no secret that the wizards of the Mage House had never liked Magon, a solitary mage who had accumulated much greater power than they could pooling their resources, and now he was saying that he could not help, Thoril had taken it as the same arrogance shown by Nasgaroth.

"And what is it you suggest?" Adokas asked.

"Well by my reckoning with the forces you have described, you will still not have enough to stand against the army described by these prophecies."

"But who else is there for us to call upon?" Asked Davkul. Solaris leaned back, his smile disappearing. He knew the answer to this question, he also knew that it would not be a very popular solution.

"There is a great force that you have not even considered, an army of vast proportions." Began Magon slowly, he was choosing his words very carefully as he too knew what reaction to expect from those gathered in his home. "Within the Four Kings mountains lies a dormant army, a great force which if roused and joined with those you have described could match anything Legion could send."

"The Four Kings? All that dwells there are orcs and goblins." Davkul snorted.

"And trolls and ogres, along with all manor of other mighty beasts." Solaris added.

"You cannot be suggesting that we seek the help of those animals?" spat Jamaan, with obvious disgust.

"These *animals* as you call them are great warriors, and I have a feeling that they too would like to stop Legion from completing his plans." said Magon sternly.

"What is this Legion you keep mentioning?" Roscoe asked.

"You do not know?" asked Magon, genuinely surprised by the question. The four new guests all shook their heads. "How much has the king told you about these prophecies?"

"Nothing more than that we need to raise an army to face some great evil force." Thoril replied.

Solaris chuckled, "The force is not exactly evil." Solaris began, "Legion is a demon, for want of a better word, his purpose is to destroy all of existence."

"That sounds evil to me," said Davkul.

"If Legion was evil he would be trying to enslave the world, not destroy it. He is not prejudice, Legion wishes to destroy both good and evil alike." Solaris explained, "If you take my advice you will go to these orcs and goblins, for you will need their help before the end."

"I would suggest a variety of roads," began Magon, "Master Roscoe, I think it best for you to go to the nomadic tribes as you are quite familiar with their people, and mister Davkul should accompany you, the tribes hold a great respect for the martial power of dwarves." Roscoe looked a little confused, how did this old man know of his familiarity with the nomads? Though he felt that now was not the time to raise this question. "Adokas and Thoril, I think you would be best served by returning to Transeen, the etharii there have a sizeable force."

"So you do not suggest we seek the help of the orcs and goblins?" Thoril asked sarcastically.

"Actually, I suggest that Jamaan makes that trip." Magon replied.

"Why me?" asked the paladin, surprised by Magon's words.

"Because my friend, you are tainted, yet still keep your goodly ways. To many in those mountains your tainted blood would be seen as a sign of strength, and keeping hold of your morality shows a conviction they will respect. You are well suited to negotiate with these warlike people, and you could lead that army out of the mountains."

Jamaan sat in silence for a moment, contemplating the suggestion before him; working with such creatures went against his principles, but he could also see the greater good in the situation. Eventually the proud man nodded his agreement to the plan.

"Stomorel, could you possibly seek out the grand druids, appraise them of the situation and seek their council?" Magon asked as he turned to the druid who had sat listening intently to the conversation.

"Certainly, I will leave immediately." Stomorel replied as she stood, and made to leave.

"We should also take our leave," Adokas said as he rose from his chair, "It would seem we have a long road ahead of us." The rest of his companions, along with Jamaan followed suit and Gregor showed them all out.

Before they left Magon called after them, "Gregor, if you would please fetch Fruril for me, I have an errand for him to run."

"Certainly my lord." Gregor replied, and followed the others through the door.

"Do you have any suggestions as to which road I should follow?" Laucian asked sarcastically.

"As a matter of fact I do," Magon answered with a grin. "I think you should search out the elemental stone of fire. There are some people currently searching for the other three stones, a search that will soon lead them here. When they are done here I shall send them to meet you in Cemulion, by which time I should hope you will have already have retrieved the fire stone."

"And where might I find this fire stone?"

"It is currently in the possession of the master of Cemulion's thieves guild, beyond that I'm afraid I cannot say."

"Then I shall prepare to travel to Cemulion." Laucian stood and took his leave to collect his travelling things.

After Laucian had left the room, and the door closed behind him Solaris began to speak in a low tone, "You know who the spy is don't you?"

"Of course, and I expect that you have worked it out too." Replied the old mage cheerfully.

Solaris laughed, he had always been surprised by Magon's constant cheerful disposition, "So you know who they are, and yet you still send them to run errands?"

"Oh no, I am simply giving them a chance to inform their masters of what is happening."

"You are playing a dangerous game wizard; do you really think you prodigies are ready to face this threat?"

"I am convinced that they will succeed in their trials. They will find their roads, and walk them to the very end."

Chapter 10
Shadowy Light

The woman crept slowly along the winding passage. She was careful to stay in the shadows cast by the few torches along the corridor. She knew this passage well, in the past few months she had been here many times, trying to find a link between this thieves guild and the mercenaries who were secretly running her home country. She had heard Deventis mention the name Pileroo when he had thought her dead.

She heard their voices approaching long before the three men came into view. The young woman smiled as she backed into the shadows. It was plain to see that these men had been drinking heavily; they were stumbling all over the passage. She could even smell the ale on their breath as they came closer to where she stood.

They were so close now, only a matter of feet away from her. She laughed silently to herself, knowing that these men had no idea she was even there. She knew it would be a simple task to kill the men, they would all be dead before they knew what was happening. There very presence in this place proved that they would have deserved to die, but how would that help he cause?

She had caused some minor disruptions to the guild; she expected her actions were beginning to annoy the guild master, Pileroo. However they had still paid little attention to her activities, leaving her able to gain much information about the guilds plans in Cemulion city, and its links to the legion of Strakstaw. If she started killing guild members however, they would be more likely to launch a more effective campaign to stop her.

One of the men was right on top of her now, he was so close that she could see the few grey hairs in his unkempt beard, yet he could not see her. Another of the men tripped and bumped into the bearded drink, sending him stumbling forward, straight through the woman without even realising she was there. She had become one with the shadows, they were hiding her, they were protecting her.

The men carried on down the corridor, and when they were out of sight the woman returned to her normal self. When she was no longer a part of the shadows she began to creep along the passage once again.

She finally arrived at an interchange of corridors, there were five new passages,all connected to this one in a small circular room. The woman was very careful now, this interchange was well lit, limiting the shadows she could hide amongst. She stopped a few feet away from the circular room, crouching in one of the shadows she waited. She did not have to wait long before a man shaped shadow came into view. Most people would not have noticed her companion approach, but she knew he was there, she could feel his presence before she saw him.

"The door at the end of the north corridor is open." The woman looked at her companion and smiled, it was about time she learned what was behind that damned door.

After Deventis had left her for dead the woman had been found by a group of travelling performers, who were more than they had seemed. The troop was made up of shadow walkers thieves, putting on a show to entertain and amaze audiences as other members of the troop helped themselves to any valuables.

The woman had spent a few months with this troop learning from them, learning the arts of the shadow walkers. She had been a perfect student, within two months she was able to rival some of the long standing members in skill, lock picking being one of the skills that she had excelled at.

Yet even with her uncanny ability to open locks, the door at the end of the north corridor had been beyond her skill to open. Now though, she would finally see what was behind this door.

"Quinn, I could kiss you." the woman was overjoyed by her companion's news. "If it were possible for me to do so."

"Ah, the pains of being incorporeal." Quinn replied. Quinn was in fact no man, and no beast for that matter. Quinn was a shadow, a creature of darkness whose appearance was that of a humanoids shadow. These creature of darkness were usually utterly evil, despising all things living, but Quinn had been summoned by a shadow walker, making him her loyal companion and friend. He was summoned with similar principles to the woman, and so had no trouble in working with her.

The pair started off down the north passage. This one was not as well lit as the others, making it an easy path to travel for the woman and her companion. It was easy to tell that this path was not often travelled, which under normal circumstances would suggest that the end prize would be nothing special. The door at the end of this passage however told the woman that whatever was through it would probably be worth the wait. It was not just an impressive series of locks that protected the door, but some powerful magic too, magic that could even stop her incorporeal friend from passing through it, and only important things were guarded that well.

It wasn't long before the woman was crouched a few feet away from the door. It looked plain, just an ordinary wooden door with iron banding, but she knew it was so much more. It was a little open now, and there was a soft glow coming from just behind it. She crept closer to the door and could hear voices talking softly coming from the room. The woman instantly recognised one voice as Pileroo's, she had seen the guild master a few times during her incursions into the building. The other she didn't recognise though, it was a strange accent, not one from Getandor or Krondmare.

"Quinn, how many are in there?" Quinn passed the woman and walked straight through the door, a few moments later the shadow returned and crouched by his companion.

"There are seven. Pileroo with four of his personal guard, a mage, and a foreign man who looks to be some kind of noble."

"Are there any shadows to hide in?"

Quinn laughed, "There are many, the room is lit by a small fire in the centre all around the edges are bathed in darkness. It appears to be some kind of ceremonial meeting place, I see nothing to warrant such a door."

The woman crept to the door and glanced through the slight opening, she couldn't see much, only one of the guards, but that wasn't what she was looking for. The side wall provided exactly what she needed. Quinn watched as she backed into the shadows of the corridor, before disappearing entirely from sight.

The room was exactly as Quinn had described it, lit in the centre but the edges were in deep shadow. It was a perfect room for the woman to observe the gathered men. Quinn was right in his assessment, the room was clearly used for important meetings, for times when Pileroo wanted to impress or intimidate his guests. Pileroo was sitting on a large wooden throne, he was a slim man wearing loose clothing and large amount of jewellery; he also had a brightly coloured tattoo up he side of his face, going all the way up onto his bald head.

Two of the guards stood by Pileroo, one at each side of his chair. The two remaining guards stood at the opposite side of the room, each just within the light cast by the fire. The foreign man stood with his back to the door, warming his hands by the fire, the mage sitting on the floor opposite staring into the flames.

Apart from Pileroo's throne chair there was no other furniture in to room. The woman agreed with Quinn's assessment that there didn't appear to be anything in this room to warrant the magical wards on its door.

"Are the tunnels complete?" asked the foreigner.

"Almost." Pileroo replied. "They will be fully accessible when the army arrives." The foreigner turned his head towards the guild master, his eyes narrowed. Pileroo shrunk back into his chair under the gaze, "I'm sorry my lord, but we ran into difficulties. The rock of the dungeon was harder to break through than we first expected."

The foreigner turned back to the fire, "Your progress is satisfactory. I will inform the general." Pileroo grinned broadly. "Is the stone safe here?"

"Of course it is." Pileroo scoffed, "You saw for yourself how difficult it was to enter this room, and that is no ordinary flame." The woman moved slightly to her side so she could get a better view of the fire, hoping to see what it was they were talking about. It was in that moment she realised just why the door was so well protected. In the middle of the fire there was a ruby about the size of an orcs fist.

The foreigner looked curiously around the room, pausing to look at each of the guards. He slowly moved his hand to the hilt of the dagger sheathed at his belt. The woman watched him closely, what was this man doing? After asking about the safety of the stone did he now plan to try and steal it?

With lightning speed the foreigner pulled the blade from its sheath, span around and launched it. Everyone stared in disbelief; he had not thrown the dagger at a person, but at the door. The force of which it struck forcing the door closed.

"Why don't you step into the light? Let us see who you are."

"What are you talking about?" Asked Pileroo as he rose from his seat.

"If you do not come into the light, we will come into the shadows for you." The guards all looked at each other, confused by the foreigners comment. The woman stayed silent for a moment, had this man heard her movement? Had he heard her take a single step to the side?

"I will not warn you again. Come into the light, or we will drag you into it by force." The woman knew now that she had been found out, but this fact did not worry her too much. With the door closed she would not be able to sneak from the room, and yet she had no intention of being caught. There were seven enemies in the room, under normal circumstances this fact would demoralise a person, but not her, she still had a couple of tricks up her sleeves. She was sure that she could quickly take out most of them before they even knew what was happening.

The two guards by Pileroo were holding swords, which they had drawn in response to the foreigners words. The other two followed suit and armed themselves, each stringing an arrow in their bows. They were all looking at each other, not entirely convinced that there actually was someone else in the room.

"Do you really think you could force me out of the shadows?" Called the woman. Everyone turned to where the voice had come from. She was close to one of the bowmen, who was now aiming his weapon where the woman's voice had come from. This unwavering attention to where the woman had spoken from would be their downfall.

The woman emerged from the shadows, but not from where the men had been expecting. One of the bowmen was standing at the opposite side of the room from where her voice had come from, and he was the first to realise their mistake. He never got the chance to announce his discovery before the woman's knife cut deeply across his throat.

The man's muffled scream caught the others attention, but by the time they had turned he was falling to the floor dead, and the woman was back amongst the shadows. One of the sword wielding guards ran to his fallen comrade, but there was nothing he could do.

"Who are you?" Pileroo yelled as he moved to stand in-between the foreigner and the mage. "I demand you come out of the shadows this instant!"

"I am your worst nightmare, and I do not suffer the demands of fools." Everyone again turned to where the voice had come from, the remaining archer loosing his arrow, but all he hit was the wall.

The woman launched herself out of the shadows, again from directly behind her enemies. She ran silently towards the swordsman who still stood by Pileroo's chair she embedded her knife in the back of his neck before carrying on back into the shadows without slowing a step.

The remaining men span around just in time to see another of their comrades hit the floor.

"There must be many of them!" called the remaining swordsman.

"How could they have gotten in without us noticing them?" asked the bowman, with obvious fear in his voice.

"There are not so many." said the foreigner with a grin.

"Antonema, you are an assassin, do something!" Pileroo ordered.

The foreigner laughed, "You do not give me orders, Pileroo. And I am doing something." Antonema drew his sword, the slender blade gleaming in the fire light as he griped tightly around the bone handle. In that moment the woman realised just how dangerous this man was likely to be, he would be her next target.

The woman drew her own sword and scraped it across the floor in front of her. Again all of the men turned to the source of the sound. The woman ran out of the darkness from behind Antonema, but he suddenly span around, easily parrying her attack.

"It is nice to finally see you." Laughed the dangerous assassin. The other men turned to see the woman, the archer aimed his bow at her but with Antonema in the way he could not get a clean shot.

The woman slashed across Antonema's chest but again he easily parried the attack. She thrust hight, thrust low, slashed and slashed again but made no progress against her foe. Antonema was easily dismissing all of the attacks until he eventually forced the woman's sword out wide, he quickly stepped in close and grabbed her by her tunic.

"You are good, and have some interesting tricks. But I am better." Antonema pushed the woman backwards where she fell to the floor. This gave the archer a clear shot. Antonema may have proved himself better than the woman, but the bowman had already seen two of his friends fall and was not taking any chances.

Before he could loose his arrow however the archer felt a cold hand on his shoulder. The man looked to his side to see Quinn. The archer's arms began to grow weak; he dropped his bow to the floor as his arms fell limp at his side. The man let out a cry as his knees began to shake under his own weight. The others turned to him, just in time to see him dragged into the shadows. Antonema turned back to the woman to see that she too had returned to the shadows.

The one remaining guard ran to where his friend had been, "He's gone! Disappeared!" He called as he ran back towards the centre of the room; he never reached his destination though as he was struck in the back by a crossbow bolt.

"She's a shadow walker," Antonema said as he turned to the mage, "Cast a light spell, there is to be no darkness in this room."

The mage muttered a few words and pointed to several places around the room, within a second the room was fully lit from all angles. With the shadows gone all eyes fell on the woman, who was now crouched in one of the corners.

"Hello again." Antonema took a step towards the woman as he spoke, "How do you expect to win now? Without your precious shadows."

The woman smiled, it appeared that no-one had noticed the two shadows that should not have been there. Both the mage and Antonema had shadows; shadows that should have been unable to exist with so many new light sources. One of the shadows was Quinn; the other was the fallen archer, a man Quinn had dragged into utter darkness.

Antonema slowly walked towards the woman, but stopped when he heard the mage groan. He turned to see the man fall to his knees, his strength drained. Antonema then noticed the other shadow by him, its hand reaching out towards him. The assassin spun away from the outstretched hand, holding his sword between himself and the creature. He looked to his allies; Pileroo had ran to the opposite side of the room like the coward Antonema knew him to be. The mage was not fairing so well, he was already loosing his human form, he was turning into a shadow.

"Do you really think that can hurt me?" Hissed the fallen archer, "I am incorporeal."

"My sword was especially forged to cut through anything, including that which is not truly there." Antonema smiled, "And that includes you." With two quick swipes Antonema had cut the shadow into three, the creature screamed in agony as it dissipated into the light. Antonema then turned to Quinn and the mage, who had now fully changed into a creature of darkness.

"Quinn go now!" Called the woman.

"But what about you?" her loyal friend asked.

"Don't worry about me. Just go and find help!" The woman ran at Antonema, but the seasoned warrior easily turned and parried her attack. "Quinn go!" She yelled again.

"You stay, help her." Quinn ordered, he watched the woman's futile attack on her deadly foe before doing as he was ordered. He ran from the room, passing straight through the door. He knew the woman had no chance of escape, hoping that they would take her captive rather than kill her, that way he could find a way to get her out of the thieves guild.

The fallen mage ran at Antonema, but the assassin was ready for such an attack. He parried an attack from the woman, forcing her backwards as he did before reversing the grip on his sword, thrusting it backwards under his arm straight into the mid section of the charging shadow. The creature screeched as it fell backwards and dissipated into nothingness.

The woman attacked again, slashing high, but the assassin easily blocked her sword. He smiled again as he forced her backwards again. With lightning speed Antonema spun around low, sweeping the woman's legs out from under her. She hit the ground with a grunt, dropping her sword which slid across the floor out of her reach.

"I advise you give up now," warned Antonema as he placed the tip of his sword to her throat, "Or I will kill you."

"You win, I give up." she said sombrely.

Pileroo now came striding up boldly to stand next to Antonema. "Kill her!" he ordered, "This woman has caused enough trouble here already." The guild master seemed to have found his courage now that the fighting was over.

"I have already told you Pileroo, I do not take orders from you." Pileroo shrank back under the assassin's gaze. "This woman will not die today. You will place her in your dungeon, and make sure there are no shadows in her cell."

"But she is the one who has been disrupting my operations, I am sure of it." Pileroo stuttered, "I want her dead." Pileroo was regaining some of his bravery.

"If she is harmed you will have me to deal with, and I will repay any pain caused to her many times over."

"But she has just killed five of my men..."

"She will not be harmed!" Antonema snapped, breaking from his usual perfectly calm persona because of the irritating guild master, who took several steps back bowing his head. "At least not until I know why the princess of Krondmare is skulking around a thieves guild in the capital of Getandor."

Chapter 11
Fear of the Gods

A gathering such as this had not occurred since the dawn of time. These beings had not all been in the same place since the time they had all worked together in the great creation.

"Has everyone arrived?" Sugalas, the sun god asked as he looked around the great chamber. The chamber was filled with his peers, it was filled by the gods.

"Yes dear husband, we are all here." Darlkeeth replied. Sugalas turned to see his former wife, the goddess of hell, approaching where he stood. Darlkeeth was holding slender sword at her side as she walked towards the sun god. Sugalas' hand fell to the hilt of his long sword.

"It has been a long time Darlkeeth."

"That it has, *my love*." Darlkeeth raised her sword, giving it a couple of test swings. Sugalas promptly drew his sword; it was a ritual these two mortal enemies went through every time they met, but never had these gods actually fought.

"Put your weapons away, we have not come here to fight," said the woodland deity Greenuff.

"Yes, of course. We are here to discuss a much greater threat." Sugalas replied as he put his blade away.

"So it is true then?" Sslishka asked with a wicked grin, "Legion's attack is at hand."

"Yes." Valkiya laughed, "And we must destroy him."

"Destroy him?" Sslishka sneered, "But his followers are such delightful schemers, just think of the beautiful chaos their betrayal will cause. Can't we just watch the fun? We can just deal with him afterwards."

"You do not understand, my unbalanced *friend*. If Legion is successful then all will be gone. If he succeeds there will be no afterwards for us to deal with anything." Explained Galan, natures guardian.

Sslishka pouted, "So what do we do?"

"We kill him." Sugalas replied.

"Looks like we will finally be fighting side by side *my love*." Darlkeeth raised her delicate fingers to Sugalas' face, causing the sun god to flinch away. The mistress of hell smiled at her former lovers reaction.

"So what is your plan?" asked Valkiya, the warrior goddess eager to end the talking and get to the action.

"His followers will summon him into this world soon," Sugalas began.

"And when they do we shall be there waiting, and we will kill the beast." Darlkeeth finished. The other gods just looked on as Sugalas and Darlkeeth, two mortal enemies, stood side by side ready to go into battle together against a greater threat.

"You will do no such thing." The voice came from the chambers entrance. All present turned to see who had spoken out against the plan.

"Elvin, you are late." Darlkeeth grunted.

"Oh, I am terribly sorry, but is would appear that my invitation was lost." the god of fear spat. "It is fortunate that I happened by though, as you are about to make a big mistake."

"And how do you come to that revelation?" Sugalas asked.

"You and your *former* wife are the deadliest of enemies, yet you never physically fight each other. Valkiya, your greatest foe, Kril'Korben, you have never fought his since he attained godhood, why is this?" Elvin asked bitterly.

"Because we are gods!" Valkiya answered.

"So?" retorted Elvin.

"It is not our place to fight each other." Kril'Korben explained, a smirk came across the undead gods lip as he thought of the absurdity of this divine law.

"Then it is not our place to destroy Legion."

"What would you know of such things Elvin?" Darlkeeth spat, "You are barley even one of us, with but a handful of worshippers."

Elvin laughed at the hell god's comment, "A handful of worshippers? Unlike you I do not need people to worship me openly. Most of your followers add to my power, with their revere of fear they too worship me."

"I should crush you for this insolence!" Darlkeeth yelled.

"Then why don't you?" Elvin asked defiantly.

"Because gods do not kill gods."

"And for that very reason you cannot attack Legion." the god of fear explained.

"There is nothing that states we cannot eradicate a demon." Valkiya added. She glanced at Kril'Korben as she spoke, remembering how she had once killed him as a boastful mortal, only for him to somehow attain godhood through death.

"Legion is no demon." Elvin snapped, "He is a god."

"How dare you compare that beast to us?" Sugalas yelled.

"What is it that makes us gods?"

"We are immortal beings, worshipped by mortals." Balil, the beautiful young looking goddess of fated life began before her visage transformed into the old haggard form of Morlil the goddess of fated death, "We use our infinite knowledge to guide our followers, and grant a portion of our divine power to our most loyal champions so they might serve us better." the twin goddess finished.

"Then by your own logic, Legion too is a god." Elvin said, "He is clearly an immortal being that is worshipped by his followers. He uses his knowledge to guide his followers, and unless I am mistaken, his most loyal general *Markus* still has the use of divine magic, which I doubt he still receives from you, Sugalas."

The sun god grunted, "Do not speak of that man! He is a traitorous fool."

"I would not say that," Darlkeeth laughed, "If you had not left him to suffer in the abyss, Jovan would never have been tempted by Legion, and you would not have lost one of your greatest warriors to the beast."

"Jovan is not the concern of this gathering!" Sugalas snapped. "We will kill Legion, and then his followers will fall." he said masterfully.

"Why are you so desperate to fight with Legion?" Elvin asked.

"The beast wants to murder my followers," Gorbalin, the abyssal beast said, in a rare moment of clarity "I wish to save them."

"You never cared for your followers safety before, as I understand you have a habit of slaughtering them. No, you want to fight because you are afraid."

"How dare you speak to me this way?" Gorbalin yelled as he smashed his clawed fist into the nearest table, "You dare to challenge my strength?"

"Calm yourself Gorbalin. I do not challenge your strength." Elvin said calmly, "I only speak the truth, you are afraid, as are we all. We fear that Legion will succeed, we fear that along with the mortal world we too shall be blinked out of existence."

"And that is why we must fight. We must kill the beast before he can attain his goal." Valkiya explained.

"No. Elvin is right, we cannot fight with Legion." Balil began, again looking like a young woman "He is a god whether we like it or not. We must find another way."

"Then what must we do?" Sslishka asked.

"We must work together; we need to convince our followers to work together against this threat."

"The elves are ready to fight," said Greenuff.

"My followers will do as I tell them." Darlkeeth sneered.

"My men will fight will also fight. One of my warriors is already on his way to enlist the aid of the orcs and goblinoids of the Four King mountains." Sugalas added.

"I will tell my shamans to follow this warrior, but they will only follow the strong." Orshanus, the god of raiders growled.

"Then it is decided, we will all go to our followers and guide them down the path to face Legion and his army." Elvin finished.

"And what of you? Who exactly are you going to guide in this matter?" Darlkeeth asked bitterly.

"One of my greatest warriors is already playing an important part in this conflict." Elvin explained, "And I foresee that he will play an important part in tipping the scales of Legion's war."

*   *   *

The music could be heard from all around the small hill, the sweet but mournful tune carrying lightly on the breeze. The small girl crept up the hill and crouched behind a small bush. She could see the musician sitting cross legged on a tree stump in the clearing, he was playing his tune on a small tin whistle. She could see his pack by the side of the tree stump, and there was a fire in front of him with a cooking pot next to it.

"There is no need to hide, I will not harm you." Laucian looked around to where the girl was hiding. She stuck her head around the side of the bush and smiled at the man. "Are you not a little young to be wondering the wilds alone?" Laucian asked as he turned back to the fire.

The girl walked past Laucian and sat on the ground directly across the fire from him. "We are very close to the city, I'm safe here." she said cheerfully.

"No matter how close you are to the city, outside of its walls can still be dangerous." Laucian replied coldly.

"So, if I was still in the city, I would be perfectly safe?" she asked coyly.

"The safest place for you would be at your parent's side. Do they know you are out here at this hour?" The girl laughed quietly at Laucian's comment. Laucian looked closely at the girl, for some reason she seemed very familiar to him. She had began to look longingly at the pot by the fire which still contained a little stew left over from Laucian's meal. "Are you hungry?" Laucian asked.

"A little, I haven't eaten yet today."

"Help yourself; I have already eaten my fill." Laucian indicated towards the food as he spoke.

"Really?" the girls eyes lit up as Laucian nodded. "Thank you."

Laucian smiled as he suddenly realised why this girl seemed so familiar to him, he also realised that she was so much more than she appeared. "I do believe we have met before."

The girl looked up from her food, "What do you mean?"

"Years ago, just before I left the monastery. You came to me that day, and gave me this." He indicated the dragon and glaive tattoo on his shoulder, the mark of Elvin's chosen.

The girl smiled, putting her bowl of stew down, "I'm surprised that you remember."

"It is not every day you are visited by a deity in the guise of a small girl, who then leaves their mark tattooed on your shoulder with but a touch. It's an event that tends to be difficult to forget."

"Oh you would be surprised. You are in fact the first of my chosen to ever remember that meeting." the girl replied with a grin. "I always knew you would be the greatest of my chosen, it is because you have always had a far greater understanding than those who came before."

"An understanding of what exactly?" Laucian asked, he found the whole situation amusing, the god of fear masquerading as an innocent young girl.

"You have an understanding of fear. All of my chosen before you have used fear, they have spread the belief of fear, but they have never truly understood the essence of fear. Fear is not about scaring people, the true essence of fear is choice."

"Those we make when we face our fears." Laucian finished.

"Exactly. You believe in fear. You use fear, much like those before you, but you also understand it. That is a rare gift, and that is why I made you one of my chosen. It is also why when you face your greatest fears and your greatest enemies you will have all my power to call upon."

"And am I to face one of these soon?" Laucian asked, now becoming very curious as to why he was being graced with a divine visit.

"The future is unclear. Certain events will soon take place that no-one can truly see." Elvin answered.

"Then to what do I owe the pleasure of your presence?"

"Guidance."

"Guidance? And why do I warrant the guidance of a god?"

Elvin smiled, "You are planning to retrieve the fire stone from Pileroo are you not?"

"I am."

"Well you are not exactly trained in the art of theft."

"Very true. So what is it you suggest?"

"I am aware that if you cannot work with your trusted friends then you prefer to work alone. On this occasion however I suggest that you seek help."

"Help from who exactly?"

"If you are trying to steal something, then it should be clear that you should seek the help of a thief."

"Ivellious." Laucian smiled as he remembered past dealings with the half-elven *rouge*, and his half-orc companion.

"Well I'm not saying who you should enlist. Only that it would be wise to use the expertise of others in this venture."

*   *   *

"A Warrior is coming." This orc looked rather peculiar; he was shorter than most, but tried to make up for this by spiking up the hair on top of his head. He was the high shaman of his tribe, which was probably the only reason he had survived as long as he had, that and the fact that the great Orshanus favoured him. His body was covered in brightly coloured cloths and paint, and he had a great many feathers stuck in his hair, and protruding from leather bands on his arms and legs.

"And what do I care about some travelling warrior, Eldrak? I have many warriors outside this very cave." Grakenster asked. Grakenster was a hobgoblin, a very large hobgoblin. He sat on a roughly carved stone throne in the cave which served as his audience chamber. Grakenster was the leader of what was regarded to be the largest army in the Four Kings mountains, unlike most of the tribes in the area Grakenter's army consisted of many different races; Grakenster had the loyalty of a large number of orcs, goblins, ogres, and many of his own hobgoblin kin.

"Orshanus say we meet warrior, he say we follow him into great battle." the extravagant shaman explained.

"Why should I follow this warrior? He is one, I have grand army." asked the hobgoblin with a wide grin.

"Orshanus say he a demon knight, follower of Sugalas but with demon blood. Orshanus say all tribes to follow knight out of mountains and destroy a legion."

"Great Orshanus wants us to help a follower of cursed sun god?"

" Orshanus say all gods unite to face common enemy. He say fight side to side with elves and men, he say enemy have army the same, he say we not able to fight it alone." Eldrak explained, getting more excited as he spoke.

Grakenster fell silent for a moment as he thought about what this shaman was saying. Fighting alongside men an elves; it seemed like madness, but he also knew Eldrak to be I high favour with his god.

Grakenster stood from his rock throne and walked out of his cave. He now stood on a ledge overlooking the camp where the majority of his army resided. "Tell me Eldrak, what is it exactly that Orshanus wants us to do?"

The brightly painted shaman ran to his masters side, "He say you to send someone to meet with warrior, to see if he strong. If he strong you follow him to great battle."

The large hobgoblin smiled, "Call for Nantic and Ardes. I will meet this warrior myself. I will judge his strength."

The shaman squealed with glee, "We have few days. Orshanus say we meet warrior at Randars pass. Orshanus say all tribes send people."

*   *   *

"My spy says Magon has sent a tainted paladin to gain the support of the creatures living in the Four Kings mountains." Deventis explained.

"This would be Jamaan?" asked Markus with a smile.

"Yes my lord, a paladin of Sugalas.

Markus laughed, "This is a surprising turn of events. I know someone who would be very pleased to learn the whereabouts of Jamaan."

"And who is that my lord?"

"The demon that tainted his blood."

"You know which demon it was?"

"I want you to summon the demon prince named Kran'slor. He currently resides deep within the abyss, a place I expect he will be more than happy to leave." Markus' smile broadened as he mused over his plan. "Tell the beast that I will give him the location of the man who humiliated him by not succumbing to the tainting ritual, on the condition that he confronts him at a time of my choosing."

"Yes my lord. Though may I ask, why a time of your choosing?"

"Because I want Jamaan to fall from grace at the time most profitable to our cause. I want Jamaan and Kran'slor to meet as he negotiates with the creatures of the Four Kings, where the presence of such a beast will send those animals scurrying back to their holes."

"Brilliant my lord. A scheme worthy of my kin." Usually Markus would not like to have been compared to viperian, but in this instance it was a fitting compliment, the viperian followers of Sslishka were well known for their devious but well thought out schemes.

"Leave me." Markus ordered. "I wish to savour this moment, for in a matter of days Sugalas will loose another of his greatest champions, either to darkness or to death."

Deventis bowed low before leaving the presence of his general. He headed off to Baknul's residence, he would need the necromancer's help in summoning such a powerful demon without it tearing him apart as soon as it entered the material plane.

*   *   *

Gregor showed the four travellers into where Magon was sitting with Solaris. Magon had been expecting this group for a while now, he knew they would be seeking the elemental stone of air which he had at the top of his tower.

"My lord, some visitors." Gregor announced.

"Thank you Gregor. Please do sit down." Magon indicated to the chairs across from him. The old man perched his glasses on his nose so he could get a better look at his visitors as they sat down.

"I am Aramil, son of Dalamar, paladin of Valkiya. This is Larenor, ranger of the forest. Kimanay, cleric of Sugalas, and the monk Delensa." One of the visitors explained before sitting down.

"Yes, I am well aware of who you all are. I also know that you are here for the elemental stone of air." Magon replied as he struggled to get his glasses to stay on his nose.

"So you will give us the stone?" Kimanay asked hopefully.

"Actually, no. You are welcome to take the stone, but I cannot just give it to you."

"What exactly do you mean by that?" Delensa asked sceptically.

"Well to get the stone you must first pass some tests. You must be able to get through five rooms in my tower. If you do this then the stone is yours."

"What is this? Some kind of game?" Larenor asked sarcastically.

"It is nothing personal you understand, but I must be sure that you are the right people to give the stone to." Magon finally decided that the glasses were not going to stay on and set them down on the arm of his chair. "But I have arranged it so that by the time you have retrieved the air stone some of my colleges should have acquired both the earth and fire stones for you. I believe you already have the stone of water."

"How is that possible?" Aramil asked.

"Some other guests at my tower have agreed to help. Fruril is currently bargaining with denizens of the elemental earth plain to gain the earth stone, amongst some other things. He should have returned by the time you have finished upstairs. The fire stone is currently in Cemulion city, where another of my friends is acquiring it. You are to meet him at the Jolly Roger tavern, where you will also be able to get passage to Krondmare. You are aware of the sceptre that you'll need to collect from there?"

"Yes, we know of the sceptre, Krondmare's king has it." Aramil answered.

"How are we to know this friend of yours in Cemulion?" asked Larenor.

"I believe that some of you have met him before." Magon smiled, "His name is Laucian Galanodel." The name caught the attention of both Aramil and Delensa.

"You are friends with that fugitive?" asked Aramil, "You realise that the authorities of my city are searching for him because of the heinous crimes he has committed."

"He has committed no crimes, the accusations are all lies." Delensa snapped, "I for one will be glad to see him again."

"Yes, well that is not your current problem. If you would follow me I will show you the way to the upper rooms." Magon rose from his seat to show his guests to the top floor of his tower, to the rooms that would lead to the elemental stone of air.

"Tell me sir knight, where did you get that bow?" Solaris asked as the visitors stood to follow Magon.

Aramil turned to face Solaris, and glanced at the silver bow strapped across his back, "We took it from some orcs just outside of Cemulion."

"Along with that sword I expect." Solaris now indicated the blade at Larenor's side. "*Sugalas' Flair* and *Fear Bringer*, you carry mighty weapons."

"The weapons make the man." Larenor replied.

Solaris smiled, "We shall see." he said. He stood to follow the group as Magon led them to face their five tests. Solaris believed that this could be very interesting.

*   *   *

It seemed like only yesterday that Roscoe was spending his evenings in the Cattle Shed. Performing for the crowd and chatting with the travellers passed through. Today though Roscoe was one of the travellers, and people were coming to ask him Questions.

"So where are you heading to next?" Jannays asked after Roscoe had given a rather flamboyant account of what had happened since they had last spoken.

"We will all be going our separate ways in the morning." Davkul explained before Roscoe could put his *artistic* spin on what was a simple plan.

Adokas chuckled to himself, knowing that Davkul did not like the way Roscoe told stories. He also knew that the gruff dwarf was looking forward to travelling alone with Roscoe just about as much as the halfling was looking forward to being alone with Davkul.

"Adokas and myself will be travelling back to Transeen." Thoril told the young barmaid.

"Roscoe and Davkul will be heading out across the plains." Adokas added, smiling as he watched the pair fidget uncomfortably.

"And I shall be taking the mountain road." Jamaan said in his deep rough voice.

"You want to be careful on that road my friend, especially alone. There be many an unfriendly creature in them mountains." Zanian warned, "I've seen entire parties of well armed travellers go into them mountains never to return. Its not just orcs out there if you catch my meaning."

"I do catch your meaning, and it is a fact I am counting on." the paladin replied.

"You want there to be lots of monsters?" asked Jannays. The surprise was not unexpected, as no-one had fully explained why they were travelling back this way.

"Perhaps we should explain." Thoril began, "We are trying to raise an army, Adokas and I will be seeking the aid of the etharii in Transeen. Roscoe and Davkul are going to speak with the nomadic tribes of the plains, and Jamaan is going to recruit those who live in the mountains."

"But there are only beasts in them mountains," said Zanian. "Only orcs, goblins and worse."

"Aye, and they'll make a mighty army." Davkul finished.

Chapter 12
Bitter Tests

"Ten gold coins," the bearded man said calmly, "Ten gold coins says you orc's winning streak ends this day."

Ivellious smiled, "I wouldn't let him hear you call him an orc."

"Ten gold coins," the man said again, "Its a good bet."

"I'll take that bet." Both the man and Ivellious turned to see who was accepting the wager. "I've seen that barbarian defeat much greater foes than that man." Laucian indicated Branack's opponent as he approached the side of the pit.

"Laucian, it's been a long time." Ivellious said, loosing a little of his usually confidant composure.

"That it has." Laucian replied as he placed a pouch of coins on the table in front of the bearded man. "Ten gold says that Branack's undefeated streak continues."

"You've got yourself a bet sir." the man smiled broadly, "But I'll not have you underestimate my boy, there be more to him than meets the eye."

"Our next match up will be the undefeated champion, Branack the hammer hand!" The crowd cheered loudly as the announcer waved his arms wildly towards Branack, who was standing calmly at one side of the pit. "And our challenger, all the way from Keglee, *Lightning Strike* Larry!" The crowd cheered again, although it was noticeably less than the cheer Branack had received.

The announcer ran to the side of the pit and quickly climbed the rope ladder which hung there. Lightning strike Larry was much shorter than Branack, and much slimmer. The fight looked as though it would be a very one-sided match. The challenger did have one advantage though, his speed.

Branack and Larry slowly paced around the pit eyeing each other, both trying to think of the best way to attack their opponent. "All bets are locked!" the announcer called, "FIGHT!"

Before the announcer had even finished the word Branack and Larry were running at each other, Branack swung his huge fist at his opponent but all he hit was air. Larry dodged down and to the side, swinging round he kicked Branack hard to the back of the knee. The half-orc's leg gave way and he stumbled forward as Larry skipped away across the pit. The crowd cheered, always loving a good fight.

Branack regained his footing and turned back to face Larry, who just stood there smiling. Branack let out a low growl as he stalked across the pit.

"Come on you filthy orc." taunted Larry.

"I am not an orc." Branack replied.

Larry charged forward, again he ducked under Branack's attack. Larry brought his knee hard into Branack's back, the half-orc stumbled forward again, this time however Larry pressed his attack. He landed hit after hit, punching and kicking his larger opponent, much to the delight of the cheering crowd. Eventually the smaller man again skipped off across the pit, grinning broadly he thought that Branack would now be badly injured.

Branack turned and smiled at Larry, "That best you got? Little man."

"Not even close, orc." Larry answered, his grin fading.

"I am not an orc!" Branack growled as he walked towards Larry, whose grin had now returned. The small man crouched down low, waiting for Branack to walk into range before launching himself forward.

"Lightning strike!" Larry yelled as he swung his fist forward, a small rune began to glow on the back of Larry's hand and sparks of lightning began to crackle around his arm. There was an explosion of energy as his fist connected with Branack's jaw. The half-orc was knocked clean off his feet, flying backwards to the ground. The crowd fell silent as they looked on in shock.

"And that is how you fell an orc!" Larry called as he danced around the ring. A murmur went through the crowd as they watched Branack climb back to his feet.

"I AM NOT AN ORC!!" Branack bellowed, his voice booming so loudly that almost the entire crowd backed away from the edge of the pit. Larry, stunned that anyone could withstand his lightning strike, spun around just in time to see the raging barbarian reaching out towards him. Larry had no chance to move before the half-orc had a large hand gripped around his throat. Branack easily lifted the smaller man from the ground, he roared loudly as he stared into Larry's fear filled eyes. Branack threw the man across the pit, where Larry hit the wall head first and fell limp to the floor.

"Branack wins!" the announcer yelled, "And remains our undefeated champion of the pit!" The crowds cheers were thunderous.

The bearded man scowled as he paid up his ten gold to Laucian, Ivellious scowled as he wished that he had accepted the bet before Laucian had. The man walked away grumbling to himself as Laucian turned to face Ivellious.

"Shall we find a table?" Laucian asked as he pocketed his winnings.

"Sure, to what do I owe the pleasure?"

"I have a busyness proposition for you." said Laucian, "Let us discuss it over a drink, our bearded friend is paying."

It wasn't long before the two men were joined by Branack, who they both congratulated heartily. Laucian then explained his proposition to Ivellious and Branack, who both listened intently.

"So you want us to help you steal a ruby?" asked Ivellious with a grin, "From Pileroo's guild house?"

"That's about it." Laucian answered. Both Ivellious and Branack laughed.

"You are quite mad." Ivellious laughed.

"Guild house well guarded." grunted Branack.

"Surly no theft is too difficult for the great Ivellious half-elven, master rouge?" Laucian asked coyly, he was trying to play off of Ivellious' pride.

"I did not say it couldn't be done, just that you're mad for thinking it."

"Just imagine the prestige. You would be the thief who out did the guild master, and along with that you will be very well paid."

The mention of money always made Ivellious feel better about a job, "Exactly how well paid?" he asked, trying to sound very nonchalant as he spoke. Laucian produced a small pouch from his cloak and placed it in front of Ivellious.

"That upon agreeing to the job, and the same again when it is complete." Ivellious opened the pouch and peered inside, his eyes widening as he did.

"How much?" Branack asked bluntly.

"Enough." Ivellious answered, "So where shall we meet you when the job is done?"

"You don't need to worry about that. I shall be going with you."

"We work better alone."

"I have no intention of leaving you alone with that stone. I remember the last time I worked with you." Laucian's lips curled into a wry smile as Ivellious laughed nervously. He too remembered the last time they had worked together. After that experience he had vowed never to double cross a psychic warrior ever again.

"So when do you wish this to be done?" Ivellious needed to know how much time they would have to prepare.

"Tomorrow night."

"That does not give us much time to plan."

"I'm sure that all the planning in the world would not make much of a difference in this case." Ivellious and Branack turned to each other and quietly discussed the proposition.

"We'll take the job." Ivellious said as he snatched up the pouch from the table.

"I have a room at the Jolly Roger, if you have any further questions you can contact me there, if not I shall meet you here at nightfall tomorrow." With that Laucian finished his drink, he nodded to the others as he stood up and then headed for the door, leaving Ivellious and Branack to their thoughts.

*   *   *

"So what are we expecting to find in these rooms?" Kimanay asked, a little sceptical at the whole prospect of having to pass tests when there was so little time.

"I could tell you exactly what you will face in each of the rooms, but where is the fun in that?" Magon began, "And what would be the point? If I tell you want you will face then you will how to overcome it. All I will tell you is that the danger is very real, and if you stray from your path then you may never find your way back."

Aramil and Larenor both peered through the first door. The room beyond seemed normal enough, four walls a floor and a ceiling and another door at the far side, so far these tests did not appear to be too difficult.

The four companions walked slowly into the room, they were taking their time as they thought there surly must be something to make this room a challenge. As they reached the centre of the room the door they had entered through slammed closed.

"This room is easy, all you have to do is reach the other side." Magon's voice sounded to be coming from all around them, "Just try to get there alive." As soon as Magon had finished speaking several panels in the walls slid open, and six minotaur's walked into the room.

All four companions readied their weapons. Aramil stringed an arrow into the Sugalas' Flair and Larenor took aim with his own trusty bow. Delensa stood with her quarterstaff in hand, and Kimanay raised her heavy mace.

"You come to our home," grunted one of the minotaurs, "Now you die." The minotaurs began to slowly move towards the four companions, although two did not get far. Aramil and Larenor loosed their arrows. Aramil's magical bow made his arrows fly strong and true, his first hitting its target in the eye staggering the beast, his second and third penetrating deep into the beasts heart. Larenor's target did not fair much better, even without the help of a magical bow he was by far the better archer. His first arrow hit a minotaur in the throat, the beast clutched at the wound screaming in pain as it fell backward, dying before it even hit the floor. Larenor was the closest of the group to the minotaurs and so only managed one more shot before he had to drop his bow and draw his sword, Fear Bringer. His aim has still been true, hitting the foul beast directly in the chest.

The fight was close quarters now, so Aramil too drew his sword. Delensa charged forward, knowing that her agile fighting style would only be hindered by staying close to the others. She quickly dodged to the side as she swung her staff into the back of a minotaur's knee making it stumble, the elven monk spun her staff round and struck her opponent in the back of its head.

Kimanay stood and waited as one of the minotaurs came towards her, the beast raised its huge fist and slammed it hard into the young cleric's shield forcing her backwards. The minotaur roared, thinking its attack would knock her clean off her feet. This was not to be the case though, and Kimanay launched herself forward, hitting her enemy in the chest with her mace.

Aramil sidestepped a minotaur that charged him. The paladin had spent many years training in his temple, and the sword and shield was where his greatest strength lay. He sliced along the beasts side, the minotaur roared in pain as it swung its muscled arm to the side. Aramil easily deflected the attack with his shield as he struck again with his sword, this time cutting deep into the beasts back. The minotaur fell to its knees leaving it wide open for Aramil to thrust his sword through its head.

Larenor was not quite as adept with his sword as he was with a bow but that did not mean he wasn't skilled, and Fear Bringer gave him a distinct advantage. With his elven agility the ranger gracefully leaped over a the minotaur he had hit with his arrow, his sword slicing across the beasts shoulders before the elf had even landed. As the blade of Larenor's magical sword cut through the minotaur's flesh a sense of dread overwhelmed the creature causing it to run off to a corner of the room where it cowered in fear, making it an easy target for Larenor to finish off.

Kimanay was easily handling her foe, blocking its slow attacks with her shield, countering with devastating force from her mace. The beast was quickly getting annoyed by the clerics relentless attack, so it backed off out of range of her mace. The beast lowered its head and charged straight it the cleric, horns first. Kimanay smiled as she jumped to the side, dropping her shield she gripped her mace in both hands and swung it straight at the charging monster's head, crushing its skull.

Delensa was not fairing quite as well as the others, she was easily out fighting the minotaur, however her staff was simply not causing enough damage. Given time Delensa could have slowly worn the minotaur down, evading its attacks with ease and striking it with her staff, butt with her friends present she would not need to spend that much time on this fight. After Kimanay had finished her opponent she turned her attention to the one attacking Delensa, hitting the beast hard between its shoulder blades. The minotaur fell to its knees giving Delensa the opening she needed. The monk dropped her staff and struck the minotaur on each side of its throat with her bare hands, striking the exact pressure points to cause the beast to clutch at its throat as it gasped for air and finally suffocated.

"Is that the best you have to offer wizard?" Larenor called as he sheathed his weapon. The others doing likewise.

"Now now my young ranger," Larenor laughed at Magon's comment, how could a mere human call him young? "You may have passed the first test, but there are four more rooms for you to explore." The door to the next room swung open as Magon's disembodied voice faded and the four companions made their way towards the second challenge.

The second room turned out not to be a room at all, as the four companions walked the door they couldn't see any walls or ceiling, instead they seemed to be standing in the middle of a desert. The door they had just passed through was still there, and they could see the previous room through it but to each side the wall was missing. Aramil reached out to touch where the wall should have been thinking it was some kind of illusion, but his had passed straight through, it was no illusion the wall simply wasn't there.

The group took a look around to assess their situation. About five hundred yards ahead of them was another door exactly the same as the one they had just passed through, presumably this was the exit to the *room*. The sun was high in the sky, and beating down hard. The group started towards the door, all four of them were used to far cooler climates than those found in the desert, and their equipment was going to make traversing the sand dunes a difficult task indeed.

They were about half way to the door, it was taking much longer than they had thought to reach their exit and the heat was severely affecting each of them. It was at this point that they noticed something catching the sunlight off to their left. When they looked hard at where the reflection come from it was clear to see that it was a crystal at the top of a shrine.

"Who would build a shrine in a place like this?" Larenor asked, almost to himself.

"Someone with a great deal of faith." was the simple answer Aramil gave.

"It is a shrine to Sugalas." Kimanay announced.

"How can you tell from this distance?" Larenor asked as he squinted to see it better.

"I am one of Sugalas' clerics, I would recognise a shrine to my god anywhere."

"And who else but the sun god would have a shrine in a desert?" Larenor added with a slight laugh. Kimanay scowled at the elf as she began to walk off towards the shrine, leaving the others standing in the sand.

"Where are you going?" Aramil called after her.

"I am going to pay tribute to my god."

"You're going to pray? We don't have time for this." Larenor said, now sounding more serious.

Kimanay turned to face the others, "There is always time to pray to my god. Someone spent timer and effort to build this shrine out in this harsh environment, it is only right that I pay tribute."

"You seem to be forgetting that this is not a real desert, we are in the tower of a mage." Delensa called after her friend, but Kimanay was not listening, she was again focused on reaching the shrine. "This is just one of Magon's crazy tests."

Kimanay ignored the monks words, she would not forsake this chance to show devotion to Sugalas. The others could do nothing but stand and watch her go.

"Now what?" Aramil asked, more than a little annoyed that Kimanay was going off mission. He understood all too well the devotion the cleric showed to her god; being a paladin himself he knew what it was like to serve a higher power, but for his order the mission always came first.

"If this is one of Magon's tests then that shrine may be a trap." Delensa suggested as she turned to the others.

"Perhaps we should go with her then, to make sure nothing happens." Aramil replied. At that moment Delensa's fears were confirmed when Kimanay screamed. The other three ran towards where the scream had come from.

As Kimanay came into view she was already up to her chest plate in quicksand. It was plain to see that the shrine was also sinking into the sand, it had indeed been a trap.

Delensa was the first to reach Kimanay, but had to quickly scramble backwards as she realised that the quicksand spread out a fair distance around her friend. The monk had to think fast, it would not be long before the cleric was completely submerged in the sand. Delensa stretched out her staff towards Kimanay who grabbed hold of the end. By this time both Aramil and Larenor had reached the scene, both took hold of the staff along with Delensa and all three of them began to pull Kimanay free of the sand. Suddenly there was a jolt, pulling the cleric back into the quicksand. Kimanay had now sunk up to her shoulders and the others were pulled forward,having to scramble backwards before they too became stuck.

"What was that?" Larenor called.

"Something has hold of my leg." Kimanay called back. The others again started to pull on the staff, but another jolt made Kimanay loose her grip making the others fall backwards. By now Kimanay was almost completely submerged, Delensa again reached out with her staff but the cleric could no longer reach it.

"Go!" Kimanay said, "I'm done here."

"We are not leaving you!" Delensa yelled. Kimanay tried to speak again but when she opened her mouth it just filled with sand, the cleric coughed as the rest of her head sank.

"No!" Delensa leaped forward trying to reach her friends sinking hand. Both Larenor and Aramil caught hold of her and dragged her back from the quicksand.

"There is nothing we can do for her now," Aramil told the monk.

"I'm not leaving her!"

"Delensa! She's gone, I'm sorry but she would want her to finish what we have started here." Larenor said, trying to calm the monk down. Delensa struggled for a few moments longer before reluctantly agreeing with the others. The three remaining companions tread carefully as the now made their way to the exit of this cursed desert.

The next room was actually a room, similar in layout to that of the first room, except this one had a pedestal in the middle with a bow resting on top. Delensa leaned against the wall and put her head in her hands trying to force back her tears. The elf had only met Aramil and Larenor a few weeks before but she had been travelling with Kimanay for a couple of years, in which time they had become close friends. Aramil tried to comfort the monk, telling her that Kimanay would want them to go on, but his efforts were not helping.

Larenor was taking a look at the new room they found themselves in, much like the first there was another door at the far side, only this one had a steel bars covering it. High above the door hung a target, it didn't take Larenor long to work out that the door could be unbarred by hitting the target based on the pulley system and chains connecting them.

The elven ranger took a closer look at the bow on the pedestal, unable to believe what he was seeing. "Doombringer."

"What?" Aramil asked, turning away from Delensa for a moment to see what Larenor was talking about.

"This bow, its Doombringer." Larenor explained, "It's my fathers bow. Both Aramil and Delensa, who had now composed herself, walked over to where Larenor was standing. The ranger reached out to pick up the bow.

"Wait!" Delensa warned, causing the ranger to stop and look round at her, "This could be a trap." The monk began to examine the pedestal closely, putting the events of the previous room to the back of her mind and focusing on the task at hand. She could find no mechanism on the pedestal, or any markings of any kind, suggesting that it was not trapped in any way.

"I'm thinking that we must shoot the target to open the door,"Larenor pointed out the pulleys and chains leading to the bars, the others nodded their agreement.

"Well you are the better archer," said Aramil. Larenor smiled as he picked up the bow from the pedestal and strung an arrow. He tested the strength of the string and sighted along the arrow. The bow was indeed Doombringer, the bow his father had made, the bow stolen by his fathers murderer.

"When we are done here remind me to ask that crazy wizard where he got this bow from." Larenor loosed the arrow, which soared with unnatural accuracy straight into the centre of the target. The target was shattered by the force of the arrow hitting it, and the pulley system began to work raising the bars that were blocking their exit.

"Good shot." congratulated Aramil, Larenor just smiled.

"You hide your shame well, elf." The three companions spun around to see where the voice had come from. To the side of the room a section of the wall had opened to reveal an ogre. This was not just any ogre however, Larenor recognised it instantly.

"You!" The ranger cried as he strung another arrow, but Doombringer began to crumble in his hands.

"Lets go, we can get out of this room without dealing with the beast." Delensa suggested.

"Yes, run, like the coward you are." The ogre taunted, "I smell your fear elf, just like the day your father died."

"I am not afraid of you, beast!" Larenor drew his magical sword and charged forward.

"Larenor! Wait!" Aramil called as he tried to catch hold of his companion, but he was too slow. The ogre laughed as Aramil and Delensa readied their weapons.

Larenor raised his sword as he ran forward swinging it at the ogre. To everyone's surprise the creature faded from view and the sword passed straight through where it had been, hitting nothing but air. Larenor tried to stop, but his momentum carried him through the secret door and into the alcove behind. His two companions ran forward as Larenor tried to scramble back into the room, but the secret door closed before anyone could reach it.

"Larenor!" Both Delensa and Aramil were trying to scrape at the wall in an attempt to re-open the door, but it was no use. They heard a loud scraping sound coming from behind the secret door followed by a blood curdling scream. Aramil and Delensa carried on trying to get the door open, neither of them wanting to accept that they had just lost another of their companions to one of Magon's tests.

The pair eventually returned to the pedestal and looked at the bow Larenor had used to shoot the target,which was now nothing more than a pile of dust. They decided that they had to continue on, neither speaking as they walked into the next room, each contemplating the fact that they had already witnessed one friend sink into quicksand, and who knew what horrors Larenor had faced behind that wall. They braced themselves for whatever Magon's next *test* would be.

The next room looked much like the first, only this one had two exit doors. In front of one door stood a slender female elf, dressed as though she was a member of a noble family. By the other door stood someone completely different, he was short with long pointed ears and nose, and his skin was a slimy green colour. He was a goblin who seemed to be wearing little more than rags.

"So where's the challenge in this room?" Aramil asked, almost to himself.

"This room is quite simple my lord," began the elf, "You must simply choose the correct door." Aramil and Delensa slowly walked further into the room.

"And how do we choose which door to pass through?" Delensa asked bitterly.

"That is easy my friend," the elf replied, "My door is the correct path."

"No! You not listen to stinkin' elf. She lie. She try to trick you." said the goblin desperately, "My door true way, my door lead forward."

"So we have to choose a door based on you words?" Delensa asked.

"Precisely." replied the elf.

"Yes, yes." the goblin chirped.

"Well this has got to be the easiest test ever." Aramil began to walk towards the elf's door.

"No! Wait! Stop! Filthy elf door not way forward!" Called the goblin.

"Aramil, wait." said Delensa.

Aramil turned to face the monk, "What is it?"

"This is one of Magon's tests, I don't believe it would be this simple."

"That right! That right! Nasty elf try to trick you!" the goblin became more agitated as he spoke, "Great Orshanus say I help you, mighty Orshanus say I show you right way."

"You would trust the word of a goblin over that of your own kin?" asked the elf.

"No I wouldn't." Aramil answered, the half-elven paladin turned to his companion, "Come on, this it the right way." Aramil walked boldly towards the elf's door followed somewhat reluctantly by Delensa. The elf smiled as Aramil walked passed her, he reached out to the handle and pulled hard, the heavy door slowly swung open.

Delensa looked closely at the elf as she walked passed, "What is that on your arm?"

"It is nothing," the elf turned away from Delensa, "Quickly now you must be on your way."

"Paint!" the goblin yelled, "It has paint on its arm!"

Aramil turned to see what was going on. Delensa grabbed the elf by the wrist and pulled her around; she pushed the sleeve from the elf's tunic up over her shoulder, revealing a tattoo.

"Aramil, this tattoo, is from the legion of Strakstaw, she's a mercenary." Aramil stood for a moment, he had fought these mercenaries before. They had tried to stop him and Larenor from retrieving the prophecies from the royal tombs, they had proved themselves his enemies in this campaign.

The elf snarled at Delensa. She suddenly span around twisting Delensa's arm and pushed her away. Now free from Delensa's grip the elf turned and kicked Aramil, the paladin stumbled backward through the open door, which slammed closed as soon as he had crossed the threshold. Delensa could hear banging from the other side of the door, but it slowly faded away.

The elf pulled a knife from her belt and walked towards Delensa, with a wicked grin on her face. She had barely taken her second step though when she fell to her knees, with a crude little knife stuck in her chest. Delensa spun around to see the goblin standing there watching as the elf fell to the floor.

"I tried to tell him. I said smelly elf lie, but he not listen, now he gone." The goblin walked up to Delensa. "You only one left now, you must go get stone now. All rest on your shoulders." Delensa looked down at the goblin, this smelly little creature had saved her life, and now it expected her to continue on alone. "Come come," the goblin grabbed her by the hand and led her to the door, "You must go now."

"Come with me." Delensa said quietly.

"No no, I not come, not my path. You go, you face final test."

"I cannot do this alone."

"You must, you not go you not get stone. You not go all is lost."

"My friends are gone, all of them. If they could not make it this far, then how can I face the final room alone?" Delensa fell to her knees, resting her head on the door her eyes filling with tears.

"You have lasted, you can go on, you must not stop so close to end."

"And what if I do go on? I cannot do this alone. Even if I succeed, how can I lead the elemental army when I cannot even protect my friends?" Delensa waited for the goblins answer, but he did not speak. There was a gurgling sound behind her, Delensa did not have to look around to know what had happened. She closed her eyes, tears rolling down her face as she felt the cold steel press against her throat.

"You couldn't even protect the pathetic little goblin." Delensa could feel the elf's breath against her cheek before everything went quiet.

Chapter 13
To Steal From Thieves

"Who's that?" Asked the rather large man standing guard outside of the guild house, "I've not seen him before."

"Him? He's my cousin, on my mother's side." Ivellious answered with a smile.

"I thought you didn't have any family." said the guard suspiciously.

"No family? That's madness, how could I have no family? Do you think I just appeared one day? At first there was nothing, and then all of a sudden there I stood." Ivellious started talking much faster than usual, "Of course I have a family, and he's my father's uncle's sister's brother's nephew's grandfather's mother."

The big man stood there for a moment, trying to make sense of what Ivellious was telling him, until suddenly he smiled a wide toothless grin, "Making him your cousin." The guard opened the door allowing Ivellious, Branack and Laucian to enter Pileroo's guild house.

"Not the most intelligent of men." Laucian said as they walked down a long corridor.

"He wasn't hired for his brain; all he needs to do is stand by the door and look menacing." Ivellious explained.

"Keeps away beggars." Branack added.

The trio eventually entered a large room filled with the sounds of music and laughter. There was a distinct smell of stale beer and smoke from all manner of dried leaves, some of which had peculiar effects on the minds of those inhaling them.

They made their way through the hustle and bustle of the crowd. It was mainly made up of drunks, men and women who had come to Cemulion seeking their fortune only to find that someone else had already taken it. Many of these people had been honourable once, but now they were thieves, brigands and con-artists, if you wanted some hired muscle for an unsavoury task then this was the place to look. This was also the place to look if you needed someone for a more delicate task, many a master thief could be found within these walls, as well as a handful of the most feared assassins.

The trio were walking passed one drunk as he stumbled up to up to a pretty young woman, "Come on baby, wanna party?" he slurred.

"Get lost." She replied. She was a pretty young woman with long brown hair, wearing a simple tan tunic and trousers. It was clear to see that she had no interest in partying with the drunk, at least not in the same way the drunk wanted.

The drunk turned to his friends, who both signalled for him to try again. The drunk turned back to the woman, brushing his hair back with one hand he approached her again, "Look love I've got good money, and I want a good time."

"Then why don't you find someone whose interested?" she said coldly, indicating the scantly dressed boys and girls working the room, offering *entertainment*.

"Because I want you."the drunk replied more forcefully.

"This is your last chance to walk away." the woman replied.

"I'm not gonna walk away until I've had some fun."

The woman smiled wickedly; "So you want to have some fun?" she stood from her chair and looked seductively at the drunk. The man smiled as he stepped closer to her, placing one hand on her waist as he reached the other around behind her.

"This is more like it." said the drunk as he leaned in to kiss her, though his drunken lunge forward did not last long. He slowly staggered backwards, his hands moving towards his groin where a knife was now embedded. The drunk fell to the floor by his friends feet, both of whom now drew their swords.

"You're dead now bitch!" One of them yelled as both advanced on her. The woman backed away slowly, knowing that she was in trouble. By now those near by were watching the scene unfold, although non would interfere, or so the two drunks thought.

Before they could get too close to the woman Laucian made his move. With both of his knives in hand he stepped in front of the two men, blocking their path to the woman.

"Put your swords down, and walk away." Laucian said in a cold emotionless tone. This drew even more attention to the situation; up until now this had been nothing more than an everyday occurrence for the guild house, but it was rare would step forward here to defend someone else. The two drunks looked at each other, not sure what to do.

"It's two against one, so why don't you back off?" one of the men said.

"That's very true," Laucian replied with a grin, "Maybe you should get some of your little friends to help you, make this a fair fight." Those stood near by all backed away, showing that non of them had any intention of getting involved. They had all heard people talking tough, but this stranger had a confidence in his voice that told them he was not bluffing.

One of the men lunged forward to attack Laucian. If he had walked away then he would not have been able to show his face in the guild again and been labelled a coward, the only way out he saw was to kill the man threatening him. His lunge was slow and sloppy, Laucian easily knocked the attack aside before he slashed the man with a flurry of attacks that ended with him embedding a dagger in the man's throat.

The second drunk moved to attack but before he could even raise his sword one of Laucian's knives was pressing against his throat.

"Drop the blade or I drop you." Laucian warned. The drunk thought for a moment, glancing at his friend who now lay dead on the floor. Deciding that his life was more important than his acceptance in the guild he dropped his sword and backed away slowly.

Laucian put his knives away and turned back to Ivellious and Branack. Most of the people in the room had already turned back to their drinks, but a few people were still paying an interest in Laucian. More than a few of assassins were now watching Laucian, they had recognised the calm confidence he had in his voice, it was the same confidence they had, confidence in the knowledge that you could easily defeat your opponent. They were curious as to who this new warrior was, and why he was willing to endanger himself by stepping up to help the woman.

The woman was also paying a great deal of attention to her *saviour*. Although she would have never admitted it, she would have been in a great deal of trouble against the two drunks, this man had possibly saved her life. He was also far better to look at than the drunks had been.

"I thank you for your assistance. She said as she got a closer look at Laucian.

Laucian glanced around at the woman, "It was nothing." he replied before turning back to Ivellious, "We should be getting on."

"My name is Stacy." said the woman as she put her arm around Laucian's shoulder.

"How nice for you," Laucian replied as he shrugged her arm away.

"Come now, don't be rude to the lady," Ivellious stepped closer, and tried to kiss Stacy on the hand, "My name is Ivellious." he said as Stacy pulled her hand away.

"How nice for you." Stacy said, mimicking the response Laucian had given her.

"Come, not have time." Branack grunted as he pulled Ivellious back by the shoulder.

"That was a most impressive display." Ivellious spun around to see Pileroo stood before him, looking at Laucian. The guild master motioned for Stacy to leave, and she did so immediately.

"Pileroo, it is good to see you again my friend." Ivellious bowed his head as he spoke.

"I have not seen you here before," Pileroo began as he walked around Laucian, looking at him carefully. "I do not like new faces in my home."

"He is my cousin, just passing through." Ivellious explained, "I thought I'd show him the finer side of our fair city."

"And I thought you were an orphan." Pileroo now turned to face Ivellious.

"I am, but that doesn't mean I don't have other relations." Ivellious answered with a smile, "Though I find that the orphan card isn't quite as effective if you tell people that you have other relatives."

"Of course," said Pileroo turning back to Laucian, "So what brings you to my city?"

"Busyness." Laucian answered, "And I wasn't aware that this was your city, I was under the impression that there was a king here."

Pileroo smiled, "Well things *may* be about to change, and *if* they do I'll be needing skilled men like you."

"I'm only passing through." Laucian replied coldly.

"Talk some sense into your cousin." Pileroo looked round at the half-elf again, "It could be very profitable working with me, for both of you." With that said Pileroo turned and walked away.

"Well done." Ivellious whispered, "In your attempt to keep a low profile you have managed to kill a man, be rude to a beautiful woman, and receive a job offer from Pileroo himself."

"We should probably get down to busyness then." Laucian suggested. Branack led the others to a quiet corner of the room. "So where would he keep the stone?"

"If it's as valuable as you suggest, it'll be behind the most secure door in here." Ivellious replied.

"And where might that be?"

"Well the story goes that Pileroo was quite the accomplished thief in his day, some say he was the best. That is up until he found a door he could not open, and so he retired." Ivellious explained.

"Your point being?"

"Well because he couldn't open the door he decided that it would be the best door to keep his most prized possessions behind, so he took it."

"Took what?"

"The door, he stole the whole door. Over time he learned its secrets, and now uses it to protect his greatest treasure."

"So where is it then?" Laucian was becoming impatient; he had no wish to stay in this place any longer than was necessary.

"I don't know." Ivellious answered bluntly.

"I thought you knew this place."

"I do but I'm not privy to Pileroo's secrets. I may be in his good graces, but that doesn't mean that he completely trusts me."

Branack laughed, "You are thief."

Laucian leaned back thinking. How were they supposed to find Pileroo's most prized possession?

"Maybe I could be of assistance." The voice was as cold as ice and as sharp as steel, but as far as the trio could see it had come from nowhere. "I know where Pileroo keeps a precious rock, and the door is well protected."

"Who you? Show self!" Branack declared. The half-orc did not like talking to people he could not see.

"I will lead you to the door, but first you must help me."

"Who are you?" Laucian asked, he too was not impressed by anyone unwilling to reveal themselves.

"The southern door, it leads to a staircase. I shall meet you at the bottom, and please be quick."

The trio thought for a moment, "That door does not lead to the stone, I can tell you that much." Ivellious said.

"How can you be sure?" Laucian asked.

"That way to cells." Branack explained, "Where Pileroo keep people he not like."

"Well it's the only lead we have on the stone. Maybe we should see what our new *friend* wants, and plan our next move from there." With that decided the trio quickly made their way to the southern door, although not too quickly as to draw attention to the fact that they were heading towards Pileroo's own private prison.

The reached the bottom of the stairs with ease; no-one paid them much attention, or they just didn't want to annoy the man who had so easily dispatched one of their peers, and they all knew Branack was not one to be messed with.

"My name is Quinn, and my mistress needs help." said the voice.

"Then why don't you help her?" Ivellious asked as he looked for where the mysterious voice was coming from, "You seem to be very good at concealing yourself."

"I am helping her," Quinn moved to where the others would notice him, "By finding someone who can at least touch the lock of her cell."

Branack instinctively reached for his axe, but raised a hand to stop the barbarian. "A shadow, showing allegiance to hat I can only assume is a mortal?"

"She is a mortal." the shadow replied.

"I thought shadows despised the living." said Ivellious who was now most intrigued by this manifestation.

"They usually do," Laucian explained, "Unless they are summoned by one."

"People can summon shadows?" asked Ivellious.

"Yes, just as my mistress summoned me." Quinn answered, growing impatient.

"She's a shadow walker," Laucian mused "Interesting."

"Yes, and she is down here." Quinn headed down the corridor and rounded a corner. The others followed Quinn around the corner to find another long corridor, this one with a row of cells down one side. About half way down the corridor they could see a bright light pouring out of one of the cells.

"She's in that one." Laucian said.

"How can you be sure?" Ivellious asked.

"The light is to stop my mistress jumping between shadows." Quinn was already near the cell, but had stopped just before the light. Laucian walked passed the shadow followed by Ivellious, Branack however stopped just short of Quinn, still not entirely trusting the creature.

"Well this is an unexpected surprise." Laucian said as he looked at the woman sitting in the cell. The woman looked up and smiled.

"Laucian, am I glad to see you." The woman jumped to her feet and stepped closer to the bars.

"Well your highness, it seems you have gotten yourself into quite the situation here." Laucian smiled back at the woman.

"You two know each other?" Ivellious asked.

"Yes, me and Tanay have been looking for the princess for quite some time."

"Stop with the royalty jokes, and just get me out of here." The woman's smile was fading fast.

"Jokes? I'm not joking, unless I am mistaken and you are not princess Elana of Krondmare."

"Are you being serious?" Ivellious asked, "This is the princess of Krondmare?" the rouge was already thinking of how he could profit from rescuing a princess.

Elana frowned, "Yes I am. Now if you don't mind could someone please get me out of this damn cell."

"Allow me." Ivellious retrieved two small pieces of metal from his pocket and started to work on the lock.

"You've made some new friends since we last spoke." Laucian indicated Quinn as he spoke.

"So have you." Elana replied, indicating Ivellious.

"There you go, you highness." Ivellious stepped back as the cell door swung open.

"Thank you..."

"Ivellious, at your service," the rogue bowed as he introduced himself, "And this is my associate, Branack." Elana paid little attention to what Ivellious was saying, she walked straight up to Laucian and wrapped her arms around him.

"I missed you." Elana said as she buried her face into Laucian's shoulder. Laucian smiled and tentatively put his arms around his old friend. Elana backed away from Laucian slightly, and looked closely at her friend, "What happened? You used to be more comfortable hugging your friends."

"I've changed a lot in the last few months." Laucian answered quietly.

"Haven't we all." Elana added.

"I hate to break up this reunion mistress, but I think we should probably be moving on." Quinn suggested.

"I agree." Branack grunted as he continued to scrutinise Quinn.

"Yes. I don't think it would be wise to be caught releasing one of Pileroo's prisoners, unless you wish to become a permanent guest here." Ivellious added.

The group made their way back up to the main hall; Elana was now wrapped in Laucian's cloak to hide her identity. Laucian had briefly explained the situation to his old friend, and Elana had agreed to help collect the stone, and so she would lead them to the room in which she had been captured.

They eventually reached the door to Pileroo's audience chamber. This time however it was closed, and all of its locks and magical wards were in place.

"The stone you described is in there, but the door is impossible to open without the keys." Elana explained.

"No door is impossible to pass," Ivellious declared, "Especially when I am stood before it." The rouge crouched in front of the door and examined it closely; he then took out his tools and got to work.

Quinn had volunteered to stand guard at the end of the corridor as he was the least likely to be noticed. Although Branack was also keeping watch, he still did not trust the shadow and so was watching it just as much as the passageway.

"This is an interesting door." Ivellious muttered.

"I told you he wouldn't be able to open it." Elana said, "I spent a month working on this door."

"Ah, but you didn't have this," Ivellious pulled out a small pouch made from a dark green silk with white runes around the rim. "How far away would you say your little shadow friend is? I can't be sure how this will affect him."

"What is that?" Elana asked.

"I'd say about thirty feet away." Laucian estimated.

"That should be far enough." Ivellious mused, "This your highness, is a very useful little item. Now when you say a few choice words, such as *tuan devcor eldar*," the door began to glow a pale blue colour, the light then began to move away from the door like a mist and started to fill the pouch. "That blue light is all the magic protecting the door, which is now stuck in my pouch." Ivellious smiled as he pulled the string to close the pouch, trapping the magic inside.

"And now all you have to contend with is the mechanical aspects of the locks."

"Precisely princess." Ivellious got out his lock picks, "We'll make a thief out of you yet." It didn't take Ivellious long to open the door now that its magical protections were all gone. "Pileroo would be so disappointed to learn that his precious door was so easily picked."

Ivellious, Laucian and Elana entered the room. It looked exactly the same as it had when Elana had been there before, the fire in the centre was even burning just as brightly.

"The ruby is in the fire." Elana said as he pointed to where she had seen the stone.

"A ruby? You never said the stone was a ruby." The thief's eyes widened as he looked for the stone Laucian had described as about the size of a fist.

"It isn't a ruby." Laucian crouched by the fire pit. "It is crystallised fire." Laucian gazed at the stone before he reached out like lightning and grabbed hold of it, pulling it from the flames. The stone was surprisingly cool to the touch, as he held it before him the flames in the pit began to die down and went out.

Now they had what they were looking for it was time for the group to leave. After the left the room. After exiting the room Ivellious shut the door before releasing the magic from his pouch, the blue light covered the door again before fading from sight, leaving no trace that the door had ever been opened.

"Hey! What are you do...?" Laucian, Ivellious and Elana looked down the corridor when they heard the voice, which had been suddenly cut off by a loud crash. They ran to where the sound had come from, finding Branack and Quinn standing over a dead thief.

"Well that is not good." Ivellious stated.

"He would have had too many questions." Quinn explained.

"What was that?" The group looked down the corridor as they realised that the dead man had not been the only person near by.

"If they see us we're done for." said Ivellious.

"Don't worry about them." Laucian smiled as a plan formed in his head.

"What are you thinking?" Elana asked, remembering the look on Laucian's face from back when she used to go on excursions with him.

"I've learned a few new tricks since we last saw each other," Laucian began, "You all head for the exit. I'll meet you at the Jolly Roger." Laucian started off to towards where to voice had come from, by the sounds of the footsteps there were four, maybe five guild members down the corridor, and they were all running towards Laucian and the others.

"No. I stay, I help." Branack grunted.

"I'll be fine, also I doubt you'd be very effective if you're struggling to breath. Now go." Laucian replied.

"What does that mean?" Elana asked.

"Trust me." Laucian winked at his old friend. Elana shook her head as she set off down the passageway which led to the exit along with Ivellious Branack and Quinn.

Laucian retrieved his daggers from his belt and began to concentrate on the air around him. The men were just around the next corner, Laucian could hear them clearly, he could hear their boots on the floor, he could hear their shouts as they ran to see what the crash was, he could hear them rushing to their deaths.

By the time they had reached the corner Laucian had called upon his ability to summon a cloud of dust. The men stopped in their tracks, each of them coughing uncontrollably as they scrambled desperately trying to escape the cloud. It was in that moment Laucian descended upon them. Because he did not need to breath Laucian was unaffected by the dust, and within seconds he had left four bodies on the floor, each with one perfectly placed killing wound. Laucian chuckled to himself as he turned to head after his friends.

"Alarm! Alarm! Sound the alarm! There are intruders!" Laucian turned on his heels and ran to where the shout had come from. As he exited the dust cloud Laucian found himself standing over the man he had let live in the drinking hall earlier.

"I knew I should have killed you." Laucian said calmly as he looked down at the man.

"You! You're Ivellious' friend." the man stuttered, as he tried to catch his breath.

"Lets keep that just between me and you." Laucian knelt by the man, he covered his mouth to muffle the scream as he cut the man's throat. At that precise moment the alarm bells throughout the guild house began to ring. Laucian stood up, trying to come up with a plan as to how he would overcome this new problem.

The alarm sounded just as the others reached the main door. "Well that could complicate matters." Ivellious said as the door guard stepped through the door closing it behind him.

"No-one leaves when the alarm sounds." the guard explained as they approached.

"We go now." Branack grunted.

"I said no-one leaves. You stupid orc." Branack smiled broadly at the guard, Ivellious shook his head knowing exactly what would happen next.

"I am not an orc." Branack calmly walked towards the guard, who just stood there and laughed.

"You're still not getting by me, *orc.*" The guard had barley finished speaking when Branack wrapped a huge hand around his throat and easily lifted him from the ground. The man struggled to break free of Branack's grip, but to no avail.

"I said I am not an orc!" Branack was growling now as he squeezed the life out of the guard. When the man was dead Branack dropped him in a heap on the floor. The group quickly exited the guild house and headed straight for the Jolly Roger tavern, leaving Laucian alone to deal with this trouble, just the way he liked it.

Laucian could hear footsteps coming from all directions, these thieves were well organised to deal with intruders he'd give them that much at least, but Laucian was no ordinary intruder. Laucian decided that he would be best served in taking the easier path, he was confident that he would be more than a match for any of the men chasing him, but he was in a bit of a rush.

Laucian put one of his daggers away, deciding that this situation called for a higher quality weapon. With a quick thought Laucian summoned his psy-blade into his hand as he headed in the direction he could hear the least footsteps coming from.

The men running towards Laucian were taken completely off guard as the rounded the corner. They were expecting the intruder to be hiding somewhere, not running straight at them with a dagger in one hand and a burning black sword in the other. The men stopped dead in their tracks, giving the charging Laucian the perfect opportunity he needed to deal with them.

Laucian barely slowed as he ran down the corridor, swinging his weapons out to the side. He buried his dagger deep into one man's chest, as his psy-blade easily decapitated another. Before the two men had hit the ground Laucian's blades were both cutting deeply into the two remaining men.

Laucian carried on down the corridor, leaving the four men where they fell. He knew that this altercation however brief would still have been heard by everyone near by, and no-one would be happy to find four more of their comrades dead on the floor.

At the end of the corridor there was a small junction, one passage led off to the left, and to the right were some stairs leading to a higher floor. Normally Laucian would have stayed on the same floor, this was the level with the exit and he was not familiar enough with the building to be traversing different levels. However he could hear what sounded like a large number of people coming from the left passage and by now he could also hear shouts from men who had obviously just found their dead friends.

As Laucian reached each new level of the building he could hear still more people running towards the stairs. Eventually he reached a level which appeared clear, though now he could hear people on the stairs, a lot of people, and they were close. Laucian headed off down the passage.

There were doors all along each wall, Laucian guessed that they were rooms for people who lived in the guild house. He realised that if he was right then there would be multiple ways to reach this floor, he just needed to find another one. He was about half way along the corridor when one of his pursuers reached the floor.

"He's here! He's here!" The man yelled, Laucian stopped and spun around, his mind blade disappeared and he dislodged a throwing knife from his bracer. With a flick of the wrist Laucian threw the blade at his pursuer, hitting him squarely in the heart.

Laucian started to check the doors closest to him, he knew it wouldn't be long before the passage was overrun by a flood of angry guild members. The first two doors were locked, but the third opened and without really thinking he entered the room. Laucian managed to close the door just as the first of his pursuers began pouring into the passageway.

"Hello again." Laucian span round to see the woman he had helped in the main hall earlier, she was lying on a large bed at one side of the room.

"How nice to see you again..." Laucian began.

"Stacy." said the woman as she sat up on the bed.

"Yes, of course. I was hoping to run into you again." Laucian was thinking fast, he needed to find a way to explain why he had just barged into the young woman's room.

"Check every room! Find him!" Yelled someone out in the passage. Stacy smiled as she slid off the bed and walked up to Laucian, she glance down at the blood stained knife in his hand.

"So you're what all these alarms are about." Stacy was still smiling as she contemplated how this situation could benefit her.

"Yes they are, and I guarantee that I could easily kill you before you have a chance to scream." Laucian warned coldly.

"Take your top off." Stacy said as she began to remove her own.

"What are you doing?" Laucian asked. He could hear that the men outside were getting closer.

"Trust me." Stacy winked as she began to remove her trousers. Laucian laughed as he realised what her plan was, he dropped his dagger and knife belt to the floor before throwing his top over them to hide the blood.

The men were outside the door now; both Laucian and Stacy could hear them. The woman put her arms around Laucian's neck pulling him forward, she fell backwards onto the bed pulling him on top of her and began to kiss him. The door swung open with a crash and three men ran into the room, each with swords drawn. Laucian rolled to the side and jumped up from the bed, Stacy quickly grabbed a sheet and wrapped it around her.

"What do you think you are doing!?!" Stacy yelled.

"We're looking for an intruder, didn't you hear the alarms?" asked one of the men as he walked further into the room, looking suspiciously at Laucian.

"We were a little pre-occupied, if you hadn't noticed." Stacy was staring angrily at the man.

"Well someone has been murdering trusted guild members, and he was last seen on this floor." the man explained, "I'm sure you won't mind me asking how long you've been here? Doesn't look like you're too far into anything yet."

"For your information we've been here for hours," Stacy smiled at Laucian, "Some men do believe in foreplay."

Another man suddenly ran into the room, "There are reports that the entrance guard has been murdered." He said quietly to the lead man in the room.

"Most likely when the intruder entered."

"No sir, it looks as though was killed as the intruder left." the lead man took another look at Laucian before nodding to the others. They left the room, the door swinging closed behind them.

"Well, what now?" Stacy asked coyly.

"Now I have to leave." Laucian answered as he retrieved his things from the floor. Stacy walked up to him, dropping the sheet to the ground, she ran her fingers through his hair, and tried to turn him round to face her.

"Sure you don't want to stay for a while? You know, until everything has calmed down."

"No, I must be leaving." Laucian was barely paying attention to the woman. Stacy laughed, she had never met a man who had turned her down so simply before, she was not used to this type of reaction from a man.

Laucian opened the door slowly and looked out into the passage, by now everyone had gone. He stepped out of the room and walked towards the stairs. Stacy followed him out of the room, now wrapped in the sheet again.

"So when will I see you again?" she asked.

"I doubt you will." Laucian didn't even look at her as he answered. Stacy laughed again before disappearing back into her room. Laucian reached the top of the stairs where the man he had killed was still lying, he bent down and retrieved his throwing knife before heading straight for the exit.

"What are you doing here?" It was the man who had burst in on Laucian and Stacy, he seemed to be in charge of organising the search for the intruder, for Laucian, "I thought you were busy."

"I can spend time with her whenever I want," Laucian began, "But right now its more important to catch the bastard killing our comrades."

"Good man. We're sending search parties out into the city."

"And what are we looking for exactly?"

"I've been informed that the intruder stole some precious stone from master Pileroo. It appears to be a big ruby, we're looking for anyone who may be trying to sell it."

Laucian thought for a moment, "I know a couple of guys who deal in that sort of thing. I'll see what I can turn up."

The man patted Laucian on the shoulder as he walked passed, "You looked like you might have been an arse when I saw you earlier, but I was wrong, get out there and find that murdering bastard."

Laucian nodded at the man before heading out into the night, where he took a round about route to meet the others at the Jolly Roger tavern.

Chapter 14
Little Song Bird

The room was dark, stone walls slowly came into view as her eyes adjusted to the dim light. There was no door or windows to be seen, she could see no source for the dim light. She wondered how long she had been unconscious, as she looked around the room she could see all three of her companions were also there, they all sat leaning against the walls, not one of them speaking.

The monk suddenly remembered what had happened to her earlier. She sat up bringing her hands up to her throat, she knew the elf had cut her, she knew that there was no way she could have survived the wound.

"So this is the afterlife?" Delensa mused. The other three all looked up at her, the thought had crossed each of their minds. Kimanay had drowned in quicksand, Larenor had been crushed behind the secret door, and Aramil had choked on the gas that filled the room he had entered. All of them new that survival had been impossible, but this was unlike any afterlife they had heard of.

"This is not the afterlife." They all recognised Magon's voice, it sounded to be coming from all around them as it had during the *tests*, "This is just a small holding area."

The group all jumped to their feet as one of the walls slid open revealing Gregor standing behind it, "If you would all follow me, my master is waiting."

Gregor led the group through the lower levels of Magon's tower; no-one spoke as they were taken back to the room where they had first met the eccentric mage, where he now sat with Solaris. The mage was grinning broadly.

"Ah come in come in, please do make yourselves comfortable." Magon indicated for the group to sit down. The mage squinted at the group as they each found seats, "I see you are all looking well."

"How? What happened to us?" Kimanay asked.

"Why are we not dead?" Aramil added.

"Well that's simple, you are not dead because my tower is a sanctuary." the mage explained, "It is quite impossible to die here, except of natural causes of course."

"So what is the point to them rooms upstairs?" Larenor asked bitterly.

"Those rooms were designed to find the flaws in all those who pass through, and then place that person in a situation to show that flaw."

"So only someone with no flaws can gain access to the stone?" Larenor snapped.

"Everyone is flawed in one way or another, my tests simply show the person what these are, so they can learn from it."

"And what exactly am I supposed to learn from picking the wrong door?" Aramil asked sarcastically.

"You my friend must learn to trust in those that you usually would not. You see the world in black and white, good and evil, there is no room for interpretation. In the troubles to come you will have to fight alongside those you would normally see as your enemies, against people you might think as friends, if you cannot learn to trust in those you see as evil then you will fail in this war."

Aramil leaned back in his chair, thinking about the mage's words. The paladin knew he had been foolish to believe the elf blindly, but warred against a neighbouring goblinoid kingdom for centuries, those creatures had always been his enemies; could he truly put trust in them?

"And what am I to learn?" Kimanay asked, "Always look where I step?"

"Your faith in your god is commendable, yet it is also your flaw."

"You are saying I should give up my faith?"

"Not at all, but you put your faith before everything else. You must learn that sometimes your quest must come first. Your god will be more than understanding if you miss a prayer or two as you work towards the greater good. Many clerics need to learn this, many have lost their way because they spent too much time in prayer instead of following their course. You failed the test because you strayed from your path."

"So I should keep my faith, but not allow it to interfere with my quest." Kimanay was almost talking to herself.

"And what of me? What was I supposed to learn?" Larenor asked coldly.

"You must learn not to rush into battle recklessly. You seek vengeance against those who have wronged you, and to do that you will charge headlong into any fight no matter the consequences. You must learn to think before you fight. You believe that you must prove yourself because of your past, but if you are not careful then your pride will lead you into a shallow grave." Larenor's face fell, he knew what Magon said was true, although his pride did not want to admit it.

No-one spoke for a while until Solaris eventually broke the silence, "And what of you monk? Do you not wish to know what you should have learned?"

"I never faced my flaw." Delensa said quietly, "I never entered the final room."

"You have the greatest lesson to learn my dear." for the first time there was genuine sadness in the mage's voice, "You lack faith. Your friends have an over abundance of it, be it in their gods, their beliefs, or in themselves. It is easy to learn how to be more careful, but you must learn to be more bold, you need to have more faith in your own abilities." Magon stood from his chair and walked to stand next to Delensa, "If you had but believed in yourself, all you would have had to do was enter the final room and take the stone." Magon dropped a clear gemstone into her lap, it was the elemental stone of air. "Trust in yourself my dear, for you truly are great." Magon turned and walked from the room.

"You now have both the stones of air and water," Solaris began, "If you wait here then you shall receive the stone of earth upon Fruril's return, and by now Laucian should have already retrieved the fire stone and awaits your arrival in Cemulion." Solaris stood and exited the room the same way Magon had.

*   *   *

They were two days out of Calamshan, Roscoe and Davkul had barely spoken to each other since parting ways with the others. Roscoe had attempted to make conversation on several occasions, but Davkul had not appeared to be in a talkative mood.

Eventually the gruff dwarf decided to talk, his curiosity about some of the things he had heard of Roscoe finally getting the better of him. "Is it true what the fire lord said about you?" the dwarf asked.

"Excuse me?" Roscoe was a little taken aback by the question, partially because he wasn't sure who the fire lord was.

"When we were speaking with Nasgaroth, the fire lord Solaris said you were a master of the Wentar words. I was wondering if it was true." Davkul explained.

Roscoe thought back to their meeting with the dragon. Solaris' proclamation had completely slipped his mind, "To be honest I don't know what he was talking about. He said that he would explain, but never did."

"Bah, that sounds about right for him. Don't get me wrong I have much respect for the man, but he often forgets to explain himself."

"Somehow I doubt he forgets. Solaris seems to me to be someone who tells you things when he feels it is the right time."

Davkul laughed to himself, not really wanting to tell Roscoe that he was right, "So you don't even know what the Wentar words are?"

"I've no idea."

"Ha, I thought you bard types were supposed to know all the legends."

"No-one can know *all* legends." Roscoe explained, "Do you know what the Wentar words are?"

"The legend says that they were the first form of spoken magic to be used by mortals." the dwarf began, "There was this chap named Wentar, some say he was elven, but no-one really knows. This Wentar lived in an area filled with dangerous creatures. One day he was attacked by some great beast, which should have killed him, yet somehow he survived, claiming afterwards not to remember how. The story goes that over the next few months this Wentar found himself in many situations which he shouldn't have been able to overcome, yet somehow he did but never remembered how. Some witnesses to these events said they heard him uttering strange words, which made stranger things happen. He would disappear from sight or fall at a slowed speed or there'd be a blinding flash of light, that sort of thing.

"Others would try using the words, but nothing happened, they would only work for Wentar. He eventually learned what these words were, and what they could do. He became a great force for goodness, travelling the lands using his newfound power to help people. He also told the words to scholars, who are said to have used them to develop arcane magic.

"There were many creatures which did not like the idea of mortals being able to use magic, they believed us to be unworthy of such power. That is why a great green dragon decided to hunt Wentar down, and kill the man who brought magic to the world of mortals. A vicious battle ensued that lasted for several days, eventually ending when both Wentar and the dragon fell. With his final breath Wentar uttered a single word. It is said that this last word of Wentar scattered his power across time, passing it on to future generations so that the mortal world would never forget their magic."

Roscoe thought for a moment after Davkul finished his tale, "So you're saying that Solaris thinks that I can use these words?"

"If he said you can, then you can." Davkul answered bluntly.

"But I've never used any strange magic, only the few arcane tricks I know."

"That probably means your ability to use the words is only recently started to present itself. Over time you will learn to control them.

Roscoe thought for a minute, still not convinced he had the power of these strange words. Thinking back there had been a couple of times in his life that he couldn't remember how he managed to survive certain situations, such as in the clearing they had fought the orcs, and Solaris had asked him what *Hashnay* had meant.

"Hold up!" Davkul was suddenly very alert. The dwarf was scanning the landscape, a little way ahead was a small hill with a few trees growing on top, but other than that it was all grassland. Davkul laughed to himself, "Clever boys."

"What is it?" Roscoe was also scanning the area now, but he could not see what had gotten the dwarf's attention.

"They want us the think they're in the trees."

"Who?" Roscoe was still looking around, trying to see what Davkul was talking about. Davkul started forward again, unhooking the axe from his belt. Roscoe watched the dwarf, his hand instinctively falling to the hilt of his own sword.

Davkul stopped by a small mound and lowered his axe to the ground, "I like your hidey hole, but it's a little obvious don't you think?" Davkul said with a grin, "Now you and your friends had best come out, we want to talk to you."

Roscoe looked at Davkul, confused as to whom the dwarf was talking to. It wasn't long before he realised exactly what was going on though.

"It looks like the little song bird has found himself a little hunting bird." All around Roscoe and Davkul the ground began to move, as did the small mound where Davkul had placed his axe. Roscoe smiled as he recognised the voice that had spoken to be one of his good friends from the barbarian tribes.

"My name is Malik the Bear." said one of the barbarian's. All of the concealed warriors had risen to their feet now, all apart from the one who still had Davkul's axe resting on his chest.

It was easy to see why Malik was called *the bear*, he was huge and well muscled, even by the standards of the nomadic barbarians. "We have been expecting you, little song bird."

"It is good to see you again my friend." Roscoe replied.

Davkul hooked his axe back onto his belt, allowing the man on the floor to finally rise. "You have been expecting us?" he grunted.

"Yes. The great hunter told us of your arrival. My father and the other chieftains are gathering all our people. We were sent to bring you to them." Malik explained.

"Then we should not keep them waiting." said Roscoe as he looked up at his barbarian friend.

Malik led the two companions to where the tribes had gathered. The large warriors walking a little ahead, although most of them knew Roscoe from his trips out onto the plains non of them had met a dwarf before, though they had heard stories. They had heard tell of these gruff little warriors, experts in weaponry and battle tactics, qualities the barbarians held in high regard. However they had also heard about how bad tempered dwarves could be, and decided to give this one a wide berth, at least until they had determined his mood.

"What's with all that bird talk?" Davkul asked when Malik was out of earshot.

"I first met these tribes when I was a travelling bard," Roscoe explained, "I introduced myself to the tribal chieftains by trading songs. Ever since then Malik has called me little song bird."

Davkul laughed. He had never seen much point to nick names, he believed a person should answer to their given name, but he had to admit little song bird was quite fitting for a halfling bard.

It wasn't long before the camp came into view; the smoke rising from dozens of fires was seen first. Then the hundreds of tents came into view.

"All of the tribes must be here," Roscoe had never seen such a gathering of the tribes, and he had been visiting them for many years.

"Not quite song bird," Malik began as he stood over Roscoe, "See there in the distance? More smoke." Malik pointed to the west, where Roscoe could see more columns of smoke rising against the backdrop of the sunset.

"How many more are still to come?" Davkul asked.

"Three more tribes. They should arrive by morning." Malik replied as he led everyone into the camp. The others began to split off, returning to their own tribes, some going to be with their husbands or wives, others their friends. Malik led Roscoe and Davkul through the camp towards a tent in the very centre.

This tent was much larger than the others; it looked to be made out of the same animal hide as the rest of the camp, only it was more highly decorated.

"Welcome to the meeting tent." said Malik with a grin. He pulled back the entrance allowing Roscoe and Davkul to enter first. They could clearly see that this tent was not used for the type of meeting that they would have with King Augustus or Nasgaroth. Inside the tent were a great many tables, all surrounding one long table in the centre. Many chairs and stools were scattered around, none of which appeared to belong to any particular table, but looked as though you would have to just find a seat and then take it to where you wanted to be. At the far end of the tent there was a large stack of barrels, this was of particular interest to Davkul as he could only think of one thing that would be stored in barrels in a place such as this.

At the far end of the middle table an older man was sat. Roscoe recognised him instantly as Mendik, Malik's father. Mendik smiled as he recognised Roscoe.

"Little song bird, you have come. Just as the great hunter told me you would." Mendik stood and walked up to Roscoe, clasping him on the shoulder. "And you must be the warrior he spoke of." Mendik turned towards Davkul now.

"Davkul Gemcutter at your service, my lord."

"I am Mendik, chieftain of the bear tribe, and if what the great hunter says is true then it is I who is at your service."

"What is it this *great hunter* has told you?" Davkul asked, curious as to whom this hunter was.

"He told me of a great battle, in which our tribes could gain much honour, and that we should follow a little warrior to this battle."

"Then you will help in the coming war?" Roscoe asked excitedly.

"That decision cannot be made without the presence of all the chieftains," Mendik explained, "But until then you shall be our honoured guests."

"And tonight we shall hold a feast in your names." Malik added with a grin. Davkul liked the sound of a feast, he had heard tales of barbarian feasts and was thoroughly looking forward to the experience. Roscoe did not have to rely on hearsay to know what this feast would entail, he had been present for several over the years. Although he enjoyed the food and drink, and the songs that would be sung, he also knew how they usually ended, and he did not look forward to spending the next few days nursing the injuries he was bound to receive.

Malik saw the slight look of dismay on Roscoe's face and smiled, "Worry not my little song bird, I will look after you this evening." Roscoe did not doubt that Malik meant what he said, but he also knew that Malik liked his drink, and many brawls had started because someone had foolishly challenged his strength.

"My son will show you to a place you can store your belongings, and sleep this night. I will send someone to collect you when the feast begins." Malik showed Roscoe and Davkul out of the tent and to the tent that they would be using for the night, where he left them to prepare for the feast.

*   *   *

It wasn't long before a member of the bear tribe arrived to collect Roscoe and Davkul, taking them back to the meeting tent. As they approached they could smell all manned of cooked meats, and outside they could see a large group of men and women all pushing and shoving in an attempt to get closer to the entrance.

The crowd parted as Roscoe and Davkul approached, giving them passage straight to the entrance, where Mendik stood along with four other men, all of whom were dressed in much more colourful clothing than the rest of the tribes people.

"Honoured guests, welcome." Mendik smiled at his guests, "Allow me to introduce my fellow tribal chieftains." The four men around Mendik all gave a slight bow.

"It is tradition that our guests should be the first to enter the feast," one of the chief's explained as he pulled open the entrance, indicating for Roscoe and Davkul to enter.

The two guests walked into the tent and were greeted by quite the site. All of the tables were full to the brim with food, there were many different types of roasted meat, bread fruit and vegetables. Much to Davkul's delight there were also several opened barrels by each table of what could only be some kind of beer.

Roscoe and Davkul were taken to sit at the main table with the chieftains and their sons and daughters, this was also the table that had the most beer. It didn't take long for everyone at the table, and in fact the whole tent, except for Roscoe, to be too drunk to realise that you didn't need to shout for the person next to them to hear.

Shortly after this level of drunkenness was reached the boisterous behaviour Roscoe had come to expect from these tribal feasts began. This behaviour came in many forms, ranging from renditions of old battle songs to drunken disagreements over who was tallest. These events stayed away from the main table for a while, until one of the chieftain's daughters proclaimed that she was the greatest warrior in her tribe. Although from different tribes Malik still saw this as a challenge and felt obliged to test his prowess against this warrior.

The challenge didn't last long, it wasn't really a fight. The basic rules were that the first to fall over lost, and you could use any means necessary to make sure it was your opponent who fell first. All those near by cleared a space around the two warriors as they began to circle each other. They began to grab at each other, each trying to pull their opponent off balance. After a few moments Malik grinned at the woman, who in that moment realised that Malik the bear had been toying with her. Malik lifted the woman easily from the ground and dropped her on her back, winning the challenge.

All those watching fell silent, waiting to see how the woman reacted. She slowly got back to her feet staring at Malik's grinning face with steely eyes. She grabbed Malik by his chest hair and pulled him close, "Finally, a real man!" she shouted before she kissed him hard an the lips and then pushed him away. Malik's face turned red as everyone erupted into laughter. "Now will someone knock this fool down?" the woman added as she grabbed a mug of beer.

This started a trend as one by one all of the other chieftains sons and daughters began to challenge Malik, each one suffering a similar fate to the first, although Malik refused to let any of the others kiss him. After they had all been defeated some of the most renowned warriors from the tribes began to challenge Malik, all of whom had excuses for loosing prepared such as Malik was cheating, or that they weren't ready.

Eventually Malik's father called out, "Is there no warrior who can knock this man down?" Mendik was answered by Davkul jumping up onto the table, holding a mug of beer in one hand and a deer leg in the other.

"I'll knock the over grown bear cub down!" the dwarf yelled. All around him laughed.

"Now now my little battle bird," Malik began, "I don't want to hurt one of our honoured guests."

"Bah, you wouldn't be able to hurt me if I was lying under a big fat boulder and you were holding a great big club." Davkul laughed.

"Now that sounds like a challenge." Malik called back.

Davkul took a bite out of the deer leg and dropped it to the table, "And I won't even spill my drink." with that the dwarf leaped from the table.

Malik stood waiting for Davkul to get close before swinging both arms towards the dwarf, thinking he'd easily be able to pick up the little warrior and drop him on his back, however he completely missed Davkul. The dwarf ran straight through Malik's legs kicking out as he went forcing Malik down to one knee. Davkul then jumped onto Malik's shoulders, forcing the giant of a man down so that he was lying on his stomach. There was a stunned silence as the tribesmen realised that one of their greatest warriors had just been beaten by someone less than half his size.

Davkul was laughing to himself, "Guess I did spill my drink."

"No you didn't," Malik's first opponent called back.

The dwarf smiled, "I have now," he laughed as he poured the drink over Malik's head. The crowd went quiet again until they heard the roar of laughter coming from Malik.

The pair got back to their feet and Malik declared "If the chief's decide not the help in your war, then I shall go with you anyway little battle bird. If only so I can make sure you live long enough for me to pay you back for this!" the huge man shook his head, covering all those near by in beer.

After Davkul's display against Malik the tribesmen had a new respect for the dwarf. They had heard about the battle prowess of dwarves, but had not seen it until today, and they had been suitably impressed.

Much to Roscoe's dismay the challenges didn't end after Malik was defeated. Now everyone wanted to test their skills against the dwarf. Although Roscoe was not taking part in this he was still sat in the vicinity of the challenges, so it was inevitable that he would eventually have someone fall on top of him. That someone turned out to be Kandar, one of the tribal chieftains, one of the *fatter* tribal chieftains.

*   *   *

It was mid afternoon by the time Roscoe and Davkul were roused by Malik, both of them feeling the ill effects of too much drink the night before.

"Come," said Malik, "You'll want to hear this."

"Have the other tribes arrived?" Roscoe asked as he dressed.

"They arrived earlier, the chieftains have already met."

"And now they want to hear what we have to say?" Roscoe was trying to think of the best ways to convince the tribes to go to war.

"No, they have already made their decision." Malik explained.

"Without hearing us out?" Davkul grunted.

"Come, my father has called for all the tribes to hear." Malik led the pair through the camp to where everyone had gathered. Mendik along with the other chieftains was standing on a large boulder.

"Not for many years have all our people gathered in one place," Mendik began, "But now we are here to answer the call of the great hunter. There is much darkness in this world, and we have been asked to stand against it. For many centuries our people have fought against the creatures of the mountains." There was a huge cheer from the crowd; Mendik outstretched his arms to quiet everyone down.

"Now we face a new threat," Mendik continued, "A threat that even out enemies fear. We must put aside our hatred of these beasts and stand with them. My people, my friends, my brothers, my sisters, we must go to war!" The crowd cheered again, many of the warriors drawing their weapons and waving them in the air.

Kandar stepped forward, "The old the sick and the young will be taken with an escort to Blain's caves where they will be safe. Every other able bodies man and woman will take arms, we leave in six days."

"We do not expect everyone to return, but those who fall will surely be welcomed by the great hunter into the hunting grounds of our ancestors." Added another of the chieftains.

Davkul smiled as the gathered tribes scattered to make preparations for war. These warriors would be a great asset in the coming battle.

Chapter 15
Old Friends

Laucian and Elana had barely left the Jolly Roger for the past few days. They knew that Pileroo's guild would be looking for them, they also knew that Boris Benard held no love for the thieves and would not give them any information about his guests.

They had spent most their time catching up. Laucian explained how he and Tanay had searched for Elana, and how somewhere along the way they had managed to get swept up in all the chaos surrounding this coming war. He also told her how he hadn't heard from Tanay since he had come to Cemulion following a new lead.

Elana told Laucian of what happened the night she disappeared, she explained how Deventis and two other legion of Strakstaw members had kidnapped her from her room. They had dragged her away into the night, and left her for dead in a ditch. Luckily she had survived the attack and was found by a group of travelling performers, who had nursed her back to health and trained her in the arts of a shadow walker.

"The people at the bar are asking about you." Sally, the young waitress whispered in Laucian's ear. Laucian and Elana were sitting at a table in the corner of the room. Quinn had elected to stay in the room they had rented, he was not fond of the bar, it was too bright for his taste.

"I think they may be the people we are waiting for," Laucian was examining the four people standing at the bar, two of whom he recognised from his past. He had grown up with the knight Aramil, and Delensa had lived in the monastery he had been sent to when his psychic abilities had started to become a problem. "Tell them we are here and that we would like a glass of wine, and a Maldraw."

Sally walked over to the bar, where Boris was denying all knowledge of Laucian's existence. He had assumed that the group were outside contractors hired by Pileroo. Sally quickly whispered something into Boris's ear.

"Oh, right. Well then, it appears Mr Laucian has been expecting you." the bar tender mumbled.

"So he is here then?" Delensa asked.

"Yes, and he would like a glass of wine and a glass of Maldraw." Sally explained.

Aramil scowled, he had not appreciated Boris lying to him, and now Laucian was demanding drinks from them. "I will not buy drinks for a criminal."

"I will. I like his style." laughed Larenor. "I'll buy those drinks, and take a Maldraw for myself. Kimanay, Delensa?"

"Just water, thank you." Delensa replied.

"Wine please." Kimanay added.

"And those who refuse to buy for others can buy for themselves." Larenor smiled at Aramil as Boris prepared the drinks. Larenor paid and took the drinks over to the table Sally said they could find Laucian, followed closely by Kimanay and Delensa. Aramil stood at the bar a little longer before joining his companions.

"It has been a long time my old friend." Delensa said as she reached the table.

"It has been too long." Laucian replied with a smile, "Please join us."

"Magon said you would have something for us." Everyone looked round at Aramil. His bitter tone catching them off guard, although very strict in his ways Aramil had always remained calm and polite to everyone.

"Hello Aramil. Will you not sit and have a drink?" Laucian replied politely. This caught Elana by surprise, although she had been friends with Laucian during a time that he seemed much happier than he was now, it had still been rare for him not to respond to a bitter tone in kind.

"I will not drink with a murderer." Aramil folded his arms across his chest and stared at Laucian.

"I am no more a murderer than you are." Laucian said, still in his uncharacteristic polite tone. "But if you can not bring yourself to drink with me then at least sit while we discuss our busyness."

"What is this murder he speaks of?" Elana asked. She had always been curious of Laucian's past, a topic he had always refused to discuss.

"He murdered several of the monks from the monastery in which he was staying." Aramil spat.

Laucian smiled, "Is that what they told you?"

"They showed us their bodies at the order, when they were seeking our aid in your capture."

"I killed them in self defence."

"You butchered them."

"They left me no choice,"

"You could have left the monastery."

"That is exactly what I was trying to do." The calmness finally left Laucian's voice and it suddenly became very clear to everyone that this topic of conversation was making him angry.

"Are you saying that they attacked you as you were leaving the monastery?" Delensa asked.

"I was never a willing resident there, you should know that."

"It was a monastery, not a prison. Everyone should have been free to come and go as they pleased." the monk replied.

"That may have been true for you, but if you remember I was kept in the private chambers. An area reserved for the training of people with psychic abilities. We were held there by force."

"So you killed them while trying to escape?" Aramil asked doubtfully.

"You know me Aramil. We grew up together, you know I would not harm anyone without good reason."

"There are people I thought better of than you whom I have witnessed turn to evil." Aramil answered through gritted teeth.

"Now don't miss understand me, this is all very riveting," Larenor interrupted, "And I really hate to be the one to say this, but shouldn't we get down to busyness?"

"Yes. The sooner we get this over with, the sooner we can leave this fugitive behind us."

"You really don't want my company?" Laucian smiled, "You are really not going to like what I have to say."

"Well just say it." Aramil spat.

"We have the stone of fire, and you are welcome to it," Elana said.

"Well that sounds good." Kimanay replied.

"We also know you are going to Krondmare next, looking for the sceptre." Laucian added.

"And we are going with you." Elana took a sip of her drink.

"Out of the question!" Aramil snapped, "I am willing to not turn you over to the authorities Laucian. We were friends once, and others seem to have faith in you, but I have no intention of travelling with you."

"I have to agree with my colleague," Larenor added, "I know nothing of your crimes, but if you cause such a reaction as this in my friend then I think it best for us to travel alone."

"Well, if that is how you feel," Laucian began, "But please do tell me how you plan to negotiate with the king of Krondmare to get the sceptre you need."

"I'm sure we will think of something." Kimanay replied.

"You will think of something? I assure you that my father will not just hand over his sceptre to anyone." Elana took another sip of her wine as she watched the reactions of the four adventurers.

"Your father?" Delensa asked, "Are you saying that the king of Krondmare is your father?"

"Yes, making me the princess of Krondmare, and heir to the throne since my mother died having never bore a son."

Larenor turned to face Aramil, "Under the circumstances she could be very useful."

"Let me guess, you won't help us unless Laucian comes along too." Aramil stated.

"Well I do have contact who can get you passage on a fast ship." Laucian suggested.

"We can barter passage on a ship ourselves." said Kimanay.

"That's true, if you wish to pay an extortionate sum of gold to travel on a fat merchant ship. A journey that would take six months to reach Krondmare, stopping off at every port on the way." The four companions looked at each other nervously, knowing that Laucian's prediction would only be true if they were lucky. "I however could get you passage on the Guillotine. The fastest ship on the coast, you may have to do a little work but it would be free, and you'll reach Krondmare in a mater of days."

"That could be useful too." Larenor said. Aramil scowled and walked away from the table, nodding his head to indicate the others should follow him.

Laucian and Elana sat and watched the discussion which followed. They couldn't make out what was being said, but it was clear they were trying to decide what to do about the situation with Laucian. Larenor and Kimanay didn't seem to have too much input in the decision, they both said their piece and then let Aramil and Delensa argue over the issue, both of whom seemed very passionate about it.

The party eventually returned to the table, Aramil stood behind the others as Delensa approached. "We have decided that your company on the voyage could be very useful and would be most grateful of any help you could provide." Delensa was smiling broadly; she had clearly won the argument.

"May I suggest that we leave the elemental stones here, where they'll be safe." Elana said, wanting to move the conversation away from Laucian accompanying them.

"Why would they be safer here rather than with us?" Larenor asked.

"Surly there's nothing to worry about if we are going to visit your father." Aramil added.

"What you need to understand is that my father's main advisor is a man named Deventis, who also happens to be a member of the legion of Strakstaw."

"They are the mercenaries that we keep running into." Larenor said.

"They are the mercenaries behind the coming war," Laucian explained, "The are the architects of this whole mess."

"My father doesn't know what they are planning, he thinks they are his allies. They have helped him with some conflicts I the past, but now they are beginning to show their true colours, there showing what they are really capable of."

"If they are his advisors then how do you suggest we get the sceptre?" Kimanay asked, "I doubt they would be willing to give it too us."

"I will speak with my father, away from Deventis, he will listen to me."

"That is a problem we can deal with later; right now we need to make preparations for sailing to Krondmare." Larenor interjected.

"You said that you have contacts on the Guillotine." Aramil said bitterly.

"Since I spent a year as a member of the crew, to say I have contacts would be an understatement." Laucian replied.

*   *   *

Laucian had left the others at the Jolly Roger as he made his way to the docks. The others were arguing over leaving the elemental stones in Quinn's care as they travelled. Despite Elana's insistence the others were finding it difficult to trust her shadow companion. If Laucian was to be honest he did not blame them, he too was still a little weary around the creature.

The Guillotine was quite a sight, although it did look as though it had suffered greatly during its last voyage. Laucian walked up to the sailor guarding the boarding ramp. He didn't recognise the man and guessed he had joined the crew after Laucian had parted ways with the ship. The sailor looked to have been in a hard fight recently, his jaw was badly bruised and he had a large cut down the left side of his face.

"I wish to speak with Janemita." Laucian said.

"Captain Urthandor is busy, and does not wish to be disturbed." the sailor replied.

"This is very important."

"The captain will see no-one." The sailor said more forcefully.

"She will see me." Laucian said just as forcefully as the sailor had been.

"The captain isn't seeing anyone!" The sailor stepped towards Laucian, trying to look as menacing as he could.

"She will see him." squeaked a voice from the ship. Both Laucian and the sailor looked up to see Benny Bignose running down the boarding ramp. Benny was the gnome who had designed the ship, and most of its weaponry. He was also one of the longest serving members of the crew.

"It is good to see you again my old friend." Laucian called. He took a close look at the gnome as he approached. Benny was looking very cheerful considering that he, like the other sailor, had many injuries. His face was covered in cuts and bruises, his left arm was bandaged, and he was clearly favouring his right leg.

"I tell ya lad," said Benny, nudging the other sailor, "This here is one of the best men ever to crew the Guillotine. Was never much of a sailor, but he killed or caught more pirates than you've ever seen."

"Sounds like he would've been useful on our last trip." the sailor replied sarcastically.

"If he had been with us then Kheldun would be nothing more than a bad memory." Benny retorted cheerfully.

"You finally caught up with the elusive Kheldun?" Laucian asked.

"Aye," replied Benny in a far more sombre tone, "We lost a lot of good men. Kheldun was not exactly what we were expecting."

"It would seem I have come at a bad time my friend, for I am here to ask for your help."

"Then you had best come with me, the captain is overseeing the repairs." Benny led Laucian up to the main deck. Laucian could see that the ship had been in a terrible battle. Although the repairs were all but complete it was plain to see where large holes had been patched and the sails had been sewn back together, even one of the masts was held up by braces and would need to be replaced soon.

"Well well, where were you when we needed you?" Laucian and Benny turned to see Galik Burns walking towards them with a big grin across his face. Galik was first mate on the Guillotine; he was a tall muscular man with dark skin and a shaved head.

"I never thought a mighty warrior such as you would ever *need* me." Laucian replied with a smile.

"Me? I don't need you, but some of these new sailors. They don't seem to know when to duck, they keep getting in the way of my club." Laughed the big man as he slapped Laucian on the back.

"I was hoping to speak with Janemita," Laucian was trying to get down to busyness.

"In that case you'd best walk this way." Galik headed towards the ships aft. "Captain! Captain! Look what the gnome dragged in!"

The slim woman looked around to see what her first mate was shouting about, as soon as she saw that Laucian was with him she quickly made her way across the deck towards them. She slowed her pace when she was getting close, not wanting to appear too eager to see her former crew member.

"Welcome aboard Laucian. We've missed you since you left the crew." Janemita said, trying to sound as formal as possible.

"Ha, she says we've missed you," laughed Galik as he nudged Laucian.

"She means that she missed you." Benny finished. Galik and Benny laughed until Janemita scowled at them.

"Yes, well. I think we should leave you to talk with the captain," said Benny, trying to hide his grin.

"Aye, we'll leave you two alone." Galik added, making no attempt to hide his smile. Benny and Galik both returned to their work on the repairs.

"So to what do we owe the pleasure of your visit?" Janemita asked, still sounding very formal. Laucian was glad of this, their relationship had become complicated before he left the crew. On a long voyage they had taken comfort in each other, an event both had known immediately to have been a mistake, it was also the event that had eventually caused him to part ways with the crew. It had worked out for the best in the end as it was when he had first been dropped of in Krondmare, where he met Tanay, Elana, and the only woman he had ever truly loved.

"I was hoping to barter passage to Krondmare for myself and five others." Laucian explained.

"This is a pirate hunter, not a passenger ship. If you want a pleasure cruse go and ask one of the merchants."

"It is no pleasure cruse we are looking for. We need to get to Krondmare in a hurry, and this is the fastest ship in these waters. We're not looking for a free ride either, you know I'm capable and my companions will have no trouble working a line, and if all else fails you could send them to sit with the crows."

Janemita laughed, she always liked sending new crew members to sit in the crows nest. They always assumed it to be an easy job, never really expecting how swaying on top of the mast would affect their last meal.

"Well we could use a test voyage. To check if the repairs will hold." Laucian smiled, he loved the way Janemita could always make it sound that she wasn't actually helping someone, but was actually helping herself, or the ship.

"So we can sail with you?" Laucian asked.

"I suppose you can tag along with out test voyage."

"That's very kind of you. I was also wondering if you would be able to give us passage back as well?"

"You're not asking for much are you." Laughed Janemita, "You do realise that we were recently in battle, and as you can see we didn't fair too well."

"I heard that you found Kheldun, and things went badly."

"He was a little more than we bargained for, although we now know why he only attacks ships at night."

"I guess it isn't for the element of surprise."

"No. Where most of his crew were men, Kheldun and a few others are vampires. We had no effective way of fighting them." Janemita turned away from Laucian, showing that she didn't really wish to discuss the battle. "Tell your companions we will be ready to sail in a few hours and can be underway as soon as they are ready."

Janemita walked away from Laucian. It was clear to Laucian that she was trying to hide the extent of her own injuries. Janemita was trying to hide a limp, and was keeping her right arm constantly by her side, he also noticed that she was gently touching her left side when she thought no-one was looking, suggesting that she had taken a blow to the ribs which was causing her some serious distress.

Laucian finally left the ship heading straight back to the others to tell them they would be leaving soon.

Chapter 16
Ghosts in the Trees

Adokas and Thoril entered the forest at the same place they had when Roscoe was guiding them. It seemed like only yesterday that they had passed this way hunting orcs. They both thought back over all that had happened since then, little of which seemed to have been in their favour.

"So how do we plan to contact these etharii when we reach the temple?" Thoril asked. He had been thinking on this question ever since leaving Magon's tower, but only now vocalised it.

"I have a feeling that won't be too difficult." Adokas was looking closely at the undergrowth around the trail they had originally used to fined the ruined temple.

"What are you looking for?" Thoril recognised the determined look in his friend's eyes, he was clearly looking for something specific.

"I heard a noise, it was over here but I cannot see what might have made it."

The pair continued on through the forest, Adokas paying a large amount of attention to their surroundings. Thoril thought he was just being overly cautious, but Thoril also thought that it was just his mind playing trick on him when he too heard noises coming from the trees.

Adokas however was sure that there was someone out in the trees, and he was sure that he knew who it was. They were back here to seek out the etharii and gain their aid, and Adokas was sure that it was the etharii who were shadowing them now, moving back and forth between the ethereal and material plains.

Little is known about the etharii, and most of that is known is thought to be only myth. None of the gods lay claim to creating this secretive race, it is said by some that they were created by something far older, something that hungered. For centuries they served this entity before finally braking free of its influence and banishing it back into the void. This left the etharii to forge forward on their own, moving away from their predatory ways to create their own civilisations.

The etharii had established a handful of cities, one of which was in the forest of Transeen. It was here that many years before the etharii had helped a paladin of Sugalas defend his temple against an onslaught from the abyss. Since gaining their freedom from their creator the etharii had become somewhat xenophobic, not trusting members of other races unless they earned it, and the paladin Jovan did just that. In the first assault the etharii had not helped, fearing that the demons would learn of their home and bring down a terrible retribution upon their hidden city.

When the demons attacked again all but one of the paladins and one of the other warriors fighting along side them fell and the temple was lost. The etharii watched the remaining warriors standing alone against the demonic army and decided that they could not just stand by and watch these warriors fall too. They rescued the men from the fight, taking them back to their city on the ethereal plane.

These two warriors were Jovan and Malkay, both of whom were favoured warriors of their respective deities. Both men charged back into their battle against evil as soon as they were able, this time with an etharii army behind them. It was a long and terrible battle which finally ended with the closing of the abyssal gate which was located deep in the bowels of the temple. Jovan and Malkay knew that when the abyssal gate was finally closed anyone within the gate room would be dragged into the abyss, and that is why they entered the room alone. They were successful in closing the gate and ending the demonic incursion leaving the etharii who vowed that they would defend the sight from anyone who would unearth the gate for any reason, be their intentions good or evil.

This was the very temple Adokas and Thoril were heading towards. They could still hear leaves rustle above them, and Adokas kept seeing flashes of movement in the undergrowth but saw nothing when he focused on the area. It wasn't until Adokas and Thoril had almost reached the temple that the etharii finally revealed themselves. It was getting late now, the sun had sunk behind the mountains and a few stars could be seen through the tree tops, and Adokas and Thoril suddenly found themselves to be surrounded by at least ten etharii. There was but one gap in the ring of etharii, leading the travellers back the way they had come.

"You may go no further!" one etharii declared.

"Go back to where you came from. You are not welcome here." spat another.

"We have come to seek your help." Adokas said as he looked around the group of etharii, trying to work out which was the ranking member.

The etharii laughed bitterly, "You want our help?"

Thoril was barely listening to what was being said, he was looking closely at the etharii, fascinated by this rarely seen race. Their wild and somewhat bestial appearance was a little frightening, Thoril shuddered at the thought of what they may be capable if they decided to attack. Their eyes though told a different story, those deep pools of silver of gold showed a great wisdom and Thoril believed they showed a longing to be left in peace.

"Please, you must hear us," Adokas continued.

"We must do nothing." Adokas spun around to see Fanell standing behind him, the same etharii Solaris had spoken with when they were last here.

"I respect that you wish to be left alone but this war is too important; we are all facing the end."

"We have faced our end before, and survived. We will do the same now." Fanell turned to one of his companions, "Escort them to the borders of the forest, make sure they leave."

"What has happened at the ruins?" Everyone turned to Thoril. Up until now he had remained silent, and his sudden question seemed to seriously unnerve the etharii.

"The ruins are not your concern!" Fanell replied forcefully. Thoril turned and walked in the direction of the ruins, two of the etharii quickly blocked his path with weapons drawn. Thoril had expected this however and had prepared a suitable counter measure.

"*Tchuva!*" Thoril extended he arm towards the etharii blocking his path and released a fine white powder. As the powder came into contact with the etharii they were forced sideways, and Thoril walked through the gap he had created between them.

The other etharii moved to stop Thoril, but he was already entering the clearing when they caught him. Thoril looked around the ruins, they had changed a lot it looked as though there had been a large excavation. "I'll ask you again," he turned to face Fanell, "What happened here?"

"Tell him nothing." one etharii spat. Fanell didn't speak for a moment, it went against everything he believed to tell these intruders anything, but a trusted friend to himself and his people had spoken highly of these men.

"Soldiers came; they took that which was hidden." The other etharii looked angrily at Fanell.

"They took the gateway?" Thoril asked to the surprise of everyone.

"How do you know of that?" one etharii asked.

"I do my research," Thoril answered. "And if I am correct, that gateway will be used to summon a creature far more terrible than anything that has passed through it before."

"That is impossible, the gateway can only be used here." Fanell explained, "That is why we have not pursued those who took it."

"The gateway can only be used as a path to the abyss from here, but Legion does not reside in the abyss." the mage replied.

"What is he talking about?" whispered one of the etharii, some of the others were asking similar questions.

"He is talking about the coming war. In which we will need your help." Adokas explained.

"You talk of wars and legions, yet all I see is you and a few soldiers who took the gateway." Fanell said sarcastically.

"I expect that the soldiers were part of the legion of Strakstaw, sent here to collect the gateway." Thoril began, "They will summon the beast into our world, and then his armies will march across the land laying waste to everything in its path."

"And you want us to stand against this army?" Fanell asked.

"The army is little more than a distraction. While his army lays waste to our world Legion will use his ancient rituals to destroy everything." said Thoril.

"So what is it you want from us?" an etharii asked shakily.

"Plans are already in motion to fight the beast, now we are raising a force to stop his army, that is where you are needed." Adokas answered.

"So you do expect us to stand against this army!" Fanell laughed.

"You will be but one part of the forces; we have emissaries travelling to all of the major powers in the region. If we don't stand against Legion's army then they will destroy everything in their path. If we let that happen it won't matter if the beast is defeated or not, our world would be thrown into chaos and turmoil."

"You have a flair for the dramatic mage." chuckled Fanell, "Do you really expect us to believe this story of yours?"

"My father wishes to speak with these men, bring them to his court." Fanell spun round to see a younger etharii who had just entered the material plane. Fanell bowed his head in respect.

"My lord, I am to take these outsiders to the palace?" Fanell sounded both confused and concerned by this.

"Yes. Take them through the hidden entrance, my father is waiting." The young etharii faded from sight as he returned to the ethereal plane.

"Blindfold them." Fanell ordered pointing at Adokas and Thoril. One of the etharii stepped towards the pair, Adokas moved to protest but Thoril stopped him by placing a hand on his shoulder.

"We are going to be taken to see their archon, but we are not allowed to know the location of their portal to the ethereal plane. If we want their help we must follow their rules." Thoril explained.

Fanell and the etharii led Adokas an Thoril through the forest for what seemed like hours. The etharii talked quietly amongst themselves in their own tongue; a language unlike anything Adokas or Thoril had ever heard.

Adokas had heard many stories of the etharii, but most had just been hearsay and rumours. However it was clear to see that Thoril had somehow found the time to do some true research into the the secretive people since their last encounter.

"What is this portal they are taking us to?" Adokas whispered.

"Although the etharii can slip between the material and ethereal planes I believe that they can only take themselves and whatever they are carrying, I would surmise that the portal is used for transporting any supplies they need for the city, and guests." Thoril explained.

"And our portals remain hidden from outsides; we don't want your kind knowing how to infiltrate our cities." Fanell finished.

Adokas did not like being referred to as *your kind* but decided not to complain, he needed to keep the etharii happy if he was to gain their help. When the etharii finally removed the blindfolds they were deep within the forest, it was dark and dense, Adokas found it hard to believe that any portal big enough to transport people and supplies to the ethereal plane could be located here.

Fanell placed his hand on one of the trees and muttered a few words too quietly for anyone to hear. There was a loud creaking sound as the bark of the tree began to peel back to reveal a glowing green vortex. Two of the etharii stepped into the vortex and Fanell indicated for Adokas and Thoril to follow them.

As the pair stepped through the portal they felt a strange tingling sensation followed by a sudden jolt. The two companions stumbled forward, Adokas easily steadied himself but Thoril's reflexes were not as finely tuned and he fell to one knee. The duo looked at their surroundings, they could still see the forest but it looked hazy and there were new structures, an entire city could be seen through the trees. A cool mist covered the ground swirling around the feet of the etharii population, most of whom were staring and whispering about the two outsiders in their city.

"Follow me." Fanell walked passed the outsiders, not fazed by the jump to the ethereal plane in any way. Fanell walked along what appeared to be the main road into the centre of the city, the other guards crowded closely around Adokas and Thoril trying to shield them from the on lookers around them.

Thoril kept trying to walk around the trees from the material plane, but with the guards surrounding him so closely he found himself having to walk straight through them. Although the trees had no physical presence in the ethereal plane Thoril still found it disconcerting to pass through them.

The pair were taken through the city straight towards a grand building that they assumed was the palace. Fanell pushed on the door which swung open easily before continuing on through a grand entrance hall. The other guards stopped just short of the entrance and bowed their heads. Adokas and Thoril stopped when the guards did, not sure if this was some custom they should follow before entering the building.

Fanell turned back to face the outsiders, "Follow me." he said before continuing through the hall. Thoril and Adokas quickly caught up with Fanell.

"Why do your men stay at the door?" Thoril asked as he looked back to see them still standing by the entrance.

"Because they are not needed in here." Fanell led the others up an elaborate staircase that spiralled around a large tree from the material plane before passing through the trunk at the top.

"What do you mean by *they are not needed*?" Adokas asked.

"They are not needed because all I need to do is nod and a moment later you would be dead." The three men continued on in silence. Adokas and Thoril had thought that by being allowed into the etharii's city they had gained some measure of trust, but it seemed they had been mistaken.

When they reached the top of the stairs Fanell walked through the trunk of the tree without hesitation, Adokas and Thoril slowed their pace still not comfortable walking through trees.

"If you could please follow me." Fanell was starting to sound irritated by the outsiders. As they came out of the far side of the tree Adokas and Thoril found themselves standing in the palace throne room. Fanell took a few steps into the room before bowing low. The visitors took in their surroundings carefully; they could see no trees from the material plane in this room. The walls were decorated by murals depicting some of the important times from etharii history.

The throne was at the far side of the room, the archon looked fairly plain compared to other rulers they had met. His cloths looked identical in style to all the other etharii they had met, the only difference being the simple crown on his head. To the side of the throne stood the younger etharii who had appeared in the clearing and extended the invitation to speak with the archon. The only others in the room were several heavily armoured guards holding large pole axes.

"So you have come here seeking our help?" the archon said as he scrutinised his *guests*.

"My lord," Thoril bowed low before continuing, "We have been sent by King Augustus of Getandor to ask for your aid..." Thoril's voice trailed off when he realised that the etharii was not listening to him. He was in fact listening to the young man from the clearing.

The archon smiled, "Save your speech's, I know why you are here. This is about the legion of Strakstaw."

Adokas and Thoril swapped a nervous glance, "That it true my lord, we are trying to raise a force to stand against them." Adokas said.

"Your wars do not concern..." The archon was cut off by the man from the clearing whispering something else in his ear. The archon frowned, "Who told you to come to us?"

The question confused the visitors, "We were sent by King Augustus of Getandor." Thoril replied. The man from the clearing whispered in the archons ear again.

"I doubt the human king even knows of our existence. Who specifically told you to seek out our help?" Adokas and Thoril looked at each other again.

"It was the mage Magon and his friend Solaris who suggested we seek your aid." Thoril answered. Both names seemed to cause a stir in everyone present.

The man from the clearing and the archon began to talk quietly, it looked as though they were arguing about something. Eventually the archon turned back to Adokas and Thoril.

"We do not get involved in the wars of others, but it seems that we have oaths to uphold here." the archon stood from his throne and left the room through a door behind where he had been sitting.

"Please forgive my father, he like many others finds it difficult to see how this war will affect us in our secluded home." said the man from the clearing. "He does however know that our people must always remain true to our word, so as to not become the same as those who betrayed us."

"I don't understand," Adokas said, "What oaths is it you speak of?"

"Many years ago my people made an oath to Jovan and Malkay that we would protect the gateway from being used for good or for evil, and we have failed in doing this. We allowed the the gateway to be taken, not knowing that it could be opened away from the temple, to fulfil that oath we must fight with you now." the etharii explained. "We also made a pledge to the one you know as Solaris; we once told him that if he called for our aid then we would answer, and it would seem that he has sent you to make that call."

Everyone was silent in the room, the guards looked to one another as they realised what their lord was saying.

"Fanell, take our guests to the garrison, give them food and a place to rest. Then rouse the army, they must prepare for battle." With his orders given the lord turned and left the room through the same door as his father. Fanell led Adokas and Thoril from the room and took them to the barracks.

*   *   *

"I have a gift for you." Markus and Deventis stood in awe of Slantary's presence. As the dragon spoke some of her knights dragged a cart into the clearing. On the cart was the gateway that had once been in the ruined temple in Transeen.

"Thank you my lady," said Markus showing Slantary all due respect. "It has been a long time since I last saw that gateway."

"You have used it before?" Deventis asked, still staring at Slantary as he spoke.

"The last time I saw this gateway, I was trying to close it."

"And now you will use it to summon the end of this cursed world." Slantary said as she raised her head and looked towards Lunda the largest of Gallisium's three moons. The pale moonlight was shining off of her deep red scales.

"Again I thank you for this gift, it shall be used well. Though I must ask another task of you." Markus said with a bow, "I would like you and your knights to lead the attack on Cemulion; I want the city to fall before the council arrives here in seven days."

Chapter 17
The Dragon's Breath

Laucian had been in the crows nest for several hours, he liked the peace that could be found there. Most people detested the job finding it tedious and boring, but Laucian was not like most. He had always liked his own space and found the cramped conditions of ship life to be highly uncomfortable, he was not overly fond of most people.

Laucian was playing his tin whistle as he watched the horizon. "Are all of your tunes so sad?" Laucian looked over the side of the nest to see Benny climbing up to join him.

"I play how I feel." Laucian answered as he put the whistle back into his pocket.

"You played much happier tunes when I gave that too you."

"They were happier times." They sat in silence for a moment as they remembered back to when Laucian had been a permanent member of the Guillotine's crew.

"Do you know what I have always wondered?" Benny asked.

"What?"

"Well since you don't breath, how can you play that whistle?"

Laucian laughed, "Just because I don't need to draw breath, it doesn't mean I cannot."

"Ah, I guess that makes sense."

"So did you come all the way up here to ask me that or is there something else?"

"Yes, of course. The captain wants you to come down from here. She is sending that elven ranger friend of yours up here for a while. She's hoping that some time in the nest will stop him from bothering the female crew members."

Laucian smiled, "If that is what she wishes." Laucian hopped over the side of the nest and joined Benny as he climbed down the rigging.

"This also gives me the perfect opportunity to show you my new invention." said Benny as they passed Larenor on his way up, "I hope you didn't have too much for lunch." Benny laughed. Larenor scowled at the gnome and carried on climbing.

Benny and Laucian were met at the bottom of the rigging by Elana and Delensa, "They have been chatting like gnome wives since you went up there." Benny whispered.

"Well we have had a lot to talk about. It seems our good friend mister Laucian has led a very eventful life." Elana said with a grin. Laucian shook his head slightly. He had not told Elana much about his past, he simply believed it to be none of her concern, but now she was happily discussing him with an old friend who had know him during what he considered to be one of the worst points of his life.

"You said something about a new invention?" Laucian turned to Benny now, resigning himself to that fact that he could do nothing to stop the others from talking. Benny grinned broadly; he was always delighted to tell anyone who would listen about his inventions.

"Yes, yes. Follow me, I'll show you." Benny ran off towards his cabin followed closely by Laucian. Elana and Delensa followed behind, still chatting and giggling to each other.

"Now of course you know that the Guillotine was the first sea vessels to carry cannons." Benny began, "You also know that it was my ingenuity which made that possible." Laucian laughed to himself, Benny loved to brag about his successful ventures, but rarely spoke of his many failed experiments.

"Well I became quite interested in these cannons. They're very useful tools, although they are a little cumbersome." They had reached Benny's cabin by now, it was overly cluttered with many of Benny's inventions and experiments. The gnome rooted through the stuff covering a large table in the centre of his cabin until he finally found what he was looking for.

"I call it a hand cannon." Benny held up his invention for all to see. It looked almost the same as the ships cannons, only much smaller and with a similar trigger mechanism to that of a crossbow. "Took me weeks to perfect the powder quantities needed to make it work, come I'll show you." Benny pushed passed the others and ran back up to the deck.

The excited gnome was waiting by the bow of the ship when the others finally caught up to him. "So you put the powder, wad, and ball in much the same as with the cannons," Benny was showing this to the others as he explained, "You pull this flint back until it clicks into position, then you point it at your enemy." Benny aimed the hand cannon off the side of the ship, "when you pull the trigger it causes the flint to spark, lighting the powder, and..." Benny fired the hand cannon. There was a loud bang and those watching could easily see where the shot hit the water.

"That seems to be a very dangerous tool." Delensa said, looking more at the gnomes reaction than at his new weapon.

"Oh it is my dear, when used incorrectly."Benny said, "But I learned many years ago that an inventor must be careful with all that he creates, as well as willing to take risks."

"I'm sure that such a weapon would be very useful on a ship like this," Elana said, "But couldn't it be dangerous in the wrong hands?"

"Oh its very useful, more powerful than the average bow, and the shot is much harder to remove than an arrow, believe me I know." Benny rubbed his shoulder as he spoke. "As for it falling into the wrong hands, you're very much right there too. Although everyone on this ship knows not to play around with my inventions, and as for anyone else I would destroy it before anyone could use it foolishly." Benny paused for a moment, "So Laucian, what do you think?"

The others looked round at Laucian, but he wasn't watching Benny's display, he was staring off into the distance. The others turned to see what he was looking at. All they could see was a dark silhouette on the horizon, a silhouette that was growing larger. Elana voiced the question they were all thinking, "What is that?"

It was but moments later when Larenor called down from the crows nest, "Dragon!" everyone on deck stopped what they were doing, hoping that the call was just the wind whistling around the mast, hoping that they had just imagined that it had said dragon. That hope was destroyed when the call came again, "Dragon!" Larenor shouted again. "Straight ahead, and coming right at us! Its a great red!"

The captain ran to the bow of her ship, telescope in hand. She looked through the telescope for a moment, "By the gods," she muttered to herself before yelling, "Prepare for battle! Archers to your places!"

"Do not open fire until I give the signal. If it does not attack us we shall not attack it." Janemita was hoping that the dragon would not consider her ship a threat and just fly by. She knew that even with a crew as strong and brave as hers they would not stand a chance against a dragon.

"You would let a red dragon just fly by?" Aramil asked.

"My ship is designed for hunting pirates, not dragons." Janemita replied.

Aramil ran his hand over the cloak he had inherited from his father. It was made from the scales of a dragon his father had slain. He had always wished that he could live up to the exploits of his father, that was part of the reason he had joined the temple and become a knight, and now he had the chance to bring down a great red. Aramil also knew that Janemita was right; in their current situation the dragon would easily decimate the ship and crew. Just a single torrent of flame from that beasts mouth could potentially sink the ship.

"Here it comes!" Galik yelled, "Everyone ready!" The entire crew and passengers alike readied their weapons, preparing for the incoming beast. There was little need for this preparation however as the dragon paid them no heed. It just flew overhead; the only person to suffer any trouble being Larenor.

The dragon passed over at great speed causing a strong wind as it did. Larenor being at the highest point of the ship, only little lower than the dragon itself, was hit hard by this wind. Larenor was blown from the crows nest. It was only because of his exceptional dexterity that he was able to catch hold of the rigging and stop himself from falling all the way to the deck.

The crew eased off their weapons, it seemed that the danger had now passed. For most on board the Guillotine this was the first time they had ever seen a dragon, and for the lucky ones it would also be the last. All that crossed the minds of the men and women on board however was that the dragon looked to be heading towards Cemulion, at great speed.

*　　*　　*

"My lord! My lord!" The soldier ran straight into King Augustus IV's throne room as the was talking with several of his noble advisors. They were now all looking at the soldier, it was most irregular for anyone to enter the throne room unannounced.

"My lord!" the soldier bowed, "We have a serious situation."

"What situation?"

"There is an army at the city gates my lord. They appeared as if from nowhere." the soldier explained. The nobles looked nervously at each other, all except Antonema Christortus, who just smiled. "They are orcs, my lord." the soldier finished.

"Are they with the men we sent looking for additional forces?" the king asked.

"No my lord, their leader calls for our surrender." The soldier replied.

"I'll never surrender my city to orcs." The king said, trying to sound commanding.

"Somehow I knew you would say that." Everyone turned to see Antonema with his sword in hand.

"What is the meaning of this?" Demanded the king, Antonema answered with actions rather than words. He moved like lightning, cutting the nobles down within a couple of heart beats. The soldier drew his sword, but he was too slow, the nobles were dead and he would be next. Antonema beheaded the soldier before he had any chance to mount a defence.

"What are you doing?" the king was on his feet now, "Drop your sword!"

"You are no longer giving orders here." Antonema advanced on the king.

"Why?" the king asked, resigned to the fact that there was no way he could hope to survive this encounter.

"Have you ever heard of an assassin named *the Shadow*?"

Augustus nodded his head, "He is said to do the legion of Strakstaw's dirty work."

"That is exactly what I do."

With a single swing of a sword King Augustus IV was dead, leaving Getandor without a ruler.

*   *   *

"Open the gates and surrender!" Kevgeon shouted, "Or we will kill you all!"

"This city will never surrender to raiders!" Commander Medlich called back. Members of the city guard lined the walls, each aiming crossbows at Kevgeon.

"Do not be foolish Medlich," Kevgeon replied, "It is not just my orcs who lay siege to your city."

"How does he know your name?" whispered one of the guards.

"I don't know." the commander answered. He looked out across the army at the gates, he knew that this force was not big enough to overrun the city, and every man and woman in the guard were well trained, he had seen to that himself. The only problem he could see was the fact that these orcs had an ogre with them, a beast that could easily demolish the gate if ordered. It was the enemy leader that truly worried Medlich however, he seemed to be more intelligent than most with orcish blood, and he also appeared to have information about the cities defences, information it should not have been able to know.

"Be gone from these walls, or I will give the order to fill your hide with bolts!" Kevgeon laughed at Medlich's threat as he turned back to his forces and yelled something in the orc tongue.

The half-orc looked back up at Medlich, "You die tonight, fool!" As he spoke the ogre walked away from the main host, straight towards the city gate.

"Open fire!" Medlich ordered, "Bring down that beast!" His guard fired their crossbows, every one of them hitting their target, but ogres have thick skin and it barely seemed to notice the attack.

The orcs began to launch arrows up at the wall, their aim was poor but the shear number of arrows meant that they were able to take out several guards in their first volley.

"Cover! Cover!" Medlich yelled. The commander looked to those around him, pointing to one of the guards he began to give orders, "Kel, you have the wall. Keep them orcs back as long as you can."

"Aye sir!" Kel replied before barking orders of her own.

Medlich turned to another guard, "Galdar, to the barracks and sound the alarm bell, rouse the rest of the guard and I want the streets clear of civilians." Galdar nodded before running off. Medlich looked over the wall one more time before heading down to street level.

Medlich made his way to the gate where a few guard were already posted. He could hear the ogre beating on the gates which were beginning to crack. Splinters of wood scattered across the ground as still more guards arrived at the gate.

Medlich took stock of those around him, each one fully armoured with weapons drawn, "The is a ogre and a hoard of orcs trying to break into our city!" Medlich yelled, "Are you going to stand for that?"

"No sir!"" the guards called back.

"Then form up!" Medlich ordered, "Lets show these fools the mistake they have made here today!" The guards formed a perimeter around the gate, Medlich knew they would fight hard, he knew they would fight well. He firmly believed that they could easily dispense of the orcs at their gates. What Medlich did not know however was that these orcs would be the least of his troubles. He did not know that the king was already dead, he did not know of the knights entering the city through he secret tunnels in Pileroo's guild house, he did not know that the dragon Slantary was on her way.

When the gate finally gave way the ogre charged into the city, alone. Kel and the guards on the wall had done an excellent job at keeping the orcs at bay. Medlich and the others were ready for the beast, a line of guards blocked its path, each one holding a long spear. The beast charged the line just as Medlich expected, he also expected that at least one spear would cause a serious wound on the ogre. As it turned out Medlich was lucky, two spears had dug deep into the beasts hide. The guards were thrown back as the ogre reared up roaring in pain, but it would take more than these wounds to bring it down and it attacked again.

"Now!" Medlich ordered, and several more guards with spears charged forward. Medlich charged in behind them with some more troops, all holding swords. The spears ripped into the beasts flesh causing the ogre to roar again, it swung out at its attackers catching one in the chest with a backhand sending him flying backwards to cash into a wall before he slumped on the floor. It caught hold of another, crushing her head in one of its huge hands. The others all fought harder, each one wanting to avenge their fallen friends, they hacked at the beast with tempered fury. Individually they may not have been able to defeat the ogre, but they fought as a unit, each small wound they caused adding up to a series of killing strikes.

When the ogre finally died Medlich surveyed the scene, it had gone better that he had hoped, although he felt the pain of any of his guard dying he still understood how lucky they were to only loose two against the beast. Medlich had the guard form up again, knowing that those left on the wall may be keeping the orcs at bay now, but it wouldn't be long before they too breached the gate. With all attention focused on the gate though, they never noticed the dragon knights approaching from behind.

As the knights approached the guards they began to kill them silently, taking out several before anyone even realised they were there. Eventually one man managed to shout out before he was cut down, alerting the others. Fighting broke out in the streets, Medlich's troops would not stand for the murder of their friends.

Despite the training Medlich's guards had received the dragon knights were cutting them down quickly. By now the orcs had finally breached the gates too, their archers having picked off many of the guards on the wall. Medlich and his soldiers now found themselves caught between two armies, the veteran commander began to bark orders. The guards were able to form up into ranks, they would not give up, Cemulion city did not belong to these foul invaders, and as long as even one guard was still able to stand it never would.

"Wedge!" Medlich yelled, "We have to break through these knights! We will make a stronger stand at the palace!" The guards reacted instantly, forming a wedge with Medlich at the front. With this sudden change in tactic the were able to knock the knights off balance and force their way though. As they broke through the knights hastily formed line Medlich and his troops were faced with yet more dragon knights charging towards them, all looked lost until help arrived in an unexpected form.

Branack's charge decimated the knights line. They had not been expecting an attack from behind, especially not an attack from a raging half-orc barbarian. Ivellious took a more subtle approach, using the shadows he would strike down the knights, then retreating back before anyone knew he was there. They caused more than enough disorientation in the knights for Medlich and the others to break through this second line.

They were running through the streets now. Trying to reach the palace to make their stand. Medlich cringed at the thought of leaving Kel and the others still on the wall, but there was nothing he could do for them now.

"Thanks for the help," Medlich said as he ran beside Ivellious.

The half-elf smiled as he replied, "Just remember this when you next find me in someone else's home."

The palace was in sight now, they had almost made it when all hope was drained from the city guard. Slantary swooped in low, landing directly in front of the running soldiers. Everyone stopped immediately, even the invading knights and orcs halted their chase, they were enjoying the fear Slantary caused.

"Now would be a good time to surrender." Antonema walked from behind the dragon, "Your king is dead, and your pitiful soldiers have no chance of survival against the legion of Strakstaw."

Medlich looked at his remaining followers, he could see the fear in their eyes and knew all was lost. He also knew that if they did surrender their enemies would simply execute every last one of them. Whatever he did the city was lost, and his guard were dead.

Medlich turned to Ivellious, "Get out. You must escape the city." He said, "Tell people what happened here, tell them we fought bravely." Ivellious nodded, Branack tried to protest but was silenced by a glance from Medlich. "Do not let the city guard have died for nothing."

Medlich walked forward, "We will never surrender to the likes of you." Commander Medlich raised his sword, "For Getandor! For the king!" The remaining guard cheered as one before charging the invaders. Ivellious and Branack faded into the shadows, it would be easy for the pair to escape the city, they knew many secret ways past the city walls. Ivellious was surprised however at how difficult he found it to leave the brave men and women of the city guard to die while he ran away.

The city guard were falling fast; the dragon was slaughtering them in droves, her great claws tearing them to shreds, and her fiery breath burning them to ash. The knights and orcs backed away from the main fight, not wanting to be killed by mistake. They formed a perimeter around the guard, cutting down any who tried to escape the dragons wrath.

Medlich fought hard despite knowing how unlikely it would be for them to kill the dragon, but he wanted to spur on his troops, he planned to die a heroes death. He had charged straight for the dragon, hacking at its taloned feet to little effect. He had managed to avoid the dragon's attacks so far, but he was beginning to grow tired. He could see the bodies of his comrades littering the streets, a sight that made him fight even harder. He caught hold of the dragons leg and dug his sword into her scaly hide, causing a wound the dragon barley even noticed.

The sword was stuck tight between the dragons scales so he used it as a step and began to climb. Medlich slowly made his way up the dragons leg, using her own scales like a ladder until he finally reached her back. He could see much of the city from this hight, the people were running scared. Most of the guard were already dead, he could only see a handful who still fought valiantly. Medlich carried on climbing until he had reached the dragons head.

Medlich pulled a dagger from his belt and stabbed it hard into the side of the dragon's head. Slantary roared in pain and shook her head violently. Medlich lost his balance and began to fall; still gripping his dagger the blade cut a deep gash down the beasts face as he fell.

Medlich hit the ground with a crash, breaking several bones. The dragon looked down at the commander, "That will leave a nasty scar," she said, almost respectfully, "But it will not help these fools, and it will not help you."

Slantary opened her jaw wide and scooped Medlich into he mouth. "I'll slit your throat on the way down!" the commander yelled, just before Slantary slammed her jaw closed, ripping Medlich in two with her razor sharp teeth.

"That's what they all say." Slantary laughed as she turned her attention back to the battle. Medlich's precious city guard were all but dead, the fight had been won. Legion would be pleased with her victory.

"The last of the guard are on the run my lady!" called one of the knights.

"Don't worry, my orcs will find them." Kevgeon added as he approached, his mighty axe covered in blood.

"And what of the civilians?" the knight asked.

"They can live for now, the city is ours." Slantary replied, "There pathetic little lives need not change much, beyond the fact that I am their new mistress."

Chapter 18
A Love Reborn

The Guillotine had been in dock for a couple of hours when the two cloaked figures approached the boarding plank.

"We are looking for Laucian Galanodel." The woman's voice was soft and sweet; she was wearing a pale green cloak while her companion wore a sky blue cloak. Both carried finely crafted bows and swords.

"Who might that be?" asked the sailor, who was under strict instructions not to talk to anyone about the ships passengers.

"We know he was travelling on this ship, and so do his enemies." the woman explained. The sailor just looked at the woman with a dumb expression on his face. It was a look he had perfected for if he was accused of cheating during games of chance.

"No idea who you're talking about," said the sailor eventually as he shook his head.

"Let us speak with the captain." the cloaked man was also soft spoken, although he still spoke with great authority.

"And who are you to ask for my attention?" Janemita asked as she walked down the boarding plank.

"Captain," greeted the sailor, "They are asking after someone by the name of Laucian." The captain looked from the sailor to the two cloaked figures.

"There is no-one of that name on board my ship." Janemita turned to walk away.

"Then maybe we are already too late to save his life." the man replied.

Janemita stopped and turned her head, "Who are you?"

The man lowered the hood of his cloak to reveal pale skin, long brown hair, and the pointed ears of an elf, "My name is Pattumal Galanodel. Laucian is my brother."

"You had best come on board."

$$*\qquad*\qquad*$$

Laucian and the others had already reached the palace by the time Pattumal had boarded the Guillotine. Laucian and Elana were leading everyone through one of the secret passages they had found whilst exploring the palace when Elana had lived there. They had decided upon this route instead of the front gate because the legion of Strakstaw had been slipping their soldiers into the palace guard for years, and wished to keep their presence secret for as long as possible.

It wasn't long before the group were walking the passage outside the king's throne room. Two guards stood by the door, one of whom looked to have the mark of the legion of Strakstaw showing slightly under his armour.

"Is there another way in?" Aramil asked, "I doubt his orders match our needs."

"Not that we can access from here, this is the only way." Elana replied with a glance at Laucian.

"Halt!" said the mercenary guard, "What is your busyness here?"

"I am here to see my father." Elana stepped up to the guards. Both men looked at each other, they had been told the princess was missing, presumed dead. Yet here she was, standing before them.

"The king has ordered that no-one be admitted my lady," the mercenary stuttered.

"I'm sure that does not include you though, my lady." The other guard added as he moved towards the door. The mercenary knew he was going to be in trouble for this. The other guard opened the door and stepped into the throne room.

"I said I was not to be disturbed!" The voice sounded strained, but still held a commanding edge.

"I apologise my lord, but your daughter has returned." the king rose his head as the guard spoke, "She wishes to speak with you." Elana and the others passed the guard who backed out of the room, closing the door behind him.

The king looked old and weak, much weaker than Elana and Laucian remembered him. He was sitting hunched over in his throne, he looked to have been taken by some wasting sickness. Elana ran to her father, kneeling just in front of him and grasping hold of his hand. The others stayed back, this was a private moment between father and daughter.

Elana talked quietly with her father for a long time, explaining to him what had happened to her. She told him how Deventis had tried to have her killed, she told him the plans of the mercenaries he thought to be his friends.

The king slowly rose to his feet, "Master Galanodel, it seems I owe you a great debt," Laucian bowed his head respectfully, "If not for you my daughter would still be locked away from me."

"I only did what I thought to be right your grace." Laucian replied.

"And you four, my daughter tells me that I should help you. She says you will bring down these mercenaries I thought my friends."

"We will do all that is necessary to protect this world." said Kimanay.

"And all you need is my sceptre?"

"That is right your grace, and we will use it to bring vengeance onto those who betrayed you." Larenor answered.

The king looked at his daughter. He had put his trust in the legion of Strakstaw for many years, but now his daughter, his own flesh and blood, was telling him they were simply using him for their own gains. She told him that they had tried to kill her because she had learned too much.

"You are welcome to the sceptre. It is in Baknul's quarters, he has been studying it." At that moment the door to the throne room burst open. Deventis stormed into the room followed by a large number of his mercenaries, along with the necromancer Baknul.

"My king," Deventis began, "Do not listen to these fools, they would poison your mind against your friends and allies."

"My friends and allies?" the king spat, "You tried to kill my daughter and have the nerve to call yourself my friend? I'll have your head for this!" the king straightened to his full hight as he spoke, regaining much of his old commanding presence.

Deventis sighed and turned to one of his men, "Kill him." The mercenary fired his crossbow at the king hitting him square in the chest, the king fell backwards. Elana dropped to the floor at her fathers side as the others drew their weapons.

"What are you planning to do with those?" laughed Deventis, "You are outnumbered three to one in this room alone, and I have a hundred more men out in the hall."

"We could take them," Larenor said as he aimed his bow from one mercenary to another.

"Maybe you could fight your way out of this room, but what then?" Deventis asked, "You would still have to get out of the palace, and then through the city, and then all the way back to your little ship, by which time I could have killed you many times over."

"He's right," Elana stood from her fathers side, "We would never make it out of the palace."

"So what do you suggest?" Aramil asked.

"Lower your weapons," Elana said, "We'll go quietly." The others looked at Elana, they could see the tears streaming down her cheeks. They knew that she was right, if they lowered their weapons they stood a chance of getting out of this alive, so they did as they were told.

"Take the princess and these four fools down to the dungeon, they can keep my son company." Deventis ordered, "And place extra guards down there." Some of the mercenaries led Elana, Aramil and his companions away to the dungeons.

"And what of him?" Baknul asked,indicating Laucian as he spoke.

Deventis shrugged, "Kill him." Deventis walked towards the door, "When you are done with him head to the dungeons, I want you watching over these prisoners personally." With that the viperian left the room.

Baknul turned back to Laucian with an evil smile. There were still a large number of mercenaries in the room, and Laucian knew it was unlikely he could defeat them all. He slowly edged towards the throne, trying to make it look like he was finding a better angle at which to engage his enemies.

"I've been waiting a long time for this." Baknul had never tried to hide his dislike for Laucian, and was overjoyed that he now had the chance to finally kill him. The necromancer reached under his robes and began muttering words of magic. As Baknul stretched out his arm again a column of fire erupted from the palm of his hand. The flames engulfed the throne, the kings body, and Laucian. The other mercenaries backed away from the heat, and when the flames finally died down the room and been decimated. The throne had been melted and the body of the king was nowhere to be seen, and the only trace left of Laucian was the charred remains of his two knives.

"Where are the bodies?" One mercenary asked.

"That is the beauty of that spell," Baknul replied, "Nothing to clean up afterwards."

*   *   *

The walk to the dungeon was not a long one; the palace layout seemed to have been designed so that anyone condemned within the throne room would not be walking the corridors for long.

The group were led into a large round room filled with weaponry, some of it old and rusted and some that looked fairly new, and still had a shine to it. One item stood out to Elana, it was a spear made out of a strange twisted orange wood. Elana recognised it immediately as the spear carried by her lover Tanay.

"Leave your weapons here." Ordered the mercenary commander. The prisoners reluctantly did as they were told, each of them feeling that this could very well be the last time they saw their favoured weapons. They were then led through a door at the far side of the room. This door led into a long corridor with bars running down both sides. They could see that some of the cells still contained the bones of previous residents. Only one appeared to be currently occupied by the living, a young man with short brown hair was sitting in the corner of one cell, his arms chained to the wall.

"Put the princess in with him, it'll be a nice reunion for them." the commander ordered, "Put the others two to a cell." Larenor and Delensa were placed in one cell, Aramil and Kimanay in another.

Elana was shoved into the cell with the man, where she crouched by his side. "Hello my love." she whispered in his ear. Tanay smiled, it had been a long time since he had heard her voice.

"I knew you were alive." Tanay looked Elana in the eyes as he spoke, "Even after all this time, I knew you lived."

"Not for too much longer though." Everyone looked round to see Baknul walk by the cells, accompanied by a couple more mercenaries. "Soon you will he joining your friend Laucian."

"What have you done to him?" Delensa asked.

"Oh he is quite dead my dear." Baknul replied with a smirk.

"Yeah, we completely disintegrated him," added one of the mercenaries.

"There was no body?" Tanay was smiling as he asked the question.

"All that was left were his burned daggers." Tanay laughed as the mercenary spoke.

"You find this funny?" Baknul asked.

"You are about to learn an important lesson Baknul, if you are trying to kill Laucian and there is no body, then he isn't dead." Tanay explained.

"Don't worry too much though," Elana added, "You are in no way the first to make that mistake."

*   *   *

Tanay had been right to doubt Laucian's death, although he had suffered some minor burns Laucian had easily made it to the secret passage behind the throne before Baknul's spell could claim him.

Laucian was now using the secret passages he had found while exploring the palace with his friends. He was taking the quickest possible route to Baknul's chambers.

<I've been waiting for you to show up.> Laucian didn't really hear the voice, it was more like the words just appeared in his mind, but he recognised them immediately. Laucian looked around and sure enough there was Coran, Tanay's familiar.

"It has been too long my friend, is your master about?" Laucian asked with a smile.

<Tanay is currently residing in the dungeon.> Coran replied.

"Well I will have to save him later, first I must retrieve something from Baknul's room."

<He told you of her then?>

Laucian was confused by the comment, "Told me of who?"

<Silvana.>

Laucian leaned back against the wall as he remembered the beautiful woman he had fallen in love with. It seemed like so long ago now, but she still remained the one true beacon of light in the darkness of his past. He remembered the day she had died, she had been murdered in front of him and he had been powerless to save her.

"What about her?" Laucian's voice almost cracked as he spoke.

<Baknul resurrected her with his dark magic,> the familiar paused for a moment, unable to carry through his thoughts, <She is Baknul's slave.>

Laucian was running now, his mind filled with both hatred for the damned necromancer, and love for Silvana. Baknul's chambers were at the highest point of the eastern tower. The door to the first room was locked, but that did not slow Laucian. As he slammed through the door he sprang several traps Baknul had in place, but by the time the poisoned darts would have hit Laucian he was already half way across the room.

"Is that you my lord?" Laucian recognised the voice instantly, it was Silvana. Laucian stopped dead as a door at the far side of the room opened and a young woman walked through. She was tall and slim with long dark hair, she was just as beautiful as Laucian remembered. The woman gasped when she saw who was standing before her.

"Silvana," it was all Laucian was able to say before the woman ran and embraced him.

"I thought they had killed you." she said.

"I thought I saw them kill you." Laucian replied quietly. A tear rolled down his cheek. The pair held each other for a long time. Silvana explained how Baknul had returned her to life only a few days after her murder. She explained that the mage now had some kind of magical control over her, she explained that she could not stop herself from doing *anything* he commanded of her.

"I will kill him for what he has done to you!" Laucian vowed.

"The you must promise me one thing."

"Anything."

"Promise me, when you have killed Baknul, promise me, you will come back here and burn my body."

Laucian's knees almost gave way underneath him, "What?"

"When Baknul dies his magic dies with him, I die with him."

"No! I cannot loose you again."

"Please Laucian, you must do this for me. This is not a life worth living. I want to know that I cannot be brought back again."

"We could leave," Laucian suggested, "You and me, we could go away, we could be together forever."

"I cannot leave, I am bound by his magic," Laucian couldn't speak, his grief threatened to consume him. "I will always be with you Laucian, as long as you keep me in your heart. Now go, do this for me." Laucian looked into her hazel eyes, he knew she was right, she was always right. Laucian looked around the room, the sceptre he had come for lay on a table by the door.

Laucian turned back to Silvana; he kissed her and said "I will do as you ask." Laucian backed away, before turning to retrieve the sceptre.

"I love you." Silvana said.

Laucian couldn't bring himself to look at her again, if he did he knew he would never be able to leave, with tears streaming down his face he said "I love you too."

Laucian walked from the room. Coran had been waiting outside, knowing it was best that he left Laucian and Silvana alone for their reunion.

"Take this to the dock," Laucian handed held the sceptre out for Coran, "There is a ship called the Guillotine, they are friends."

<And what of you?>

"I go to free your master," Laucian answered, "And I have a promise to keep." Coran gripped the sceptre in his claws and flew out of a window as Laucian headed for the dungeon.

*　　*　　*

Baknul sat on a chair by the door leading into the corridor of cells. There were another ten mercenaries scattered around the top few cells. Most were talking quietly amongst themselves. The prisoners all sat in silence, not seeing much need to talk to one another.

Everyone looked round when they heard a loud scraping sound coming from the far end of the corridor. The mercenaries squinted to see what the sound was, it looked as though the wall was moving, it slid open to reveal another passageway behind it. Laucian walked out of the darkness, much to the surprise of Baknul and the mercenaries.

"I did tell you," Tanay laughed, "No body, then he's still alive."

"Well I won't make that mistake again." Baknul stood from his chair, outstretched his and muttered a few words of magic. This time a green gas erupted from his fingers. The gas travelled down the corridor with unnatural speed, passing by the mercenaries before engulfing Laucian. Everyone listened as Laucian roared in pain, they even thought they could heard the sound of bones cracking. Tanay shook his head and laughed.

"What is so funny?" Baknul asked, "Your friend is dying and you laugh?"

"I just find it amusing that you would use poisoned mist, on a man who doesn't breath."

Laucian's roar stopped, and was instead replaced by a deep throaty laugh. The smile disappeared from Tanay's face, he had heard that laugh only once before, and he had no wish to recall the scenes that had followed.

"Laucian! No!" Tanay yelled, but it was too late.

Laucian launched himself out of the gas cloud, straight at the closest mercenary, his arms outstretched. Laucian's face had changed greatly, he had called upon his psionic abilities to transform his jaw into one which resembled that of a wolf, with an elongated snout, black fur, and razor sharp teeth. His finger nails had also been elongated too, becoming claws which he embedded into the mercenary's chest.

The man fell backwards to the floor, Laucian crouched over him with his claws still cutting deeply into the man's chest. Laucian sniffed at the man's face, "I can smell your fear," Laucian growled, "It's like an elixir to me, it intoxicates me."

"Laucian, please don't do this." Elana was standing by the bars, she was afraid for her friend, she was afraid that if he gave in to his primal rage then he would be lost forever.

Laucian looked at her for a moment, nobody mover, nobody dared. Laucian let out a low growl before turning his attention back to the man he was crouching over. Within the blink of the eye he wrapped his jaws around the man's throat, biting down hard. Still gripping the throat Laucian reared up to his full hight, leaving the man lying dead on the floor, as his blood was sprayed across those cells near by.

Laucian stood there for a moment, blood dripping from his claws and bits of flesh hanging from his mouth. The mercenaries could only stare at the scene before them, they had only seen such brutality before from the wildest of beasts, and they knew that they would be next.

"Kill him!" Baknul yelled as he tried to think of a suitable spell to deal with this new threat. Laucian had killed another three mercenaries before they had even been able to draw their weapons, ripping out each of their throats. The rest faired no better. Laucian was too fast, he was jumping from one side of the corridor to the other, slashing with his claws as he went and biting down on any who got too close.

It wasn't long before Laucian was standing face to face with Baknul. The entire dungeon was covered in blood; the prisoners had turned away, some feeling nauseous from the carnage they had just witnessed.

Baknul was shaking with fear, he was trying his hardest to think of a spell, but the stench of blood was driving them all from his thoughts.

"I saw her wizard!" Laucian growled, "She told me what you made her do!"

"Laucian, what are you talking about?" Tanay asked.

"Tell them! Tell them how you resurrected Silvana," Baknul tried to back away, but only managed two steps before he was up against the wall. "Tell them how you used her as your slave!" Laucian growled.

"Laucian please, you're not a murderer." Elana pleaded.

"TELL THEM HOW YOU USED HER AS YOU PERSONAL CONCUBINE!" Laucian roared, "YOU COULDN'T HAVE HER IN LIFE, SO YOU RAPED HER IN DEATH!"

"Kill him." Larenor said calmly.

"I would." Aramil added.

"She loved me," Laucian said quietly, "She still loves me. You could only have her through magic."

"If I die, then she dies with me..." It was all Baknul could think to say, hoping to save his own life.

"I know. She told me. She told me to kill you. She would rather die than live any longer as your slave." Laucian ran a claw down the side of Baknul's face. "She would have killed you herself, if not for your sick control spell."

"Please..." Baknul begged.

"I do this for her." Laucian rammed his claws into Baknul's chest, digging them in deep. "I do this for vengeance." Laucian ripped his hand back out of Baknul's chest. The last thing the necromancer saw before he slipped into oblivion was Laucian biting into his heart.

No-one moved for a moment, a deathly silence falling over the dungeon. Eventually Laucian took the cell keys from Baknul's corpse and threw them to Elana, "Let yourselves out and head back to the ship. I have sent Coran ahead with the sceptre."

"Where are you going?" Tanay asked.

"I have a promise to keep."

Chapter 19
Fight or Flight

By the time Laucian had gotten back to Baknul's chambers the last sparks of life had faded away from Silvana. Laucian found her lying on the bed. She looked like she was sleeping, but Laucian knew she would have died only moments after he had killed Baknul.

Laucian leaned over Silvana, his face and hands returned to normal, though still covered in blood. He couldn't bring himself to touch the woman; he didn't want to ruin this perfect image of her.

Eventually Laucian rose from Silvana's side, he picked up a lamp from Baknul's table and poured the oil over the bed and Silvana's body. "I love you." Tears filled Laucian's eyes, "I'm sorry." He lit the oil, standing and watching it burn for a moment before he turned and left the room.

As Laucian made his way down the tower he splashed more oil on the walls and floor. When he finally stepped outside he turned and lit this oil too. The flames spread quickly throughout the tower, and Laucian stood and watched as the tower was consumed, destroying all the research of the foul necromancer who had called it home. Thought's of Silvana were running through his mind, memories of the happiest time of his life, a time that was now over.

Laucian finally turned away. Walking back towards the ship he called upon his psionic abilities once more, the claws and wolf jaw returning. He was not expecting this to be an easy trip.

*　　*　　*

"Where is Laucian?" Janemita asked as the others boarded her ship.

"He had some busyness to attend to." Aramil replied.

"He will be here." Elana added.

"Captain," Janemita turned to see her first mate, "Laucian may be here, but they'll be here first." Galik was pointing back up towards the palace, smoke could be seen rising from the far tower, and a small army was emerging from the gates.

"Prepare to make sail." Janemita said quietly.

"You cannot just leave my brother here." Pattumal said as he walked up to everyone. Most of whom were shocked by his announcement, except Aramil who recognised Laucian's brother from his childhood.

"I have no intention of leaving Laucian, but I plan on being ready when he arrives." Janemita snapped. "Now can you use that bow? Or do you just carry it for decoration?"

"I can use it." Pattumal replied.

"Galik, get the crew ready, this will be a hard fight."

"Aye captain." Galik ran across the deck barking orders as he went, the sailors were quick to respond. Men and women ran into position, they loaded cannons and readied the sails. A row of archers lined the side of the ship, joined by Pattumal and his companion, along with Laucian's companions.

It didn't take the soldiers long to reach the docks, stopping a little away from the ship. One man stepped forward from the others. "You will surrender your ship to me," he called, "If you fail to do so, we will take it by force."

Everyone looked around, the crew of the Guillotine was a formidable force, but they would not be able to hold back this many soldiers for long.

"I am waiting for your answer!" The soldier called.

"He wants an answer captain," shouted Galik with a smile, "Should I give him one?"

"No." Janemita replied, "As captain of this ship, that duty is mine." The captain strung and arrow in her bow and drew it back. Her aim was perfect, the soldier was dead before he hit the ground.

There was a moment of silence before another of the soldiers shouted, "Take the ship!" With that the small army surged forward, just as Janemita's crew opened fire.

The archers took out the front lines of soldiers, Benny's hand cannon proved to be a devastatingly effective weapon, and the cannons tore through the soldiers. The most effective attacks however came from Tanay. The young sorcerer was using some of his most powerful spells, he detonated balls of fire in the middle of the soldiers killing dozens at a time and sent torrents of lightning causing through others.

The Guillotine's crew were doing an excellent job of holding their attackers at bay, but there were just too many, and they were starting to get dangerously close to the ship.

"There he is!" Larenor shouted, pointing towards the palace. Sure enough they could see a lone figure charging towards the rear of the soldiers. The soldiers were not expecting an attack from behind, and were woefully unprepared for such an attack to come from a seemingly psychotic man with claws and a wolf's jaw.

"Cover him!" Janemita ordered. Several of her archers fired at the soldiers closing in on Laucian, but he didn't need their help. Laucian was cutting a bloody path straight towards the Guillotine, and it wasn't long before he broke though the front line of soldiers.

"Set sail!" Janemita ordered. Sailors began to pull the main sheet as others cut the mooring lines, within seconds the ship was moving. Janemita dropped her bow and ran to the aft of the ship, grabbing a rope as she did. The ship pulled away from the docks as Laucian got close, he sprinted along the pier and launched himself off the end. As Laucian jumped Janemita threw the end of the rope, Laucian caught hold and swung to the side of the ship and began climbing.

The soldiers stopped short of the water, they knew that the ship had escaped, there was nothing in their navy that could match the Guillotine for speed. By the time Laucian had climbed the rope the was a small welcoming party waiting for him, Janemita, Galik, Benny and all those he had rescued from the dungeons.

No-one spoke, they all just stared at Laucian. He was covered in blood, and had bits of flesh hanging from his jaw. He walked straight past everyone and across the deck, the claws and wolf jaw returning to normal as he did. As he crossed the deck Pattumal approached him.

"Hello brother, it has been a long time." Laucian glanced at the elf and let out a low growl as he passed him. Pattumal turned to follow but was stopped by Tanay placing a hand on his shoulder.

"Let him be for now." Laucian had reached the side rail as Tanay spoke; he was leaning over the side, being sick.

"I have never seen someone affected by sea sickness so quickly," Pattumal said.

"That is not sea sickness," Tanay replied, "What you need to understand is that all the blood in and around his mouth, it is not his own."

Nobody approached Laucian for a long time, after he had finished being sick he had sat leaning on the rail. Eventually someone did approach, but it was not someone he would have expected.

"I may have been wrong about you." Laucian looked up to see Aramil standing in front of him. "I was told not very long ago that I needed to put my trust in people that I wouldn't usually, I think that includes you."

"What are you talking about?" Laucian's voice was quiet and withdrawn.

"I was told that you had murdered people, I was told you were a cold blooded killer." Aramil explained, "But now I find myself asking, if you are this evil man then why are you helping us? Why are you risking your life to help those who insult you?"

"I'm not here to help you." Laucian answered as he got to his feet, "I am here because even with the evil this world holds, despite the fact that innocent people can be murdered and even abused after death, I still believe that this world is worth saving." Laucian walked passed Aramil.

Aramil caught Laucian by the arm, "I was wrong about you, I see that now. I may not agree with the methods you used in that dungeon, but I do understand. You are a good man." Laucian shrugged Aramil's hand off his arm and began to walk away. "Even if you do hide it so well." Aramil called after him.

Laucian retired to his cabin, where he found a bowl of warm water left there by Benny. The gnome had know Laucian would want to wash the blood away.

"We need to talk." Pattumal had followed Laucian to his cabin.

"What do you want?"

"Father has sent me to bring you home."

"We both know he is not my father." Laucian finally turned to face Pattumal.

"He may not be your true father, but he still raised you as his son. You may not be my brother by blood, but I still love you as one."

Laucian laughed, "I see you still wear the cloak made for you by the human girl."

"And wouldn't you wear the cloak made by the woman you married?" Pattumal's female companion walked in behind the elf.

"It is good to see you Maria." Laucian said as he looked at the woman, "I imagine father did not approve."

"He's dying Laucian." Pattumal said, "He wants to see you before the end; he says there are things he must tell you."

"What is wrong with him?" Laucian asked, a little concern showing in his voice.

"Both he and mother became ill, no-one could find the cause." A tear came to Pattumal's eye, "Mother died a few weeks later, but father held on, he sent me to find you. That was three months ago."

"Then he has probably died already."

"No. The healers put him into a magical sleep; he will live until we return." Pattumal explained, "But we must go now."

"I am sorry Pattumal, but I am not returning with you."

"What? Why?"

"I am involved in something here. I cannot just turn my back on this war." Laucian said, "Father always told me I had to see things through to the end, and that is exactly what I must do."

"Well I am not to return without you." Pattumal smiled, "So you had best tell me about this war of yours."

"What about your father?" Maria asked.

"The magical sleep will hold until we return." said Pattumal, "Besides, from what I have already heard, this war seems to be of great importance."

"So we finally get to have a grand adventure together, just like we planned as children." Laucian added.

"So tell us Laucian, what exactly are we fighting for here?" Maria asked. She may have been but a child when she last saw Laucian and Pattumal together, but she still knew that despite their differences when they decided to do something together, they would see it through to the end, no matter what.

*   *   *

Randars pass was was rarely used any more. Men did not pass this way because it led deep into the mountains, where they were likely to find little more than the tip of an orcish spear, if they were lucky. The creatures of the mountains never came this way because it only led them to the grassy plains below, and away from the relative safety of their mountain home.

Randars pass was busy this night. The pass itself was little more than a clearing between the some rocky slopes and some cliffs. Tonight the clearing was filled filled by all manner of beasts and creatures, most standing in awe of Grakenster and his two ogre body guards, Nantic and Ardes. The hobgoblin was speaking to all those that had gathered, even if this demon knight proved unworthy Grakenster would still profit from this gathering, he would gain more followers into his army.

Those gathered did not have long to wait for Jamaan's arrival. He boldly walked into the centre of the clearing, exactly as and when Orshanus said he would. Everyone present fell silent as they watched the knight, even Grakenster stopped trying to coerce people into his army.

"I am Jamaan son of Jameel, and I am here to call you to action!" Jamaan announced, "I am here to lead you to war!" There was a low murmur in the crowd as the creatures of the mountains discussed Jamaan's statement.

"Why we follow you?" one goblin yelled.

"I not bow to puny human!" a hobgoblin added.

"I do not ask you to bow to me. All I ask is that you follow me into battle, a battle to defend your lands as well as mine."

"Defend our lands against what?" Grakenster asked, making sure he would be a part of discussion.

"There is a mighty army on its way," Jamaan explained, "And if we do not stand against it as one then it will destroy us all in turn."

"I do not see any army," Grakenster walked up to Jamaan, "All I see is you, and you do not impress me."

"I am not here to impress you," Jamaan replied, not backing down as the hobgoblin growled at him. "You will follow me out of these mountains into battle, or you will all die in your holes."

"You are very brave to threaten me, human." Grakenster smiled, "Or very foolish."

"He is both!" Everyone scattered as the demon prince swooped into the clearing, even Grakenster and his body guards fled before the might demon. Only Jamaan stayed barely flinching as the monster landed in front of him.

Jamaan recognised the beast instantly; he had been looking for this monster ever since it had tainted his blood. The demon stood almost twice the hight of Jamaan, its red scaled hide shining in the moonlight. The demon folded its bat like wings behind its back and snarled with its canine like face as it drew a huge sword.

"I have been looking for you," the beast growled.

"I'm sure you have." Jamaan snapped.

"Did I find you at a bad time?" the demon laughed, "I seem to have scared away your little army." Although the orcs, goblins, and other creatures had fled at the sight of the beast, they all watched now from a safe distance. They wanted to see if this knight was as strong as their god Orshanus had claimed.

"They will be back." Jamaan replied calmly.

"And why would they do that?"

"Because they are going to follow me out of these mountains."

"You still do not understand your role in this world do you?" the demon laughed again, "You are my slave, you will bow to my will, or you will die."

"I will never serve you!"

"So be it." The demon struck fast, slashing hard with its sword. Jamaan was barley able to raise his shield quick enough to block the attack, though this did little to help Jamaan. The strength of the blow threw the paladin across the clearing as well as breaking his shield in two.

"You are weak!" the demon yelled. Jamaan saw the demon leaping across the clearing and quickly rolled out of the way as the beast's sword cut deeply into the ground where Jamaan had been lying.

The paladin was back on his feet now, sword in hand and ready for any move the demon might make. The beast attacked again and Jamaan parried the blow, knowing he could not match the demon's strength he moved with the attack, spinning to the side in an attempt to attack the demon from behind. The balor was prepared for this however, it lashed out with its tail catching Jamaan in the chest, again launching him across the clearing. Jamaan hit the ground hard, dropping his sword and loosing his helmet as he did.

The demon walked slowly towards the fallen paladin, "I offered you such power, such strength." said the prince of the abyss. "And this is the thanks I get?" Jamaan tried to get to his feet, but the demon kicked him back into the dirt. "All I asked is that you accept the gifts I have given you. Wake up the demon inside you and serve at my side. Instead you have chosen weakness, you have chosen death." The demon raised its sword above its head, before bringing it down and stabbing it through Jamaan's chest.

It was at this point Grakenster made his move. The hobgoblin did not want to look a coward in front of so many who could fill the ranks of his army, and he was sure that he had a better plan than this knight had.

Grakenster charged across the clearing, flanked on either side by his ogre bodyguards. The demon span around to face them, just to be hit in the chest by a volley of arrows from others who had stayed to watch. The beast roared, more in frustration than pain.

It easily avoided Grakenster's attack by side stepping the hobgoblin, but this led it straight into the path of Ardes who struck his spear into the demon's side. The beast grabbed hold of the ogre by the throat as Nantic attacked from behind. The demon spun around faster than should be possible for a beast its side, it dragged Ardes in front of Nantic's charge. Ardes screamed in pain as Nantic's spear ripped though its back. The demon threw the dead ogre to the side before punching Nantic in the face with the hilt of its sword, sending the ogre sprawling to the floor.

Grakenster was attacking again, but the demon caught hold of the hobgoblin's head and threw him backwards. The demon stalked over to Grakenster, "You mortals really are quite foolish." The monster laughed as it stood over the hobgoblin.

"Leave him be!" The demon looked over its shoulder to see Jamaan stood across the clearing with sword in hand. The demon could see that the knight was taller than he had been, and had leathery wings sprouting from his back. The beast smiled.

"You have finally accepted the gifts I offered you." The demon walked towards Jamaan slightly, "Now we shall hunt these pathetic little creatures together, as it should be."

"You will hunt nothing this day; I shall make sure of that."

The demon's smile faded and was replaced by a look of confusion, "You accept my power, yet still defy me?"

Jamaan laughed, "What's the matter? Has the world become a scary place, now that you've woken up the demon..." Jamaan charged forward, "IN ME!"

The beast braced itself for Jamaan's attack, but at the last moment the knight sprang to the side, bringing his sword in low. He sliced his holy sword across the demon's stomach, the beast doubled over in pain as Jamaan reversed the grip on his sword slashing it across the back of the demon's knee. The beast howled in pain again, not understanding how this mere mortal was able to bring him down to this level so easily. Jamaan swung his sword back again, this time aiming for the demon prince's throat. The mighty demon fell dead to the floor as its head rolled away from its body. Jamaan walked up to the demon's decapitated head and plunged his sword through it, impaling the loathsome thing to the ground. Jamaan stood there for a moment before he too fell to the ground.

Grakenster was by Jamaan's side almost instantly, he could see the huge hole in the paladin's chest where the demon had impaled him earlier. The hobgoblin watched as Jamaan's skin lost its red colour and returned to dark tone it had been when he was fully human. The bugbear watched as the last sparks of Jamaan's life drained away from his body.

The others who had fled began to return to the clearing, they all wanted to see what remained in the aftermath of the battle. Grakenster got back to his feet and turned to face the crowd.

" Orshanus said we should follow this knight if he proved worthy." the hobgoblin began, "Well he proved himself to me. I will fight his war." The others looked on in silence as Grakenster continued, "My army will march out of the mountains in three days. Who is brave enough to help me avenge this mighty warrior?" All those in the clearing cheered loudly.

"I bring my tribe! We follow you!" An orc yelled.

"The goblins of Deephole pledge you allegiance!"

These declarations of loyalty continued for some time. Grakenster smiled, not only was he going to war but he knew that every tribe would be going with him, under his banner. Now the Four Kings mountains would have but one king, and his name was Grakenster.

Chapter 20
Legion

"Why are we here?"

"What do you want?"

"Who is the beast?"

"Where is the honour guard?"

"When will the client arrive?"

Markus hated it when the council spoke like this. He knew full well that it was all for show, they only ever spoke together like this when they were trying to impress of confuse those present. Only today they impressed no-one.

The five council members looked to one another, they were not used to being ignored. They were the leaders of the largest mercenary force Gallisium had ever known, but still their words seemed to fall upon deaf ears. Instead Markus just appeared to be overseeing a large creature positioning an oval ring made of gold and silver interlocking links, while Deventis was drawing strange symbols on the floor.

"Why are we here?"

"What do you want?"

"Who is the beast?"

"Where is the honour guard?"

"When will the client arrive?"

"Oh do be quiet." Markus turned to face the council.

"You will not speak to us this way."

"You will answer our questions."

"As you wish." Markus smiled as he spoke, "You are here because I summoned you. What I want is to sacrifice you along with the blood of an innocent to open the gateway for Legion to enter our world. The beast is a willing servant of our true master, and the honour guard along with the clients of this area are all dead."

The council looked to one another again, "We do not understand."

"This is not how the legion of Strakstaw works."

"You do not give the orders."

"You serve us."

"We command you to submit."

"They always talk too much," Havak laughed, "That is one thing that never changes."

"The runes are complete my lord." said Deventis as he walked up behind Markus. The general smiled as his companion spoke; he had waited for this moment for so many years.

"Bring the innocent." he ordered. Deventis nodded and walked from the room. "As for you, I think you should notice that amongst the runes my colleague has drawn there are five circles. I would appreciate it if each of you could go stand in one of them."

"What is the meaning of this?"

"How dare you..."

"You will do as commanded!" Havak interrupted, "Or I will tear you limb from limb." The council members looked to one another again before they each gazed at the menacing form of Havak. It was plain to see that the beast could easily make good on its threat, so they decided to do as they had been ordered.

The five council members remained silent as they stood in the circles drawn on the floor. Each one studied the runes around them, attempting to decipher their meaning in an attempt to find a way out of this sacrifice Markus had spoken of.

It wasn't long before Deventis re-entered the room, he was pushing a pixie in front of him. The poor creature has both its hands and wings bound behind its back. The pixie stood no mare than two foot high, with long pointed ears. Her brightly coloured clothes set against the grim expression on her face; the usual joy and prankster nature found amongst pixies had been sapped entirely from Deventis's prisoner.

Deventis pushed the pixie to the middle of the room, just in front of where general Markus stood. "I doubt this is what you expected to happen when you first crossed my path." Deventis chuckled. The pixie looked up at Deventis as he backed away. The viperian was right, the pixie had first crossed paths with Deventis a few months previous and had decided to set free the horses belonging to him and his companions. The pixie had judged them to be of ill intent and thought it would be amusing to slow their expedition, only to find that their security had been far superior than she had expected. Since then the pixie had been locked away in a dark room, away from her precious sunlight.

Markus started talking in a strange language that only Havak recognised, he had heard these words many times before. The pixie and council members watched the general as he spoke. Markus pulled out a knife from his belt, the long serrated blade shining in the torchlight as he held it above his head. As Markus continued to speak a bolt of lightning shot out from the top of the gateway, it struck the blade which began to hiss and spark with the lightnings power.

Markus took hold of the pixies clothes and hoisted her into the air, the poor creature closed her eyes knowing full well what was going to happen next. Markus called out another word of power as he stuck the knife deep into the pixies stomach. As Markus stabbed the pixie five more bolts of lightning erupted from the gateway, each one striking the council members square in the chest. Each of them screamed in pain as the flow of the lightning reversed its direction, drawing the life force out of each member of the council. As the council members began to wither up Markus held the pixie up in the middle of the gateway, its lifeblood dripping on the floor, Markus spoke one final word of power before slicing the pixies head clean off in one quick movement.

The general was forced backwards as a blinding flash of light erupted from the gateway. By the time Markus could see again the pixie had vanished, and the council members were little more than piles of dust. The gateway itself now had a shimmering light in the centre of its interlocking rings.

Havak was smiling broadly as his master came into view. A clawed hand reached through the gateway, digging deeply into the floor. Muscles tightened on the green scaled arm as it pulled the rest of the beast through the gateway. The metal rings creaked as the monster's body pressed against the edge's of the gateway, forcing them wide enough for his body to pass through.

When the beast had fully made its way though the gateway it stood about ten feet tall, his muscular torso, arms and head were covered in deep green scales, and his legs in dark brown fur, and it had large brown bat like wings on its back. A huge sword hung at the beasts side, it had a black hilt and a blood red blade with golden runes along its edge.

Markus asked, "What is thy name?"

The beast answered, "My name is Legion, for we are many."

Markus, Deventis, and Havak all kneeled in the presence of their master, bowing their heads in respect. Legion stretched out its fingers and craned his neck, his bones cracking loudly as he laughed to himself.

"Arise my loyal servants," Legion's voice was deep and rough, and yet also sounded comforting, "Take me to my army."

* * *

Laucian woke with a jolt, sweat pouring down his face. This night the dream had been different, he had not seen the war of elements, he had not witnessed himself be run through by the demon. Tonight he had witnessed the death of an innocent, he had seen the life ripped from a council of five, he had seen the beast pull itself into his world. Laucian knew that Legion had arrived, time was running out and there was still so much that needed to be done.

Laucian walked up on deck, the sun was shining and the wind was light. Tanay had been using his magic to summon up a wind to help speed up their journey. Janemita was standing near the aft talking to someone Laucian didn't recognise. He could also see that that another smaller ship was tied up along side the Guillotine.

"The city has fallen." said the stranger, "Overrun by orcs and dragon knights, and the dragon itself. She's taken up residence in the palace. They've already killed the entire city guard."

"They're all dead?" Galik asked sounding both shocked and concerned.

"Aye, those who survived the initial attack were rounded up and executed. There are rumours of some who escaped, but I doubt its true."

"And Medlich?" Larenor asked.

"Dead. Killed by the dragon, but he left a scar she'll not soon forget. He died a true hero, however little good it did."

"And what of the populace?" Aramil asked.

"They continue as usual, well as usual as can be expected with a dragon as ruler." the stranger explained, "No-one really knows what's going on. Red dragons ain't really known for taking over cities, they usually just burn them down, right?"

"How did you get out?" Janemita asked what everyone was wondering.

"We were able to slip out to the docks last night; the orcs were sleeping at their posts."

"How are we going to get the elemental stones back?" Kimanay voiced the concern.

"Is it possible for anyone to get into the city?" Laucian was formulating a plan as he spoke.

"Probably after nightfall, maybe a couple of people could sneak in through the docks." the stranger replied, "But what could be worth so much to risk going back into that city?"

"I'll go," Elana said, "Quinn is guarding the stones, and he won't give them up to anyone but me."

"I will go too." Laucian said.

"And you two are not going anywhere without me." Tanay added.

"Then it is decided," said Aramil, "You three enter the city tonight, we will wait for you at the totem of elements."

*   *   *

Ivellious and Branack were not expecting to find the encampment. They had thought they'd need to travel all the way to Faknell before finding any semblance of Getandor's army. To find those who must know of Cemulion's fall.

"Hold! Who goes there?" It was plain to see from his uniform that the guard was a Getandor soldier, but those around him were clearly not soldiers of the empire.

"My name is Ivellious, and my companion is Branack. We bring word of Cemulion." Ivellious lowered his gaze, "The city has fallen."

The soldier stood there for a moment. He looked around hoping for someone to tell him what to do with the information Ivellious had just given him, but he was not that lucky.

"You had best follow me." The guard said eventually, then led Ivellious and Branack through the camp. The camp seemed to be made up of three different armies, there were the Getandor soldiers who were happily socializing with the large barbarians who made up the second army. The third army was keeping itself separate from the others; Ivellious had never seen anyone like them before, he found these horned soldiers most intriguing.

The soldier led Ivellious and Branack into a large tent in the centre of the camp, "Captain Holdak, these men bring word from Cemulion." Everyone turned to face Ivellious and Branack. The tent was already quite crowded, Holdak was there along with Aramil and Thoril who had brought the etharii, Fanell was also present. Davkul and Roscoe were also there, sitting with Malik the bear.

"What word do you bring?" Captain Holdak asked, taking a closer look at the pair.

"The city has fallen," Ivellious answered solemnly, "The guard is all but wiped out, and I believe the king has also been murdered.

"How is that possible?" Roscoe asked, in shock from the news.

"Who could do such a thing?" Holdak said quietly.

"The legion of Strakstaw." Thoril spat.

"There was an army of orcs and knights." Ivellious paused for a moment, "And a dragon." All present fell silent for a moment. It was because of King Augustus IV that many of them were here, and now he was dead and a dragon ruled his capital city.

"And what of the civilians?" Holdak asked.

"I cannot be sure. During the battle they were left alone, but now the city guard is defeated who knows what those beasts are doing?" Ivellious replied, "Commander Medlich told us to get out of the city, to tell others what happened, and that is what we did."

"And what of Medlich?" asked Roscoe, deeply concerned for his friend.

"I'm afraid he fell. He died fighting the dragon, he fought well but the beast was just too powerful." Everyone fell silent again, no-one knowing how they could stand against a dragon.

"We cannot fight such a monster." Fanell said coldly.

"But we must try." Roscoe said.

"He is right. I doubt our current force could match the legion of Strakstaw's army," Holdak explained, "But a dragon, that would destroy us."

"Do not give in to despair." Everyone turned to the tents entrance to see Magon and Solaris enter.

"Then what would you have us do, wizard?" Fanell asked, "If we try to stand up against the full might of the legion of Strakstaw their army would march straight over us."

"That is why you must find more allies." Solaris stated flatly.

"But who else will come?" Malik asked.

"I will go to my father; the elves of Landorn will join this fight."

"Even with their help we will still loose." spat Fanell.

"Has there been no word from Jamaan?" asked Thoril, "What of the army he was sent to raise?"

"There has been no word as of yet," Magon answered with a smile, "But his army should be arriving soon, very soon indeed."

"And if the sceptre of elements was successfully retrieved then those that remain of my world will be summoned soon." Solaris added.

"Will that be enough?" Roscoe asked hopefully.

"Probably not." Magon replied.

"What of the dwarves?" Solaris turned to Davkul, "Will Nasgaroth allow his *servants* to fight?" Davkul grunted in reply, but gave no real answer.

"I was told that this battle is but a diversion," Fanell began, "If that is the case then why do we bother to fight it? Why not just kill the demon and avoid his army?"

"The demon will be dealt with, but if his army runs unchecked it will damage this world so that it can never be repaired, even if the beast is destroyed." Magon replied.

"I do not understand," Malik said, "How is the army a diversion?"

"The demon's true goal is to use his ancient magic to remove all evil from the world." Magon explained.

"And what is so wrong with that?" Holdak asked.

"Without evil the balance would falter."

"I know little of what you speak," Malik said, "But I see no harm in evil being destroyed."

"I have walked this land since the dawn of your time," Solaris began, "I have seen both the good and the evil it has to offer, and both shall be saved. For without one there cannot be the other." A silence fell over all everyone; Solaris' words had struck a deep cord in all those gathered. No-one knew why, but each of them knew that he spoke the truth; deep down in their souls they knew that if all evil was truly gone from the world then it would fall apart at the seams.

"Then why do we focus on this army, and not more on the beast?" Holdak eventually asked.

"I will face the beast, along with a few select warriors. You must stop the army before it decimates your lands."

There was a sudden commotion outside the tent, people were shouting and weapons were being drawn. All those gathered ran outside, each of them holding their weapons, all except Magon and Solaris.

Everyone watched in disbelief as an army of orcs and goblins, trolls and ogres, hobgoblins and many other such creatures marched through the camp. They were being led by a large hobgoblin, it was followed closely by four orcs carrying a stretcher. They could see that someone lay on the stretcher, although they were completely covered by a cloth. The hobgoblin stopped a little way in from of those who had exited the tent, and the orcs placed the stretcher in front of their leader before joining returning to the rest of the army.

"I am Grakenster, leader of this army." the hobgoblin announced. "We answer your call to war. We will fight in the name of Jamaan son of Jameel, a warrior of true strength."

"We welcome you to our camp, and thank you for your aid," Holdak stuttered.

"Please tell us," began Roscoe, "Where is Jamaan?"

Grakenster bowed his head and looked at the stretcher, "The brave warrior fell in battle. He died protecting my kin from a mighty demon. He will be remembered by my people as a great warrior and a powerful man. I return his body to you; so that you may observe any rituals you have for the dead."

"You have our thanks." Solaris said as he crouched by the body, he placed his hand on the dead warriors head, "I hope you now find the peace in death that you sought so much in life."

"Our army is almost complete," said Adokas, "I will set out at first light to my father's kingdom, the elves will be here soon."

"But what of the dragon?" Malik asked, "How can we bring down such a monster?"

"I know one thing that could bring it down." everyone looked to Roscoe as he spoke, "I too will leave at first light, I will bring Nasgaroth to this fight." The others were shocked to hear such a bold statement from the halfling.

Solaris looked to Davkul, whose head was bowed, "I will travel with you." Davkul said quietly, he raised his head and met Solaris' gaze, "I will bring the dwarves to battle."

"Then tomorrow's plan is set," said Magon with a smile, "Come morning we will begin to set plans for the battle, but tonight we must honour our fallen friends."

"Your warriors have travelled far Grakenster," Holdak began, "I will have my soldiers help you set camp."

"You help is well appreciated." Grakenster replied.

Within the space of one evening alliances were formed between races that had been mortal enemies longer than anyone could remember.

Chapter 21
Earth Fire Wind and Water

Getting into the city had been a surprisingly easy task, as was retrieving the elemental stones from the Jolly Roger. Getting back out of the city proved more difficult, they were going to use the docks again, but the number of guards posted there had been increased as a fleet of ships could now be seen on the horizon, it was safe to assume they were carrying the bulk of the legion of Strakstaw's army. Finding another route was not too much of a problem, a quick spell from Tanay, a silent kill from Laucian, and their escape covered by shadows provided by Elana.

"What do you think will happen when they find the dead guards?" Elana asked as the trio walked the road towards the totem of elements.

"I expect they will start a search for us." Laucian replied.

"And when they don't find us?" No-one answered Elana's question. She looked to Tanay and Laucian but both avoided her gaze. Elana then turned to Quinn, her shadow companion who had dutifully guarded the elemental stones, but he too avoided her stair.

"What will happen when they don't find us?" Elana's tone was sharp, she would have an answer to her question, she would not be ignored.

"They will probably execute some of the civilians." Laucian replied coldly.

"They are going to execute people because of us?" Elana stopped as she spoke, as did Tanay and Quinn. Elana watched Laucian as he continued walking, not even noticing that the others had stopped. "Does it not even bother you that people are going to die because of us?"

Laucian stopped and looked round at Elana, "I don't like it any more than you do, but if a few must die so we can save everyone else, then it is a trade I am willing to make." Laucian turned and began walking again, followed by the others shortly after. The travelled in an uncomfortable silence from that point.

It was going to take a little more than a day to reach the totem of elements. None of the trio had ever been there before and so were not entirely sure of its location, and the rough map Aramil had drawn them was difficult to follow.

"Greetings travellers, do you have far left to go?" The group looked to see where the voice had come from. Laucian's face dropped as soon as he saw the druid Stomorel leaning on a tree up ahead.

"Hello again, what brings you so far from home?" Tanay asked in a cheery voice.

Stomorel scowled at the viperian, "Magon wanted me to show you to the totem."

"We already know how to get there," Laucian spat.

"I'm sure you do." said Stomorel, who was smiling again. "But I know a short cut."

"Well that could prove most useful, but who exactly are you?" Elana asked.

"This my dear is Stomorel," Tanay explained, "She is one of the residents at Magon's tower. She's also quite a fan of Laucian." Tanay whispered the last part of his introduction, though it was still loud enough for Laucian to hear, who scowled at the comment.

"What is this short cut?" Laucian asked.

"Tree walking," Stomorel replied, "Its an old druid trick. We can travel with a few passengers through trees. I can take us through this tree here to one mere yards away from the totem of elements. It would save you a whole days travel."

"That's impressive." Tanay replied. Stomorel placed her hand on the tree and muttered a few words under her breath. The bark of the tree seemed to lose some of its texture and became liquid.

"If you would fellow me." Stomorel turned back to the tree.

"My lady," said Quinn, "I cannot travel this way."

Elana turned to her shadow companion, "Why not?" she asked sounding concerned for her friend.

"The dark magic that creates my kind cannot exist in the same space as the natural magic she uses on the tree." Quinn explained.

Stomorel looked closely at Quinn, she had not noticed the shadow until now, "You really do pick your friends unwisely Laucian, first a viperian and now that monstrosity."

"Watch your tongue!" Elana snapped.

"Do not worry about her," Tanay said with a smile, "She has trouble seeing past people's appearances."

Stomorel scowled at the comment. "Are you coming or not?"

"I will not leave Quinn here."

"Do not worry my lady, you go this way and I shall find you after nightfall. Travelling in this sunlight is painful for me, it shall be easier for us both this way."

"He's right Elana, we have to reach the totem as soon as we can." Tanay added.

"Fine." Elana sighed, "But be careful my friend."

"As always my lady," Quinn replied, "As always."

"Then shall we go?" Stomorel asked bitterly. The druid stepped into the tree and vanished from sight. The others walked up to the tree, looking to each other before following. Laucian entered the tree first followed by Tanay and Elana. The trip was a strange sensation; it felt like they were being dragged through mud, it wasn't long before the trio were standing in a clearing surrounded by dense woodland. As Tanay and Elana emerged from the tree they were greeted by the sound of Laucian laughing.

"And you insult the company I keep." Laucian was still laughing as he spoke, while Stomorel and the assassin Aluthana looked at him smiling.

"Did I forget to mention that it was me who let my good friend here into Magon's tower?" Laughed Stomorel as a great many soldiers began to surround Laucian Tanay and Elana.

"Now I feel it is my duty to inform you that there are about five bows aimed at each of you." Aluthana explained with a grin.

"So why don't you just kill us then?" Laucian asked.

"Because of you actually." Aluthana replied, "Now don't miss understand me, you are all going to die, but first I want to have another shot at you. One on one." Laucian smiled and walked towards the assassin. Both of them dropped their cloaks to the ground as Stomorel and the soldiers moved to give the two of them room to fight.

Aluthana drew her sword as Laucian summoned his mind blade and they began to circle each other. They had fought on two occasions before this and they were both well aware of how well trained their opponents were.

Laucian made the first move. He struck hard and fast bringing his blade in a low arc, but Aluthana easily parried and spun away. Aluthana's counter came quickly, aiming high for Laucian's shoulder; he was barley able to avoid the attack.

The pair continued in their usual dance, neither able to gain the upper hand. The fight raged for what seemed like hours,with both combatants scarcely avoiding the others deadly attacks. Eventually they both began to grow tired, their attacks slowing and loosing strength.

Laucian finally found an opening, one of Aluthana's attacks had left her off balance. Laucian kicked out low, catching her in the back of the knee. Aluthana stumbled forward, as she did Laucian spun around behind her holding his mind blade to her throat.

"Looks like you failed to get your kill." Laucian whispered, "Again."

"Are you sure?" Aluthana gave a quick glance to one of the soldiers as she spoke; Laucian looked up at the man just in time to see him loose an arrow. Laucian moved fast, but not fast enough and the arrow tore through his shoulder. The sudden pain caused Laucian to loose his concentration and his mind blade began to fade, giving Aluthana the opportunity to escape.

Tanay and Elana both went for their weapons, but each found several swords at their throats before they could do anything. Laucian staggered backwards as Aluthana regained her footing, she suddenly ran forward and kicked Laucian in the chest sending him sprawling to the floor. Within seconds both Aluthana and Stomorel were standing over him.

"Looks like I finally do get my kill." Aluthana laughed.

"Such a shame to kill a fine specimen," Stomorel drew her scimitar and crouched by Laucian's side, "But if he must die then I will take great pleasure in cutting his throat."

Everyone suddenly froze as a loud wolf like howl was heard from beyond the tree line, a howl too loud to be from any natural animal. The distraction gave Laucian the chance he needed to escape his attackers. He punched the crouched Stomorel in the jaw sending her falling backwards, Aluthana thrust her sword at Laucian's chest but he kicked her in the stomach and rolled away. Laucian was back on his feet in an instant as several soldiers stalked towards him, he tried to summon his mind blade back into his hand but the pain in his shoulder was still breaking his concentration.

Tanay and Elana looked to each other, both trying to think of a way they could help their friend without being instantly killed by the soldiers around them. Their help was not needed though, as the soldiers moved in on Laucian a huge beast leaped from the tree line. The creature was easily seven feet tall despite the fact it was standing hunched on its hind legs, it was covered in thick brown and had strong canine features. The beast howled before launching itself at the soldiers around Laucian.

The soldiers did their best to fend off the beast but it was too fast and too strong. The creature was easily throwing them around, or tearing them apart with razor sharp claws. Those who were guarding Elana and Tanay also ran to join the fight, they did not get far before they were hit by a shower of small rocks. The soldiers armour deflected most of the rocks but those those unlucky enough to be hit in more vulnerable places suffered greatly, men were left rolling on the floor in pain and some were even killed.

Those who remained standing turned to see where the attack had come from, just in time to see five druids running out of the tree line. Their attack was fast and hard, coming at the soldiers armed with clubs and scimitars. The soldiers were falling fast as Laucian, Tanay and Elana could only stand and watch. Both Aluthana and Stomorel could see that their ambush was falling apart and made a run for the tree line.

A druid blocked Aluthana's path, this was little trouble for the seasoned assassin who easily side stepped the man blocking her way, spinning around him she stabbed the druid through the back before making her escape. Stomorel was not so lucky, as she fled the beast pursued her. It caught hold of Stomorel by the back of her tunic and threw her back into the clearing.

The beast stalked towards Stomorel seemingly shrinking as it did. Its fur began to thin and the canine features faded until it finally stood over Stomorel, and was just a man.

"A werewolf." Tanay said as he stared at the man standing over Stomorel.

"Not just a werewolf," said the nearest druid. "That is Arch Druid Duranas, the head of our grove."

"I am very disappointed in you Stomorel." Duranas crouched over the fallen druid, "You had so much potential despite your association with that damned legion. You could have been one of the greatest of our order."

"It is my membership of the legion of Strakstaw that makes me great!" Stomorel spat.

"It is your membership with them that has brought you to this. Lying on the floor surrounded by enemies, enemies who could have been friends."

"Friends?" Stomorel laughed, "Why would I be friends with fools? Can't you see what we are doing? This is the only way to create true harmony, true balance."

"By destroying everything?" Duranas asked, "That is not the druid way. We seek balance with nature, you seek balance with nothing." Duranas stood to his full hight and nodded to two of the other druids; they walked over and lifted Stomorel from the ground. "There is only one punishment for your treachery." Duranas bowed his head as he spoke, "I am so sorry." The two druids holding Stomorel dragged her towards the closest tree and held her up against it.

"What are they doing?" Elana asked one of the druids standing close, but she did not answer. Duranas walked up to the tree and placed his hand on the rough bark, he then began to mutter a few words under his breath. Stomorel screamed as the bark began to grow around her limbs, the two druids holding her backed away quickly neither wanting to be caught by the bark. It wasn't long before Stomorel had been completely engulfed by the tree, all that remained of the druid was the faint outline of her face under the bark.

"By the gods," Tanay muttered.

"I thought druids weren't supposed to kill their prisoners," Elana added.

"She is very much alive." Duranas walked up to Elana, "In fact she is now truly at one with nature. Stomorel is now a part of that tree, it will feed and water her, she will live for as long as the tree itself lives." Elana didn't say anything to this; to her this seemed to be a far worse punishment than death.

Duranas turned to Laucian, "That wound looks angry." the arch druid took a small container out of a pocket, "Pull out the arrow and rub this over the wound, it will be as good as new in no time."

"Thank you," Laucian took the small container, "And thank you for your help."

"A good friend of mine has a lot of faith in you, he says that you are destined for great things. It is my honour to help you on your path." Duranas replied. "My druids must return to our grove, but I shall take you and your friends to the totem of elements, it is not far from here."

*   *   *

It didn't take the group long to reach the totem of elements. Aramil and his friends were already there waiting, along with Janemita and Benny, Pattumal and Maria.

"Did you retrieve the stones?" Aramil asked as they approached.

"We did," Tanay replied, "Is all ready for the summoning?"

"Everything is ready." Kimanay answered.

"Who is your friend?" Larenor was looking at Duranas.

"This is arch druid Duranas, head of the druid order in these parts." Laucian explained, "He helped us on the road."

"There was trouble on the road?" Janemita asked, trying not to sound too overly concerned.

"The legion of Strakstaw," Elana explained, "They set a trap, which we blindly walked into."

"If they know of our plans then they will most likely be on their way here," Benny said, "Perhaps we should begin the summoning ritual."

The totem of elements appeared to be little more than five standing stones, with the largest in the middle and four smaller ones around it. The centre stone had a hole in the top where Aramil placed the sceptre of elements. Larenor, Delensa, Kimanay and Aramil then each took one of the elemental stones and each stood on one of the smaller standing stones.

When they were all in position they held out the elemental stones before them and began chanting "Earth, fire, wind, water," over and over again in every language they knew. After a short time the four elements began to erupt from the sceptre, each striking the corresponding elemental stone. The four stones shattered in a blinding flash of light. As everyone began to regain their vision four units of elemental warriors were standing before them.

In front of Aramil stood the earth warriors, their large rock forms standing as tall as the paladin despite the fact that he was still on top of the standing stone. "Warriors of earth, I ask for your allegiance in the coming battle of Legion's war."

The large rock like warriors answered in unison, "We pledge ourselves to your service."

In front of Larenor stood the slim, pale skinned archers of the air warriors, "Warriors of air, I ask for your allegiance in the coming battle of Legion's war."

"We pledge ourselves to your service." The archers replied in unison.

In front of Kimanay stood the blue scaled mages of water, "Warriors of water, I ask for your allegiance in the coming battle of Legion's war."

In unison the mages answered, "We pledge ourselves to your service."

The red cloaked assassins of fire stood before Delensa, "Warriors of fire, I ask your allegiance in the coming battle of Legion's war."

The fire warriors stood there in silence. Delensa looked to her friends as she realised no answer was coming. "Warriors of fire, I ask your allegiance in the coming battle of Legion's war." Delensa repeated, but still received no reply, "Warriors of fire, I ask your allegiance in the coming battle of Legion's war."

One of the fire warriors stepped forward, "We cannot pledge our allegiance to you." The statement shocked all present. "We see into your heart, it is full of doubt. How can we follow you when you do not believe yourself to be capable of leading us?"

"She is more than capable of leading you!" Larenor called.

"It is not you who needs to believe those words." the warrior replied, "If she does not believe in herself then how can we believe in her? We will not follow you into battle." Fire began to swirl around the assassins and eventually consumed them before fading away.

Delensa stood staring at the empty spot where the assassins had been, unable to move. Her three friends all rushed to her side, helping her down from the standing stone. Delensa sank down and sat with her back to the stone, tears filling her eyes.

"I cannot do this," she sobbed, "I'm not strong enough."

"Of course you are," said Kimanay comfortingly.

"What do those fools know?" Larenor added.

"We don't need them." said Aramil.

"Yes we do!" Delensa snapped, "And I wasn't strong enough to gain their allegiance." Delensa forced her way passed the others.

"Delensa wait. Where are you going?" Larenor asked as he followed the monk.

"Let her go." Larenor felt a gentle hand on his shoulder, the elf turned to see Duranas standing by his side. "Your friend is out of balance, she is filled with self-doubt. Only alone can she find her true self, only alone can she regain her balance."

"But we need her," Larenor said longingly. "She is a great warrior." He added quickly.

"She will be back, that I promise you." Duranas said with a smile. "However, now you have other things you must do. You must lead your new allies to join with the rest of your army, you have a war to fight."

Chapter 22
A Formidable Force

It was late dusk and a wave of excitement crossed the encampment. Whispers could be heard, the elements had come, almost every culture had legends about the elemental races from before time began. All of these legends spoke of the elements return in a time of war, when they would sweep across the battlefield destroying any whom opposed them. Now they were here, walking into this camp and pledging allegiance to its cause.

"You are most welcome to our camp." Holdak didn't know how to react to the appearance of these warriors. He had never truly believed in their existence, and now here they stood before him, ready to fight for his cause, under the command of people he had not thought all too special when they had passed through his town.

"Where are the warriors of fire?" asked Magon as he approached the gathered warriors.

"They deemed the one chosen to lead them unworthy, they would not follow her." answered one of the air warriors.

"And what of her?" Solaris asked as he walked up behind Magon.

"Lord Flameheart!" the air warrior and other elemental warriors all bowed their heads upon seeing the immortal.

"Where is the woman who was to lead the warriors of fire?" Solaris asked again.

"What does it matter where an unworthy warrior has gone?" one of the water mages asked.

"Even the strongest can have moments of self doubt." Solaris said, "She is a great warrior. Even if she does not see that herself the warriors of fire should have."

"The girl will be back," said Duranas, "As soon as she finds her balance she will return."

"You all must be tried from your journey, I shall have some of my men help set some tents for you." Holdak announced, "Adokas should be back by morning with the elves, then we can begin our preparations for the battle."

"You are most kind," Aramil said as he followed Holdak along with his companions and the elemental warriors.

"Laucian, I must speak with you." Solaris said as the others left.

"About what?"

"We are not destined to fight in this battle," Solaris explained, "As these people fight their war I must go and face Legion himself, that is why I have the power of the immortal."

"And what has that got to do with me?" Laucian asked as his friends came to listen to the conversation.

"The dreams you are having, they show you the war to save my world. They show you the fight with Legion when he was defeated last. You of all people should see that even with the power I possess, I cannot defeat him alone."

"You wish for me to fight along side you?" Laucian looked to his friends and then back to Solaris, "If you are so powerful, then what could I possibly do to help?"

Solaris laughed, "Like most of your world you do not fully understand your potential. The fact that you are having the dreams tells me that you are strong enough to help me in this fight. Not only that but you also have the favour of possibly the greatest power your world will ever know." Solaris glanced at the tattoo on Laucian's arm, "All life succumbs to fear,those who understand it and wield it wisely are seldom defeated. You are one of the god of fears chosen, I see no-one better to help me."

Laucian smiled at Solaris, this fight would probably be the hardest battle he would ever face in his life, and he planned to face it head on. "When do we leave?"

"First thing in the morning." Solaris answered.

"Well I guess we should get some rest," Tanay stretched as he spoke, "Sounds like we're going to need it." Laucian and Solaris both looked at the viperian.

"You don't expect us to let you fight Legion alone do you?" Elana smiled at the pair.

Laucian laughed, "No, of course not."

Everyone began to make their way into the encampment, "Well I guess our first battle together is going to be an important one." Pattumal put his hand on Laucian's shoulder.

Laucian bowed his head, "No." he turned to face Pattumal with sad eyes. He and Pattumal had been raised as brothers, it had not been until he was sent away from his family that Laucian had learned they were not truly related. Even so he still loved Pattumal as a brother and longed for nothing more than fight side by side with him, but this was not the time for that battle. "You cannot come with me on this one."

"What are you talking about?"

"Look around you," Laucian began, "These men and women will be marching soon, many to their deaths. I am needed to fight another battle, but you would be better served here with them." Laucian looked at the faces of the people sitting around camp fires. "You and Maria are two of the greatest archers there are, how many lives could be spared because your bows are on the battlefield?" Pattumal remained silent, he too looked around the camp. He knew Laucian was right but still did not want to leave him to go and face Legion.

"Do not worry about me," Laucian continued, sensing Pattumal's concern, "I will not be fighting alone."

"Fine." Pattumal said eventually, "You go and fight your demon in some dark place that no-one can see. I will stay here and claim the glory of helping to win a great victory in battle, where everyone can see."

"Don't be to overconfident brother, I don't want you getting killed because of some careless mistake. We still need to have our grand adventure."

*　　*　　*

"My lord, I am honoured by your presence." Slantary said as she stood before Legion. The demon god's ship had arrived in Cemulion only a few minutes before. The dragon had not expected him to arrive so soon which meant that her knights had not yet completed the preparations on the alter needed for Legion to conduct his ritual.

"You have done well in taking this city," Legion began, "Now tell me, how go the preparations for the ritual?"

"The alter is almost complete," Slantary explained, "We did not expect your arrival to be so soon; I will have my men double their efforts."

"There is no need, I wish to have Deventis oversee the final preparations." Legion said as he strode into the city.

"As you wish my lord, and what of me?"

"You are to serve general Markus. You are to help him prepare my army for battle."

"As you wish." Slantary smiled; she was growing tired of this city and longed for more action.

"Deventis, come we have work to do." Legion strode of followed by Deventis.

"It is good to see you again my lady." Markus bowed his head as he spoke.

"Welcome to my new city," said the dragon, "How may I assist you?"

"The fleet will be landing within the hour; we will need lodgings for the army."

"I will have my knights procure them some residence."

"How will they do that?"

"They will kill the current residents." Slantary laughed.

"Very good." General Markus began to walk into the city followed by Slantary. "What do we know of the enemy force?"

"Not much at the moment." Slantary began, "A ship was seen sailing up the coast, looked like the pirate hunter. There is also an encampment to the west, the shadow has gone to scout it, he is expected back soon."

"Then we shall make our plans upon his return. Is there somewhere I can rest while we wait?"

"I will have one of my knights show you to some comfortable quarters. I will summon you when the shadow returns.

Markus did not get much chance to rest before one of Slantary's knights was banging on the door to his room. The knight explained that the shadow had returned and was waiting for Markus. The general walked boldly into the palace throne room, which had been converted into living quarters for Slantary as it was the only room in the city in which the dragon could move around in. Although the dragon could take on the form of almost any living creature, making finding a suitable room for her easy, she despised reducing herself to the form of *lesser* creatures and so she tolerated the cramped conditions.

"General Markus, please allow me to introduce Antonema Christortus, also known as the shadow." Slantary said as Markus approached.

"It is a pleasure to finally meet you," said the general, "I have heard much of your exploits."

"My lord," Antonema bowed his head in respect, "I bring news of our enemy, their army is more advance than we believed."

"How do you mean?"

"They have most of the Getandor army, along with a large number of barbarians, and a force of etharii. They also have an army that marched out of the mountains, orcs, goblins, all manner of such beasts. I also believe that they are expecting the elves of Landorn to arrive soon."

"That sounds like quite an army. Isn't it lucky then that we have brought the full might of the legion of Strakstaw." Markus smiled knowing that the army Antonema had described could still not match the size of his army.

"That is not all, they also have the elements, the warriors of the previous world have come for this fight. Even with the might of the legion of Strakstaw, and the power of Slantary we should not underestimate this army. They are not as chaotic as we first thought, fighting together they make quite a formidable force."

*   *   *

"So, you got any idea how you're going to bring Nasgaroth to the battle?" Davkul and Roscoe had not long arrived at the mines which were home to the gold dragon and the dwarves of Davkul's clan.

"I have no idea." Roscoe said bluntly. The truth was that he had been trying to figure out how he would handle this situation since he had declared that he would bring Nasgaroth to the fight, and now he was standing at the entrance to the mines still not knowing what to do.

It didn't take them long to reach the entrance to Nasgaroth's chamber. Two dwarves stood blocking their path, "Lord Nasgaroth is not taking visitors at this time."

"Stand aside," Davkul ordered, "He will see us."

The two guards looked at each other, "Fine, but you will have to leave your weapons here." Davkul snorted as he walked up to the guard.

"Stand aside." Davkul said calmly, the guards just looked at each other again. "You have a simple choice to make now." Davkul continued, "Move, or be moved."

The guards shared another nervous look before deciding it would be in their best interest to move. Davkul walked past them and pushed the door open, "Go on Roscoe, I will be back shortly."

"Wait, What?" Roscoe looked a little scared, "You can't let me go in there alone."

"It was you who claimed to be able to bring Nasgaroth to war. I have other things I must do." Davkul pushed Roscoe through the door before turning on his heels and walking off along the passageway.

"Who dares to disturb my rest?" Roscoe froze where he stood. The last time he had been before this dragon it had not been too friendly. Nasgaroth had refused to help in the war and now Roscoe had to try and change his mind.

"What do you want little man?" Nasgaroth asked as he came into the light. Roscoe stared at the huge creature, its golden scales gleaming in the light. "Well, are you going to explain this intrusion? Or just stand there like a fool?"

"I am here to seek your aid," Roscoe stuttered, "We need your help in the coming battle."

"I have already told you, the wars of mortals are no concern of mine."

"This war concerns all life, Legion plans on killing us all."

"Do you really believe he could do that?" the dragon laughed.

"He is going to use ancient rituals..."

"There are no such rituals!" Nasgaroth snapped. "Draconic magic was the first magic; if there were any such rituals then I would know of them."

"Legion is from a world before this one. His magic pre-dates anything of this world."

"I grow tired of your presence little one, I suggest you leave."

"I'm not leaving until you agree to help us."

"You will leave now!" Nasgaroth snarled as he closed in on Roscoe. The halfling reacted quickly, drawing his sword and holding it up at the dragon.

Nasgaroth laughed loudly, "What do you expect to do with that?"

"Whatever I must." Roscoe replied shakily.

"Guards!" Nasgaroth yelled as he turned away from Roscoe. Four heavily armed dwarves ran into the room, "Remove this insect from my presence."

"Yes my lord." The dwarves moved in on Roscoe, who now turned his sword towards them. Roscoe was thinking fast, how could he get out of the predicament? It wasn't long before an answer presented itself.

"Anyone who touches the halfling will have me to deal with!" Bellowed a voice. Everyone looked round to see Davkul standing in the doorway. The dwarf was no longer wearing the dragon armour had had before. Now he wore an intricate shirt of silver rings and a silver helmet that looked to have a crown moulded into it, and his shield now bore the largest perfectly cut emerald Roscoe had ever seen at its centre.

"What is the meaning of this?" Nasgaroth demanded.

"I have come to tell you dragon," Davkul stepped further into the chamber, "We will suffer your rule no longer. These are dwarven mines and I, Davkul Gemcutter, am lord and king under this mountain."

"Your ancestors passed their rule to me generations ago, bowing to my wisdom."

"Wisdom?" Davkul laughed, "I see no wisdom in hiding away while the fate of our world is decided on the battlefield."

"So what do you plan to do?" Nasgaroth chuckled.

"I will lead *my* clan into battle." Davkul turned to one of the other dwarves, "Sound the great horn, have my army gather at the gates."

"Yes my king." the dwarf replied, grinning as he ran from the chamber.

"And Nasgaroth, if you do not help in this battle then I do not expect to find you in *my* mines upon my return." Davkul turned and walked from the chamber, followed closely by the other dwarves and Roscoe.

It didn't take long for Davkul's army to assemble, despite being a peaceful race the dwarves were always ready for war.

"My kin," Davkul yelled as he walked down the line in front of his army, "We go to fight the greatest battle of our time. For the first time we will be fighting alongside our sworn enemies in a common cause. We fight to protect our homes! We fight to protect our loved ones! We fight to protect our world!" A huge cheer erupted from the soldiers, "I do not expect all of us will return, but know this, those who fall in glorious battle will be remembered as the true heroes of our time!" Everyone cheered again, even Roscoe.

Davkul stopped in front of the halfling, "I am sorry my friend, but you cannot come with us today."

"But..." Roscoe protested.

"I am sorry Roscoe, but halflings have no place in the battles of men and dragons." Roscoe tried to protest again but was silenced by a look from Davkul.

"Come my brothers, my sisters," Davkul yelled, "Let us show our enemies the might of a true dwarven charge!" Davkul turned and began to sprint down the mountain, followed by hundreds of cheering dwarves.

Roscoe could only watch as the army disappeared into the distance. The halfling looked up as a shadow descended over him.

"So, you beg me to join your fight and then get left behind when it comes to the fighting." Nasgaroth smiled at Roscoe.

Roscoe turned back to the departing dwarves, "Davkul says that halflings have no place in the battles of men and..." Suddenly Roscoe knew exactly how to get Nasgaroth to fight. He quickly spun around to face the dragon, "You say that you will not fight the battles of mortals?"

"I have no interest in them."

"But what if I told you that our enemy has been joined by a dragon?" Nasgaroth suddenly looked interested, so Roscoe continued "When Cemulion fell it was because they were attacked by a great red, the sworn enemy of gold dragons, unless the tales are wrong."

"How do I know that you speak the truth?"

"Draconic magic was the first magic; one of your power should easily detect such a deception."

Nasgaroth chuckled, "A great red you say? The certainly would warrant my attention." Roscoe smiled as he realised that he had in this moment succeeded in bringing Nasgaroth to the battle.

"Tell me Roscoe; are you truly a master of the Wentar words?"

Roscoe was taken aback by the question,"I'm not sure. I had never heard of them until Solaris spoke of them. Sometimes I do say words I don't know and strange things happen."

"Yes, that would be how they usually work." Nasgaroth turned back up to the mountain, "Come little one, we must prepare for battle."

"We?"

"But of course. If you truly are a master of the Wentar words then your place is in the midst of this battle. Now come quickly I have much to teach you of your gift, and very little time in which to do it."

Chapter 23
War

It was still dark as the armies gathered, both hoping to gain the upper hand by setting the battlefield before the other. However their was little to manipulate to any advantage on the planes east of Cemulion. Captain Holdak had been surprised when all of the gathered armies of his force had allowed him overall command of the army, despite the fact that until now some of those gathered he had considered mortal enemies and others had a higher rank in their armies than he did.

Both armies were still in formation, neither wanting to give away their battle plan to the other. Legion's army greatly outnumbered that of those allied against him, he had spent years growing his forces while those he faced had only a matter of weeks. To look at the armies Legion's force should have been able to decimate those they faced with ease, especially with Slantary among their ranks.

As was tradition for battles of this magnitude the leaders of each army met at the centre of the battlefield with two of their lieutenants. General Markus had been joined by Antonema and Kevgeon, where as Holdak had taken Grakenster and Fanell in an attempt to strengthen the alliance with both their armies.

"Have you come here to surrender?" Markus asked as he removed his helmet, the sight of his face causing Fanell to gasp in surprise.

"We are here to demand your withdrawal from our lands." Holdak was calm but firm. Although Holdak had not been in combat for some time this was what he lived for. He had trained all his life for moments like this. Despite the fact his enemy looked to clearly out match his own army Holdak showed no fear.

"I do not think you are in any position to be making demands captain, you are greatly outnumbered." Antonema scoffed.

"Numbers matter not. Our warriors are strong." Grakenster spat.

"Your soldiers may be strong, but so are mine." Markus explained, "This is the only chance I will give you to surrender, it is the only way to prevent hundreds of people dying needlessly."

"We will never surrender to you. These are our lands, this is our home, we will defend it to the very last."

"I am glad to hear that captain." Markus smiled as he replaced his helmet. "I am looking forward to crushing your little army." Markus and his lieutenants turned to head back towards their ranks when Fanell spoke.

"Do you think your ancestors approve of your actions general?" the etharii asked.

"My ancestors?" Markus turned to Fanell, "And what do you think you know of my ancestors?"

"One thing all our races have in common is that we resemble our ancestors, and you general are the image of an ancient friend to my people."

Markus knew exactly what Fanell was talking about and found it amusing, "Please do explain your point."

"Many generations ago a man of your image fought alongside my people to save this world from a demonic attack. Now you, his obvious descendant, are leading an attack that could destroy all he fought to protect."

Markus laughed as he spoke, "My views of this world have changed a lot since those days."

"Your views?"

"Yes, my views. When I fought alongside your people I was young. I still thought that this world was worth saving."

"This world is worth saving." Holdak said.

"Are you sure? A world full of corruption, where evil runs rampant. A world filled with murderers, rapists, and worse, do you really want to save all that?"

"It is true, there is much in the world that does not deserve saving, but there is much good here too. Look at who stands against you, mortal enemies fighting side by side in a common cause."

"Yes you will band together when it suits you, but when you no longer need each other you will return to your petty little wars. I was a fool when I saved this world before, I will not make the same mistake now."

"You were the one who fought alongside my people?" Fanell asked in disbelief, "That is not possible; Jovan would have dies many years ago."

"I am the one who fought alongside your people. You would be surprised how much the beasts of the abyss know of mortal physiology, such as how to stop our ageing so they can torture us for longer."

"Is that why you are so bitter toward our world? Because you suffered?"

"I am not bitter towards this world. I am simply creating a perfect, evil free world, in the only way possible. By ending it." Markus explained, "When Legion saved me from the abyss he showed me how he planned to destroy evil forever. That is when I stopped being Jovan paladin of Sugalas and became Markus, general of Legion's army. It is in this position as general that I will give you this final chance to surrender before my army destroys you."

"We never surrender." Grakenster spat.

"You may have lost your faith in life, but we have not." Fanell added.

"Then prepare yourselves for death." Markus turned and returned to his army.

Holdak and his lieutenants did like wise, each of the barking orders to their soldiers, preparing for immanent battle.

It had not been difficult for the small group to get around Legion's army, and the city had been left all but unguarded. All that remained now was to find where Legion was conducting his ritual.

"Legion is in the palace somewhere." Solaris stated.

"How do you know that?" Elana asked.

"It is one of my abilities as the immortal. I can sense Legion's presence, well that and the fact it is the only building to retain any form of guard."

The main entrance to the palace had a minimal guard posted; just two men stood one at each side of the door. Laucian and Tanay easily dispatched the guards; one died with one of Laucian's throwing knives in his throat, the other choked as Tanay used his magic to remove all the air from around his head.

The group was inside, now all they needed to do was locate Legion.

*   *   *

Both armies began to break formation in preparation for the battle. Holdak's soldiers along with the earth warriors led by Aramil would take the centre charge, where as Grakenster's army along with the etharii would take the left flank, and the Landorn elves and Malik's barbarians took the right. The regiments would be covered from the rear by each armies archers along with the air warrior archers with Larenor and the magic users of the water warriors led by Kimanay. The etharii griffin riders would act as air support, aiding whichever area of the battle needed them most.

Markus had his army in a similar formation. He would be leading the centre, with Kevgeon leading the left and Antonema the right. Markus' army was not as segregated as his opponents, his regiments were not made up of single races, but an even mix of different races so to have no one unit more powerful than another. Markus also had archers and a few magic users to back up his soldiers. Although the general had no units like the etharii griffin riders he still had no doubt that his army would maintain aerial superiority, there was nothing his enemy had that could stand up against Slantary.

Both armies stood ready for a while staring at each other, the soldiers saying quick prayers for help to any god they thought might listen. Both armies new that many would die today, but it was a cost they were both willing to pay for their causes.

Holdak was the first to make a move, "Now is the time of our destinies!" he called, "Fight! Fight like you've never fought before!" Holdak paused for a moment, "FOR GETANDOR!" The captain charged forward, followed closely by his troops and the earth warriors. Markus' army remained still and silent. Aramil used his magical bow as he ran, each arrow finding its targeted, but still Markus gave no orders for his own troops to move.

As Holdak's charge got close the general finally gave an order. Markus cried, "Havak! Let slip the war dogs!" Havak smiled broadly as he released the chains holding the beasts he had bred for this very moment.

The war dogs tore through Holdak's ranks, killing dozens within seconds. His soldiers moved their attention to the hounds, spear-men crowded the beasts trying to keep a safe distance from the teeth and claws of the animals as they attacked. The earth warriors didn't have as much trouble with the war dogs, using their extreme strength and durability to beat the dogs into submission.

As the soldiers looked to be finally getting the war dogs under control they heard general Markus bark another order, "Charge!" In that moment Holdak realised what Markus had done. The war dogs had thrown his men off guard, they were busy fighting the beasts as the rest of Markus' men attacked.

The charge was brutal, but it didn't take the seasoned warriors under Holdak's command to adapt to this new onslaught, though many were lost in the initial confusion. The earth warriors weathered the new attack well, taking minimal losses, but when Havak hit their ranks they began to suffer.

The warriors of earth relied on their size and strength in battle, Havak however was both bigger and stronger than they were. They were not used to this type of opponent, leaving them woefully under prepared for Havak's attack. The monster laughed as he smashed his way through his enemy, he knew his target and these rock men were just an inconvenience to overcome to reach it.

*   *   *

Grakenster's army and the etharii met with heavy resistance to their charge, but it was nothing they could not handle. The etharii attack was as deadly as it was graceful, each warrior slicing up there opponents and dancing away before anyone else could respond. Grakenster's troops took a more simple approach to battle; they hit heavy and hard, killing anything that bore the marking of the legion of Strakstaw.

Antonema's troops retaliated to the onslaught with equal force. His soldiers were systematic and brutal in their approach. The assassin had made sure that every combatant under his command were highly trained, he had personally taught them the art of death. Despite Antonema's style of killing relying greatly on stealth, the precision of his style proved to be highly effective, with all of his soldiers able to kill their opponents with the minimum of strikes.

The two forces seemed evenly matched; neither side able to gain any kind of advantage over the other. This worried Grakenster and the etharii, if they could not gain the upper hand and turn things to their favour they risked loosing the battle to Antonema's superior numbers, and if their line was broken it would leave the archer open to a direct attack.

Antonema however was not worried that he had gained no real advantage against his foes, he knew his line would not be broken. Although it looked as though both sides were even Antonema had very specific plans, plans he knew would easily tip the flow of battle in his favour.

*   *   *

Malik the bear and his barbarians along with Branack led the charge on their flank, the elven infantry following closely behind. The barbarians hit Kevgeon's troops hard, barely even slowing as the crashed through the front ranks.

Kevgeon had built his army on the concept of strength and the ability to overwhelm their enemies, but Malik's barbarians were strong too and it looked as though they were going to easily overwhelm Kevgeon's troops. This coupled with the elven infantry cutting a swath through Kevgeon's soldiers with ease made the battle for this flank look to greatly favour those allied against Legion.

Malik smashed his way through the enemy line, each swing of his great club sending men flying across the battlefield. The huge barbarian lived for moments like this. He had been in many battles, most were small skirmishes against rival tribes or any goblinoids that ventured down from the mountains. In this battle though he could earn great honour, his exploits here would be sang about for generations.

Branack too broke through the enemy lines with ease, his axe cutting men down wherever he swung it. Anyone foolish enough to refer to Branack as an orc suffered an even worse death than his axe blade through their skull. Those who ventured too close to the half-orc were caught in his iron grip, many died that day due to Branack squeezing the life out of their throats.

Kevgeon tried to spur his troops on by example, and the example he set was exemplary. Kevgeon's huge double-ended axe tore his opponents apart. He killed both barbarian and elf alike, showing no mercy to anyone, his warriors revelled in his butchery. Those close to Kevgeon were whipped up into a frenzy, each one trying to match their leaders ferocity. They began to push back against the barbarians and elves, but it didn't look to be enough, this still seemed to be a loosing battle.

*   *   *

Archers and magic users protected the opening charge. The archers had little effect after this, it quickly became too dangerous to fire at the enemy as they risked hitting their own forces. The warriors of air had no trouble with this however, their aim seemed to supernaturally accurate. The magic users had become largely ineffective in a combat sense too, their spells also risking killing their allies. Instead the mages of water along with Kimanay used their magic as healers, patching up any wounded that could make it back out of the melee.

The only support which had any real effect on the battle was the etharii griffin riders. Led by Fanell the griffin riders dive-bombed their enemies, attacking with spears and bows they killed dozens with every pass. The riders luck was running out however as they were about to face the wrath of their enemies most fearsome warrior.

Slantary let the battle rage for a while before entering the fray. When she finally attacked the dragon went after the griffin riders, she would not suffer these lesser creatures to sully her sky. The great red launched herself high into the sky before swooping down towards her targets. She caught hold of two griffin riders on her first pass, her blade like talons ripping through both the etharii and griffins with ease before she dropped them to the ground in pieces.

Fanell began to bark orders to his unit, trying to get them into some kind of formation that could deal with this new threat. The etharii knew that they had little chance against the dragon, but he had no intention of going down without a fight. The griffins were faster and more manoeuvrable than Slantary, which Fanell planned to use to his advantage. Keeping the unit in close formation they swung around behind the dragon firing their bows at the beast, trying to find a weak point in her armour like scales.

Slantary swung round quickly whipping her tail out as she did. Fanell dived down narrowly avoiding tail, but the rider next to him was not so lucky. The griffin took the full force of the hit and fell to the ground in a heap, crushing its rider. Slantary swooped again catching another griffin in her claws, as the dragon crushed the life out of both griffin and rider she unleashed her fiery breath on the others as they flew by. The inferno engulfed most of the remaining griffins, sending both riders and mounts screaming to the ground like meteors. Fanell now only had one griffin rider flying by his side and knew full well that the monsters next attack would most likely see them both dead, but he still had no intention of backing down.

The etharii coaxed their mounts in for another attack, they dived under Slantary firing their bows at her exposed underbelly. The scales on Slantary's belly were not as thick as those on her back, but they still stopped most of the arrows, and those that did penetrate her hide were little more than insect bites to the mighty red dragon. Fanell swung round behind the dragon, his comrade by his side. They were chasing the dragon now, each gripping their spears hoping that they would be more effective against the beast than their bows had been. As the griffins drew close to Slantary the dragon suddenly outstretched her wings and incredibly stopped almost immediately in the air, leaving the griffins to fly straight past her. Fanell looked back over his shoulder just in time to see the jet of fire that would engulf him and the other rider, sending them both crashing to the ground like comets.

*   *   *

The monk could see the fighting from where she sat. After leaving her friends Delensa had walked into the foothills of the mountains north of Cemulion. She didn't want to watch the battle, but couldn't bring herself to turn away.

"Help me! Help!" Delensa looked around, she couldn't see where the scream had come from but it sounded be from behind some large boulder. The monk leaped from the outcrop where she sat and ran in the direction of the scream.

As Delensa ran around the boulders she could see that the cry for help had come from a young girl who had been cornered by three orcs. The orcs laughed as they closed in on the helpless girl, she was pressed up to one of the boulders. It looked as though the girl was trying to pass through the stone in an attempt to escape, but the hard rock would never give way.

"Walk away now and your lives may be spared!" The trio of orcs looked around to see Delensa standing a little way behind them, staff in hand.

"Look at this lads," said one of the orcs, "Another brave little slave girl for us to take home."

"All you will be taking home today is a broken bone or two." Delensa said with a wicked smile, "If you make it home that is."

"You get that one; me and him will show this cocky elf that orcs break bones better than she can." Two of the orcs began to advance on Delensa as the other turned back to the girl.

The monk turned to her side and shifted her grip on the staff in preparation for the orcs attack as the two approaching her drew their crude swords. Delensa waited patiently for the orcs to get close before leaping into action. The first orc slashed at Delensa who easily blocked the attack before spinning between the two orcs, hitting the second in the stomach with her staff. In an instant the monk reversed her spin and brought her staff down hard on the back of the orcs head sending the beast sprawling to the floor. This left Delensa standing face to face with the first orc.

The orc looked at his friend lying on the floor before he attacked again. Delensa easily blocked the orcs barrage of attacks before striking out with a barrage of her own. The monk danced around the orc with such speed and grace that the orc had no chance of keeping up with her onslaught of strikes, and it wasn't long before he was lying on the ground next to his friend.

Delensa now turned her attention to the orc who had gone after the young girl; he had her cornered by one of the boulders. The orc was laughing as he taunted the girl, he would give her an opening to escape but then quickly block her path as she tried to run. The orcs laughter ended abruptly when Delensa hit him across his back with her staff making him stumble forward. The orc looked back over his shoulder just in time to see Delensa quickly sidestepping towards him. She kicked him hard in the back, sending the orc running face first into the rock in front of him where he slumped to the floor.

"Quickly, this way." Delensa motioned for the girl to follow, leading her away from the unconscious orcs. Delensa finally stopped when they were back at the outcrop from which she had been watching the battle.

"Wow. That was amazing." said the girl, "You must be a great warrior."

"Not as great as you would think," Delensa was checking the girl for injuries, "They weren't the most challenging of foe."

"But you beat them so easily." the girl smiled, "I bet you're going to the great battle aren't you?"

Delensa was taken aback by the comment, "No. I'm not strong enough for that fight."

The little girl laughed, "Of course you are. I saw you beat them orcs so easily."

"Defeating three orcs is not as tough as you think. Fighting in a battle like that though," Delensa walked to the edge of the rock face and took in the scene before her. "In a battle like that all my presence would achieve would be to hinder my friends, I would just be in the way."

The girl laughed again, "How can someone with elven grace ever be in the way?"

Delensa smiled, "It is not that simple. I may be a good fighter, but I am not good enough to fight in this war."

You are better than my daddy, he would not have beaten three orcs like you did, but he has still gone to fight."

"If your father has gone to fight then he is a better warrior than me."

"Daddy says that in battles like this it doesn't matter how good a warrior you are, but how noble your sole is."

"I don't understand."

"Daddy says all you need in battle is the will to do what is right. If you have the will to stand up for the greater good then no matter how strong you are you can still help to win, you can help to inspire others to fight with you."

"Your father is a wise man."

"Then you will go to the battle?" Delensa looked closely at the girl, she new that she was right. It didn't matter if she doubted herself, it didn't matter that the warriors of fire had not followed her. All that mattered was that she did all she could to help her friends. She had to stand up for what was right.

"Yes, I will go to the battle, I will do what is right." Delensa said, "But first I had best get you home."

"Don't worry about me, I live near by." The girl smiled before turning on her heels and running off, "You go help my daddy."

Delensa started after the girl, but after following her around a large rock the girl seemed to had disappeared. Delensa looked around for a moment before she gave up on finding the girl and began to make her way out of the foothills towards the battle.

The little girl watched Delensa run off into the distance, smiling broadly as the three orcs approached her from behind.

"Did your plan work my lord?" asked one of the orcs. As it spoke the three orcs began to change, they lost their brutish forms and seemed to become less solid. They kept their humanoid shape but seemed to be made up of little more than smoke and light.

Elvin glanced around at his loyal servants, "My plan worked perfectly." replied the god of fear. Elvin too began to change form, shedding the guise of the young girl and reverting to his true form.

Chapter 24
Deception

"It is time little one." the dragon said, "I have taught you everything I can about your power, now it is time to see if you can use it.

"Are you afraid?" Roscoe looked up at the dragon, "As powerful as you are do you still feel fear before a battle?"

"Not as you do. I do not fear death in battle, I only fear not defeating the evil that I face." Roscoe stared at the huge beast. It was not long ago that Nasgaroth had been refusing to fight, and now he spoke so nobly of defeating evil. The halfling found it amusing how Nasgaroth had changed his stance so completely, but still made it sound as the he was doing exactly what he had always planned.

"Come now little one, it is time." Nasgaroth lowered his shoulder so that Roscoe could climb up onto his back. The halfling found himself a comfortable place to sit between the dragons wings before Nasgaroth launched himself towards the battle.

*   *   *

The four moved quickly and quietly through the halls of Cemulion's palace. Since the two guards at the palace entrance the group had met no resistance as the searched for Legion. They entered one of the many ballrooms which was empty like every other room so far. They were about halfway across the room when the group realised they had walked straight into a trap.

"Halt!" The four companions looked up to the balcony surrounding the ballroom. About fifteen soldiers stood around the edge of the balcony, all aiming crossbows. "We've been expecting you, move and die."

"Well this is a predicament" Tanay said as he looked around, trying to think of a suitable spell for the situation.

"Our lord Legion has been working on this for some time now," one of the soldiers explained, "He has learned from his past mistakes, such as leaving himself unprotected from the so called *immortal*."

"So he set set a trap for us." Laucian spat, feeling foolish for not seeing this coming.

"Legion may have anticipated out approach, but he obviously has no idea of what he is dealing with." Solaris said boldly.

"Don't try to frighten me *immortal*, a crossbow bolt through the heart will kill you the same as anyone else."

Solaris smiled as he turned to his companions, "Be ready to run," he whispered, "Straight for the door when they drop their weapons." The others gave him a confused look.

"All four of you lie face down on the ground and place your hands on your heads."

"No." Solaris replied calmly.

"You really are confident aren't you?"

"Drop your weapons!" Solaris spoke loudly, with great authority. As he spoke the each of the soldiers let their crossbows fall the the ground. "Go now!" Solaris and the others all sprinted for the door. Laucian was the first to reach the fancy double doors and slammed hard into them with his shoulder. The lock broke and all four barrelled through, slamming the doors closed behind them just in time to hear a series of bolts hitting the other side.

"Well that is an interesting talent you have there." Tanay said as he tried to catch his breath.

"Yes it is, and I will explain but I feel that we should move on from here first." The others agreed and set off down the new corridor.

When the group finally decided they had safely eluded their pursuer Solaris decided to explain what had happened in the ballroom. "Ever since I became the immortal my own innate powers were increased in strength. Along with that I gained *a power of the beast*. My predecessor told me that each of the immortals gain something. She had been imbued with Legion's strength, I however gained a limited control over those baring his mark. If Legion is to give one of his followers a command they cannot disobey it, I can give them simple commands and they will follow them for a few moments until Legion's hold returns."

"So each immortal gains a different ability?" Elana asked.

"That is how it seems."

"How many immortals have their been?"

"I cannot be sure, it is somewhat difficult to keep track of how many new worlds their have been what only a handful of beings survive from one to the next."

"So where do we go now?" Laucian asked.

"I'm not sure." Solaris replied.

"I thought you could sense Legion's presence."

"I can, but that is not much help when you don't know the layout of a building."

"I believe that you need to go this way." Everyone span around with weapons in hand as they heard the icy voice.

"Quinn!" Elana was excited to see her shadow companion.

"Greetings my lady." Quinn said with a bow, "After I left you with the druid I felt I could be most useful scouting the city for you."

Quinn led the others to the lower part of the palace, through winding tunnels. Eventually they reached an area where the tunnel widened into a round junction where four more tunnels joined it. A hooded man stood in the centre of the junction, Tanay Elana and Laucian moved out to the sides to flank the man where as Solaris approached from the front, each of them instinctively moving their hands to their weapons.

Quinn silently drew near to the man, hoping he would not notice the shadow. The man had noticed though, and as he drew close the man raised his hand unleashing a blinding flash of light. The four companions shielded their eyes before readying their weapons.

"Hold!" the man called. No one moved. Elana scanned the junction desperately trying to spot Quinn, but the shadow was no-where to be see.

"I truly am sorry for your loss my lady, but the shadow could not have survived the light. He was a brave servant, but his presence would only have hindered you in fighting Legion."

"Who are you?" Solaris asked as he moved closer to the man.

"I am both your friend and your enemy." The man replied, "As a follower of Legion I must obey his commands, but as a willing follower I am allowed some measure of free will."

"I don't understand," said Elana, who was trying to hold back tears for her fallen friend.

"I think I do." said Tanay, "This is why you brought me here, this is why I was never inducted into the legion of Strakstaw."

"Yes my son, this is why." Deventis lowered his hood now his identity was known. "I needed to escape our people and the evil goddess the follow, I tried to raise you to be different from them, and the fact that you are here now has proven that I succeeded. You must understand my son, Legion offered me a way to escape our people, he gave me a chance to do some good in this world."

"You think what you are doing is good?" Laucian spat.

"No, he knows what he is doing is evil," Tanay explained, "The good he did was to bring me with him."

"Exactly," Deventis smiled, "I agreed to join Legion, but only if I could bring my son. I knew I would have to follow Legion's orders, but if I raised my son right, if I placed him with good people to fight alongside, I knew if I could get you involved in this endgame then you would cleanse the world of the evil I had to perform." Deventis turned to Elana, "You know princess, you are lucky that it was Markus who ordered your death and not Legion himself. If Legion had given me the order I could not have spared you, or paid the travelling shadow walkers to collect you and train you in their arts."

"You arranged for them to find me?"

"I arranged many things in your life, and some in yours Laucian. Who do you thing sent Silvana to the market on the day you met? Who do you think hired the men to stage a robbery so you could save her?"

"And who arranged her death?" Laucian asked coldly.

Deventis looked down, "That was never a part of my plan, but you all insisted in exploring those catacombs. I cannot be blamed for the impetuous of youth." Deventis turned to Solaris, "I also had no control over you, the immortal, luckily you are easy to predict."

"So what now?" Solaris asked.

"I have manoeuvred you all here because I knew Legion would order me to stop anyone from entering the chamber, but I'm sure you realise that I cannot stop you all."

Tanay pulled a small stone from the pouch on his belt, "I'm sorry father." He threw the stone, Deventis raised his hand to protect himself but he was too late. The stone hit him in the shoulder, it exploded on contact sending Deventis sprawling to the floor.

"Go!" Tanay commanded, "Stop Legion, I will deal with my father." the others looked to each other.

"Do as he says, this is why I rescued him from our homeland."

"Go Now!" Tanay's three companions did as they were told, leaving Tanay alone to face his father.

"Don't hold back my son. You must do whatever it takes to defeat me. I am under orders from Legion, I now must stop your friends and I will do whatever it takes to stop them, even if it means killing my own son."

*   *   *

After defeating the griffin riders Slantary turned her attention to the archers and magic users. She swooped over them, burning many with each attack. The archers and magic user changed their focus and began to attack the dragon, but to little effect. The arrows just shattered on the dragons scales and the spells seemed to be little more than an annoyance to her.

The battle seemed to be going in the way as that with the griffin riders until salvation showed itself in a way no-one expected. As Slantary swooped in for another attack she found herself to be under attach herself, from above.

It hadn't taken long for Nasgaroth and Roscoe to reach the battle. The gold dragon had flown at full speed and even though the dwarves had set out hours earlier the dragon and the halfling had arrived ahead of them.

Nasgaroth's attack was swift, he slammed himself into Slantary's back, the great red didn't know what his her and she began to plummet towards the ground. The huge dragon would have crushed and killed many of the archers if Nasgaroth hadn't caught her in his claws and thrown her away from the soldiers. Slantary quickly regained her senses as she searched the sky for her attacker, she saw Nasgaroth circling overhead. The great red let out a loud roar before launching herself into the air, aiming to tear out the gold dragon's throat.

*   *   *

Markus could see all aspects of the battle from his vantage point. He could see that Kevgeon's army was fighting a loosing battle. He could also see that Antonema seemed to be in a stale mate in his battle. The general had the up most confidence in his lieutenants though, he was sure that they would prove themselves victorious. Markus turned his attention back to his area of battle, it was going well for his forces but he felt it could be better. Markus decided that it was time to make his presence know on the battlefield.

Until now Markus had stood back from the fight, keeping a close eye on the field. Now Markus unsheathed his sword and strode fearlessly into the thick of the battle. The general easily cut his way across the field knowing exactly who his target was. The general had always believed that to kill the body of an army you had to cut off its head, which was exactly what he planned to do. Anyone who came even close to Markus was easily dealt with by the seasoned warrior as he drew closer and closer to his target, Markus was heading straight for captain Holdak.

"It is your time captain!" Markus yelled when he was close enough for Holdak to hear. The captain looked to where the shout had come from just in time to see Markus cut down a young soldier, enraged by the sight Holdak ran straight for the general.

Markus easily sidestepped Holdak's charge sweeping his sword around at the captains head. Holdak ducked under the blade as he tried to change the direction of his charge, but Markus kicked him in the side causing Holdak to stumble uncontrollably before falling into the dirt.

Markus laughed as he walked up to Holdak, "So you are the one chose to lead this rabble? I am not impressed." Markus raised his sword, ready to bring it down in a killing blow but Holdak was not going to die so easily. The seasoned warrior rolled to the side leaving Markus' sword nothing but dirt to kill. He kicked out catching the General in the knee and forcing him to stumble to the side, giving Holdak the time he needed to get back to his feet.

"So there is some fight in you." Markus laughed as he raised his sword before him. Holdak attacked again but Markus easily parried the strike before slamming his mailed fist into Holdak's jaw. The captain spun away, blood dripping from the side of his mouth.

"This must really upset your men," Markus taunted, "Seeing their leader so greatly outmatched." Markus began a barrage of attacks on Holdak; the captain parried most until Markus forced his defence out wide before kicking him hard in the gut making him fall backwards to the ground.

"Time to kill your armies body," Markus placed his boot on Holdak's gut to keep him in place, "By cutting off its head." The general raised his sword ready for one final killing blow.

Holdak laughed as he looked up at his killer, "You think my men will falter if I die?" Markus held off on his attack, curious as to what Holdak had to say. "My army is like no normal beast, my troops fight like a hydra. If you cut off one head two more shall grow in its place. Kill me and they will only fight harder, that is how I trained them."

"We shall see." Markus buried his sword deep into Holdak's chest. "You were a worth adversary captain Holdak, if outclassed. You have died well fighting for your misguided world, for that you have my respect."

"You truly believe what you are doing is right," Holdak spat, "And for that you are a fool." He finished with his dying breath.

*   *   *

The faith Markus had in his lieutenants was not miss placed, both Antonema and Kevgeon had plans in place to help tip the flow of battle in their favour. Kevgeon's plan was simple, unleash a secret weapon. This secret weapon came in the form of a powerful orc shaman who specialised in fighting close combat battles.

At Kevgeon's signal the shaman unleashed his devastating attack. The magic the shaman used was very potent and he was able to direct it so precisely that he could kill his targets without harming the people they were fighting. It didn't take long for the shaman to turn the tide of the battle putting both Malik's barbarians and the elves on the back foot for the first time. Many tried to reach the shaman in an attempt to regain control of the fight but those who did manage to get close were cut down by the shaman's bodyguards, four large ogres.

Kevgeon laughed as he watched the elves and the proud barbarians running and hiding from the shamans magic. Kevgeon knew that as long as his shaman remained safe this battle would be his.

Antonema also had a simple plan, though his had taken much longer to prepare. The assassin waited for the precise moment that his plan would be most effective against his enemies, and when that moment arrived he signalled to one of his men. The soldier blew on a horn hanging around his neck.

The horn made a low rumbling sound that once heard made some of Antonema's troops leap into action. It was in that moment that Grakenster's army and the etharii realised that Antonema had obviously had his troops setting the field of battle long before they had marched out this morning.

Antonema's army almost doubled in size in a matter of moments. Antonema had spent a great deal of time on this field since he had moved to Getandor, and he had sent many of his followers out to this very spot each night. He had them digging holes, a great many holes perfectly hidden in the ground with wooden trapdoors covered with turf. When the horn had sounded the trapdoors had been flung open revealing more of Antonema's troops, all of whom had been sitting in wait since the night before.

Grakenster's army and the etharii now found themselves surrounded and greatly outnumbered. Many were killed in the confusion, but it didn't take the warriors long to regain their composure. Even though they managed to put up a good defence they were now facing overwhelming odds.

*   *   *

"What exactly happened back there?" Laucian asked as he descended deeper into the palace cellars with Solaris and Elana.

"I thought everyone in the legion of Strakstaw had their memories erased before joining." Elana added.

"That is not always the case," Solaris explained, "Legion always has a handful of followers who join him willingly. They are usually the most dangerous of his disciples, they are true believers in his cause. If we defeat Legion most of his followers will regain the memories of their previous lives, many of them spending the rest of their lives trying to atone for their part. His willing followers however will spend their time trying to complete their masters work, or seeking revenge on those the see as responsible for Legion's downfall."

"But how does that explain Deventis?"

"It does not. I have never heard of one like him before. He has somehow managed to deceive Legion. He must have convinced the beast of his loyalty to have been allowed to retain his memory, he must also be a part of Legion's inner circle to have been here in the palace as what seems to be the last line of defence for Legion. He is a brave man to go against Legion like this; it is a shame that your friend will have to kill him if he plans to survive himself."

Chapter 25
Turn of the Tide

"This is the first time one of my followers has managed to deceive me." Legion said as Solaris, Laucian and Elana entered the room. "Some may think I would despise him for what he has done, but I do not. I am proud of him. It takes a great man to do this to me and that is why I recruited him. He has done too much to help my cause for me to be angry at him for turning on me now."

Laucian and Elana moved to flank the beast while Solaris strode boldly forward, each one of them with weapons in hand. The three warriors glanced at each other, making sure they were all in position before attacking. Solaris was the first to move, he ran forward aiming his sword for Legion's lower back. The beast span around with unnatural speed, easily parrying the attack with his own sword.

Laucian and Elana attacked at the same time, Elana with her crossbow and Laucian with his throwing knives. Legion ignored the attack, allowing the knives and bolts hit him. Any of the weapons that penetrated his scaly hide seemed to cause no reaction in the beast, it was almost like he had not been attacked at all.

Legion swung a huge fist at Solaris who ducked under the blow and span away. Elana fired at Legion again, but the bolt had no effect like before. Solaris closed his eyes for a moment, as he opened them again it looked as though a fire burned behind them. Within a instant yellow flames had spread over his entire body making him look to be a man made completely of living flames.

"I have seen that trick before, I am still unimpressed." Legion pressed forward as he spoke. Solaris easily parried and dodged the onslaught until he eventually worked his way under Legion's defences. Solaris leaped forward hitting Legion in the chest with his shoulder, the sound of sizzling could be heard as the monster's green scales burned, it was clear to see from his reaction that Legion was in pain but he still kept his stern composure.

"As I told you before," Legion caught hold of Solaris by the throat, "Your flames cannot harm me."

"Oh come now, they hurt a little." Solaris said as he tried to break free of Legion's grip. The beast laughed before he flung Solaris towards a wall.

"Pain is in the mind little man." Legion taunted as Solaris tried to rise to his feet, "But your flames still lack the intensity to burn through my scales."

"Lets see if this will break though your hide!" Laucian called as he ran forward slicing his mind blade up Legion's back, directly between the beasts wings. Legion roared in pain and anger as he span around to face his attacker. Laucian ducked under a wing but as he rose again Legion caught him in the chest with a huge arm, sending Laucian flying across the room.

"That cut deep insect. I doubt you will get to do that again." Legion snarled as Laucian slowly climbed back to his feet. He staggered backwards trying to shake the grogginess from his head.

Elana ran to her friends side, firing her crossbow as she went. Laucian waved her away as he regained his composure; he summoned his mind blade back to his hand. Laucian tested his grip on the black flaming sword before he moved forward again. Solaris moved in on the beast too, Legion's attack had reverted him back to his normal form so the immortal began to summon the flames around his body again. Elana kept firing bolts at Legion, hoping to cover her allies attack.

The renewed attack proved to be of little effect. Solaris and Laucian attacked from opposite sides but Legion was ready for them. Solaris stabbed low, but his blade was knocked out wide as Legion parried the strike. As he blocked the attack from Solaris Legion also caught hold of Laucian with surprising ease. He held Laucian by the throat, lifting him from the ground before he had even managed to make his attack.

Elana's attack was going largely unnoticed by Legion. Most of her bolts simply bounced off of the beasts thick scales, and those which did penetrate Legion's hide barely dug into the flesh underneath. Solaris continued his attack, which was becoming increasingly difficult as Legion was beginning to use Laucian as a shield. Solaris now had to defend against Legion's attacks as well as try to avoid injuring his companion with his own.

Laucian was fighting to loosen Legion's grip on his throat. The fact that Laucian didn't need to breathe was the only reason he was still alive, but Legion's grip was tight and getting tighter, it wasn't going to be long before Laucian's neck would break. Elana decided that her crossbow was useless in this fight and so drew her slender sword an ran forward. As she did Legion span quickly and threw Laucian. Laucian flew straight into Elana, hitting her with enough force to send them both tumbling across the room. Elana tried to get up, but fell straight back to the floor. She glanced over to her friend who was not moving at all. This left Solaris fighting Legion alone.

"So you are the best your world had to offer?" Legion mocked as he slammed the hilt of his sword into the side of Solaris' head. Solaris staggered backwards, the flames covering his body disappearing as he did.

Legion laughed, "Your flames really are quite disappointing. As I recall you couldn't keep them burning the first time we fought. Your predecessor would be ashamed if she realised how pathetic her chosen successor has turned out to be."

"My flames have improved since we last met." As Solaris spoke he concentrated on his flames which returned across his body, he focused harder on the fire and as he did the flames burned brighter, with greater intensity.

"Impressive," Legion kicked out at Solaris, hitting the immortal in the chest he sent Solaris flying backwards. "That was actually quite painful. Shame you seem to be quite defenceless while you *heat up*." Legion was laughing as Solaris again returned to normal.

*   *   *

Deventis picked himself up from the floor, laughing as he got back to his feet. The fight between him and his son had raged since the others had left. Both sorcerers had suffered some brutal injuries; both were bruised and bleeding from where they had failed to avoid bolts of energy, flaming arrows, or other such spells.

"You are still holding back." Deventis created a small ball of light in his hand and threw it at his son. Tanay's spear glowed as the young man used it to knock the glowing ball into the wall. "I told you not to hold back my son. If you don't kill me then I will kill you."

Tanay hesitated for a moment, he knew that his father had done terrible things that he needed to pay the price for, but a part of him was still a good man. Everything Deventis had done was in preparation for this moment, where his deception could help save the world from Legion. Tanay wasn't sure if he could take his fathers life.

The moment of hesitation cost Tanay greatly. Deventis did not hesitate and began to throw a series of spells at his son. Tanay was hit by a barrage of small energy bolts causing him to stagger backwards. With Tanay off balance Deventis created a pale blue orb about twice the size of a cannon ball and launched it at the young sorcerer. Tanay was hit in the chest by the orb and sent crashing into the wall behind him where his head cracked on the stone.

Deventis walked over to where the young man was now slumped by the wall. Deventis crouched by Tanay's side, "I truly am sorry my son. I never wanted things to end this way, I always believed that you would be able to defeat me. It seems I was wrong. Now I must go and kill your friends, helping Legion complete his task." Deventis stood and began to walk towards the corridor leading to Legion. "It is quite amusing, this war of Legion's. If no-one stood against him, if there was no battle then his rituals would not work." Deventis glanced back at his slumped son before carrying on, "Yes his army would have decimated the land, but his ritual would have had none of the power it gains through the battle."

"You were right." Deventis turned to see his son standing again. Tanay was leaning heavily on his spear. It was clear to see that he was badly wounded but he was not willing to give up the fight. "I was holding back father. I will not make that mistake again."

Deventis smiled as he took a few steps towards his Tanay. The sorcerer created several more energy bolts and began to throw them at his son. Tanay let go of his spear and dropped to his knee, he pulled a small green gem from a pouch and threw it at his father as the energy bolts flew over his head. The gem exploded a little in front of Deventis covering him in a sticky resin.

Deventis staggered a little as he tried to wipe the tar like resin from his face. The old sorcerer managed to clear the substance from his eyes just in time to see a small ball of fire heading towards him. Deventis tried to dodge the fireball but it was too late, as it struck him the stick resin caught fire. Deventis screamed in agony as the flames engulfed him. He tried to concentrate through the pain to summon up a spell to douse the fire, eventually managing to summon a small torrent of water. Deventis fell to his knees, his body covered in burnt flesh.

Deventis looked up at his son who was standing over him leaning on his spear again, "That's better my boy, but I'm not beaten yet." Deventis grabbed for the spear but Tanay yanked it away making Deventis fall forward to the floor.

"I'm afraid you are father." Tanay crouched over his father, the burnt man rolled onto his back and looked up to Tanay who was holding a small curved dagger. "I know you are a good man father, trying to do what you can in a dark world. I am grateful for everything you have done for me."

"So this is how my story ends." Deventis smiled.

"Exactly how you designed it to. I hope you find the peace in death that this world would not allow you in life." Tanay stabbed his father in the chest, cutting straight through to his heart. Deventis fought the urge to call out in pain.

"Thank you, my son." Deventis stuttered as he died. Tanay used his spear to pull himself back up to his feet before starting off to help his friends fighting Legion.

*　　*　　*

Nasgaroth and Slantary battled furiously above the armies. Each biting and clawing at the other. Roscoe was holding on tight trying to avoid being burned by Slantary's fiery breath. The little halfling was trying to keep a close eye on the battle below, he could see that it was not fairing well for his friends. It was Kevgeon's shaman who really caught his attention though.

"We have to help them!" shouted the halfling. Nasgaroth glanced down at the battle for a moment. Slantary took advantage of the laps in concentration and slammed herself into Nasgaroth's side. The gold Dragon began to plummet towards the ground barely saving himself and swooping over the heads of the warriors below.

"I'm afraid I am a little busy with my own fight." Nasgaroth growled, "If you want to help the other you will have to do it yourself."

Roscoe thought about how he could help, thinking over all Nasgaroth had taught him about the Wentar words and how he could use them here. "Can you at least swoop over there?"

Nasgaroth looked to where Roscoe wanted to go before swooping towards the shaman. Roscoe waited for the perfect moment before he jumped from Nasgaroth's back. The halfling called out one of the words Nasgaroth had taught him and his decent began to slow. He landed softly on his feet a little way behind the shaman, luckily avoiding the notice of the shaman's four ogre bodyguards. They were all focused on the retreating enemy leaving Roscoe open to attack the shaman directly.

He drew his sword and ran up behind the shaman, stabbing the wild magic user in the back. The shaman screamed as he spun round, yanking the sword out of Roscoe's hand. The halfling backed away as the shaman stared down at his murderer. The four ogres reacted quickly to the scream, realising that they may have just failed in their one job in this battle, to protect the shaman at all costs.

The shaman tried to curse Roscoe as he fell to the ground, unable to understand how he had been brought so low by a mere halfling. Roscoe took another step back as the shaman died, suddenly very aware of the fact there were now four raging ogres charging at him and his sword was still stuck in the shamans back. Despite his predicament the halfling couldn't help but smile, knowing that he may well have just shifted the course of this part of the battle in his friends favour.

Malik could see what was unfolding with Roscoe and the shaman and couldn't believe that the little halfling had just achieved what he and his barbarians had failed to do. "Do you fools want to be out fought by a little song bird?" Malik yelled, their was a large roar from those around him. "TO THE HALFLING!!" Malik charged followed closely by Branack and the barbarians, who were in turn followed by the elven infantry.

Roscoe began to panic as the ogres closed in, the first swinging a huge club at the halfling. "*Hashnay*!" Roscoe called, turning him intangible so the club passed straight through him. The magic wore off however just as the ogre ploughed into him, sending Roscoe tumbling to the ground, tripping the ogre who rolled to the floor behind the halfling. Roscoe quickly shook off the dizziness of the impact knowing that there were three more ogres running at him, and the other would not take long to regain its composure.

Roscoe leaped to his feet just as the other ogres reached him, calling out another of the Wentar words he vanished completely from sight. The ogres stopped dead in their tracks looking to see where the halfling had gone.

Roscoe was now behind the ogres next to the dead shaman. He quickly retrieved his sword, planning to run back to his allies, though he never got the chance. Roscoe had been paying so much attention to the ogres that he hadn't noticed Kevgeon's approach. The half-orc grabbed hold of the back of Roscoe's shirt and lifted him from the ground, the halfling struggled to get free but to no avail.

"You killed my shaman," Kevgeon grunted, "You are either very brave, or very stupid." Kevgeon looked over to the ogres, who all now stood waiting for their commander's orders. The half-orc laughed, "Either way about to become very dead."

Kevgeon threw Roscoe over to the ogres, each of them smiling broadly as the halfling landed at their feet. Roscoe looked up at the ogres, trying to think of some way out of this deadly situation.

Kevgeon now turned his attention his enemies new charge. "Hold the line!" Yelled the half-orc. Kevgeon's troops ran to his side, forming into ranks ready for the coming onslaught.

Malik and Branack were the first to reach the enemy line. Malik swung his huge club, smashing those before him out of the way. The barbarian didn't slow in his charge, he was heading straight for where Kevgeon had thrown Roscoe, determined to reach his friend. Branack had a different mission in this charge, as he reached the enemy line he swung his axe straight for Kevgeon. The two half-orcs had been looking for each other during the course of the battle, though they had only met once before they had taken an almost instant dislike to one another. Branack had forsaken his orcish heritage, where as Kevgeon had forsaken his human half.

Kevgeon blocked the attack spinning round with his double-ended axe,aiming for Branack's gut. Branack easily avoided the attack by skipping away backwards. As he did the rest of the charging barbarians and elves reached the enemy line. The attack was devastating, the ranks of Kevgeon's army were all but shattered. Without the shaman to protect them Kevgeon's army appeared doomed to be overrun by the superior force.

*   *   *

Havak was running across the open space of the battlefield, his target was the archers covering the forward infantry. The running giant caught the attention of a man who up until now had just observed the battle, waiting for the right moment he felt he could best serve in the fight.

"I think it is time to show that beast the feral strength of our world." Arch-druid Duranas stepped forward slightly, calling upon his ability to change into a huge werewolf. The transformation took a matter of seconds, turning the unassuming man into an eight foot tall monster of muscle and claws covered in thick brown fur.

"There was a time I would have said I'd take the beast, but you know what, he's all yours big guy." Duranas looked down at the elven ranger, Larenor winked at the werewolf, "I'll cover you."

Duranas laughed as he tuned back to Havak, and began his own charge. Larenor left the air warriors to cover the infantry and moved out to flank Havak, firing arrows as he went. Havak slowed slightly as the arrows hit home, the elf's aim was perfect but it would take more than a few pointy sticks to stop Havak.

Havak had easily crossed the battlefield so far by using his superior strength to force his way through anyone who had gotten in his way, but Duranas planned to stop his run. The werewolf was still smaller than Havak but his taught muscles held a great amount of strength. As the two colossal beasts neared each other they both prepared for the assault. Duranas crouched low, ready to tackle Havak.

Havak expected to do the same to Duranas as he had everyone else, planning to simply knock the smaller opponent out of his way and carry on to his real target, the archers. Duranas was not to be underestimated though, he launched himself forward hitting the beast at about waist hight with his shoulder. Much to Havak's surprise he was knocked clean off his feet and landed hard on his back as Duranas rolled away.

Duranas quickly got back to his feet, ready for any counter attack that may be coming from the beast. Havak smiled as he too climbed bat to his feet, he realised now that he was about to face his first real challenge in this battle. Duranas charged again, this time however Havak was ready for him. The beast side stepped the werewolf, though Duranas still managed to slash his claws across Havak's side. Havak growled as he caught hold of Duranas by the shoulder.

"You're strong," Havak laughed, "But I'm stronger." Havak pulled hard on Duranas' shoulder and threw him to the ground.

"You may be stronger," Havak began to advance on Duranas, "But I do not fight alone." As Duranas spoke Havak was hit by another barrage of arrows, although they did little harm to the beast the seemingly supernatural speed and accuracy of Larenor's attack made Havak stumble back.

The moment of respite gave Duranas the time he needed to get back to his feet and regain some composure. Havak was becoming annoyed by the elven archer, he reached down and picked up a rock which he launched at Larenor's head, but the ranger easily dodged it. Duranas took this chance to renew his attack on Havak. No longer having a clear shot at the beast Larenor drew his sword Fear Bringer and charged forward.

The werewolf dug his claws deep into Havak's gut, as the beast doubled over in pain Duranas bite down hard into its shoulder. Havak howled in pain before taking hold of Duranas and forcing his away, ripping a large chunk of flesh to be ripped away from the beasts shoulder as he did. Havak threw the werewolf to the ground and was about to leap onto it when Larenor attacked.

Larenor ran up behind Havak and sliced Fear Bringer across the beasts hamstrings. Havak's legs gave out under him and he dropped to his knees. Larenor's next strike sliced up the beasts back, Havak roared as he arched his back. Larenor skipped away as Duranas ploughed into the the stricken Havak. Duranas grabbed hold of one of Larenor's arrows that was stuck in Havak's chest and pushed hard, forcing the arrow deeper until it pierced the beasts black heart.

Havak fell to the ground clutching the arrow. The beast began to writhe around, he tried to get back to his feet but all his tremendous strength was leaving him. The beast began to cough violently as it struggled with the arrow, inadvertently forcing it deeper into his chest.

Duranas and Larenor stood over Havak, watching the beast struggle to get up. It was clear to both of them that Havak was dying, very painfully.

"I never could watch a creature in distress." Larenor said as he sliced his magical sword across the beasts throat, killing Havak quickly and cleanly so to end it's suffering.

Chapter 26
Elvin's Champion

Laucian opened his eyes, blinking a couple of times to adjust to the light. He was no longer in the room with his friends and Legion was nowhere to be seen. Laucian climbed to his feet staggering slightly, he was almost overwhelmed by dizziness and his head throbbed with pain.

Laucian took a moment to look at his surroundings, or lack of them. There was nothing to see in any direction, it was just white. If he had not been standing on it he could have easily believed that there was no floor as it looked to be the same endless whiteness as all around him.

"No, you are not dead."Laucian span around at the sound of the voice to find himself face to face with an almost double of himself.

"Who are you?" Laucian asked. He thought of summoning his mind blade, keeping the idea close to his mind ready for any danger.

"You are the first mortal to ever see my true form." The double replied. Laucian looked closely at the man before him. He was wearing loose fitting cloths; they were almost like robes in a pale blue colour. The only physical difference between the pair was their hair. Where as Laucian's was black the doubles hair was streaked both black and white.

"You are Elvin aren't you?"

"Yes." the double replied, "And I have brought you here because I wanted to help."

"You may have rescued me by bringing me here, but you have left my friends to fight alone. I would have preferred to have been left there."

"And that is why I am making you my champion, because even facing the fear of death you still choose to go back to fight along side your friends."

"I do not fear death."

"What are you afraid of?" Laucian was stunned by the question. "What is wrong? It is not a difficult question."

"I am not afraid of anything."

Elvin laughed, "Think of whom you are speaking with. I know that anyone who claims to fear nothing is either a fool or a liar, and you are no fool."

Laucian thought before speaking again, "I am afraid that I will fail." he began, "I am afraid that I will let my friends down."

"But what do you fear the most?"

Laucian looked the god in the eyes, "I am afraid of myself."

Elvin smiled, "You are going to face many trials in your life, as long as you survive. So to help you on your path I grant you the title of Elvin's champion, and with it the blessing of a god."

As he spoke Elvin reached out and touched Laucian's arm. The tattoo on his shoulder came to life in that moment; the dragon and glaive pattern began to change. The glaive became larger with four runes on the blade. The dragon too changed, it became the image of a monstrous roaring beast with scales of red and orange. The image of the dragon was clutching onto the glaive with its tail coiling around the lower part of Laucian's arm and disappearing under his bracer.

"I also give you these." Elvin handed Laucian a pair of gloves, "These will enhance your mind blade ability. They will give you the ability to create any weapon you choose, as long as it has no moving parts."

Laucian removed his bracer's making visible the lover part of his newly extended tattoo, showing the dragon's tail ending on the inside of his wrist. Laucian put on the gloves; they were black leather with cut off fingers. The back was slightly padded to give a little extra protection to his hands and the palms had been designed to help with grip.

"Did I also mention that with these you will also be able to summon one weapon per hand? As long as they are both single handed weapons of course."

Laucian smiled as he summoned a knife into each hand, they both looked similar to his mind blade, black with a translucent flame covering them.

"And with these gifts I send you back." As Elvin spoke Laucian vanished from the white space, leaving Elvin seemingly standing alone.

"Are you sure this course of action is wise?"

"Are you questioning me?" Elvin turned to face his servant as he spoke.

The servant shrank under Elvin's gaze, "No my lord. I only feel that it may be dangerous to play the brother's against one another in this way."

"The signs show that one of them will attain some kind of ultimate power, and whichever one it is will be within my influence."

*   *   *

Pattumal and Maria were working hard to help the armies archers cover the infantry units. Even with their superb accuracy though, there was little they could do to help their allies from being overrun by Markus' army.

Pattumal eventually noticed a sound coming from the forest behind them. He turned to see what it was but could see nothing through the trees. The sound was getting louder as it drew closer; it became clear to the elven archer that it was a battle cry. By now Maria and a few others had heard the sound too, all of them growing worried that they were about to be attacked from behind by some previously hidden enemy.

Pattumal started barking orders, he had a number of the archers form up in ranks ready to face this new threat. The elf moved forward of the others as the noise grew closer, he wanted to make sure he had room to move, planing to take as many of this new enemy down before they could reach the other archers. The battle cry was getting close now, it sounded as though hundreds of warriors were about to come charging out of the forest.

Pattumal was sighting down an arrow as a lone dwarf came running out of the tree line. He looked back at Maria who seemed to be as confused as he was at the sight of the dwarf.

"Get out of the way! Ya damn blasted elf!" Davkul yelled as he ran straight towards the elven archer, who just stood there with a dumb look on his face.

Pattumal's expression soon changed to panic as about twenty paces behind the first dwarf the rest of his army charged out of the forest. The elf sprang into action, he was running much like his wife and the other archers, all of them trying to get out of the way of the dwarves. Most managed to avoid dwarven army, and fortunately for those who didn't the dwarves showed surprising agility in avoiding knocking them to the ground and trampling them to death. The dwarves all followed their king's lead, heading straight for the centre of the battle.

Davkul hit the enemy hard, killing several in his opening attack. He swung his axe with such precision that those who did survive his attacks still fell to the ground clutching severe wounds, most surviving only long enough to be trampled by the following army. The dwarven charge managed to force their enemies to begin falling back, giving their allies a much needed chance to regroup.

Even with this new dwarven onslaught it didn't take general Markus long to get his troops back into formation so they could renew their attack. Davkul had quickly made his way into the thick of the battle trying to find his allies commanding officer. The dwarf eventually fought his way to Aramil's side; the paladin was shouting orders to both the huge warriors of earth and the Getandor soldiers in an attempt to take full advantage of the dwarves opening attack.

"Where's Holdak?" Davkul called out.

"Already fallen." Aramil replied. Both warriors were fighting back to back now, each fending off enemy troops as they spoke.

"His followers still fight hard?" Davkul was worried about the soldiers moral after the death of their captain.

"They fight harder," Aramil explained, "They fight to both honour and avenge their fallen leader."

Davkul smiled at the sentiment, "So these bastards tried to defeat the troops by killing the leader, what do you say we return the favour?"

"I was having the same thought." Aramil was glad to have the dwarf with him now. He had little experience leading so many in battle, but this dwarf seemed to be well versed in the art of war.

"So who leads this rabble?"

"His name is Markus." Aramil pointed the general out to Davkul.

"Then shall we?" Davkul started to make his way towards where Markus fought.

Aramil smiled, "It would be my pleasure."

*   *   *

Delensa stood at the edge of the battlefield; she still doubted how much good she could really do but decided that she had to at least try. She dropped her staff to the ground, knowing that in this close quarter combat she would not have the room to use the weapon to full effect.

The monk could see that Antonema's force greatly outnumbered Grakenster's troops and the etharii. If the battle continued as it was then Antonema's troops would soon wipe out those allied against them. Delensa ran into the battle, using her extensive training in unarmed combat to quickly kill of immobilize anyone who drew too close. As she fought her way through the mass of soldiers many thought they saw clouds of smoke appearing and disappearing around her.

Eventually the monk's initial charge began to loose momentum as Antonema's troops began to adapt to this new threat. In a one on one situation the soldiers had not chance against Delensa, she was far too quick and well trained for them to match her but there were more than enough soldiers to surround her, and work down her defences.

It wasn't long before Delensa found herself in a very dangerous position, while she was occupied by two soldiers another made his way behind her. The soldier raised his sword as he stepped forward, but the blow never fell. Instead the soldier drooped to his knees, wondering why he suddenly had a hole in his chest. Within a few seconds any enemy soldiers close to Delensa found themselves to be in a similar situation.

"Now you set an example we can follow." It took Delensa a moment to realise that all of Antonema's soldiers around her were now dead, and she was in fact surrounded by the warriors of fire.

"You came back." Delensa was shocked to see these noble warriors after they had refused to follow her into battle.

"We never left. We were waiting for you to realise that you are capable of leading us." The warrior placed his hand on Delensa's shoulder, "Now, what do you command of us?"

Delensa glanced around at the battle before smiling, "Lets go win this war." As soon as Delensa spoke the words the warriors of fire reacted. They quickly spread out across the battlefield leaving a trail of dead enemies in their wake.

Grakenster watched his new allies slicing their way through Antonema's troops and saw this as the perfect opportunity to make his move against the enemy commander. The assassin had been massacring Grakenster's troops and the hobgoblin decided it was time to put this human in his place. He yelled for his troops close by to form a tight wedge formation around him. The hobgoblin began a charge across the field, using his troops as a shield Grakenster quickly made his way towards Antonema.

The assassin had built up an impressive body count during the battle. He had easily despatched anyone foolish enough to get too close to his deadly sword. Antonema saw Grakenster's approach and was not entirely sure what to expect from the tightly packed unit heading in his direction. The assassin called out to those around him, quickly preparing them for Grakenster's attack.

Grakenster finally gave the order for his troops to break formation; they spread out quickly and attacked those around Antonema. This left a clear path between the hobgoblin and the assassin. Grakenster charged straight forward, holding his large curved sword out to the side he raised his crude shield planning to ram it into the assassin's smug human face.

Antonema easily avoided Grakenster's attack, spinning around behind the hobgoblin. Antonema moved in to kill his opponent thinking he had found another easy target. Grakenster had no intention of dying so easily though, quickly twisting round the hobgoblin managed to use his shield to block Antonema's strike before bringing his own sword in low aiming for the assassin's gut. Antonema leaped backwards, smiling as he did. It seemed this hobgoblin was going to provide a greater challenge than he first believed, but the assassin was still confident he would have no real trouble.

The pair fought back and forth, Antonema using very precise attacks to try and wear down his opponent. Grakenster however was much more random with his attacks, there was no real style to his onslaught but he still managed to keep the assassin on the back foot. Antonema was struggling to find an opening in Grakenster's defence, despite the seemingly confused fighting style of his enemy Grakenster always seemed able to have his shield between him and the assassin.

When Antonema was eventually able to force Grakenster's shield out wide and he took full advantage of the opportunity, he quickly pressed forward slicing the hobgoblin across the gut. Grakenster staggered back until he caught his boot on one of the many corpses and fell to the ground as blood began to soak through his armour. The cut wasn't deep and would probably not even scar, but Grakenster knew that if he didn't find a weakness in Antonema's defence soon then it would not be long before he suffered far worse.

Grakenster tried to get back to his feet, but Antonema was stood over him and kicked him back to the ground. Antonema went for a killing blow but Grakenster was not finished yet. The hobgoblin dropped his shield a grabbed a handful of dirt which he threw in the assassin's face before rolling away. Antonema took a couple of steps backwards as he wiped the dirt from his eyes. Grakenster made it back to his feet and charged again. The assassin barely had chance to defend himself but just managed to dodge out of Grakenster's path.

The hobgoblin growled as he skidded to a halt, angry at the fact he had just run passed his enemy. He turned just in time to see Antonema was right on top of him, the assassin elbowed Grakenster in the face breaking his nose. Grakenster stumbled again, blood pouring down his face.

"And I thought you might prove to be a challenge." Antonema laughed. He moved to strike Grakenster again but stumbled as he did, falling to one knee. As he had moved he was kicked in the back of the leg and now Delensa skipped passed him to stand by Grakenster's side.

Antonema rose to his feet, smiling as he did, "Two against one, this should make things more interesting."

*　　*　　*

Kevgeon swung his huge double-ended axe with incredible precision, trying his damnedest to kill Branack. The two half-orcs were in a fierce battle; both had flown into a rage when they had met. Anyone foolish enough to stray too close were brutally cut down by one of the huge axes being swung around freely.

"You are weak!" Kevgeon yelled, "You have denied your true strength!"

Branack growled as he pushed forward, punching Kevgeon in the gut as he did. "If I'm weak why are you hurting so much?"

Kevgeon charged forward forcing Branack to leap out of the way. Kevgeon quickly spun, bringing his axe round in a low arc aiming for Branack's gut. Branack managed to block the swing, pushing hard he forced Kevgeon's weapon to the side before striking him in the side oh the head with his axe's handle.

Kevgeon stumbled as Branack raised his axe above his head. Branack brought his weapon down with all his strength, Kevgeon raised his own weapon to block the swing but Branack's axe smashed through the weapons handle before it was embedded deep into Kevgeon's shoulder. Branack ripped his axe free as Kevgeon roared in agony and fell to his knees, dropping his broken axe to the ground.

Kevgeon looked up at Branack who was now standing over him. "You may kill me today, you may think this some great victory over the dark side of your soul, but it will not change anything. You are still an orc!"

Branack smiled as he looked down at his helpless opponent, "I am only half orc." Branack swung his axe again, this time aiming for Kevgeon's neck. The axe tore through Kevgeon's flesh and bone, easily separating his head from his shoulders.

All those near the fight watched with awe, none had ever seen a fight between two so enraged combatants. Now it was over there was a great deal of confusion among the ranks. Kevgeon's troops were all but overrun, and those left had lost the will to fight. Now that their leader was dead and with Legion busy fighting his own battle they were beginning to break free of the demon gods control. They were beginning to remember who they truly were, they were remembering their lives from before they had been recruited into the legion of Strakstaw. It wasn't long before what remained of Kevgeon's troops were laying down their weapons and surrendering themselves to the barbarians and elves.

Branack made his way to Malik, the huge barbarian was kneeling on the ground surrounded by four dead ogres. Malik was kneeling over the halfling Roscoe.

"Alive?" Branack asked as he drew close. Malik looked up at the half-orc and shook his head as tears rolled down his cheeks. Malik picked up the dead halfling and carried him over to the his tribe.

"He will be remembered as a true hero. My people will sing songs of his bravery for generations to come." Malik handed Roscoe over to a member of the bear tribe before he went off to help round up the last few of Kevgeon's soldiers. Those who surrendered were bunched together, surrounded by both barbarians and elves. Those who did no surrender were soon caught or killed by an angry and grieving barbarian.

Chapter 27
Victory?

The battle had been raging for hours, the day was just dawning when the armies had met but now the sun was at its zenith. Countless men and women had already died fighting for what they believed in, each one a hero for their respective cause. Nasgaroth had no time to consider the fallen now, he had to focus on the living and most prominently his enemy Slantary.

The red dragon was proving to be a fearsome foe, far stronger than Nasgaroth had given her credit for. Slantary had managed to swoop behind the gold dragon, clutching onto his back with her hind legs she began to tear into his left wing with her talons. Nasgaroth roared as he began to plummet to the ground, the gold dragon managed to guide his decent enough to avoid landing on any of the soldiers below but still hit the ground hard as Slantary launched off his back moments before.

Nasgaroth tried to stand but his legs gave out under his own weight, he was fairly certain that at least one had been broken when he collided with the earth. Slantary had landed too, she was laughing as she ran straight at her injured opponent. Slantary was about to pounce when she stopped dead in her tracks, she had just been struck in the side and head by numerous bolts of lightning and ice.

The mages of water spread out around Slantary hitting the beast with everything they had, the dragon backed away a little but the attack was little more than a distraction to her. The distraction was all that Kimanay needed though. The cleric had run up the back of Nasgaroth and when she reached his shoulder launched herself at Slantary. Swinging her heavy mace Kimanay struck the red dragon in the side of her jaw before falling back to the ground, one of the water mages quickly cast a spell so that the cleric landed softly on her feet.

Slantary staggered back, shocked at how painful this mere mortals attack had been, "How dare you? Pathetic insect!"

Kimanay swung her mace back and forth, "Go and help the dragon, I'll deal with this beast." The water mages nodded before running to try and heal Nasgaroth.

"You will deal with me?" Slantary laughed as she examined the warrior before her. "The sigil on your shield, you are a priest of Sugalas?"

"I am."

The dragon looked up at the sun, "Then shouldn't you be running off to you midday prayers?"

"I doubt my lord will mind if I miss them today."

"Why don't you ask him." Slantary tilted her head back as she took in a sharp breath before unleashing a fiery torrent at Kimanay.

The flames engulfed Kimanay and Slantary had to give her credit, the cleric didn't scream. As the flames cleared the ground had been scorched black, all that remained was Kimanay, who much to Slantary's surprise was not a burnt corpse. The cleric had hidden behind her shield which glowed red from the heat, but beyond this she appeared completely untouched by the flames.

"It seems that even without today's prayers I am still have my god's favour."

"Impossible!" Slantary roared as she stared at the sun priest.

"They say that dragon fire is the hottest thing in our world, lets see how it stacks up against the brightest thing in the heavens." Kimanay swung her mace at her side, the metal head of which had now changed into what appeared to be a miniature sun.

With a smile to herself Kimanay charged forward. Slantary swiped at the cleric with one leg but she ducked under the attack and kept going, swinging her sun mace at the dragon's other fore leg. The dragon screamed as the miniature sun burned through her usually fire resistant scales. Kimanay had to dive out of the way of the dragon's bulk as its leg buckled and she came crashing to the ground.

Kimanay move fast, running up the side of Slantary in much the same way she done with Nasgaroth earlier, only this time she was striking the dragon with her mace as she went. As she reached the monster's neck the dragon shook herself and Kimanay lost her footing and fell hard to the ground. The cleric got back to her feet just in time to see the dragons tail coming at her, she managed to raise her shield in time but was still sent flying across the field.

When Kimanay rolled to a stop she lay still, her entire body in agony. She looked up to see the dragon pouncing towards her, she tried to raise her shield only to realise that she must have dropped it. Just as the dragon should have landed on the cleric the colossal beast was struck hard in the side. The water mages had managed to heal Nasgaroth enough for him to re-enter the fight.

The gold dragon rammed his full bulk into Slantary's side sending her back to the ground. Before she could do anything Nasgaroth was on her. Latching his jaws onto her throat he bit down hard before ripping away a huge chunk of flesh. Nasgaroth stood over Slantary as he spat his enemies blood and meat to the ground.

Slantary's strength was leaving her, but she had enough left for one more attack, one final act of defiance. With one sudden movement she launched herself forward, aiming one of her horns for Nasgaroth's heart. The gold dragon howled as the horn tore through his flesh. Nasgaroth took hold of Slantary's head and forced it to the ground, he snarled as her horn was pulled free from his body.

"Enjoy your time in the abyss." Nasgaroth said. Slantary tried to break free of his grip, but her strength was all but gone. Nasgaroth began to squeeze Slantary's head, the red dragon began to seize violently as he skull was crushed. Nasgaroth took a few steps away from the dead dragon before he too collapsed to the floor. Kimanay and the water mages ran to his side, preparing healing magic as they did.

"Do not worry about me, I shall live." Nasgaroth rasped, "Go and help the others, I shall still be here when this battle is won."

*   *   *

Delensa helped Grakenster back up to his feet, the hobgoblin held his stomach in pain. Antonema rushed forward before his opponents could ready themselves to face him. Delensa easily leaped out of the assassins way, Grakenster however was not as agile though he did barely manage to parry Antonema's sword.

The assassin skipped away before Grakenster could make a counter attack, but he was not expecting Delensa to be attacking as he moved. The elf kneed Antonema hard in the back sending the assassin stumbling forward, straight to where Grakenster was waiting. The hobgoblin hit Antonema across the face with a strong backhand. Antonema quickly backed away, he was shocked at how easily Delensa had blind-sided him. The assassin shook the dizziness from his head and spat blood as he faced the two unlikely allies. The assassin ran forward again this time moving in on Delensa, he planned to keep her in his sights, this elf was too quick for him to risk turning his back on her again.

Antonema swung his sword in a wide arc which Delensa easily ducked under, the assassin suddenly reversed the swing this time keeping his blade low forcing the monk to flip backwards in order to avoid the attack. The assassin spun on the spot ready to face Grakenster who thrust his sword at the assassins chest but the blade was easily blocked. Delensa was back in the fight quicker than Antonema expected, glancing over his shoulder to see her moving in fast. The assassin forced Grakenster backwards before turning to face Delensa, but he was not quick enough and the monk punched him in the face.

Antonema stumbled again, this time straight into Grakenster's grasp. The assassin tried to twist himself free but the hobgoblin held him tight. Antonema managed to free his sword arm swinging his weapon for the advancing Delensa but the monk caught hold of his wrist. Delensa twisted the assassin's wrist forcing his arm out straight before striking hard, shattering bone. Antonema screamed in agony as he dropped his sword.

Grakenster released the assassin, pushing him to the ground as he did. Antonema rolled onto his back just as Grakenster brought his crude sword straight down, stabbing the assassin through the gut. Antonema called out again in pain, many of his soldiers turned to see their leader laying on the ground in agony. They had never before seen their leader injured and now he looked defeated.

Grakenster crouched over the fallen assassin, "You were a worthy opponent. Alone I could never have beaten you, but you are beaten." The hobgoblin smiled as he drew a small knife, "It is the custom of my people to leave a dying enemy on the battlefield so that their suffering will last as long as possible, but I respect your power and so will end your suffering."

Grakenster placed the tip of his knife over Antonema's heart; he forced the blade through he assassin's light armour killing him where he lay. Grakenster walked over to where Antonema had dropped his sword and raised the slender weapon above his head.

"Your leader is dead!" Grakenster shouted, "I claim his weapon as my own and offer you this one chance to surrender or you too shall suffer his fate!"

As had happened with Kevgeon's troops, Legion's hold over Antonema's soldiers began to fade with their leaders death. After a few seconds thought they began to throw down their weapons and surrender themselves to their enemy. A loud cheer erupted from both Grakenster's army and the etharii as they began to round up their prisoners. The warriors of fire remained silent as they surveyed the battlefield and made their way to Delensa's side.

"What now my lady?" One of the fire warriors asked. Delensa took stock of everything going on around her before answering.

"I think these can handle the surrender. There are many of our friends still fighting for their lives, our place is by their side."

The only force still fighting was General Markus' troops. Although they had all but overrun their enemy to begin with the appearance of the dwarves and the extra help from other allies on the battlefield the fight had begun to swing against Markus. Aramil and Davkul were cutting a quick path across the field, easily making their way to where Markus was fighting. They arrived by the general just as he was killing another of the Getandor soldiers.

Davkul charged at Markus with his shield held high. The general was too busy with those around him to notice the dwarf approaching from behind. Davkul's shield slammed hard into Markus' back sending the warrior staggering forward. Markus quickly shook off the attack turning to face the dwarf just in time to see Aramil swinging his sword in an arc above Davkul's head. Markus managed to parry the attack but was unprepared for Davkul's second charge, this time hitting Markus in the stomach with his shield and sending the big man falling backwards. Davkul didn't let up and swung his axe for the general's chest but Markus managed to roll away.

"Finally," Markus laughed as he got back to his feet. "An enemy who knows how to fight." Markus gripped his sword tightly as Davkul and Aramil moved out to his sides. Markus swung his huge weapon at the dwarf who raised his shield to block the swing, but the sheer force of the blow made the sturdy dwarf stagger.

Aramil saw his chance to strike and ran forward. Markus was ready though; turning with unnatural speed the general brought his sword round at mid hight. Aramil stopped and raised his shield in defence. In a fluid movement Markus moved his sword up high and arced it down over Aramil's shield. The paladin backed away slightly raising his own sword to parry the attack.

Davkul was moving again, he tried to ram Markus with his shield again. The general saw the charge coming and dived out of the way leaving Davkul to run straight into Aramil. Markus laughed as the pair tried to regain their composure.

"If only all of my enemies were so willing to attack each other, this little battle would be over by now."

"You really are enjoying this aren't you?" Aramil spat.

"I do take pleasure putting over confident self righteous fools such as you in their place."

"You seem a little overconfident there yourself." Davkul retorted as he ran forward again, Markus swung his sword at the dwarf. Davkul blocked the sword with his shield swinging his axe as he did. The blade caught Markus on the side as he jumped backwards. A line of blood appeared on the generals side soaking through his armour as Davkul moved off to the side.

Aramil ran in after Davkul swinging his sword in a high arc. Markus ducked under the swing and caught hold of the paladin's leg, pulling hard he tripped Aramil sending him tumbling to the ground. Davkul began swinging his axe in a fury forcing Markus backwards. The general was trying to get himself into a position where he could strike back but Davkul's attack was relentless constantly keeping him on the defensive.

Aramil quickly jumped back to his feet and charged forward again, dropping his shield as he did. Davkul suddenly dropped to one knee as Aramil leaped over him, the paladin showed amazing agility as he landed on Davkul's shield before launching himself at Markus with an extra boost from Davkul. Aramil hit Markus squarely in the chest with his shoulder sending both men sprawling to the floor. Markus lost the grip on his sword as he hit the dirt and it skidded away from him. Aramil rolled to the side as Davkul stood over the fallen general.

"I will give you this chance to surrender." Davkul said coldly. Many were watching the events unfold now from both sides. None of Markus' troops had expected to see the mighty warrior bested.

"I will never surrender!" Markus quickly sat up, he shoved Davkul over as he forced himself to his feet. The general found Aramil stood before him now; the paladin thrust his sword into the generals gut. Markus doubled over in pain as Aramil withdrew his sword.

"You should have surrendered." Aramil said calmly as Markus fell to his knees. Davkul was standing behind Aramil now, both watching as Markus tried and failed to get back to his feet. It wasn't long before the general was lying on the ground in an ever growing pool of his own blood.

All of Markus' troops that witnessed his downfall threw down their weapons and surrendered the instant he died. It wasn't long before the generals entire army had given themselves up, and those who refused to surrender were soon cut down by the armies allied against them.

The battle was finally over; with the defeat of Legion's general his hold over the troops was finally broken. They began to return to how they had been before joining the legion of Strakstaw; the memories of their stolen lives began to return to them, many of them felt great shame and remorse for the atrocities they had been forced to perform.

All of the gathered armies began to collect their dead, many of the generals soldiers offering to help. Others swore allegiance to the various aspects of the victorious army. Most of the orcs and goblins made their way to Grakenster's army and the humans went to the soldiers of Getandor or Malik and his barbarians. Others still begged to be allowed to stay in Cemulion, wishing to help rebuild what they had destroyed.

*   *   *

"Well what do you know, they actually won." Magon was sitting in a comfortable chair watching the events unfold in a large crystal ball.

<It is not over yet.> Coran replied.

"Very true. The battle for Getandor is over, but the battle for the world still goes on." Magon waved his hand over the crystal ball and the image began to change. It became darker as the outside battlefield faded and became the image of the catacombs under Cemulion city, where the fight with Legion still raged.

<Do you ever wish you could help them?>

"I do help them, I guide them on their journeys."

<But you have so much magical power; don't you ever want to help them fight?>

"It is not my place to fight my charges battles for them."

<That isn't what I asked.>

"Why aren't you helping them?"

Tanay's familiar smiled as he thought of his answer, <It is not my place to fight my charges battles for them. That doesn't mean I don't want to though.>

"Why did you choose Tanay as your charge anyway?" Magon sat forward as he spoke, "The boy never seemed all that special to me."

<You always focused on those destined for the great battles, I see the potential in those destined to help them. Your prodigy Laucian wouldn't get anywhere if it wasn't for Tanay and Elana, they truly are unsung heroes.>

*　　*　　*

Tanay finally reached the battle with Legion and quickly took in the scene. Laucian was lying on the ground with Elana kneeling over him, whereas Solaris was fighting Legion alone. Tanay made his way into the room still leaning heavily on his spear. He began to think of what spell he should use to suitably announce his arrival.

Tanay pulled a few components from a pouch and muttered a few words over them before throwing them into the air. There was a flash of light and a ball of energy appeared in front of him, the young sorcerer pointed at Legion and the energy ball shot of straight for the demon. Tanay's spell struck Legion in the back, but the energy seemed to just spread out over the demon's scales and do no actual damage. Legion smiled as he clenched his fist and punched Solaris. As Legion struck the immortal all the magical energy from Tanay's spell was expelled from the demon's body through his fist sending Solaris flying across the room and crashing to the floor where he lay motionless.

Legion turned his attention to Tanay now; the sorcerer think of another spell to his the demon with, hoping another would have more effect on the beast. Legion crossed the room with unnatural speed and caught hold of Tanay by the throat before he could do anything.

"Your petty spells may have beaten your father, but they will do little to help you here." Legion lifted Tanay from the ground, squeezing as he did. Tanay struggled to break free of the monsters grip as Elana took hold of her sword and ran to her lover's aid, but Legion swatted her aside like a fly.

Elana fell backwards to the ground as Laucian leaped over her. Elana was shocked to see her friend leaping through the air, only moments before he had been all but dead yet now he appeared healed and refreshed. He looked a little different too, his tattoo had changed and he was wearing gloves instead of his bracers.

Laucian summoned a psionic knife to each hand; using them to slice at the arm Legion was holding Tanay with. The demon screamed, dropping Tanay as it did. Tanay dropped to his knees, trying to catch his breath. Laucian continued his attack on Legion, he ducked under a heavy backhand from the beast cutting Legion across the gut as he did. Legion backed away, trying to get out of reach of Laucian's mind blades.

"What's wrong beast? You've stopped telling us how pointless our attacks are." Laucian taunted.

Legion laughed, "Do you think you are winning? Don't be foolish boy." Laucian ran forward again but this time Legion was ready. The demon swung his huge sword for Laucian who dived and rolled under the attack.

Elana made her way to Tanay's side, the sorcerer tried to get back to his feet but fell back to the floor. His fight with Deventis and the vicious attack from Legion had almost completely drained his strength. Elana tried to make her love comfortable before turning her attention back to the fight.

Elana ran forward, Legion had his back to her trying to catch Laucian with his sword. Elana stabbed the demon in the side as she passed by him. Legion leaped to the side, more out of surprise from the unexpected attack than from any pain. Legion let out a low growl as he looked from Laucian to Elana.

Both Laucian and Elana moved forward, Laucian was the first to attack. He leaped to the side where he kicked off a wall, as he flew through the air he dismissed his psionic knives and summoned a large axe in their place which he brought down aiming for Legion's head. Legion blocked the axe with his sword and forced Laucian off to the side. The demon spun quickly as Elana ran in, hitting her in the side of the head with the hilt of his sword sending her skidding off along the ground.

Laucian pressed on with his attack, swinging the axe for Legion's stomach. Legion blocked again with his sword before swinging his weapon around high. Laucian ducked under the sword dismissing the axe and summoning the knives again. Laucian cut Legion across the thigh as he skipped passed and away from the demon.

Elana looked around as she tried to stand but the room was spinning and she collapsed to the ground next to Tanay. The sorcerer was stirring again now. He climbed to his feet using his spear for support. Elana tried to stand again but was overcome with dizziness and fell back to her knees. Tanay was at her side in an instant, checking her head which was bleeding heavily.

"Go, help Laucian." Elana said. Tanay looked up to see his friend skipping around the demon, trying to find a weakness in its defence.

"You can not help him now." The voice came from behind Tanay. It sounded like Solaris but it was somehow different, it sounded more distant. The sorcerer didn't move. He stood watching his friend fighting, knowing that Solaris was right; there was nothing he could do to help.

Laucian was ducking and weaving around Legion. He moved in to cut the beast whenever he could, but his attacks were doing little more than annoying the demon. Laucian knew that he couldn't keep this up much longer, it would only be a matter of time before Legion caught him with an attack of his own. Laucian jumped backwards, throwing both his psionic knives as he did. Both mind blades hit their target, one catching Legion in the shoulder and the other in his chest. Laucian ran forward again, the two knives vanished as he moved and his psionic sword appeared in his hand.

Legion readied himself for the charging psychic. Using his sword he knocked Laucian's weapon out wide, and caught hold of Laucian with his free hand. Legion lifted the psychic from the ground and impaled him with his sword. Laucian called out in pain as Legion dropped him to the ground, ripping his sword free as he did.

"Did you really think that you could beat me?" Legion asked with a smile.

"I never had to beat you," Laucian laughed, "I just had to stall you." Laucian glanced over his shoulder, Legion followed his gaze to see where Solaris was stood. Solaris' body was again made of flames, but they were no longer the orange yellow glow of normal fire. The flames covering Solaris burned brighter than any Legion had ever seen; they were white and burning with greater intensity than any celestial body in the heavens.

Legion moved quickly against Solaris, swinging his sword at the burning man. Solaris caught hold of the sword by its blade. Although Legion could not feel the heat coming off of Solaris the sword still began to melt, it wasn't long before the top half of the blade crashed to the ground. Legion dropped what remained of his sword and backed away. For the first time in his life Legion felt true fear. The beast had summoned into and banished from countless worlds but he had never before truly feared an opponent.

Solaris left a trail of smoking footprints as he followed Legion. Everything Solaris touched began to melt, but the heat was not felt more than a foot away from his body. He punched at Legion, the demon raised his arm to block but this did nothing to help. As soon as Solaris' fist connected Legion's scaled flesh began to burn, the beast roared in agony as he backed away again. Solaris pressed forward, every attack leaving the demon severely burned. Legion tried to fight back, but every time he blocked an attack or struck Solaris the white hot fames simply burnt him.

Legion was beginning to panic, there seemed to be no way for him to win this fight. Even when he managed to hit Solaris it was him who suffered. Legion eventually had his back to the wall. With nowhere for the demon left to go Solaris pressed on, punching and kicking the demon with lightning speed.

Legion's body had caught fire by now, his flesh began to melt off his bones. He tried to hold back his screams of agony, but he knew that his time in this world was running out. He knew he had failed again. Legion fell to his knees, leaning forward he braced himself with one arm. Legion looked up at the immortal who was standing over him.

"If you kill me, it will be the end of you as well," the demon pleaded, "Spare me and you will live forever."

"I've lived long enough." Solaris raised his fist, Legion roared in anger. Solaris punched Legion in the side of the head with all his strength. The fist burned through Legion's flesh and deep into his skull. The demon fell to the floor, flames spreading across his body. Within seconds the beasts body was completely engulfed by fire, burning itself away until Legion was little more than a pile of ash on the floor.

"Is that it? Is it over?" Tanay staggered over to the side of Solaris, trying to help Elana walk with him.

"Have we won?" Elana asked.

"Legion has been banished but it is not over, he will return in the next world." Solaris returned to his normal form. "This war may have been won but the damage to your world will not soon be healed." Solaris walked to Laucian's side, the psychic lay motionless on the floor in a pool of his blood.

"Is he..?" Elana couldn't bring herself to finish the question.

"He couldn't have survived that wound." Tanay said quietly.

"He may not have survived, but that does not mean he will die." Solaris kneeled on the floor next to Laucian. He placed his hand over the wound and spoke a few ancient words. Laucian suddenly sat upright clutching at his stomach as he did, instinctively checking the wound only to find that it had been healed.

"I pass my power to you," Solaris said, "You are now the Immortal, destined to survive whatever fate befalls your world so that you may protect the next."

Solaris fell backwards; everyone quickly made their way to his side. "I give you this warning." Solaris said, looking Laucian in the eyes, "With the power of the immortal your natural abilities will increase in power. The power of the immortal has never before been given to a psychic such as you. I do not know how your abilities will be affected by this, but any changes to the powers of the mind can be dangerous." Solaris closed his eyes and laid his head back.

"Thank you my friend, for everything you have done for us." Laucian said quietly.

Laucian stood from Solaris' side with Tanay and Elana next to him. Solaris' body began to burn in much the same way Legion's had until he too was completely consumed by the flames. Each of them quietly said their goodbyes to the dead immortal before they began to make their way back outside. All of them now wondering how their friends had faired in the battle, hoping and praying that they had not been lost.

Chapter 28
The Smallest Grave

Legion sat on his throne, the dimension he had been banished to was a dark desolate world. It was a perpetual night with a black starless sky, the only light coming from a large moon. Dozens of small creatures were scurrying around the clearing; they were running back and forth from cave in the large cliffs surrounding the clearing to their masters throne.

The creatures were bringing ointments and potions to their master, trying to heal the burns still covering his body. Legion's eyes were focused on a pool of water on a large stone platform in front of the throne. The pool showed images of the battle outside of Cemulion, Legion always watched to see how the battle went after he was banished from each world, trying to see where he had failed and what he could do different in the next world. He felt a great shot of sadness when he saw Havak die, Havak had been by his side since the beginning and despite their failures had always found a way to survive. Havak had been the son of Legion's twin Havoc, and with his death Legion had nothing left of his closest brother.

"Do you not grow tired of always loosing brother?" Legion looked to to see where the voice had come from.

"What is the meaning of this?" Legion tried to stand but his injuries were too severe.

"Calm yourself dear brother. I only wished to see how you were doing."

"Phobia?"

"Why do you always use the old names? I am called Elvin in this world."

"Why do you appear before me in this form?" Legion snorted turning away from his brother.

"I appear before you as I always do, in my true form." Elvin smiled as he spoke, "It would seem that my true appearance changes with each new world."

"Your *true appearance* has never changed before."

"Indeed. In the past I have always appeared in our fathers image, until this world."

"And now you appear as that Laucian, with whom I have just done battle."

"Not exactly, but that is another tale and not the reason I am here."

"No, I expect it isn't. You are here to gloat about your victory, as you always do."

"That is not true," Elvin said with a wry smile, "I am here out of concern for my older brother. It was never my intention for you to suffer."

"You didn't want me to suffer?" Legion spat, "It was you who first betrayed me, it was you who first banished me to this forsaken place!"

"It may seem like that, from a certain point of view. I prefer to believe that I saved your life, I gave you true immortality."

"You snatched victory from my grasp!"

"I stopped your insanity!" the god of fear snapped, raising his voice for the first time. "I always agreed with you, I always believed your war was right and just." Elvin paused for a moment, "When you decided that the only way to stop our enemies was to destroy everything though, it was clear to see that you had lost your mind."

Legion growled, "If that is what you think then why banish me here? Why not just kill me?"

"You are my brother and I love you, I could not kill you."

"Instead you plan to spend eternity fighting against me."

"Not eternity dear brother, only until you come back to your senses."

Many who had fought in the battle had left over the past few days. The elemental warriors had disappeared almost as soon as the battle had ended, returning to wherever they had been summoned from. This left their commanders to decide what they would do next. Aramil had chosen to stay in Cemulion; the Getandor soldiers had a lot of respect for the paladin after the battle and offered him the position of temporary commander. Kimanay had decided to stay with him and try to help bring some stability to the now leaderless country.

Larenor and Delensa both decided to travel to Krondmare, they wanted to help calm the chaos there after the death of Krondmare's king. Larenor had managed to barter passage on a merchant vessel leaving a couple of days after the fighting ended.

The etharii were the next to leave, staying only long enough to collect their dead before heading back to their homeland. The elves and most of the dwarves left after a couple of days. The dwarves taking the injured Nasgaroth with them so they could tend his wounds back in his home. Some dwarves stayed behind to help rebuild Cemulion, Slantary had done a great deal of damage in the brief time she ruled there.

Grakenster had stayed for a few days before leading his army back to the Four Kings mountains. The hobgoblin had tried to recruit as many as possible before leaving, happily taking any who did not wish to remain in Getandor. He had tried especially hard to get Branack to join with him, offering many treasures and high ranking positions amongst his troops. Branack had no intention of leaving Cemulion city though, it was his and Ivellious' home and they planned on helping to rebuild. Grakenster even thought about abducting the half-orc but eventually decided that it would probably be bad for his own health to try.

Malik and his barbarians collected their dead and prepared them for the journey home to be buried with their ancestors, but none were willing to leave yet. They had no intention of going home until they paid their respects at one of the many funerals that were taking place. Most of the funerals were small private affairs, with close friends and families of the fallen warriors present. One funeral in particular pulled a large crowd though, all of the barbarians were present along with Adokas and Davkul, Thoril and Aramil, Laucian Tanay and Elana, even Magon made his way to this funeral.

Malik carried the coffin of the brave halfling, many had offered to help but Malik had insisted on carrying Roscoe to his final resting place. The huge barbarian had always liked the little halfling, he liked Roscoe's view on life, always seeing the good in everything. Malik kneeled by the side of the newly dug grave and placed to coffin on some rope which had been stretched across the hole. Malik thought back to all the times Roscoe had visited his tribe, he had always thought the halfling would out live him and sing songs about his great deeds. Now it looked as though Malik would be singing the songs about Roscoe's great deeds, Malik would be telling the stories about how Roscoe's glorious death in battle had saved him and many of the tribes warriors.

Davkul and some of the barbarians lowered Roscoe's coffin into the grave with the ropes it had been placed on. No-one spoke after the coffin was lowered, everyone stood and silently remembered how the halfling bard had affected each of their lives. Davkul and Malik began to fill the grave, the barbarian tried to hide the tears rolling down his cheeks but nobody cared as most in attendance were shedding tears of their own.

When the grave had been filled Thoril stepped forward, the young mage held his staff up high and spoke a few words of magic. There was a bright flash light as a stone slab appeared on top of the grave. The magical stone had a constantly changing inscription, telling the tale of Roscoe's life and of his heroic death.

People slowly began to leave the funeral until only a handful remained. Some of others stood by the graveside for several hours. They did not want to leave Roscoe's side, as if they stood there long enough Roscoe might crawl out of the ground and tell them he was just a heavy sleeper. They eventually started walk away one by one making their way back to their homes, the very homes made safe by the actions of all those who died in the battle against Legion's army, the brave men and women like Roscoe who proved themselves to be heroes when they fought and died to protect those who could not protect themselves.

*   *   *

A lone figure watched the funeral from the cover of some trees in the distance. The woman was not interested in who was being buried, she was trying to find one man in the crowd. She was trying to find the man who had humiliated her time and again. She was trying to see the man she blamed for the defeat of her beloved master Legion.

Aluthana had been more than willing to follow Legion. He had saved her from a dark past and promised to destroy everyone who had ever hurt her. Legion had not been able to fulfil that promise and Aluthana blamed one man for this, the one man who had fought so hard to stop her master.

Aluthana watched as Laucian walked back towards Magon's tower. He was with his friends, all of them smiling, overjoyed with their victory. Aluthana was enraged by their mocking laughter. The assassin strung an arrow in her bow, it was an easy shot for her and she planned to savour this kill. She pulled back the string and sighted down the arrow but before she could loose the arrow a knife cut her bowstring.

Aluthana spun around, drawing her sword as she did. The assassin stumbled backwards when she saw who was standing there. She was looking at an almost exact double of Laucian, the only difference being that the double had white hair whereas Laucian's was black. The doubles tattoo was different too; it was on his right arm instead of left and although a similar design instead of a glaive it was a sword with five runes on the blade and the dragon looked more wise and regal in purple and blue.

"I am sorry if I startled you, but I cannot allow you to kill him." the man said, "My name is Mykhaylo, and if you will allow me I can help you find a new path."

Mykhaylo reached out his hand to Aluthana, the assassin stared blankly at him for a moment before tentatively taking his hand.

Epilogue

It was uncharacteristically quiet in the tavern area of *The Travelling Rest*. The few patrons present this night along with the staff were all silently staring at the inn keeper who took a sip of their drink and smiled back at them all.

"What then?" a young goblin asked excitedly.

The inn keeper looked over and smiled, "What then? I'm afraid that is the end of this tale."

"But it can't end like that," an elf stated, "There are too many unanswered questions."

"Aye," a dwarf piped in, "Like what's goin' on with that fella lookin' just like Laucian?"

"And what did he do with that assassin lady?" A halfling added.

"Also what happened with Laucian's dying father?" a human asked, "Did he go with his brother to see him?"

"Speaking of brother's" a hobgoblin put in, "What's going on with that Elvin being Legions brother?"

The inn keeper laughed and took another sip of their drink. "These are all good questions my friends." The inn keeper glanced around the crowd again "But it is growing late and I know many of you have to be back on the road early in the morning."

It was at this time the satyr like resident bard of *The Travelling Rest* stepped up and whispered something into the inn keepers ear. "It also seems I have duties to perform."

A general groan of disappointment crossed the room as those present realised they would not be able to convince the inn keeper to tell them any more this night.

"Do not fret my friends, perhaps I will continue this tale the next time you find your way to my door," the inn keeper explained before adding, "Or my door finds you." winking to the crowd.

With that being said the inn keeper finished their drink and took the glass to the bar where the bar tender passed them a some flowers. With the flowers in hand the inn keeper walked across the tavern and out through the inter-dimensional door of their extraordinary establishment.

The inn keeper looked out across the small oasis, wondering if any of the patron this night would ever come across the moving entrance to *The Travelling Rest* again, would they ever get to hear what happened next in the story. With a knowing smile the inn keeper began to walk towards the centre of the oasis, their thoughts moving away from their new *friends* and back towards those of old.

Bonus

Graw

It is believed that when evil and chaotic elves died and their souls passed onto the abyss they were tortured by the demons that make the plane their home. In time these elven souls became so twisted and corrupted that they became demons themselves, the hedonistic sadists known as the Graw. Although the graw are far weaker than much of their demonic brethren they do hold one advantage, they breed and multiply at an alarming rate. This means that if another more powerful demon attacks them they can even the playing field through shear weight of numbers.

The first time the graw witnessed the rampaging Gorbalin slaughtering his way across the abyss they became obsessed with the demon god. For countless years the graw followed *The Abyssal Beast* revelling in the slaughter he wrought, some even going as far as to throw themselves into the path of his huge axe so they could feel the sensation of being destroyed by the great blade, sending their twisted souls into oblivion.

In a brief and rare moment of calm Gorbalin finally took notice of the graw and found them to be a wonderful example of chaos, so he granted them a great gift. Using all of his tremendous might Gorbalin swung his axe, cutting a small hole between planes. Although too small for Gorbalin or any of the other more powerful demons of the abyss for the few seconds that the hole remained in place thousands of graw were able to spill through, making their way to the material plane, to Gallisium.

Upon entering the material plane the graw scattered all across Gallisium, seducing and slaughtering mortals where ever they went, using especially brutal tactics against elves, who they despise above all others.

The primary goal of the graw has always been finding a way to bring their god Gorbalin to the material plane so he can bring his terrible wrath against the mortals across Gallisium. However due to their chaotic nature and an obsession with causing and experiencing both pleasure and pain the graw have never come close to achieving their goal, that is until the rise of Ulsagan, the first graw queen.

Ulsagan is a powerful graw sorceress who managed to bring thousands of other graw to her banner with the promise of power and excess. With her new army Ulsagan invaded one of the southern kingdoms of Gallisium burning it to the ground, and from its ashes grew the graw nation of Zil'Toroth.

Appearance and Age

On average graw sand between five and six feet tall and usually have a slender build. They have long pointed ears suggesting elven ancestry, but their pale red skin, razor sharp teeth and a ring of small horns around their heads clearly shows they are of demonic heritage.

As demons the graw do not age in the same ways as mortals. Any graw born through more traditional reproductive methods grow at a greatly accelerated rate, becoming a fully grown adult within a matter of hours, they are also effectively immortal living for an indeterminate number of years.

Society

The graw who still reside within the abyss to this day continue to follow Gorbalin on his eternal rampage, hoping that he will either grant them the ecstasy of being slaughtered or grant them the opportunity to follow their brethren to Gallisium. They are always willing to answer the summoning call of wizards from the material plane, thinking that they can break free of any mortals bonds and join with the other graw an the material plane.

The graw who escaped the abyss live in one of two ways. Many live as nomads, travelling in small groups, wreaking havoc on any mortal communities they come across, staying until they become bored of an area or they are forced to move on by mortal champions.

The remaining graw are those who follow Ulsagan and created the nation of Zil'Toroth. The graw of Zil'Toroth live out their every sadistic whim within the borders of their new homeland, keeping the mortals who survived the initial invasion in breeding pens and sending out raiding parties to capture more from their neighbours, meaning they have a constant supply of victims to torture and toy with. It is within this nation that Ulsagan has made great strides toward releasing Gorbalin onto the material plane, but has of yet always fallen short. This is primarily due to the chaotic nature of the graw, she has yet failed in keeping them focused on her great task. If Ulsagan was ever to succeed in her plan then the mortals of Gallisium would taste the edge of Gorbalin's mighty axe.

About The Author

Jon Roe

Born in Keighley, West Yorkshire. Jon was first introduced to fantasy when a parent read The Hobbit and Lord of the Rings to him and his sister as children. This lead to a lifelong obsession with the genera, be it books, films or games such as Dungeons & Dragons. Now he is putting his own humble offering out into the world.

Twitter - @JerichoLives
Instagram - jericho_lives

Printed in Poland
by Amazon Fulfillment
Poland Sp. z o.o., Wrocław